buzuner@superonline.com
www. buketuzuner.com

BUKET UZUNER, was born in Ankara in 1955, is an author of short stories, travelogues, and novels. Her books have been on the Turkish National Bestseller Lists since 1992, and translated into four languages. She is one of the most prominent and acclaimed writers of contemporary Turkish Literature.

Ms. Uzuner's *Mediterranean Waltz* was awarded as the *Best Novel of 1988* by the *University of İstanbul,* and she won *The Yunus Nadi Prize* for her novel *The Sound of Fishsteps in 1993.*

Ms. Buket Uzuner was selected among the *75 Most Influential Women* of the Republic of Turkey, for Mimoza-Sabah Magazine by well-known professionals civic leaders, members of the press, and academia to celebrate the Republic of Turkey's 75th anniversary. She has been presented as honorary fellow writer by The University of Iowa, in 1996.

She has travelled and lived widely in North Africa, North America and Europe. Buket Uzuner lives in Istanbul with her animated cartoon film maker husband and their son.

Buket Uzuner's published books:

Short Story Collections: My Name is May, The Most Naked Day of the Month, The Sun Eating Gypsy, The Sorrow of the Northwest Wind, The City of Poets

Travel Writing:The Travel Notes of a Brunette; The Diary of an Urban Romantic, New York Loogbook

Novels: Two Green Otters, Their Mothers, Their Fathers, Their Lovers, and the Others; The Sound of Fishsteps (1993 Yunus Nadi Novel Award), *Long White Cloud: Gallipoli* (in progress).

PELİN ARINER, was born in Ankara in 1976 and grew up following her bureaucratic-nomadic parents around the world as the daughter of a diplomat.

She has lived in Sudan, Greece, Turkey and for the last 10 years, the United States. She received degrees in both creative writing and double bass performance from The University of Oberlin, USA. Pelin Ariner lives in California and works at Lonely Planet Publications USA.

In writing this book, the author has benefited from several articles, books, and individuals' experiences. These are: the articles of Robert Elbish, "Peering Into the Nanofuture" (*Sky*, March '97); Cengiz Bektas, "Kuzguncuk" (*Istanbul*, June '92); Douglas Waller, "Onward Cyber Soldiers" (*Time*, August '95); "Soldiers-file" (*Fokus*, January '96); and Senay Kalkan, "Alev is" (*Radikal*, December '96); and the books of Hans Magnus Enzensberger, *Civil War Scenes* (trans. Ersel Kayaloglu); Sun Tzu, *The Art of War* (trans. Sibel Ozbudun, Zeynep Ataman); Yves Michaud, *Violence* (trans. Cem Muhtaroglu); John Keegan, *The History of the Art of War* (trans. Fusun Doruker); Robert F. Burges, *Ships Beneath the Sea*, Thomas Hobbes, *Leviathan* and Thucydides, *History of the Peloponnesian War*.

My thanks to everyone who helped me in the writing of the book, especially Juliette Binoche, Can Dundar, and my mother.

BUKET UZUNER

MEDITERRANEAN WALTZ

*1998 Novel Prize
of Istanbul University*

Remzi Kitabevi

MEDITERRANEAN WALTZ / Buket Uzuner • 2000
The Original Title: *Kumral Ada ~ Mavi Tuna*

© Buket Uzuner, 2000
© Remzi Kitabevi, 2000

Translation: Pelin Arıner

Cover illustration: Ali Murat Erkorkmaz
Back-cover photograph: Karen Thirman
Cover design: Ömer Erduran

ISBN 975-14-0772-9

FIRST EDITION: November, 2000
Reprinted July, 2001

Remzi Kitabevi A.Ş., Selvili Mescit Sok. 3, Cağaloğlu 34440, İstanbul.
Tel (212) 513 9424-25, 513 9474-75, Faks (212) 522 9055
WEB: http://www.remzi.com.tr E-MAIL: post@remzi.com.tr

Printed by Remzi Kitabevi, Turkey.

MEDITERRANEAN WALTZ

For Attilâ İlhan...

"Mind, love, and soul!
Theirs is a trinity.
It cures every ill, soothes all calamity."

Mevlânâ Celâleddin Rumî

TUESDAY MORNING

I awoke one Tuesday morning.
In all the papers, the woman dearest to my heart was
 accused of murder.
I had not expected this at all.
I was stunned.
I was caught completely off-guard.
I had known the truth all along, but no one had asked
 me.
They had convicted her!
There was a knock on the door.
Two soldiers had come to get me.
Civil war had erupted, and the country was being
 mobilized.
This, I had expected.
I was not the least bit surprised.
I had been expecting this for a long time, in fear and
 suspicion.
I packed my things and left the house that Tuesday
 morning.

FREEDOM

"Man is born free, yet lives everywhere under chains."

Jean Jacques Rousseau

Everyone has their own miracle, and she happens to be mine!

"Freedom is being able to do the same things every morning when you get up!" I said, as I stretched and smiled broadly.

"Only the same things you choose to do!" she corrected.

"Freedom is being able to do the same desired things when you get up every morning!"

She produced a self-satisfied smile, as she always does in her moments of triumph. My heart rejoices when she laughs. I grab on to life from wherever I might have left off.

"Think about it Duna, there are billions of people who, everyday, are 'obliged' to do things they don't want to do. That in itself makes daily life lousy, horrible, and very... very boring!" she said. "Nevertheless, the rules that seem the least boring are the ones we make ourselves."

"If only we lived without rules, free and unattached!" I sighed.

"People are creatures of contradiction. Just look at us: we live in self-styled prisons, only we call them 'home, family, relatives, and tradition.' Then we suffocate and go insane within these walls, but guard their collapse with our own lives. Hah ha ha!"

She has always been this way. From the outside she looks arrogant, impudent, and sarcastic, but it is well known that the closer you allow her to get, the more sensitive, fragile, and deadly proud she becomes.

Nevertheless, she has three qualities which remain constant regardless of how close one might be to her: 1) she is attractive 2) she has personality, 3) she has very distinctly Mediterranean colors.

"Plus Duna, just think of how there would neither be any leisurely mornings, nor freedom, if a man as addicted to the productivity of early mornings as yourself, and a woman as covetous of her morning sleep as I, were to wake up in the same bed!"

Once again, the same laugh out of the corner of her mouth!

This woman, who seems somewhat opinionated, haughty, and overly self-confident to some people, and who might therefore be difficult to handle, is for the same reasons unique and very special to me.

Still, her depiction of us waking in the same bed together did not amuse me as much as it amused her. On the contrary, it conjured up painful images. I felt a pang of sorrow. Taking care to conceal it, I changed the subject:

"Yet Uncle Poet tried to teach us for years that freedom is realizing your obligations. Maybe we'll only be free once we learn that," I said, smiling wryly.

"I hope you're not making fun of Uncle Poet. You know I couldn't stand that."

I was making fun of us, and she knew it. The Poet Dogan Gokay was one of the very real aspects of my life; a person who had always taken us seriously, who had been the chief architect of our intellectual thought, and whom I loved very much.

Like all passionate people, she was fond of stressing the sanctity of those she loved, and that was the reason behind all this fuss. Besides, the Poet Dogan Gokay was her real uncle, I was the one who was the "pretend" nephew.

"We were so young then. If Uncle Dogan had given us the same definition, prefacing it with 'Karl Marx says' we'd either have been intimidated and inattentive, or we'd have been stuck on the name, like label-freaks. But he wanted us to think, Duna."

She was right.

"I was in high school by the time I realized that that phrase he dropped every so often, 'you grow more free as you begin to know yourself' was Sartre," I said, shaking my head like a person suddenly aged.

"To reach the point of self-awareness is to become a free being!" she corrected in a theatrical voice.

She paused and looked at me attentively, as if she had remembered something.

"I knew a Canadian man, an atheist, who used to be a devout Christian. He once told me there was a saying in the New Testament that 'the truth shall set you free,' " she said.

Suddenly she became distant, and lost in thought. I was just starting to wonder, a little grumpily, about who this Canadian might be, when my mind intercepted:

"My mother is a devout Moslem, but she won't say 'amen' to any prayer she doesn't understand," I said.

"Pardon?" she fixed her surprised eyes on my face.

She had come back to me, and with what beautiful brown eyes!

"I was saying that my mom reads the Qoran very frequently, but from its Turkish translations. Especially after that incident...you know...you can't catch the poor woman without a Qoran..."

As soon as I had said it, the embers of "that incident" fell somewhere between us, but I acted swiftly to keep them from starting a fresh fire:

"Mom says, 'according to Islam, humans are born free,' " I quickly added.

We fell silent and contemplated.

"I guess they are all saying the same thing...But he is the one who first got us involved in these matters!"

True. Something of a teacher, a father, a brother, but most of all a friend...

"Uncle Dogan's greatest strength has always been the sincerity of his self-confidence."

Our eyes met, and we shared someone we both loved dearly in each other's beloved eyes. Emboldened by the assumption that I too was a person she loved passionately, I tried to charge my gaze with all my adoration. But my eyes could not bear the weight of this electricity and grew cloudy. I averted them.

"Americans," she said with the exaggerated mannerism of a volunteer who first runs to aid in a difficult situation, "Americans say that 'freedom is like money, you have to earn it before you spend it.' But since we have no interest in this subject, our dictionary of proverbs sorely lacks the word freedom under F. In our culture it is a luxury to create proverbs regarding freedom."

She knows exactly how to get me started. I was hooked instantly.

"Maybe we don't have proverbs on freedom, but there's Nesimi who was skinned alive for its sake, and then there's Dadaloglu, Sheik Bedrettin, and Nazim," I said.

"Oh yes, of course, I must have forgot," she rejoined melodramatically, " 'this freedom is a bitter thing under the stars,' says our great poet whose freedom was wrenched away, and who was imprisoned because of his thoughts."

Those who fail to recognize that she aims the sharpest stabs of her sarcasm at herself are those who have not understood her at all, and she could not care less about these people. Yet if someone she loves falls prey to the same misperception, her heart is shattered. The scene I have absolutely the least tolerance for, and would go to any length to prevent, is one where she gets hurt, where she feels the slightest pain.

"Of course one shouldn't forget Fikret's definition: 'A poet with an independent mind, independent knowledge, and an independent soul.' Perhaps it would be more appropriate to search for freedom under 'I' in our dictionaries?"

"Come on Duna!" she protested. "Naturally, we can't encounter a spirit of individual freedom in either Fikret or Nazim. Even if they're poetic geniuses, in the end their writing is affected by the conditions of their country. So, even though it might be for different reasons, I think those two are poets of a collective spirit of independence. They were not children of the French Revolution or the American Civil War…Look at us, don't you see? We are, in turn, their children."

She gave her speech with gestures and expressions copied from her uncle. She was pleased with what she had said. She looked at me. She saw the effect her loud voice and tense manner had on me. I was preparing to burst into that laugh characterised by puffed cheeks and snorting noises which we had practiced since our childhood, everytime she came out of one of her tirades. She joined me in sharing one of those exaggerated moments of hilarity, right out of our childhood in the mansion's garden. But our laughter died quickly. Perhaps because our generation was not ready to joke about freedom, we fell silent, slightly envying our successors.

"Who knows, maybe you're right Duna. Maybe freedom is being able to repeat what you want every morning, huh?"

"Maybe," I said sadly.

"Whoever finds it first, tells the other, okay?"

"Alright," I said.

All of a sudden I remembered how when we were kids, we would laugh like crazy at grandpa's endearing accent which swallowed the "l's" and most of all at the way he said "wiberty." How hurt grandpa would get, refusing to talk to us...

I smiled faintly.

She smiled too. My heart rejoices at her smile.

We looked at each other, smiling at different things.

SOMEONE IS DYING OUTSIDE!

"In fact, civil war has already pervaded the metropolises, its metastases have become part of daily life in big cities."

Hans Magnus Enzensberger

As usual, he got an early start that day. Taking care not to wake the woman sleeping next to him, he got out of bed, picked up his glasses and quietly slipped out of the room. He fell to repeating the things he liked to do every morning.

He always woke up at the crack of dawn, no matter how late he might've turned in or how tired he might've been, in order to catch the final rehearsal of the day, before it was revealed to the public. So far, neither his mind nor his body had presented any obstruction to his habit of being an early riser, regardless of the season or the day of the week. In his childhood it had been a family tradition, in his youth a considerable amount of time saved for homework, and now it was simply one of his characteristics.

First he picked up the basket from outside the door. Their two-story apartment did not have a doorman, but the grocer's boy had, with a small tip, agreed to make the morning's first delivery to their house. He took the fresh bread and bottle of milk from the straw basket and went into the kitchen. The papers had not yet arrived. He checked the expiration date on the red aluminum cap of the milk bottle, and, unable to resist the fresh, crusty bread, broke off the heel and munched on it.

As he bent down to pour milk into the bowl marked "Brunette," a dark calico cat appeared in the kitchen and proceeded to rub herself against his legs, purring cheerfully. The young man asked the cat how it was doing in a soft voice, as if talking to a young child, but his subject had already buried her entire head in the milk-bowl.

He lit the stove, and put the large kettle filled with drinking water on the burner. On top of this he placed a smaller kettle which contained three measured spoons of looseleaf tea.

"Here it is, Brunette, the Turkish samovar!" he called to the cat.

The cat remained non-plussed. Mechanically, he pressed the *play* button on the small radio-cassette player. A soft jazz melody spread across the kitchen into the whole house and he quickly turned down the volume. When he opened the door to the small kitchen balcony he felt the breath of a warm summer morning on his face. He prepared breakfast for two on the balcony which was filled with flowers. He steeped the tea. From the gentle thump at the door he figured that the grocer's boy had brought the papers, but when he went to open it the kid had already disappeared, leaving his delivery on the doormat. He received two papers daily, but it seemed that this morning the little rascal had left every paper in circulation at his doorstep.

"What the...Now, why would he do that? He's going to get it from Musa..." he muttered as he picked up the bundle and went inside.

He took the papers to the balcony, but just as he was about to glance at them a helicopter roared past above him. Annoyed, he raised his head but couldn't see the helicopter. He turned back to the papers only to be startled by the sound of breaking glass coming from the kitchen. When the cat had clambered up on the conter hoping for seconds, she had tipped over the milk bottle and smashed it to pieces.

"Brunette, you're so clumsy!" he cried, even more annoyed.

Frightened, the cat ran away. He took the broom and dustpan out of the closet and started to sweep. Then he heard the bathroom door shut.

"See what you did, Brunette? It was the poor girl's day off, and you couldn't let her sleep!"

The cat grumbled from her hiding spot. She was never one to be put down. In the same instant, the room was filled with the ferocious rumble of several planes tearing past.

"What is going on, for God's sake? Can't I have a moment's peace?" muttered the young man.

He still had on the shorts and t-shirt that constituted his pajamas, and ortheopedic slippers on his feet.

After cleaning up the kitchen he poured tea into the slim-waisted glass and went back out on the balcony.

"Now if I could only have a cup of tea without something going wrong…" he thought. It was his habit to read the papers starting from the back. He did the same that morning.

"BursaSport's Egemen leaves for Belgium for a promised 125,000 marks and three years of higher education."

"Escobar, defense player for the Colombian National Team which was eliminated in the first round of the World Soccer Championship, has been murdered. It is suspected that pari-mutuel betters and the drug mafia are behind the killing of Escobar who scored a goal against his own team in their 2-1 losing game with U.S.A."

"The civil war in Rwanda rages on fiercely. It is estimated that 500,000 peple have already been killed."

"The civil war in Algeria extends to foreigners. Seven Italian sailors found with their throats slit open."

"Southern Yemen has declared its secession from United Yemen where a violent civil war is ravaging the country."

"Israeli planes have bombed the Hizbullah camp located in the Bekaa Valley of Eastern Lebanon."

"Taliban and Barzani forces continue to fight in Halepce. At least 600 people reported dead."

"Azerbaijan declares a peacefire on all fronts last night after Russia's call for peace."

"The FBI has opened a new bureau in Russia's capital, Moscow."

"A mosque in Hamburg, Germany is attacked. A firebomb is thrown into a Turkish locale in Hamburg."

"The fifteen year old civil war in Angola between the official army and the armed opposition movement UNITA has erupted in renewed violence."

"Civil war continues in Liberia, the Land of Savages. The political regime and native tribes are in struggle against each other."

"Over thirty thousand people are estimated dead in Sri-Lanka's civil war, which has been going on for the last eleven years."

"The Caucasus is a bomb waiting to explode! Reports of death arrive daily from Georgia, Abkhazia, and Chechenya."

"The operations held in the Southeast are reported to have killed 3905 PKK militants. The amount spent for security forces in the area has reached 400 billion Turkish liras."

"PKK militants have executed the six teachers they kidnapped earlier."

"Sarajevo, which is described as the greatest concentration camp of the modern world, is approaching its thousandth day under siege. According to UN sources, 10,068 people have died in this time period, 1,572 of them children."

"God damn it!" he spat from between his teeth. "Someone is always dying outside!"

Then he glanced at the small photograph under one of the articles. A woman with jeans and sneakers was lying face down on the ground. The small shoes of the child she had apparently dove to protect before she got killed were floating in a dark pool of blood.

"God damn it! God damn you all!" he groaned.

The insides of the papers were filled with capital letters.

IRA, ETA, FNLA, PKK, IBDA-C, TIKKO, THKP-C, SPLA, UNITA...

And the list of the countries at war kept going.

The news made him sick to his stomach. He took a sip of his perfectly cold tea. No sooner had he done this that he felt the same unbearable repulsion for the taste in his mouth. Sensing he was about to throw up, he spat out the tea on the balcony. He left, went into the empty bedroom and got dressed. As he was putting on his light blue shirt and jeans, the entire neighborhood shook once again with the sound of planes flying overhead.

"What's going on, for the love of God? What is this ruckus? Now mom's going to get all anxious," he said, glancing at the floor below.

When he emerged from the bedroom, the bathroom was empty.

"Weird, she didn't take a shower today," he mused. He started to shave hurriedly, but heard the phone ring. "Oh, she'll get it," he thought, and went on with his grooming. Meanwhile, the increasing racket of the planes was making him extremely edgy.

"God, so many someones are dying outside," he sighed, and cut himself. He looked in horror at the blood pouring from the tiny nick. He felt queasy, lightheaded. The sight of blood made him nauseous. He averted his eyes at once and pressed the towel tightly to his face. After keeping his eyes away from the mirror for a while he groped for a band-aid and put it on. He combed his hair, put on his aftershave, and cleaned his glasses.

When he went back out on the balcony, washed and dressed, the woman wasn't there. She had not touched her breakfast, and only half her tea was drunk. The newspapers he had left on the table made a disorderly heap. The mess irritated him even more.

"Merich! Merich are you home?" he called. "She never leaves without saying goodbye, I wonder what happened?"

Then he saw the note. It was scrawled hurriedly on yellow grid paper:

Duna, I got a phone call and had to leave right away.
Take care of yourself and don't lose hope.
Also, ignore the article in the paper, it's just tabloid junk.
Duna, I'm leaving you some antibiotics, painkillers, and sedatives
   in the bedroom.
Take good care of yourself. For my sake!
Meric

"Huh? What could this mean?" he said as he sank on the balcony table. "What sort of note is this? Has she gone crazy?"

Once again the sky started to rumble with the maddening roar of airplanes.

"Don't get me started!" he yelled, and shook his hand up at the sky as if asking for an answer. "Why is everything bombarding me this morning? God, why is everything going wrong? I'm going to suffocate right now, yes, I'm about to pass out!"

That was when the front pages of all the newspapers caught his eye. More accurately, a powerful magnet drew his eye in the direction of the headline repeated in all the front pages. First, he read one and couldn't understand a single thing. He stood frozen. He looked at the other front pages slowly, as if he'd been numbed. He became dazed, he felt his body shake and his chest constrict. He leaned back all his weight in the chair and started to breathe deeply. He tried to calm himself by swallowing repeatedly.

He looked once again at the newspapers which had filled their front pages with huge color pictures. Her picture was in all of them. He read the bloated headline once again and felt his heart sink.

"FAMED MURDER KEPT SECRET FOR MANY YEARS!"

"How could there be a famed –" he was about to say, but froze.

"The beloved daughter of the famous screen couple, Sureyya Mercan and Pervin Gokay, has confessed to having committed the murder, which was covered up as an accident years ago. The well-known young beauty has turned out to be a murderess!"

The attractive, intensely brunette woman in the accompanying picture wore a confident, yet wistful smile. She held a cigarette in one hand. The picture had been taken in a restaurant, and there was a clean-shaven young man with curly hair and glasses sitting next to the woman. His hands were empty.

"But that's me!" he cried. His voice sounded like a nightmarish whisper. "How could they be this unfair?" He leapt up from his chair. "That's the worst picture they could have found of her, she doesn't even look like herself! Besides, where did they get it?"

Just then, the cat came back out on the balcony, began rubbing up against him and purring. Duna looked at the cat and then at the newspapers on the table. Then Merich's note caught his eye again. He felt very tired, almost on the point of collapse. It was as if all of his inner organs were ready to burst and explode into tiny pieces.

"You see, Brunette! They've convicted her! They've declared her a murderer…They've not even given a thought to how hurt she will be! No justice, no law! They simply wrote it up and sent it to press…"

Still purring, the cat settled down and began her morning grooming.

"They should've asked me. I was there, and –"

Suddenly the sky was filled with trios of low-flying fighter jets. The noise was unbearable.

The cat ran inside with marked meows of protest.

"Of course, I'd forgotten about those!" he snorted, and followed suit. "But, before I do anything, I have to call her. She must be going out of her mind by now!"

He went over to the phone and dialed a number obviously well-lodged in his muscle memory.

"I have to find her, I simply must find her! Oh God, she must be so hurt right now."

He reached her answering machine, but was not greeted by her usual bilingual message. Her voice, tinged with the freedom of a wildflower, did not declare over the background music of Native American flutist Carlos Nakai:

"Good morning or good evening! If it's morning I'm sleeping, if it's noon I'm not home, and if it's evening that means I'm working. Anyway, please do bother to leave a message. Thanks!"

Instead, there was a new message in which she spoke fast, and sounded anxious:

> *"Dear Mabel,*
> *I'm leaving this message only for you.*
> *Terrible things are happening.*
> *I saw the papers. I find it extremely disturbing.*
> *I am leaving town for now.*
> *How many more times do we have to go through hell?*
> *Try to stay in one piece. I mean it!*
> *You are my only witness!*
> *Oh Mabel, how exhausting it is for us to always have to remain strong…*
> *Farewell…Farewell…"*

He dialed the number again and got the same message. Then came a knock on the door.

"That's her, that must be her, she must've come to me!" he said, as he ran exuberantly toward the door, but it was not she.

There were two soldiers at the door. The handsome, fresh-faced first lieutenant flashed an official smile, and inquired:

"Good morning! We are looking for Duna Atacan, the teacher."

"Yes, that's me."

"We've come to get you."

"Excuse me?"

"You mean you haven't heard?" The soldiers were surprised.

"But she's not a murderer! It's a lie of the newspapers! This is media violence!" protested Duna.

The soldiers looked at each other, now completely puzzled.

"You misunderstood us, sir, we came to draft you into the army."

"But...but I already did my military service!"

The two soldiers sighed and exchanged glances once again, shaking their heads.

"You must not have heard. It didn't make it into today's papers but all the radio and TV stations have interrupted their programs. In fact the whole country, if not the whole world is talking about this."

"About what? What's everyone talking about?"

"Sir, the nation is being mobilized, we are recruiting reserve soldiers."

"Mobilization? When? Where?" Duna asked, turning up his palms. "I mean, who are we fighting against? Who's the enemy?"

"Er, um, this is a civil war, sir."

"A civil war? Oh my God, so it's finally happened..."

The soldiers looked at each other with suspicion this time.

"We should leave immediately, sir," said the lieutenant, gathering himself. "You can take a small bag with you."

"I was expecting this," said Duna, looking ahead thoughtfully. "I was expecting this...I'd been suspecting this for years... For, with all those 'someones' dying outside, none of us could have remained 'civil' on the inside!"

He turned around.

And all his inner chords snapped.

BRUNETTE ADA: MABEL!

"The fairest of the maidens fair
Didst choose with Kays her words to share."

Fûzûlî

From the first moment I saw her, I sensed that she would occupy a very important place in my life. It was just like figuring out an entire movie from the first scene.

I had sensed from the first that she would be very important to me, and I had been frightened.

From that point on, my life would change, and nothing would ever be the same. I remember well how strongly I felt this and how shaken I was. There was nothing I could do. I had been drawn into a strong magnetic field, I had become spellbound. What's more, it was with an uncanny pleasure that I had surrendered to this "witchcraft." It had everything to do with my will and my person.

When I first saw her she was talking to herself. After a little scrutinizing, I realized that she was actually talking to something I could not see from where she crouched. I could not stop looking at her, and despite my curiosity, could not turn my gaze toward the object of her attention. I was utterly bewitched. She was one of those people who can only be conveyed through metaphor, whom words fail to do justice.

It would be insufficient to describe her with words like "pretty," "striking," "fair," "dark," or even "gorgeous." You could only come close if you said she was as distinctive as one not from this world, impressive as a shooting star, addictive as well-brewed coffee, defiant as a silkworm, and unique, since she was sent to this planet alone. Her beauty was of a calm and settled nature. Most important of all was the powerful, almost magnetic pull she had over me, and the striking contrast of her very fair complexion to her dark hair.

Of course, I was too young to name these thoughts when I first saw her, but I was old enough to feel them.

I had stationed myself right by her side and, unable to see what it was that she was talking to, had fastened my gaze upon her. All of a sudden she turned around and saw me. It was there that I was first introduced to her great brown eyes, and learned how important eyes could be.

Her eyes were rivers, the color of pine-honey, running under her dark eyebrows. When observed closely, the green that combined with a fine brown to give the hazel to her eyes sometimes betrayed the gold and blue of its origins. I stood, locked into her brown gaze which was constantly alive with the flicker of green, or gold-blue. In all my life, never had I seen, and never did I see another girl born bathed in such hues of brown! No woman's eyes have ever been more beautiful since that moment!

She got up and looked me over. She thought for a while.

"Ada," she said.

Her voice smelled of freedom, like wildflowers, and had a hint of olive paste.

" 'Scuse me?" I asked, staring dumbly.

"Ada!" she repeated.

She looked at me expectantly. I started to panic. I simply stood there, not knowing what I was supposed to say. She said "Ada," and nothing more. What on earth did she mean?

"Ada, eh?" I said, trying to buy time.

She remained unperturbed. She'd fixed those magnificient brown lights on me and waited impatiently. She was strange.

There was such defiance, such magnetism in her attitude that it rose in one a desire to be with her forever rather than to run and hide. The muscles of her body were as taut as fillies ready to bolt, her mouth was on the verge of a sorrowful smile, and her eyebrows were brown question marks.

Ada.

I thought about the first associations "Ada" had in me. This was a distant, cool, mysterious, elliptical word.

Ada.

It had to do with the sea. We used to go to the "ada" by ferry, we rode the phaeton on the "ada," then there were "ada songs," but in my current predicament I couldn't figure out what other meanings "ada" could have had besides that of "island." I stood there, sweating from the effort. Plus, I hadn't been able to make out if she expected an answer or a reaction. I bit my lips, looked away, and of course, swallowed hard with shame.

"A-da!" she reiterated angrily.

I was stunned. I began to fear I'd stay frozen for years, unable to move an inch from that spot. I'd been waiting to get this chance for days. How was I going to forgive myself for ruining it with such a fiasco?

She turned around, with a pout that expressed her exasperation with me, and picking up that thing from the ground, started to walk away. So she was leaving. I had to do something, I had to stop her at any cost and prove to her that I wasn't stupid. Quickly, I checked my own vocabulary. I went through all the far, elusive, and attractive sounds in my memory.

"Mabel!" I suddenly cried out in delight. Actually, it was more of a scream than a cry. She stopped and turned towards me with those question marks on her face.

"Mabel?"

There! Now it was her turn to be puzzled. At least I'd saved face, and I'd prevented her from leaving.

There, I had a difficult, mysterious word too!

Mabel was the name of the my favorite bubblegum at the time, but what was special to me was the picture on its wrapper. The picture was of an enigmatic, though somewhat intimidating, pretty black woman whose image appeared on a light mustard-yellow mirror, on a brown background. Right below this picture, in a rectangular box, it said in large red letters:

M A B E L
Bubblegum

The chocolate-skinned woman who had a red, pinstriped scarf tied pirate style around her head, wore a large red hoop in one ear. A wistful, pearly white smile exuded from the wondrous red lips of Mabel, who looked to a distant place or person with her languid eyes. She had three rows of pearls on her bare neck, but due to a printing error, these had come out as light brown.

In all the packages I bought, Mabel never changed her stance or her smile. I'd never seen her get mad at me or show sadness over anything. It was always the same Mabel who smiled at me from the packages I bought; winter or summer, day or night.

Mabel was a cheerful, healthy, beautiful young woman. Nevertheless, when you peered closely you could distinguish the sorrow she hid in her eyes, so I did not study them very often. Even then I recognized and reveled in the pleasurable aspect of sorrow, but I knew it was a delicate balance… The light vanilla scent and the rich sugary taste, as well as the superiority in size to all other gums, but most of all Mabel's distant, mysterious, and sightly frightening specter…I guess these were what attached me most to Mabel bubblegum. Her name was the word that taught me to read before I even started school: MABEL!

And her color: Until that age, I had never seen a black person before. In the culture I grew up in, people with black skin were either genies with lips reaching from here to high heaven, or pitch-dark "arab girls" who looked out of windows in nursery rhymes. I repeated proudly:

"Mabel!"

"Is your name Mabel?" she asked, astonished.

"Of course not! My name is Duna!" I cried.

"But you said Mabel," she pouted.

That maddening defiance came back into her eyes. She began to stroke that thing in her hand. I finally saw what it was: a white, elliptical stone, about four inches long, with thin red veins. It looked like a little, hard-to-lay egg. So this girl had been talking to a pebble!

"But you yourself said Ada…" I began, but understood before the words were out of my mouth. "You mean your name is Ada?"

That's when she smiled. She nodded in a proud, self-satisfied manner, with a smile that showed she had long loved her name.

"Ada, huh?" How weird, I never heard of anyone else with that name!"

Ada once again presented me with her glorious smile. That smile was a beauty I would never tire of watching, a masterpiece I'd be afraid to touch for fear of causing damage…And despite all its brightness it seemed to hide a secret sadness. How and how much this sadness factored into that smile was a riddle.

What could it be that makes one smile different, and unparalalled?

Maybe it's simply the smile itself!

So we stood staring for a while. She was smiling and I was gazing at her in pure admiration.

"From now on, I'm going to call you Mabel," she said. "Mabel suits you very well."

I hid my eyes in the stone she held in her hand. I hadn't yet noticed that she held the stone in her left hand, and that she was left-handed. After I noticed I always envied lefties.

Ever since that day in the mansion's garden, Ada has always called me Mabel. No one knows this except us two. Ada only calls me Mabel when we are alone. Her letters begin with Mabel.

Oh dear beautiful Ada!

Oh my sweet, my brunette girl!

Ada.

Ada.

A-da.

A.

Da.

Ada: Ma belle!

WE ARE AFRAID, WE ARE SUSPICIOUS!

"If we hope to understand anything about the world, we must purge ourselves of hate and anger."

Jean Genet

"Utter obedience must have a certain irresistible appeal to it…" mused Duna.

He went into the bedroom to do what the soldiers had asked him. He took, out of a closet, the small backpack which he usually packed with a thermos, books, and candy when they went on a weekend hike. This time he packed his shorts, underwear, and socks. He was moving very quickly, mechanically. Then he caught sight of the medicine bottles on the dresser. A few bottles of antibiotics, painkillers, multi-vitamins, and the psychosomatic adjusters he'd lately been using were stacked on top of each other, waiting for him with stickers that read: *physician's sample- not for resale.* He tossed these into the bag. He opened the drawer of his bedside dresser, took out a volume of poetry by the Poet Dogan Gokay called "Brunette Ada," and stood stroking the cover for a while. He placed this carefully into his backpack. Then he picked up from where he had left off, like a robot whose switch had been turned back on. From the same drawer, he took a chocolate bar with nuts, and added this to his belongings. He checked the contents of his wallet: some money, identification, ATM card, license, and phone card.

"I have everything I need for a long trip!" he thought. As he did, he saw his own reflection in Merich's full-length mirror. It was a young man whose curly black hair and glasses rested on an unimpressive, frail frame. The doubt embedded in the blue eyes of the young man reminded him of a newspaper story he'd read in horror some years back.

It was the story of a strange, humiliating game, staged on a local Istanbul ferry by a weekly magazine. Two men in black trenchcoats and shades (with turned up collars and hands in pockets) had suddenly appeared on deck and in a strict voice, ordered the passengers: "Quick, hit the ground!"

The passengers had followed this order without exception, and without a word of protest. The experiment had succeeded, and the conventional wisdom had once again been proven correct in a live laboratory:

"Turks are afraid to ask questions!"

"Turks don't know how to stand up for their rights!"

"In Turkey one only gives or receives orders!"

"Turks have lived trembling, oppressed and meek for fear of being punished now or in the future by either a divine being, or a few choice persons from above."

"But will Turks always stay this way?"

....

"Isn't it true?" Duna had yelled. "If the experiment had yielded the same results during the Ottoman monarchy it might've been understandable, but when a hundred years later, not one of these passengers living under a democracy, dares ask who these men might be... man, it makes my blood boil! It drives me crazy to think of it!"

He had turned around, and started chewing on his lip to control his frustration, but the words had fallen with an even greater force from his battered lips:

"This is simply Pavlov's dog reflex, and these are our people... And face it, we're no different!" He was trembling. Ada had finally opened her mouth and said:

"Oh Mabel! It hasn't even been a hundred years yet...We're just learning. We'll learn freedom by hurting, by bleeding both on the inside and the outside. Just like you and me."

Duna had pretended not to hear.

"To ask- to ask requires courage! It requires independence, and that's the courage we lack! I don't count slashing yourself with razors and running to greet death as courage, that's just madness!"

"And isn't that what I'm telling you my sweet Mabel? But...how can I say this? I think what bothers you most is that if we had been there we would've hit the ground like everyone else."

How that remark had hurt him. It was not that Ada's reaction came as a surprise. She always explained things by weaving together theories of the abstract, the historical, and the emotional with a maddening coolness, then presented these ideas to people around her in a self-congratulatory manner! She was exactly like her uncle, the Poet Dogan Gokay: to those who loved them, both were rare, sincere intellectuals of addictive depth. What irked Duna in earnest was the dumb obedience displayed on the ferry, and most importantly, the possibility that Ada was right...He had carried this incident in his head for days and suffered from it.

"But we should be able to ask! By this time, we should be able to!" he now said aloud in the bedroom.

His image in the mirror had come alive, and the estrangement he felt from it had disappeared. He picked up his backpack with a determined gesture, and headed toward the main door. When he opened it, the two soldiers were still there. (Ah, so it hadn't been an illusion...)

"Just a minute!" said Duna in a slightly harsh but intent voice. "How should I believe you are who you say you are?"

The soldiers stood staring in surprise.

"I mean I want documents, proof of identification! You could very well be people disguised as soldiers, you could even be terrorists!"

Once again, the lieutenant was first to collect himself.

"You're right, sir," he said, smiling. "We are all so suspicious these days that we should have shown you the documents before you even asked. Here's your mobilization draft order."

Duna took the computer printout that was held out to him.

"Actually, the public TV and radio stations have been broadcasting special news of mobilization since four fifty a.m... Private stations have also been completely informative of the situation – that is, those which could continue to broadcast."

"Those which could continue to broadcast?"

"Yes. Here, this is my own identification. I'm First Lieutenant Birol Onay, and this is private Demir!"

The ID card had a serious looking passport picture, a cold stamp, logos and acronyms symbolizing the Turkish Armed Forces, and a date of birth on it.

"You're five years younger than me!" exclaimed Duna in surprise.

First Lieutenant Birol smiled.

"Can we go now, sir?"

"The cat!" Duna suddenly remembered. "I have to prepare dinner for the cat, she gets hungry around five in the evening."

He ran hastily into the kitchen. He got a can of cat food from the cupboard. The cat instantly appeared when she got a whiff of the liver smell. She dove into the surprise meal with appreciative purrs.

"I guess I'm really leaving, Brunette," Duna whispered.

The cat didn't pay any attention. Duna crouched next to her and stroked her hair. Ignoring any linguistic expert who might protest that "Cats don't have 'hair' in Turkish!", he stroked the brown hair of his cat. He petted Brunette, knowing full well that cats don't like being touched while they eat.

"So, they really do come and take you away to a civil war... Well, don't you find this a little odd?"

The cat stopped abruptly and, licking her mouth, looked at Duna. She blinked, and waited as if listening to him.

"See girl, the time has come for me to face this civil war which I have been dreading for years! You understand, don't you?"

The cat left her food and sat down.

"Maybe, Brunette, who knows, maybe it's impossible to run away from a necessary war? What do you say, huh? And I suppose it's time I learned that."

The cat blinked, as if she'd understood everything, and meowed restlessly. Cats can feel the tension in a house.

After checking Brunette's water bowl one last time, Duna stood in the kitchen doorway. The cat had turned her yellow gaze directly into his eyes.

"Goodbye Brunette!"

Suddenly he remembered something. He ran into the living

room, opened the glass display case, and tossed a small white, elliptical stone into his bag. He rejoined the soldiers who were still waiting for him at the door, and said:

"Gentlemen, I'm ready!"

He shut the door behind him.

As they descended the narrow stairs with First Leuitenant Birol in the lead and Private Demir bringing up the rear, Duna felt like a convict walking between them. But the question of whether he was an innocent man under slander, or whether he was truly guilty seemed too complicated even for himself. He'd just began a new inner argument as to who was guilty and who was innocent in civil wars, when First Leuitenant Birol spoke:

"We do not know much about you, but you are related to the famous Gokay name-"

"You mean you conducted research on me?" asked Duna, irritated.

"As much as everyone else. We know that you are a high school teacher, that your wife is a doctor, that you served a short-term military service, that –"

"Oh damn!" Duna stopped dead in his tracks. The soldiers also stopped. "Merich! Of course…how could I forget? I should have left her a message…Now my mother's going to be worried too. Damn!"

"We notified the missus, sir," said Leuitenant Birol in a friendly voice.

"When did you tell Merich?"

"This morning. She said you were in the bathroom at the time."

"But she didn't tell me anything," muttered Duna, as if in a dream.

"When men are going to war, their wives and mothers become extremely emotional," whispered Leuitenant Birol, as if letting him in on a secret.

They resumed their descent. On that Tuesday morning, the stairs of the tiny, two-story apartment building seemed to Duna as endless as if they had been a skyscraper's.

"I didn't see Merich at all this morning. She practically fled the house. And that odd message, as if…"

"Women aren't like us, sir!" said First Leuitenant Birol.

This time Duna halted very consciously. The soldiers followed suit. He looked at the Leuitenant's face in indignation. He searched carefully, but could not find a trace of mockery, disdain, or exclusion in that handsome young face.

"They do not have standard reactions like us men," Leuitenant Birol felt the need to explain.

"They all have their own reactions. It's us men who act homogeneously, and who immediately accuse women of being unpredictable and inscrutable when we feel threatened by them!"

"A woman is like a stormy sea, commander!" grinned Private Demir. Then, thinking that he'd spoken out of bounds, he somehow managed to stand to attention in that narrow stairwell.

"Commander, sir!" he cried.

His voice echoed in the bright emptiness of the building. Completely confused, Duna looked suspiciously at First Lieutenant Birol. Dense, slippery clumps of thought were running through his mind at a great speed.

"Is it possible that a military officer should think in such a modern, universal way? Besides, is he allowed to express his thoughts so freely? If being a soldier means following the rules down to the letter, then what's this Lieutenant doing? There can only be two answers: either this Leuitenant is not entirely assimilated yet, or... none of this is real!"

Before they reached the landing, he'd already wholeheartedly embraced the latter theory: "Of course, none of the things that happened this morning are real! It didn't even seem real...All this is a dream! I'm dreaming...Yes, yes, this is all a nightmare...Soon I'll wake up, and the nightmare will be over! It's just a mean trick my brain is playing on me...A trick of my own brain..."

His eyes were dazzled by a sudden glare, but he forced them open.

KUZGUNCUK, ISTANBUL

*"A man who works in Beykoz should live in Beykoz
Yet Kuzguncuk is a sweet place
And quite superb are the rose preserves of the pensionist
Madame, and her daughter Rachel..."*

Nazim Hikmet

I was born in Kuzguncuk.

If you ask me, Kuzguncuk is still a village on the Bosphorus.

It used to be a village in 1776. It is shown on the Kauffer map as a triangular settlement with the seaside as its base. Elder people tell of how Chengelkoy was mostly Armenian, and Kuzguncuk predominantly Jewish. The Moslems were minorities back then. It had not been a rich neighborhood, and still isn't. It can politely be called "middle-class," or "of limited means."

This is the reason behind the saying:

"Famous is Kuzguncuk's refuse,

Beylerbeyi's manners

and Chengelkoy's produce." It's true, our Kuzguncuk has many junk collectors, artisans, and merchants, and I was born here into one of these families.

Naturally, when four different cultures were kneaded into the native charm and abundance of as magnificient a Mediterrenaean city as Istanbul, the already existent joys, tastes, and beauties of this town were increased four-fold. Just like explorers who grew wise and erudite from their travels to far-off lands, the people of Kuzguncuk had combined the four separate tastes of the cultures that came to their feet...I am part of the last generation of Kuzguncuk-

ites who've managed to see a mere hint of this fading cultural pan-
orama.

The Kuzguncukite has learned how to eat a scorpion fish from
the Armenians, and a rockling from the Jews. The Greeks cook a
mean silverside, their salt bonitos are famous, and their vegetable
dishes in olive-oil are superbly delicious, not to mention ornate.
Grandpa could never stop praising Armenian stuffed mussels. The
Jews were also renowned for their fig preserves, and their pear and
apple desserts. My mother had first seen a chocolate-machine at
Madame Esther's, and tasted her first home-made chocolate there.

My grandmother, who'd grown up with the Moslem cooking of
Istanbul, brought the incredible delicacies and wealth of Ottoman
cuisine to our tables with her artichokes in olive-oil, buttered lamb
kabobs, fragrant chicken pilafs, saffron pudding, dilled chick-peas,
mince-meat pastries, stuffed grape leaves, famed mullah-pleaser
and sultan's favorite, which are stuffed and charred eggplant
dishes, respectively. Despite the fact that she had been raised with
cooks and nannies, and had been blessed with a father intelligent
enough to value her education as much as that of a son's, my
grandmother used to toil for hours to cook these dishes for us with
her own dear hands.

My grandmother's true specialty was in desserts, though, and
we kids were spoiled with her creations. The first ones that spring
to mind are her pear and apple desserts cooked with musk mallow,
icy sherbets that refreshed us in the summer, starch wafers, rice-
pudding with finely shredded chicken, and those illustrious desserts like almond baklava that were only made on religious holidays
with the help of neighbors, to be served to guests.

I still don't know if grandpa was not as good a cook as he was a
tailor, or if he simply did not want to compete with my grandmother.
While the latter was still alive, grandpa would sometimes be persuad-
ed by my father's pleas to make Bulgarian bean stew. After my grandmother's death he proved to us that his culinary skills were not half
bad. My mouth waters when I think of his fruit tortes.

I never saw my father cook. My father never showed us that he
was passionate or adamant about anything. My mother, on the
other hand, presented us with tastes she brought with her from the
East. She was famous for her Circassian chicken with walnuts, vari-

ous flat breads, tender lamb in bulgur, and her raisin-grain pudding.

When I was young I'd give candy and meat to our non-Moslem neighbors during our religious holidays, and they'd bring us painted eggs, sweets and breads during Easter and other holidays. No one was wealthy among us, but no one was belligerent, condescending, or boastful either.

I'm one of those who were lucky enough to witness the years when Kuzguncuk resonated with the live music spilling out of peoples's houses. It is not surprising that those who consider playing the accordion, piano and violin to be an essential part of life should also know how to enjoy life itself. Grandpa used to say that during the notorious fire of Arapzade, a piano had been found in every house.

Both my grandma and grandpa played the tambur, which is a Turkish lute. Some evenings our neighbor, Uncle Yahya, would improvise on the zither, and the violinist Yorgo and grandpa would drink raki, eat fish, bean stew, and sing Greek, Bulgarian, and Turkish songs together. We kids loved music. Because music entertains, because grown-ups who make and listen to music don't have any time to fight.

Later, Ada's father started inviting the musicians over to his mansion for musical sessions which he joined with his superb voice. But these were largely family events.

Nevermind today's mansions, which are more like self-styled prisons with their towering walls and security guards. Those people aren't from Kuzguncuk anyhow, their address is the Bosphorus. You cannot live in Kuzguncuk and not feel it! Nowadays, people around here say that the waterfront mansions have turned their backs to Kuzguncuk. The real Kuzguncukites live on Kuzguncuk's Charshi Avenue, where life still goes on in an axis balanced by Icadiye Avenue.

Yet when I was a child, the mansions were also Kuzguncukites. It was improper to show one's wealth, and to talk about money; it was considered bad manners. Humanity and neighborliness were alive and well, but no one poked their nose into each other's business, or tried to enforce their own traditions and values. No one's belief, or lack thereof, was any more holy than anyone else's, as long as it did not harm anyone. Maybe that was the main reason that during the separatist riots of September 6-7, outsiders who infiltrated neighborhoods to start trouble were least successful in Kuzguncuk.

Back then, mansion owners would purposefully keep their doors open to neighbors, in marked contrast to their current counterparts. When we kids made a friend from the waterside-mansions, we wouldn't feel at all lacking; rather, we'd be glad to have found a new place to swim. In fact, the mansions were built facing Kuzguncuk, with their backs towards the sea.

"It would've been rude of them to have their back to the Sultan when he went by, so they turned their face to the street, and their back to the water, m'boy," grandpa used to say.

When someone pointed out that there were no seaside roads on old maps, he'd get mad and grumble that "them scribblings must be from Byzantine times, not from the Ottoman era!"

We had lots of springs to swim in, endless meadows to run around on, and plenty of trees to climb. We used to play to our hearts content in Mocan Grove (now called by its old name, Fethi Pasha). The stream would flow nearby, and families would picnic around pine and walnut trees. No one would disturb or abuse anybody else with their music, their noise, their trash, their food, or their persistent stares (and to think that these are simply the memories of a thirty-something!).

I was born in Kuzguncuk. In other words, I was born and bred here, unlike Ada. True, her family's move into Kuzguncuk had attracted the attention of several previously oblivious artists to our unpretentious but polyphonic village. Consequently, some newspapers had even written articles about Kuzguncuk, which was more than likely the reason why some of the gorgeous, abandoned houses were renovated and saved from demolition. Furthermore, it could easily be said that Ada's well-known mother, father, and uncle contributed an amount of classy fame, and even respectability to our neighborhood. Yet it was on one particular local family that their move had its largest effect. The relocation of Ada and her folks irrevocably changed the entire fate and future of one Kuzguncukite family: My own!

The people of Kuzguncuk can never forget the popular fate of these two families. If Ada's family had never moved to Kuzguncuk, my family's life would have been completely different. Theirs too, of course. How would it have been, where would it have gone? No one will ever know.

All we know is what has happened.

My great-grandfather, Osman the tailor, was a Bulgarian Moslem who emigrated to Anatolia after the 1913 War of the Balkans. Kuzguncuk had never been a popular neighborhood for Thracian immigrants. His story is somewhat like those of captains who change their routes due to a coincidence. While his relatives were largely settling in Silivri, my great-grandfather was staying with his wife and son at a friend's house in Uskudar. Grandpa was only six years old then, and says that he constantly used to miss the friends he'd left back in Bulgaria.

Upon meeting Master Johannes the Kuzguncukite tailor, my great-grandfather had taken his young wife and son Muharrem, and made his way to Kuzguncuk, and there it was that he'd stayed. He'd opened a small dress shop here. With a shop adjacent to Master Johannes, who was famous for his hand-made neckties, my great-grandfather had started working on shirts, and built up a reputation. They'd had very hard times during the war years, and lived on the brink of hunger after he miraculously returned alive from the War of the Dardanelles. But once the Republic was established, the "fine gentlemen of Istanbul", who had heard especially about young Muharrem's craft, had begun frequenting Kuzguncuk to buy their shirts and neckties, and business had recovered.

In those days, the Jews, Greeks, and Armenians were considered natives of Kuzguncuk. Even though Muslim and Turkish families were a minority, they could live together without trouble and were allowed to intermarry. A non-Muslim who married a Muslim would usually convert, but continue to practice his own religion as long as it did not disrupt what was considered the common traditions of Kuzguncuk. Since those who were more educated and well-to-do favored Ortaköy, our Kuzguncuk was a modest neighborhood even in those years. There are very few neighborhoods in Istanbul which possess such a sense of tolerance and understanding among diverse populations. I am a firm and proud believer of this fact, as are all Kuzguncukites.

While learning the family trade at his father's side as a young man, grandpa fell in love with one of Kuzguncuk's Jewish beauties, by the name of Rozita. The story of Rozita and grandpa still carries a sense of magic for those who were around to see it.

The love affair between Rozita of Kuzguncuk, then a curly, red-haired girl of sixteen, and blue-eyed Muharrem of Plevna, himself only nineteen, had reached such legendary proportions that everyone knew about it. The poems penned by grandpa, Rozita's dreamy expression, the love-letters sent by private messengers…The nights they went to the Easter fair, during which Icadiye Avenue was closed to traffic and covered with carpet…The way they'd danced for three nights and three days to the celebrated barrel-organ at the fair, and carved themselves into people's memories…

Their families, who were Kuzguncukites enough not to see any choice except marrying them in the face of their famed love, had organized a modest wedding the following year. Rozita had converted and assumed the name of Gulkiz, but no one touched her name: everyone still called her Rozita.

My grandmother is not Rozita, but Mrs. Murshide, who became a bride to Kuzguncuk much later. With Rozita's death from tuberculosis, one year after their marriage, grandpa had retreated into years of mourning, dedicating himself solely to his work. Grandpa was a truly fine and sensitive person; a man who was generous enough to allow his young wife, whose death he simply couldn't comprehend, to be buried in a Jewish cemetery.

Besides being considered by European Jews to be the last stop before reaching the Promised Land, Kuzguncuk also has another attribute. It is said that Jews who die before reaching Jerusalem wish to be buried in Kuzguncuk. That's especially the reason why I find grandpa's decision, made during a period of great youth and grief, worthy of respect.

The refinement of spirit that the Plevnian tailor Muharrem possessed was reflected in the clothes he sewed, and his work immediately drew attention, as if it had been a work of art. I think of him frequently, and greatly miss him. Grandpa has always been younger and closer in thought to me than my father. My father was an introspective, quiet, patient, and hard-working man. Grandpa always likened him to Mrs. Murshide.

The shop where grandpa spends all of his time, having withdrawn from the world after the consumptive death of his young wife, soon bears his own name:

Plevnian Tailor Muharrem Atacan.

Now he has rich customers from Sisli, and Mecidiyekoy, he's making a neat sum, and it's his turn to provide for his parents. Not long afterwards, he buys the Greek house, adjacent to the one his parents had bought with the gold and the meager savings they'd brought over from Bulgaria. Greek houses are built of stone, like their Armenian counterparts, except that the upper stories of the former are built on wood frames, with wood slating, and make tasteful residences. But there are no bathrooms in Christian houses (they went to the baths). Of course, like all other Muslims, grandpa has a bathroom built right away.

One of grandpa's wealthy patrons has a modern, educated, and graceful daughter who has been widowed, and one day this girl comes to grandpa's shop with her gentleman father. Mrs. Murshide falls in love at the first sight of the Plevnian tailor Muharrem, who is seven years her junior, and who, like herself, is widowed. In time, she succeeds in unlocking grandpa's painfully shut heart with great patience, cultivation, and love. They get married and my father is born a year later. My grandmother remains forever embarrassed about reaching motherhood at an age that would be considered late in comparison to her contemporaries.

Ah dear Mrs. Murshide, my dear grandmother, there have emerged those Turkish women who, two generations later, found the opportunity to care for their occupations, educations, and themselves more than the act of mothering, and who were not ashamed. May your mind be at ease, and your soul rest in peace!

The grandson of one of Rozita's cousins who lived in Ortaköy would always get a grand reception at our house, when he came to visit his relatives in Kuzguncuk. Nesim, who was a couple of years older than me, was well loved by all of us. Grandpa treated him no different than us, I suppose he saw him as his own grandson.

Yet grandpa did not have any affection for Nesim's grandmother, who'd say things like "Ortaköyans wake to the cock's crow, and Kuzguncukites to the donkey's bray!" Apparently Rozita's cousin looked down on her relatives who lived in Kuzguncuk. Me and Nesim used to giggle at these words, while grandpa grumbled ominously.

Perhaps owing in part to grandpa's influence, I still love Nesim at a comfortable median between a close friend and a close relative. Sometimes we talk about the young girl with the dreamy eyes whom neither of us ever met, and whose old, tattered black and white photograph is a keepsake from grandpa…That girl who gives us both the feeling of a common, warm, peaceful past, and who bears the colors of affection, friendship, and love…His grandmother's cousin, grandpa's first wife, Rozita!

And whenever we meet or talk on the phone, we promise ourselves to visit her grave, but somehow we never succeed. Maybe it's because the idea of visiting a cemetery is none too pleasant, or because today's Ortaköy and Kuzguncuk do seem further apart from one another…

When the Surname Law was declared, making it mandatory to have a last name, most of our Bulgarian emigré relatives had preferred trade related names like "Tailor," or "Tailorson." My great-grandfather on the other hand, had chosen "Atacan" because of his admiration for Ataturk. My grandfather had always been proud of this choice. Perhaps due to this pride, he'd always address my grandmother as "Murshide Atacan."

"My, my, how lovely you look, Murshide Atacan!"

"That's your kind opinion Mr. Muharrem!"

I remember my grandmother faintly, dressed in stylish two-piece suits made by grandpa. When I combine all that I've been told of her with the photographs in my possession, I can say that she was a modern, chic, shy and distanced woman. Once, grandpa let it slip that even when the two of them were alone, she did not release the passion in her heart. I suspect their relationship was not much like the one grandpa had with Rozita.

"Murshide Atacan was like all girls who were well-educated back then… she couldn't let herself go, Duna, m'boy!"

Kuzguncuk is a love-hungry Bosphorus village. By the time my father is ten years old, this time it is being racked with stories of a young doctor's hopeless devotion to an older, married woman. The poems written by the young doctor are read on European Hill, the young girls sigh with envy, and this love story becomes a famous song, spreading through Istanbul in Fehmi Ege's doleful voice:

> "Eighteenth of July
> made us both cry
> may the moon impress
> its trace on the Bosphorus.
>
> O heavenly lover
> I loathe to say goodbye
> and what I call our love
> is a yellow butterfly…"

This love song which reminded grandpa of Rozita, must have so wounded my grandmother that later, when my mother learned and started to sing it, she is said to have ran out, slamming the doors behind her.

My grandmother died when I was young. What I remember of her death is more of a reserved sorrow than tears and wails. In a manner befitting her character, her death was greeted with the utmost calm and respect. Grandpa had given her tambur to my dad, her mostly Ottoman books to us, and her embroideries to my mom. After the prayers on the fortieth day of her death, a concert had been given of Murshide Atacan's favorite classical Turkish music, and candy had been distributed to the neighborhood kids.

The absence of my grandmother who always preferred to stay in the background, and to love from a distance, was not openly felt in the household…It was as if she was still in her upstairs room, reading and drinking coffee, and would soon call to me with that angelic voice I faintly remember:

"Blue Duna, my grandson, would you care for some ginger cookies?"

My grandmother's presence had remained in the house, and it never left…

Grandpa did not mourn after his second wife, but rather, taught me and my older brother Aras, songs that she'd liked, and had us read the books she had read. To this day, when I read Tevfik Fikret's poem "Ferda," or hear Ismail Dede Efendi's song, "Sana ey canimin cani efendim," I feel as glad as if grandma had promptly appeared and held my hand. Yet grandpa himself preferred folksongs and airs, which he'd get up and dance to every so often.

"Grandpa, why did grandma die? Was she sick?" I would ask
him, and he would succeed in quickly changing the preoccupied look in his eyes into a blue twinkle, and say:

"Eh, why do you think, because she didn't eat enough yoghurt! We were used to eating bowl after bowl of yoghurt in Plevna, my blue Danube boy, and mind you, yoghurt keeps away all sorts of ills!"

I guess these words have had some effect on my still present affinity for yoghurt. As I've gotten older, I have started to think more and more of my grandmother. I have tried to understand her, to read the meanings behind the face masked with calm in photographs. I have come to believe that she felt lacking, owing to her seniority over her husband, and her belief that she was not as beautiful as Rozita, that the more she suffered, the more she withdrew into her shell. I always think, how many people have gone to waste since we based our world culture on the young and pretty woman, and the young and strong man...

The story that my father, while stationed in Kars during military service, fell in love with the dark-eyed, dark-haired, willowy, defiant Zubeyde is not false, but it is incomplete. For it was my mother who saw my father, and got it in her head to marry him. It was also my mother who managed to persuade her father to let her come to Istanbul as a bride. My mother was an intelligent and determined girl who succeeded in gaining the acceptance of her great, venerable Istanbulite mother-in-law, (whom she still refers to as "good-mother") and her Ottoman, world-weary father-in-law, ("gentle-father").

My mother's father, Hadji Ali, had been one of the small, progressive merchants of Igdir, and a supporter of Ataturk's revolution. Igdir, which was at the time attached to Kars, always saw itself as "the rose of the East." Grandpa, who grew sugarbeets, had sent his two boys, Mustafa and Kemal to military school, and when my mother, Zubeyde, came as a surprise at a later age, greatly spoiled her, allowing her to go to school bare-headed.

Her father never told his son-in-law that he'd hoped little Zubeyde would marry an officer or a teacher, instead of a tailor. Nevertheless, my dad always felt its crush in his heart. I would sense this from the bright yellow hurt that appeared in his eyes everytime he said that he wanted me and my brother to get a higher education.

Our relatives on my mother's side always remained distant and unknown to us, with the exception of my uncles. Sometimes we received packages from Igdir, containing great rolls of sheep-cheese in tin boxes, dried plums and apples (which my mother called "kak"), pure honey in the comb, dried fruit paste, and walnut "sausages", which are actually rolls of dried fruit paste and walnuts. My favorite was the great head of sugar. This was a gigantic, two-pound slab which my mother would chip away at with a pair of sugar tongs and use sparingly in her tea. And then there was "kesmece," which grandpa could die for. He said it reminded him of Plevna. Kesmece was similar to baklava, but it was cooked with pure fruit starch, then laid out to dry in the sun, placed in a baklava tray, and served just like baklava.

Whenever a package of provisions arrived from Igdir, my mother would grow so overjoyed that, like all kids, I would get excited from her sheer gladness. My brother Aras would attribute my happiness to the food, but the true reason I still love the fine tastes of these Eastern foods might be my mother's joy.

My mother would savor the food. My grandmother, with her great goodwill, would praise these dishes to high heaven, thus bolstering my mother's pride.

To us, Igdir was very far away, it was almost a place in Neverneverland. Igdir, to a Kuzguncuk kid like me, lives, just like Plevna, as a mysterious part of my past. Every year me and my mother plan to go there...

Oh Kuzguncuk! Witness of my childhood, my boyhood; partner to my pains and joys; o town that gave Ada to me, you are, in my view, the most boisterous of Bosphorus villages! Magical, comfortable, good friend Kuzguncuk!

Kuzguncuk is a place to love. One does not have to force himself to like it; Kuzguncuk is already expert at endearing itself. And I guess the love of living somewhere, coupled with the desire to stay, is what defines being "from" a place.

In short, however you look at me, you'll find traces of Kuzguncuk. For, your life is a portrait of the place(s) you've lived in. Mine's first name is Kuzguncuk.

THOSE WERE NOT FAIRYTALES!

> "Civil war is not a virus that is contracted from foreign lands, from unknown sources; it is an internal process. It is always initiated by a minority, for if one person out of every hundred did not want you, it might be enough to render living together in a civilized manner impossible."

Hans Magnus Enzenberger

When they were kids, swimming hours began with the dawn of the summer sun. The sea was clean then, and they were kids...Nesim, Musa, Sefer, Aret, Kosta, Aras, Ada, and Duna... Actually, Ada and Duna only joined the others every once in a while. During summer vacation, these two preferred to stay in the mansion's garden, drawing pictures, playing games, and daydreaming in the shade of the fig trees. It had only been twenty years since then, but things were as different as if it had been a century ago.

Upon dropping the arm with which he'd shielded his eyes from the dazzling Kuzguncuk sun, Duna came face to face with a military truck. Could this huge truck, parked in front of his house on Uryanizade Street also be an illusion?

When he raised his head and squinted around, he could see people leaning from their windows and balconies. They were all women and children.

He never knew there were that many women and children living on his street. But was this possible? Could this many women and children fit into these houses? Perhaps relatives had gathered together with the announcement of mobilization, and had already started forming a peaceful world, comprised of the women and children left by themselves, after the men had gone off to fight a civil war... But could such a thing possibly be true? Were men and testosterone, as it was always claimed, the source of this cursed violence, this waste as old as history itself? Were men alone burdened with the sin of so much blood and death? No, no, that couldn't be....Women and children had their own civil wars, and war was the invention of human beings. It was specific only to humans, women and children included.

"Didn't Golding describe in *Lord of the Flies* how children, and not only grown people, were capable of creating evil?" he whispered to the person next to him.

And suddenly a new question exploded in his head.

"Well, what if the children on that deserted island had been girls?"

When he turned to look at the person next to him, he met the handsome Lieutenant Birol, who was watching him with sad eyes. (So, the dream goes on!)

"Go on, sir, get in the vehicle, we have a long way to go!" said the Lieutenant, gently patting his back.

Before he boarded the military truck, Duna raised his head one last time. The expression he saw on the faces of the women and children leaning from their windows and balconies was that of people about to watch a formidable horror film: half tense and half suspicious.

"Either they can't believe it yet, or they too know that this isn't real!" Duna whispered once more.

It was as if the tens, dozens, hundreds of faces suspended in the sky were a still from a Fellini movie. And just like the theatricality and simulated surrealism of these faces, civil war seemed to be an imaginary disease caught by foreign countries in movies, novels, and television; not something that would happen to you or your country...(but what if it's not a dream?)

As he took a large leap into the military truck covered with khaki-colored canvas, an old woman caught his eye in one of the windows. She had a beatific face, a gauze kerchief covered her hair, and her lips were moving. When he stuck out his head to look again she was gone.

"Good God, isn't that Mrs. Murshide?" he murmured in excitement, but immediately changed his mind. "But grandma never used to cover her hair…"

Mrs. Murshide would pray five times a day, and frequently read the Qoran and Yasin. However, she was very averse to showiness and exaggeration, and that was the reason Duna had never seen this deeply religious Muslim woman with her head covered. She would gather her pure white hair in a bun at her neck, and wear dresses with long, close-fitting skirts. She had a very sparse, individual sense of style.

Duna was half-blind during the time it took his eyes to adjust to the dimness of the truck. He groped for the wooden bench, and perched on its edge. Just then, his hand touched a man's leg, making him realize he was not alone. Quickly withdrawing it, he apologized. The man didn't make a sound.

Duna shut his eyes tightly and began to take long breaths. He could hear Lieutenant Birol's voice coming from outside. Even though he couldn't make out what the leuitenant was saying, he sensed from the rhythm of the voice that Birol was receiving an order, and replying "Yes, Sir!" in a determined tone.

'So there's a higher-ranking officer in the front of the truck," he thought.

He was glad to realize that the soldier who nimbly leapt unto the vehicle right as it started moving, and took a seat next to him was First Leuitenant Birol. (Why should he be glad?) Private Demir had sat across from them.

When Duna tried to move over and make more room for Leuitenant Birol, he bumped into the same man.

"Excuse me, I'm bothering you," he mumbled without looking at the man. Once again there was no response.

"I thought civil wars were times when houses and stores got looted and sacked, when the streets echoed with stray bullets, when people ran for their lives over the strewn bodies of the dead and dying…When fires were started… and child murderers, rapist freaks, and opportunistic fanatics ran amock…When you could only smell fear, and burnt, crushed hope. I mean, that's how civil wars are portrayed in movies and books, isn't it? Like those views of Bosnia we saw on TV…isn't it, Mr. Birol?"

"Unfortunately, some parts of town are in the state which you describe, lieutenant. These here are areas where the curfew is still observed, and which are still under control. Oh, and, lieutenant," whispered First Lieutenant Birol, "you need to call me 'lieutenant, sir.' Even though it's not what I would prefer, those're the rules, you know…"

"Oh, of course, of course," Duna assented, feeling slightly embarrassed. Then he thought, "not only does he want me to call him 'leutenant,' but "leutenant, sir," because he wants to prove to me that I am a part of all this! Birol is not to blame of course, it's my own brain that's planning all this!"

"In a civil war, it is much more difficult to determine who's against who, and one must be constantly alert and prepared for every situation, lieutenant," Birol said.

"To be constantly alert!" sighed Duna. "So it's finally happened! I have to face what I've feared and anticipated for years!"

"Strategically, lieutenant, wars where the enemy is clearly discernible, present a comparative ease and homogeneity of effort, whereas the most difficult ones are civil conflicts, which Hobbes calls 'everyone's war against everyone else'."

"So, the murderer and the victim are blurred!" murmured Duna.

Suddenly he felt exhausted. He felt the weight of years of weariness, anxiety, and sleeplessness on his body. At the same time an unease was spreading through his brain, like that of a person slowly realizing he was having a nightmare. Yes, the nightmare was snowballing as it approached, and he had to do whatever he could to wake up, to avoid the oncoming torture now. Right now! But he was just sitting in the military truck, utterly clueless as to a method of escape.

"My brain will protect me!" he thought cheerfully. "The human brain is powerful, and bears the instinct to preserve its body!" he muttered.

But his rejoicing was cut short. His thoughts surged with an incredible speed and intensity, more like deadly pieces of stray shrapnel than actual thoughts. They attacked from every direction, hurting him almost physically, and draining his energy.

Actually, the assault he was experiencing was nothing new. For a while now, his thoughts had been relentlessly pestering him to the point of exhaustion. He could not get away from his thoughts, or free himself from the feelings of fear, anxiety and alarm they created. He felt as if he was in the mercy of his thoughts and worries. The only person he could talk to was Ada, but he was afraid of exasperating her. Everything was alarming. The things that happened at home, at school, within himself, on the street, in the city, in the country, and the world in general, were at times too complicated, barbarous and ugly for him to handle, and at times too meaningless and terrifying to be explained by any law of reason, nature, or physics. He would try to bring about solutions by coming up with new ideas and projects, and would even succeed in giving hope to himself, his family, and his students, but would just as soon relapse with the emergence of a renewed outburst of violence, exploitation, or insensitivity.

All the values he'd been taught by people who sincerely believed in them had collapsed, and been discarded as worthless, empty, and ridiculous notions. Friendship, love, affection, humanity, equality, loyalty, common sense, forgiveness, freedom, trust, belief, justice, the way of reason...all, every single one of them had dropped out of use, or had had their contents changed, and were furthermore prohibited from being taken seriously by social law. As a result, Duna had known for a long time that his civil war was imminent. He had been waiting for the knock on his door.

Duna was waiting, like many others. Waiting was a staple of this age anyway. But not with fear. He waited more with suspicion, wondering "when, and in what guise will it knock on my door?"

Later, he waited impatiently, thinking: "Let it happen, whatever it is! Let us face each other and get it over with!"

So finally whatever was had come to be; there had been a knock on the door that Tuesday morning, and they had enlisted him, saying "Mobilization has been declared." In truth, he knew very well that he was starting on a journey which could help him reach the sense of peace he'd been longing for, by facing his inner fears, and paying their price. Therefore, these tales of mobilization and enlistment could only have been hatched by his own brain. They were not, and could not be real!

Just then, he felt Leuitenant Birol's hand on his shoulder, and heard him ask:

"Are you alright, lieutenant?"

"I'm fine, thank you, lieutenant, sir…I was just beginning to think that my sense of reality was damaged."

He smiled at the Lieutenant who'd fixed his puzzled brown eyes on his face.

"Seferberlik, eh?" he mumbled, musing on the word for 'mobilization.' "An Arabic word. It means preparation for war. The root of the word, 'sefer,' is used by itself to mean journey. And of course there's my childhood friend, Sefer the baker…" he said, smiling. Yet he'd always disapproved of people who tried to relax by pattering on and on.

He thought of his grandfather. Of the times he had called Duna and his friend, Sefer, the baker's son, in from the street where they had been playing, to tell them his stories of mobilization…The way he had sat in front of the stove during Kuzguncuk's dry, chilling winters, with his older grandson Aras, the family genius, on one side, and his younger grandson, his darling "Blue Duna," on the other…The way Duna's mother had warmed over the fruit paste from Igdir on the stove, and wrapped it with toasted apricot seeds to give to the children…

"Those weren't fairytales!" he muttered to himself.

First Lieutenant Birol turned to look at him anxiously. Assuming that Duna the teacher was undergoing a slight shock, he left him alone.

"The mobilization stories my grandfather told weren't fairytales, but they seemed like that to us back then," explained Duna.

Having emigrated to Istanbul after the Ottoman defeat in the War of the Balkans, his great-grandfather had gone off to fight in the Battle of the Dardanelles before he was even properly settled, and had returned miraculously safe and sound from a war that claimed one hundred and ninety thousand lives…

Fifty-five thousand martyred, ten thousand missing, one hundred thousand injured, and twenty-five thousand ill…Among the things Duna remembered were tales of poverty, hunger, and scarcity. The way his great-grandpa and family first stayed with relatives in Silivri, and then in Uskudar, until they finally settled down in Kuzguncuk…

And the deep impression left on him by his grandpa Muharrem, who could never restrain from weeping when he sang the song: "In the Dardanelles they shot me/ Before I died they buried me/ Alas, my youth, alas!"

Although the dates and the wars in which their grandfather and great-grandfather fought were often mixed-up, in those days the two brothers only cared about the heroics of their elders during the mobilizations. These stories featured feats of such supernatural proportions that they resembled the miraculous adventures of mythological heroes.

Grandpa Muharrem would exaggerate everything, either because he knew the impact of these tales from having listened to his father's Balkan War stories as a boy, or out of sheer willful fancy. Aras and Duna were still in grade school, and they loved to identify with the infinite, abstracted courage of the burly Turkish soldiers, whom they likened to fairytale heroes. But it was always ruined when Ada joined them in the audience, and kept interrupting the stories which the boys listened to with cheers of "hooray!" and "ta-da!" with her singular: "Just a minute, uncle Muharrem!"

"There were no tanks back then! Besides, people can't be nine feet tall, and in my opinion, creatures without wings can't fly!"

"But, my girl, everything seems different during a time of war!" their poor grandfather would say in a pleading voice.

"Look, we know all that! But we like the stories this way," Aras would interject sternly, protecting his grandfather.

Duna would smile. He'd voluntarily switch sides, giving into Ada's rebellious and reckless charm. He'd always think that hers was not a show of ill-will, but rather one of kind correction. The love and devotion he had for his grandpa would then be channeled into an admiration and passion for Ada.

"Womenfolk don't like war stories!" his grandfather would whisper after Ada left. They would understand that he had forgiven her for this reason, and would keep silent.

"If someone doesn't like war stories, can he not be a man, grandpa?" Duna would ask hesitantly.

"You're still young, my Blue Duna," his grandfather would say, and taking him into his arms would hug and kiss him.

Duna remained as Plevnian Tailor Muharrem's younger grandson, whose differences would always be tolerated.

"We became one fist, my boys!" his grandfather would pick up, making a fist. "We did not let the Enemy Boot trample over Turkish land; thanks first to my magnanimous God and next to the great Ataturk, we became one fist and punched the infidels on the face!"

The more concrete, realistic parts of his grandfather's wildly exaggerated stories were about the National War of Independence, which the old man had taken part in.

"Well, the occupying forces had gotten so out of hand, my boys, that they didn't hesitate to crack their whip upon the faces of Turkish police on the ferryboats. Oh, my little ones, may God never leave a man without land or country! May He never again let this nation be trampled on by enemy boots! May God protect you! O my great God, may he never banish anyone from their country and make them hapless!"

His grandfather's trembling voice and watery eyes would sadden Duna, who would lean on the old man's arm and stroke it gently in the hopes of providing comfort.

"How did you shoot, grandpa? Did you kill many enemies? Bang, bang, bang! Aargh!" Aras would ask excitedly, and then act out the scene, finally falling dead on the floor.

"What a calamity there is, my boys! The battlefield rings with cries of 'Allah Allah!' Your heart tears away, and runs ahead of you…Die, and you're a martyr, live and you're a *ghazi!* Nothing holds you back…You think of love of God, and country…your mother and your betrothed…if you have a kid, his face appears before you…and Ataturk, we would think of him. But finally, when you're running toward death you become blind, deaf, and dumb…You're no longer the one who's crying 'Allah, Allah!' and raging like a torrent!"

"What was your horse's name, grandpa?" Duna would ask.

"What horse are you talking about, boy? There was poverty, destitution! We would line up stove pipes next to each other like cannons, trying to trick the enemy, we'd put on our bayonets and charge ahead on foot."

The unmounted soldiers would take away all the magic of the tale, and spoil the mystery of the children's universe. The two brothers would begin to giggle.

"Eh, why do you laugh, my boys? Never forget: once your country is lost, nothing has any meaning left! Wiberty is as sweet as life itself!"

The fact that their grandfather couldn't pronounce "liberty" would strike the boys as even more funny, and soon they would be rolling around on the floor from laughter. And this would make the immigrant Tailor Muharrem really mad, whereupon he would start shouting angrily, forgetting that his grandsons were still children.

First their grandmother, and later their mother would rush to interfere and make amends. But grandpa, who prided himself on being "stubborn as a mule," would play it up for his wife or daughter in law, and things would get worse.

"Mr. Muharrem, their incessant laughter is because they are mere children. Such accidents would occur in our childhood too."

"What do you care about them, gentle-father? They're just little brats!"

Following a considerable period of grumbling, grandpa would appear to pardon the tomfoolery of his grandsons only after being bribed with a cup of slightly sweet Turkish coffee, and that on the condition that it be prepared on a stove or brazier. His daughter-in-law would always mutter,

"As if I wouldn't make him coffee without all that acting! How he becomes a kid himself with the kids! Oh well, old age, I suppose…"

For some reason, the smell of that coffee would seem much more full and enticing to Duna. He was too young to have any, but he'd beg his mother to make him the same coffee when he grew up.

"Just you grow big and strong, like a lion, then you'll see what coffees I'll make for you my Blue Duna, my sky-eyed boy," his mother would say, stroking his curly black hair.

Duna promised himself that he'd have some of his mother's superb coffee as soon as he got out of this nightmare.

"Why is there war, grandpa?"

"If you lose your wiberty, if your land is occupied, you become enslaved, my boy," his grandfather would reply, weeping silently as he remembered those years.

When their grandpa cried on the subject of enslavement, Aras

would get put off and leave the room, unable to reconcile his heroic, *ghazi* grandfather with this vulnerability. Yet these were the
times when Duna felt especially close to his grandfather, managing
to sense, if not fully grasp the importance of words like "liberty"
and "independent nation." The fact that his venerable old grandfather cried, just like a kid, would create in him a feeling of camaraderie.

"But who's the enemy now, grandpa? Who's occupying where,
and what freedom are we going to die for?"

"Are you alright, lieutenant?"

"Wha –?"

First Lieutenant Birol was now looking at Duna with outright
concern. That was when Duna noticed the machine gun Private
Demir was holding upright on his lap.

"Is it loaded?" he asked, pointing.

"Is what loaded?" Private Demir shot him a stern glance, trying
to determine whether he was serious.

"Sir, you're not well!" sighed Lieutenant Birol.

Duna simply sat hunched over, with his worried eyes fixated on
the gun opposite him, and his small backpack on his lap. He frequently adjusted his wire-framed glasses and, thinking that he was
the one really responsible for all this, fought back a shortness of
breath.

"Don't you worry, sir," whispered Lieutenant Birol. "I've seen
people who've experienced this shock much worse than you. Everything will be alright when you fully face reality."

"What reality?" asked Duna.

"Why, the reality of arriving at the barracks and surviving the
physical conditions," replied Lieutenant Birol, slightly surprised.

"Oh, the things this brain makes me put up with!" groaned
Duna.

"Everything is up to God's will, teacher Duna!" said the man
who had so far been sitting next to him silently.

It pleased Duna enormously to hear his name being pronounced. Turning sideways, he took a close look at the fellow next
to him. What he saw was a middle-aged man with a slight pouch
and thinning hair, whose black beard reached almost down to his
belly.

"What's the matter, don't you recognize me 'Blue Duna?' " the man said, taken aback. "Have we become such strangers?"

"Musa, is that you? Must be the beard, 'cause I swear, I couldn't make you out at all at first," Duna answered joyfully.

Musa had been a childhood friend of his, though he was actually the same age as Aras. He continued his father's business, running the grocery shop at Kuzguncuk. In the past few years he had gained a lot of weight, started losing his hair, and devoted himself completely to religion. He grew angry at those who did not go to the mosque, pressured his old friends on the subject, and even went so far as to stop saying hello to those who didn't.

"We thought we'd be seeing more of your face since the schools let out but you don't even, come by the store let alone the mosque!"

Musa's voice bore a trace of hurt rather than a reprimand.

"And yet we love both you and your family…What's there to it, we grew up together, thanks be to God, we're all Muslims!"

"There isn't always time, Musa! School, exam papers, homeworks, and you know, once you start tutoring over the summer…"

"But you've become too introverted, Duna. You never even show your face in public anymore! You never come to the mosque, or drop by the store…It isn't right, you know."

Musa's voice had softened up a little, with an affection born towards a young person not utterly beyond hope.

"It's so hard to believe what's happening, Musa," Duna began to confess.

"You were always this naive, Duna!" Musa said piteously. "Open your eyes, dear brother. All these are tricks, heathen tricks! Christian and Zionist imperialism is always playing tricks against the Ottoman. Furthermore, there are traitors amongst ourselves…Spirituality is out the window, there's no fear of God left in people!" Then, leaning down, he whispered in a softer voice: "What you are in is called a witless slumber, Duna, wake up, wake up or you'll be in sin, upon my word!"

"I too want to awake and return to reality, Musa. Here, let me tell you something, come closer," Duna beckoned, and said in his friend's ear: "I know that all this is actually my own nightmare. A scenario concocted by a vehemently pacifist brain, wracked by feelings of anxiety and panic... Do you understand, Musa?"

Musa made a face in response. He scratched his ears for a while. Then he checked Duna's forehead, saying: "Duna, brother, are you alright? Oh no, you're practically in flames, my poor brother! You must be raving from the fever."

"This is all my fault... My own fears, my hate towards war and violence caused all this... None of you are really here... This is simply my nightmare, and none of you are real, as you appear right now!" Duna sadly admitted.

There was a laughter from the men in the truck. (So, there were many of them!)

"What's this guy saying?"

"Poor thing must've lost it from the start!"

"Silence, fellow brothers! Can't you see that our brother the teacher is ill, and raving in his fever? For God's sake, don't bother him," Musa spoke up in defense. Then, to Duna he whispered: "Of course, you fell sick after reading the morning papers, isn't that right? That news about the movie stars' daughter must've driven you crazy... Want me to tell you something, my dear brother, God forgive me, I never quite liked that girl...Nevertheless...look here, it's a great sin to slander! Forget it, Duna brother, the media has made a pact with the devil anyway. These people would declare their own father a murderer if it'd help them sell better... Neither any religion left, nor any faith... God keep us all!"

"Ada!" Duna suddenly remembered.

His voice had the ring of someone who recognizes he has been shot as he is already falling down.

"But of course, how can I still be here? I have to find her right away!"

He leapt to his feet and yelled at the top of his lungs for the driver to hear:

"Stop this truck, I have to get off right now, right this instant!"

"Sir, please, relax, sit back down!" Lieutenant Birol tried to intervene, but Duna did not even hear him.

"I have to find Ada, I've got to find her! She needs me!" he was hollering.

"Hold him, he's going to jump!"

"This guy is nuts!"

When he jumped off the truck, after struggling free of the tight grasp Musa and Lieutenant Birol had on him, Duna was still screaming:

"I have to find Ada!"

WHERE DO THE STARS FALL?

"Those who first discovered and named the constellations were storytellers."

John Berger

We had misunderstood!

As a nation, we were demonstrating the far-reaching effects a small misunderstanding might have.

Those were the years when we all wanted to modernize as quickly as possible.

A lot was changing in due speed.

We were under the impression that throwing away all remnants of the past would transform us into new, different beings. Everything that was wrong and insufficient would be dumped out with the past, and from this clean slate a perfect country, as well as a brand new culture, would spring forth. In other words, it was the regrettable heyday of the misunderstanding that in order to become modern, we had to abandon many of our qualities. We didn't like anything about ourselves!

This fact, coupled with monetary greed, was the reason that the centuries-old beauty of Kadikoy and Uskudar were being destroyed. Erenkoy, famous for its Pembe Chavush grapes, pretty Moda adorned with nettle trees, Salacak that sent heads spinning with its fragrant pine and figs, and Fenerbahce, famous for its lilacs, hyacinths, and Joshua trees: these places were all being paved with concrete at an incredible speed. Not just ours, but both sides of Istanbul were striving to completely erase their history and nature.

Even in Kuzguncuk, which was known for its strawberries, the gardens had diminished, and instead of restoring those lovely two-story houses, people had chosen to have ugly apartment complexes built. Impatience, avarice, and tastelessness bred the highest degree of crudity. As I said before, we had misunderstood.

My mother wanted an apartment to be built in place of the three-story, wood-framed house my great-grandfather had once bought from a Kuzguncukite Armenian. For my mother, who had been born and raised in Igdir, "cement" meant modernity, and "apartment" meant comfort.

Grandpa was violently opposed to the demolition of either his father's house, or the adjacent one which was being used as a tailor's shop at the time. This was the first time he had fallen at odds with his daughter in law, for whom he had always professed a great fondness.

Dad was stuck between his wife and his father, and seemed resigned to leave everything up to either Providence or happenstance rather than take any initiative.

In the end my mother partially triumphed, and our house was turned into a three-story grey apartment building. Grandpa protected the two-story Greek house until the end, leaving us every night, as if he was a guest, to go next door to "his place" above the tailor shop.

While we were trying to modernize with all our might, the abandoned mansion across the street, rumored to have been built a hundred years ago by an Ottoman governor, began to witness a hustle-bustle.

"Finally they've wizened up. Together with the garden, you can fit two apartment buildings into that space," my mother said.

"Whoever cuts down those gorgeous fig trees will not be welcome either on this earth or in heaven, Zubeyde girl," grandpa muttered.

My dad stayed silent.

All through the winter and spring a surprising number of workers toiled on the house. Despite common expectation nothing had been torn down, but rather, that ruin of a mansion had been painted, restored, and transformed into a dazzling creation. Even the little fountain in its garden was working, spouting water out of fishes' mouths. The reparation of the garden had taken almost as long as the house itself, but had turned it into a dreamlike place, with a carpet of grass, colorful flowers, a vine-covered arbor, and swing.

"You could buy an apartment in Nisantasi for all this expense, gentle-father!" my mother exclaimed.

"There's no place better than Kuzguncuk in Istanbul, my girl!" grandpa answered.

My father kept quiet.

"Maybe these people are fortune-hunters or something."

"I heard they were smugglers, where else would you get all that money?"

"They say Americans bought the mansion."

"Oh come on, what would Americans have to do in Kuzguncuk?"

As the ornateness of its wood-carvings and the delicacy of its decorations emerged, the dazzling pink and white mansion became the talk of Kuzguncuk that spring. People continued to guess at its owners, but in the meantime two truckloads of furniture were brought to the door, a pure-breed Sivas kangal puppy, only a few months old, was introduced to the garden, and a plump, middle-aged couple settled into the house. While whispers that those were the gardener and the cook started spreading around, that girl who always walked together with a dark-haired, fussy, and smiling lady appeared in Kuzguncuk. Just as soon as we had learned that the accompanying woman was called "nanny," the real news was dropped like a bomb:

"It's Sureyya Mercan and Pervin Gokay who bought that mansion!"

"Oh my God, get out of here! Oh, I swear, I'm going to faint right now!"

"Come on, who'd come here when they can just as well live in Nisantasi, Sisli, or Bebek?"

I had gathered that the owners of the mansion were important and well-loved people, but I hadn't quite been able to figure out what it was they did. The wave of joy and excitement was greatest at our house, where my mom rejoiced as if we'd won the lottery, and kept my father informed while he, silent and steadfast as an ant, continued to labor at the sewing machine.

"I wouldn't believe it in my dreams, Naim! Just think, now you and I are going to be neighbors to Sureyya Mercan and Pervin Gokay! They say that these people have two maids, one gardener, and one cook! Plus the girl's nanny..."

"But mom, doesn't that girl have a mother? Why's she always going around with a nanny?"

My mother didn't even hear me.

"Stars are raining down on our neighborhood! If only my gentle-mother, may she rest in peace, had been able to see these days..."

"Mrs. Murshide would not have been able to live in this concrete house, she would have withered away from grief!" grandpa grumbled.

My father remained mum.

Everytime mom failed in her efforts to catch a glimpse of Sureyya Mercan and Pervin Gokay by hiding behind a curtain, she would heave a sigh and exclaim disappointedly:

"I suppose stars must have very irregular schedules..."

"Mom, doesn't that girl have a mom?"

"Sweetie, both that girl's father, and mother are stars!"

So she was a daughter of the stars! A stargirl!

"Stars are real busy people; they travel, they shoot movies... they go to parties and things... what else... I don't know... they're just not like us, they have different lives!"

Wow, so not only was she a daughter of the stars, but she was nothing like us!

"Remember that movie 'Fisherman Osman', the one that played at the summer theater last year? Well, that was Sureyya Mercan!"

"So that girl's dad is a fisherman? But mom, I thought you said he was a star!"

"No, my Blue Duna, my innocent boy. Sureyya Mercan was the handsome man who acted like the fisherman in that movie. He's a different person in every movie!"

Oh my God, what kind of girl was this that filled me with such mysterious joy and excitement? I was dying to get a better look at her, and to talk to her, but I could not muster the courage.

"Mom, doesn't that girl have a brother?"

"She's an only child, Duna dear."

My timidness was further increased by the mixture of reverence and longing that fell into my mother's voice whenever she talked about them.

My brother Aras had, as always, weighed, pondered, and firmly made up his mind on the issue. I might add that I never saw him regret any decisions. The logical, agile, smart and strong Aras!

My well-loved, successful, and self-confident older brother.

"That girl's just stuck-up!" he had said, and dismissed the whole matter.

My mother laughed at Aras, but she was also proud of the decisiveness of her son, whom she thought most resembled her own recently deceased father. Nevertheless, she couldn't allow her stars to be harshly judged.

"Well, of course, girls who grow up with nannies are supposed to be haughty," she had said.

"Eh, why do you say so Zubeyde girl, was Murshide Atacan spoilt, now, tell me that?"

"Good-mother was one in a million, gentle-father, may she rest in peace!"

I didn't care. I was very curious of this girl, and couldn't wait to meet her. Yet she had no idea that I was even alive, and I was too shy to make myself known to her.

Ever since the daughter of the stars had alighted in our neighborhood, my admiration and interest towards Aras had waned, and he had started to grow restless because he knew that "that girl" was the reason. I had given all my thoughts up to this girl; I wandered around, repeating her name as if in a dream, and gave up eating.

Aras was never in want of friends. He was brave, Aras. Bold and brash. Intelligent, and just. He was a true leader. It was an honour in the neighborhood to play with him, and to gain his approval. Sometimes other kids would challenge his throne but no one could beat Aras in any game or race.

Aras was talented. He would labor for hours, making toys out of cardboard. The model planes and ships he worked on for days awed people with their fine details. He was crazy about submarines and ships, he was a superb swimmer, he could climb the highest branches on trees, and lift the biggest rocks.

My older brother would secretly look out for me, but he was

never partial. I was proud of him, and placed great trust in him. I never did outgrow these feelings. But I was never like him. Instead of climbing trees or playing cowboys, I loved to daydream, watch movies, and listen to stories. Rather than participate in games myself, I liked to watch the children play and make up stories about them.

I had already thought up hundreds of stories about the daughter of the stars who had just moved into the mansion. I would muse that she was a princess one day, and then decide she was a cloud, or flower, or a fairy the next, all the while talking to her in my dreams. My state of melancholy provoked annoyance from Aras, a slew of giggles from my mother, and grandpa's heartfelt sympathy, as he sighed:

"Well, youngsters age faster these days!"

My father frequently had me help around the shop, partly to divert me from my troubles, and partly to prepare me for taking over the business. Our tailor store, which now bore the sign

MODERN TAILOR
NAIM ATACAN

at its door, was losing its business to the growing ready to wear industry, and the sole financial source of our modest lifestyle was depleting in strength.

It was around midsummer. One morning, I marched out of my father's store with a determined stride, and headed for the mansion. It was as if the battle between my obsession and my shyness had rendered me impervious.

The main door of the mansion was open as always, and the gardener, Uncle Shakir was singing as he worked. He brightened up when he saw me, and greeted me by taking off his straw hat.

"Finally, our very first guest!" he said.

Just then the Kangal puppy, who was still unaware that he was there to guard the premises, appeared by my legs, wanting to play. He was jumping up and down, and wagging his tail deliriously.

"Sivri! Hold on, boy, leave our guest alone, here pooch pooch, here Sivri!"

I don't know how I managed to avoid wetting my pants from

fear. As I waited with feigned calmness for Sivri to get used to my scent, I was furiously biting my lips. There was no turning back now. I was going to find the stargirl! It was the gardener's wife, Ya-shar Kalfa who stepped out into the garden at that moment with a vase in her hand, and came to my aid. At first she was surprised, and looked me over carefully, and then, stroking my hair, pointed to the backyard. It seemed that everyone I had met at the mansion that day had approved of my presence, and encouraged me by act-ing as if they'd been expecting me all along.

And at last, I found her in the backyard. She was alone under the arbor, just a few feet away from me. As soon as I saw her, I sensed that she would occupy a very important place in my life. It was just like figuring out an entire movie from the first scene.

When I first saw her she was talking to herself. After a little scrutinizing I realized that she was actually talking to something I could not see from where she crouched. I could not stop looking at her, and despite my curiosity, could not divert my gaze toward the object of her attention. She was one of those people who can only be conveyed through metaphor, whom words fail to do justice.

Soon I had found out that she had been talking to a white, 3-4 inches wide, semi-circular stone with thin red veins. And before long she had christened me Mabel.

I had known from the first that she would occupy a very dear place in my life, but she was not aware of it yet. To keep her from finding out, I hid my eyes in the stone she was holding. She must have understood somehow, for she gave me the stone as a gift, and in doing so, returned my eyes.

I was five years old when I met Ada. She was two years older than me, and possessed a very classical Mediterranean beauty. Ada always stayed that way.

RED IS THE COLOR OF PASSION

"Time flowing in reverse causes agitation."

Friedrich Nietzsche

Duna was dazzled by the brilliance of the blood on his hands. How pleasant it was to think that red coursed through the human body with such lovely lustre. Perhaps the passion that man, and womankind had for the color red signified a defiance of death itself. Perhaps, if blood had been yellow, or green, red would not be the color of passion…

"Red is the color of passion," he whispered.

Even though he only had a faint recollection of jumping from the moving truck and being violently dragged along, the wonder he felt at the bright red blood on his hands was very clear in his memory.

Yet the sight of blood made him sick. So the moment he realized that the substance on his hands was blood, his own blood, he fainted. When he opened his eyes he was lying in a bare, white-washed room. His head was being pummeled by a horrible number of aches, while his bandaged left arm and right leg, too timid to move, lay stretched out, motionless. Everything was white, pure white, and cloudy. He could not see another color no matter how hard he tried.

"And white must be the color of eternity," he murmured.

"It won't last long!" said an impersonal voice.

That's when Duna was able to make out, as if through a fish-eye lens, the pale white face leaning over and peering at him through an eyelid held open. The man's white labcoat covered all his field of vision.

"This is going to hurt a little but-"

Duna felt the pain immediately, clamped his teeth, and grimaced. He waited for it to recede. It was a horrible pain, as if hundreds of pins were being impressed into the right side of his forehead. It hurt terribly. Awfully.

"All right, that's all for today," said the man with the white shirt. For today? How long had it been?

"You are much better now, sir, but believe me- it was a close call. It's an utter miracle that you are alive! If the driver hadn't slammed on the brakes at the last moment, and if your friend hadn't held on to you with the help of the first lieutenant, there would be nothing left of you to piece together..."

"The cats," thought Duna. His mother used to say that every cat that you fed and took care of was bound to protect you in the future.

"Cats saved me," he whispered, trying to smile. But the muscles around his mouth hurt too much.

"Pardon?" asked the man in the white labcoat.

His face was blurry.

"I gave you some painkillers, so you should feel better soon," he continued, getting over his initial surprise. "Today you can start eating soup and jello."

"How long have I been here?" Duna asked, gathering up the courage to move slightly.

"Oh no, sir, please, have a little more patience!" cried the doctor, as he ran to the bedside. "It's only been three days since you arrived at the infirmary. Tomorrow we'll take out the stitches in your eyebrow, and your leg and arm will heal slowly."

"Three days!" Duna yelled. His voice had spilled rashly from his lips, like a sudden flood of long imprisoned light.

The doctor anxiously tried to calm him down.

"Don't you worry, you're recovering fast. You'll be out of here before you know it."

Duna winced and looked at the doctor, but he still couldn't see clearly.

"Is this also a military hospital?

"Yes, it is," said the doctor, somewhat relieved. "I am doctor Major Kutlu Chechen, and this is the brigade infirmary."

"I knew you'd say that," whispered Duna.

As he scribbled something in his notebook, doctor Kutlu remarked,

"So, I hear your wife is also a doctor."

"Yes," said Duna, wincing from a pain he could not exactly locate.

"In time, the pains will stop completely. What is her branch?"

"Whose branch?"

"Your wife's of course."

What was his wife's branch? What was that area Merich had wanted to specialize in, and ended up abandoning for something entirely different?

"Pathology," Duna heard himself say.

"Uh-oh! God help you, it's hard for women!"

That was when Duna really wished to see doctor Kutlu's face. It was a habit of his to look carefully at the faces, and especially eyes, of people who possessed definitive ideas and judgements on men and women, trying to determine where they had been hurt, how they had reached this state.

What he saw was a thin, rather young man of average height, but the image was still unclear. His eyes hurt when he tried to squint in the hopes of regaining focus.

"My glasses! I don't have my glasses! Where are my glasses?" he asked in panic.

"Ah," said Doctor Kutlu, remembering. "The glasses were broken, we will try to fix them in a couple of days."

"Doctor!" whispered Duna. "Is it true that there's a civil war? Has mobilization really been declared?"

It was difficult to gather any clues from the icy voice of the doctor, whose face expression was already inscrutable to Duna.

"Yes," said doctor Kutlu.

Duna waited. He waited for something more, but the room was quiet. Yes? Was that all? Definite answer to the question posed: Yes! What else could he say? "Yes" might contain whatever you want, but most of all it indicates clarity.

Just then an orderly entered the room with a tray. He left his burden on the portable table next to the bed. He cranked up the head of Duna's bed with a mechanism and placed the portable table in front of the patient.

"Hope you like it, sir!" he said, grinning. His breath smelled of garlic.

Duna observed the food which consisted of white soup and pink jello.

"I'm not hungry," he said, averting his eyes from the tray.

"You have to eat!" insisted doctor Kutlu as he left the room. "Our dishes are delicious."

The orderly approached Duna as soon as the doctor left and said:

"The good doctor's right. You ain't gonna get any better if you don't eat. See, you'se already skinny as a reed. God help me, you'd fall over if I so much as breathed your way…C'mon, eat!"

"Is it true that war has been declared? Civil war?" asked Duna, completely ignoring his meal.

The orderly, whose features were indistinguishable except for the fact that he was round faced, dark haired and somewhat chubby, stood staring at Duna for a while, and then approached the bed.

"I reckon you still think this's a joke? You'se really somethin' else, sir! They did say that you was a little…but never you mind."

"What did they say about me?" Duna angrily tried to leap out of his bed, but the sudden movement punished his face and body with an incredible pain. Then he hit his funny bone on the portable table and the unique pain that shot through him took his breath away.

"Now, jest you stop that thrashing around, please, sir. Get your wits about you and eat your meal!"

As he waited for both his pain and his anger to recede, Duna asked:

"What kind of soup is this?"

"It's noodle soup and strawberry jello. You'll see, they'll be good for your intestines… You'se gonna have to do with these for a few days, sir, and then we'll find you a good bite to eat!"

Duna took an unwilling spoonful of soup, which his hungry stomach gratefully accepted, and before he knew it, he was polishing off the plate. Even the light, bland taste of the jello seemed pleasant.

"There you go! Good for you, sir! My hand to god, life comes from the throat and leaves from the throat. You got to eat to get better!" the orderly said as he picked up the tray with a grin. "Sir, if you don't mind me asking, what do you teach? Science, math or some such thing?"

"I'm a literature teacher," said Duna with secret pride.

"Oh," came a disillusioned sound from the orderly.

Duna pretended not to hear. Even though he was still unaccustomed to the fact that literature and art were seen as unimportant in an increasingly ignorant consumer society, he tried not to let that get to him. Naturally, he failed.

"Lookere, I'm Hasan the orderly. Sergeant Hasan. If you need anything, press that there button and I'll come right away."

"Hasan," said Duna, feeling a little better, "Hasan, where do you think we are?"

"Mercy! Don't you know, sir, we're in the military hospital!"

"I know that much! I'm just wondering if you're aware of where we really are!" Duna bristled.

"Oh dear god, help me! You're going off the deep end, mister teacher. What we gonna do with you? Hold on, let me give you some of them sedatives the doctor ordered so you can get a little ease…"

"I don't want to sleep!" Duna wanted to shout, but instead a moan came out of his lips. "On the contrary, I want to wake up, Hasan. You tell me there's a civil war out there, that mobilization has been declared, and then you put me to sleep and take away my glasses to prevent me from seeing clearly. No! On the contrary, I would like to wake up and get out of this place, this nightmare!"

The more he shouted the louder his voice grew, his pains surged, his irritation increased, and his anger multiplied. Despite the claims, shouting had never been a source of relief for Duna.

Upon hearing his voice, Major Kutlu Chechen and another doctor rushed inside and scolded the orderly after asking him a few questions. Doctor Kutlu hurriedly administered Duna some sedatives.

"None of this is real? Don't you understand? This is all a nightmare! I have to get out of here and find Ada! Don't you understand, she needs me!" Duna was still yelling. "Besides, this is my nightmare, and you are all players in it. I created you in my head, out of my fears and anxieties. You are all a figment of my imagination, a dream!"

By the time he heard doctor Kutlu's chilly voice say, "Alright, professor. You just rest a little and everything will be alright, believe me, it'll be alright...Calm down, and don't tire yourself out like this." Shapes and voices had already started fading away, and rhythms had begun to slow down.

"I'll wake up soon! How much longer can you keep me asleep, anyway? I will surely wake up at one time or another! And then this nightmare and its contents will all disappear... That's why you're all so worried! You want the nightmare to go on, and you want to try me in every way by prolonging my sleep. If the nightmare goes on, those who benefit from it can live longer! But no...oh no! You can't keep us asleep like before!

No..o...I...re...fuse...I...won't...fall...a...sleep...no...sleep...a...ny ...more!"

As his eyes and mouth began to close he could hear his voice very faintly, from a great distance.

"Night...mare...dream...this...I...want...to...wake...up...ga me...this...is..all...a...game..."

His head fell back. He dozed off.

LIZARD TAIL

*"Grown-ups never understand anything on their own. What a
chore it is for kids to always be explaining things to them."*

The Little Prince
or
Antoine de Saint-Exupèry

"If you want to play with me you have to drink the juice of
three lizard tails!"

I thought it was a joke, but she wasn't smiling.

"Lizard tail juice?" I said, surprised.

"Yup, that's right!"

In later years, I did learn the expression of devotion: "to eat raw
chicken for someone's sake," but "drinking lizard tail juice," never
seems to have caught on in Turkish.

"What do you mean? Is that something like medicine?" I asked,
making a face.

"It's very simple. You catch three lizards, cut off their tails, and
put them in water. This becomes lizard tail juice. And that's what
you'll drink!"

"Eeeew," I said, holding my stomach.

"Don't worry, lizards don't die, they grow new tails."

"No, no, what if I swallow the tails?" I asked, frightened.

"Well, you don't have to swallow the tails, silly!"

You could clearly hear in her voice the admiration she had for
her vast knowledge, and for her graceful willingness to share it. I
had never seen a princess before, but I thought this was exactly
what one must be like. I suspect that she too thought the same. Be-

cause she had declared that she would allow one of the masses to play with her, and was now returning to her palace with her heart at ease. (must princesses be cruel?)

At first I felt as if I might cry, then, abandoning my pout, I sniffed, gnashed my teeth, and began to fear the test. I wanted to scream and yell, to ask her "Who do you think you are?" But I kept silent. After all, I was the only boy who had dared to enter the garden of the mansion, even though the door was always open. I had allowed her to call me "Mabel." Therefore I had to go all the way, I had to really deserve her!

Of course I did not realize until much later that I had fallen into the midst of an invaluable lesson at such a young age. In all my five years there had never been, and there would never again be anyone whom I sought so much to please, whose love and interest I went through so many pains to acquire. Only her. Only Ada.

Ada!

Brunette Ada.

Now I know that we allow this privilege to only a few people in our lives. We spoil and appease her, let her walk all over us, and even submit to her. She, for her part, knows this from the very beginning. If you're not lucky, the person becomes spoilt and out of control. You end up hurt, regretful, disillusioned, and you suffer. Sometimes, though rarely, you are lucky and you experience a miracle. Because you have met someone who's familiar with your language. (God how we love miracles!) It doesn't matter at all how old you are at that point. (No it does not!) And I was lucky!

"Okay Ada!" I called after her, my eyes burning as I squeezed them tight to keep from crying. "Okay, three lizard tails' juice!"

"All right Mabel, see you later!" she said without looking back, and entered the mansion.

I left the garden with self-assured steps. That hadn't been so bad. Once again, I'd refused to be defeated in front of her. Not in the least! Besides, keep in mind that she was a whole two years older than me, as big as my brother Aras, and she was a daughter of the stars.

I remember very well how cheerful I was that night. I had told my mother all except the lizard tail and "Mabel," though I suppose these two were at the heart of everything. Being her "Mabel" would always affect my life. And if I didn't drink lizard tail juice, I couldn't be her friend.

My mother listened to me with the utmost pleasure. She was completely overwhelmed by the fact that her "shy little Blue Duna" was friends with the beloved daughter of such magnificent stars. (Ah if she had only known about the lizard tail juice, I wonder if she would have been pleased.)

In both physique and personality, my mother combined the classical Anatolian woman's dark hair and eyes, sturdiness, and patience, with the long elegant features of her ancestors from the Caucasus. After elementary school she had, with her father's support, gone to live with her relatives in Kars in order to complete junior high. It still grieved her to think of how she couldn't stay and attend high school because her mother's death necessitated her return to Igdir. Even though she helped my father out with the tailoring, she was unmistakably a housewife. She took pride in her thick black hair; in Igdir, "the Rose of the East"; and in us.

Pervin Gokay, on the other hand, was seen as one of the most European and modern movie stars of Turkish cinema. Famed for her blond hair, slim figure, and Fine Arts degree, she seemed utterly different and inaccessible to my mother.

It was as if Pervin Gokay was a surreal visitor to our country, from a planet other than the one we and the neighbors inhabited. A mystical, enigmatic, and wonderful creature! Besides being a beautiful and educated woman, she was also successful. She was an artist who had the opportunity to continue her desired profession and maintain a family at the same time. Her life had not ended once she became a wife and mother; she was still alive! A product of Turkey at European standards. Ataturk's ideally envisioned Turkish woman! She was an excellent image!

Sureyya Mercan, for his part, was a husband fit only for a star, with a pencil thin Gable moustache, and a knack for directing his passionate gaze straight into women's eyes.

Defying that unwritten law which all husbands obey, he was brave enough to continue wooing his wife after their marriage. ("Because there's a gleam in his wife's eyes, and only content women have that sparkle!" my mother used to say. And I never forgot it; I looked for that gleam in the eyes of women whose happiness I was interested in determining. Because my mother is right.)

What's more, Sureyya Mercan was a stunningly handsome man with jet black hair, a flirtatious sideways smile, and a Mediterranean complexion.

And now the precious daughter of these two divine beings was becoming friends with my mom's little son. Zubeyde, who was already an excitable person, must have been seeing the stardust she believed had rubbed off on me, as she blissfully gazed at my face. (Ah if she only knew about those lizard tails!)

The next day and the following, I couldn't find a lizard anywhere in sight. It was the height of summer, and I had searched the corners of walls for hours. A few more days passed unsuccessfully and cheerlessly. Just as I was becoming morose, thinking I must have been forgotten or cruelly mocked, I heard her call me from the garden gate of the mansion. My heart leapt to my throat.

"Duuuna! Don't hurry, I'll wait!"

So she hadn't forgotten, and she'd kept an eye on me.

"I'll find them, don't you worry!" I said, trying to be cool. But instead, my voice came out weak and tearful.

In fact, I knew very well that I couldn't catch a lizard if I found one. I wasn't one of the wild, aggressive, leader-types. And I never have been. I was good at one-on-one relations and more successful in calm, stable environments. While Aras and the other boys climbed trees and hunted birds with slingshots, I used to paint my father's leftover spools and make toys out of them by stringing them up. While Aras and his friends played soccer and wrestled noisily, I would cut pictures out of old magazines to paste in notebooks, and make model dresses out of construction paper.

Thank goodness Aras had more than enough of the qualities that are expected from a boy, so that, with the help of that lavender-scented understanding shown to the youngest members of a household, I was saved from being seen as a problem.

"An order of the reptile family, possessing four legs, five toes, and retractable eyelids."

My father, who was patiently repeating the lines he had read umpteen times in the only encyclopedia in the house, thought my passion for lizards was related to the profession I'd choose in the future.

"Zubeyde, it looks like this kid's going to be a *baytar* when he grows up…"

"An animal doctor? Forget it, I'll have no such thing!"

"What's wrong with being a *baytar,* eh? Let me tell you, there's no thing as a good or bad profession! The country needs people of all trades, Zubeyde girl!" grandpa objected.

"Characterized by protruding eyeballs and long, forked tongues, lizards also have backs covered with hard scales."

"It's veterinarian, grandpa, not *baytar*. Veterinarian!" Aras corrected him.

"Well you're always fiddling with this lovely language, my boys! I swear, one needs a lexicon to understand it nowadays, like some foreign tongue!"

"The term lizard encompasses fifty species of reptiles which share cone shaped heads and highly developed tails."

So, they had highly developed tails, did they? And I was to drink the juice of three of these highly developed tails. Oh God, why did I have to try and befriend a girl who had prerequisites for playing, instead of making do with naturally formed friendships?

One cannot carry many images from his formative years into his adulthood. Among the clearest ones I can remember is the picture of grandpa's face. Specifically, I must have preserved this kind, loving, infinitely hopeful face with the smiling blue eyes as it was during the lizard crisis, for I can hardly remember it any other way. Grandpa sighing, and watching me with a bewildered expression, as I tirelessly filled sheets of paper with hundreds of lizard drawings.

"In my day boys were interested in horses and donkeys. Now it's lizards. I tell you, I don't understand it!"

I remember my mother as she hands me the picture of a lizard she clipped from a magazine, rather than in the exhausted state she was in after doing cooking, housework, and helping out my father with stitches and buttons. She has a funny smile on her face.

I can clearly see my shy, calm, hardworking father, not with the bloodshot eyes he had after staying up sewing all night, but wandering around with the L volume of the only encyclopedia in the house, reading me the article on lizards.

Those who are surprised by the clarity of my childhood memories do not know that they all have to do with Ada. How could they know? They haven't met the miracle!

"Stop blubbering and think about what you'll ask for in return!"

After we moved into the three story apartment building erected in place of our old wooden Armenian house, I had lost the pleasure of sharing a room with grandpa. He had moved to the second floor of the tailor shop next door. Although he spent most of the day with us, he went back to his authentic Kuzguncuk house at night, thereby trying to ward off his growing feeling of estrangement. I now shared the room with Aras.

"What am I supposed to ask for, and from whom?" I sniffed.

"From that girl of course!"

We looked across at each other from our beds.

"You know," he said in an irritated voice. "what are you going to ask for once you find the lizards?"

"She's going to play with me!"

"That's not enough!" Aras shouted. "You should ask for something in return from that spoilt girl!"

In one leap he came over to my side, sat down on the bed and put an arm around my shoulder. Now I was safe. Those who have experienced it will remember the feeling of brotherly support. Particularly those who have a strong, brave, and smart older brother like mine...(the three tenets of older-brotherhood!)

"You decide what you want from that girl until I catch a lizard, alright?"

"But how do you know Ada wanted a lizard from me?" I asked, finally relaxed, though still sniffling.

"I know these things!" he said boastfully.

When, in the light of the streetlamp, I saw the confidence, pride and beauty on his face, I fell in awe of my brother for the thousandth time.

The next day two lizards had already been caught and their tails had been put in a box. Despite all of Aras' protests I had insisted on cutting one of the tails in two so as to make it seem like we had three tails in all.

The gate to the mansion's garden was wide open, as always. I went in and found her. This time she was with her nanny. Her face lit up when she saw the box in my hand. Meanwhile Sivri, who'd joyfully jumped on me, was barking and bounding about as if he'd been reunited with an old friend. I couldn't admit that I was afraid of dogs to Ada, so I had to grin and bear poor Sivri. (Besides, fear of dogs is nothing compared to drinking lizard tail juice! The things I have to put up with for this girl's sake! Ha! How was I to know that this was only the beginning?)

We went into the backyard and sat down under the fig tree. After stroking my hair and smiling at me, her nanny told us, "Alright children, you go and play," and fell to conversing with Uncle Shakir the gardener on the front lawn.

"Did you find three of them?"

I nodded. She opened the box and peered inside.

"Good job, Mabel!" she whispered. (What a great moment that was!) "Now, let's get some water."

"Do I have to drink it?"

"Yes!" she snapped. (Since all princesses are required to be heartless!)

"Aunt Cihan! Will you bring us a glass of water? Duna's thirsty!"

When her nanny, who'd been watching us out of the corner of her eye, ran inside, I gathered up all my courage and asked her.

"Well, what're you going to do for me in return?"

Ada was very taken aback. Of course, she had always been the one who made requests.

"I'm going to play with you!"

"Forget it!" I said, with a determination borrowed from Aras.

"Alright, what do you want then Mabel?"

"You have to come over to our house to play!" I said.

"Fine. I'll come with Aunt Cihan," Ada replied, breathing an audible sigh of relief.

Soon the water had appeared, the lizard tails had been added, and now the concoction was waiting for me. Ada was holding my hand and smiling. (God what a pretty hand, what a lovely touch, what a warm feeling!)

"Wouldn't it be okay if I just pretend to drink it, Ada?"

"Of course not, Mabel, my dear!"

I brought the glass up to my lips twice, but couldn't do it. I kept freezing up when I saw those tails right there in front of my nose.

On one hand the fear of losing Ada, on the other, the impending death from drinking lizard tail juice… I was being crushed under hundreds of pounds of pressure, and my lungs felt like they might burst from lack of air. Everytime I was about to cry and run away, I would see Ada's almond eyes dripping over me like honey and would remain sitting under the fig tree in the backyard of the mansion, hopeless, and infinitesimally small. I wanted to vomit, but was embarrassed to.

Right then I heard my rescuer's voice.

"Leave him alone, he's just a little kid! If you really want, I'll drink it!"

Aras was sitting on the low, ivy covered wall surrounding the garden, and had fixed Ada with a challenging stare.

When Ada saw him she froze. My brother's beauty was so striking, so immediate, that strangers on the street would look at him and say "*Mashallah!* May God keep him from envious eyes!" These phrases must sound familiar to all handsome men.

"I suppose you don't know that the entrance to the garden is through the front gate!" Ada reprimanded Aras.

"Who wants to enter your garden? I came to protect my brother from you!"

They tried to stare each other down. God, how alike they were! But Ada was actually buying time to gather herself together. She was badly struck. I saw her struck once more: years later!

Ada was struck as soon as she saw Aras, and unfortunately I had seen and perceived this before either one of them. There was a great clamor inside me as the glass sheets of my childhood came crashing down. I yelled loudly so no one could hear the noise:

"Stop, stop! I'll drink this, okay?"

Having finally recovered, Ada got on her feet, assumed her proud posture, and immediately took the offensive.

"I wasn't going to let him drink that anyway, I was just testing to see if he would keep his word!"

"Hah! You all turn into cowards when you're in trouble!" said Aras with the air of a comic book hero.

"Who, me? No way! Who do you think you are?"

By now they'd forgotten me. It had happened; two strong characters, the male and female lead had met each other and had already forgotten about me, the one always doomed to play a minor role (for I can't bring myself to say "extra"). You didn't need to be a rocket scientist to figure out that they could never again part with one another. But you did have to be perceptive.

I chugged the disgusting water in the glass and cried:

"Stop fighting! There, I drank it!" (Please don't forget me!)

Then I must have fainted.

LET THE WATER REACH THE SEA!

> *"Certainly a bud feels pain as it unfolds,*
> *Everything struggles, hurts as it grows."*
>
> Karin Boye

The worst nightmare is the one you awake into.

When Duna woke up he was extremely frustrated to realize that he was still lying in the infirmary. The whiteness that quietly occupied everything around him, and the ever-present smell of lysol…

His eyes met those of a man who was standing over him in a labcoat and studying him.

"I have good news for you, Mr. Duna," said doctor Major Kutlu in his cold voice. "You're being released!"

"You mean I've recovered?"

"Almost… They'll transfer you in a couple of days."

"To the front?" Duna cried.

"To the campaign operation station!" doctor Major Kutlu corrected with the same icy and non-participatory voice. "Oh and one more thing, I had your broken lenses replaced. However…"

"However what?"

"They didn't have any negative five degree lenses left, so they put in three degree myopic lenses instead. Given, we're in a time of war, but later, we'll even take care of that!" he said, and held out the glasses.

"Thank you," laughed Duna. "It's a good trick, if a little cheap!"

"Pardon?" asked doctor Major Kutlu, surprised.

"It's a good nightmare trick!" Duna said, as he put on the glasses under the puzzled gaze of the doctor. "With defective lenses I can discern everything pretty well, but I can never see clearly. You understand, don't you?"

The doctor stared blankly.

"It's a technique used in horror films!"

" ... "

"Remember how I was sucked into this nightmare because of my doubts and fears? Well, it wants to terrify me even further, through blurry images!"

Doctor Major Kutlu sighed deeply.

"Who do you think wants this?"

"My brain of course!" said Duna, laughing bitterly. "Look doctor, I've grown up admiring two very intelligent people. I loved both of them dearly and still —"

He stopped and averted his eyes. He briefly travelled to a time known only to himself. Then he revived and went on:

"My love and admiration for them was so great that I never even thought of envying their talent and intelligence. Do you understand this? Have you ever imagined what it's like to live with the infinite tolerance that a fierce love brings? Think about it... What is it like to love someone fiercely? But think about it without going insane!"

Doctor Major Kutlu Chechen had approached Duna's bed, and was listening intently.

"I was so close to them, to those two, that I had neither a thought nor a complaint about myself or my abilities. None! Ever! If you really want to know, doctor, I didn't grow up with Ada and Aras. I didn't simply love those two miraculous people. I lived them, I became them, I existed in their bodies for years! And one day..."

He fell silent again.

"Yes, one day?" the doctor asked in his icy voice.

"One day when they weren't with me any longer...that day, yes, that must've been how it happened...of course! I must've realized in those days that I despised my own brain and intelligence... Yes, there, doesn't this all make sense?" He took off his glasses and stared. "And now my brain is taking its revenge on me! This is my punishment for disdaining my own brain and my capacities, for admiring others far too much! Hah hah ha! How ingenious, isn't it, doctor?" He put his glasses back on. "Look, I can see everything, but not quite well enough. A good plan indeed!"

"A plan?" doctor Kutlu interjected suspiciously.

"The plan my own brain and subconscious hatched against me! The greatest blow comes from the closest quarters!"

"Lieutenant, you should rest a little now. Try to relax, and stop thinking. Take off your glasses so we can remove that stitch on your forehead. Don't worry, this won't hurt at all."

His voice was cold and distant.

Duna meekly did as he was told and waited for the stitches to be removed.

"There, that's it! It might leave a small mark but it won't create an aesthetic problem. Do you feel any dizziness?"

"No, I'm fine doctor. Thanks," said Duna, forcing a smile.

"I'm going to give you a painkiller and a sedative. Neither of them are very strong so you can use them without worry. I'll see you once more before your transfer."

A deep silence ensued when the doctor stopped speaking. The kind of intense silence that is difficult to emerge from. The two young men stayed this way for a while, not knowing what to do. Duna reached over and got his glasses from above the dresser, then peered carefully at doctor Major Kutlu Chechen from behind the faulty lenses. He looked him over, thinking his subject tried very hard not to give away what kind of person he was. What he saw was a serious looking man who would not be considered ugly, but who could not be called handsome either. He was of average height, with a receding hairline which revealed a widow's peak.

"Literature was one of my favorite classes in high school," said the doctor, surprising Duna with a pastel colored smile. "It was because we had a wonderful literature teacher. I can safely say that he taught me to love books, to hunt for clues in them, and to use them as a place to hide."

So, he admitted to an affinity for secrecy...

"We boys considered literature, especially stories and novels, to be a trivial, overly emotive business which we identified more with girls. However, Mr. Vasfi taught us that good literature was a product of skill and intelligence. He explained how literature is the science of words and meaning. There could be no thought or civilization without good communication. It was thanks to him that we learned to respect and enjoy literature!"

"He's trying to win me over, he thinks he can cajole me because I'm a literature teacher," thought Duna. "What he says is intelligent, but it's just flattery." Then he asked himself, "But why should he do that?"

"In later years I found literature to be a great source of help in both my personal life and in my psychiatric training. What I'm tring to say is, I know what a good teacher is worth."

"Psychiatry?" Duna asked.

Just then Hasan, the orderly, came in with his ever present smile and his devil-may-care attitude.

"With your permission, major, I came to get our teacher!"

Despite Duna's protests, they plopped him down in a wheelchair.

"As I said before, we need you, Mr. Duna! A good teacher doesn't simply teach, he makes his students love the subject, he facilitates the application of knowledge. And that's why you're going to take care of yourself!" said doctor Major Kutlu in his frigid voice.

"Weren't you a surgeon, doctor?" Duna inquired suspiciously as Hasan the orderly wheeled him out of the room.

"Aren't we all a little?" the doctor replied, but Duna could barely hear him from the corridor.

"What's your rush, Hasan, I couldn't hear the doctor's answer because of you!" he barked. Then he got offended at the anger in his voice. Why on earth had he gotten so mad at Hasan?

"Scuse me but you'se getting plucky for nothin', sir! I'm hurrying up 'cause they're bringing in the wounded... They say there's already many dead!"

"Many dead?" shuddered Duna. "Dear god, someone is always dying outside!"

His voice had become hoarse with desperation.

"Now hold on, don't you freak out again sir, you'll get up your blood pressure or something, and then what'll you do?"

The narrow white corridor seemed like it would never end.

"Yet the road should seem shorter when one's sitting down," he said.

"Oh my good sir, why you go around tirin' your mind out like that, huh? See me for example, I'm an Anatolian soul, I don't poke my nose into nothing I can't understand. But in the end, everything is God's will. Whatever's writ on your forehead that's what will be your fate. Listen to this here Hasan and don't worry your blessed heart. *Mashallah,* you're a fine young lad, though you do need a little meat on your bones, but nevermind, you'll be back on your feet soon enough."

"I wish I could think like you, I wish I could believe in fate, Hasan! Don't you think I envy that? What you say is true, the plain and small is beautiful. But it's already too late; once your mind and consciousness are engaged, there's no turning back!"

"Well, sir, you're a pretty good talker, you speak fine and fancy, but, if you'll excuse me, seems like you don't say all that much. You worry for nothing! Don't you strain yourself; let flowing water reach the sea! What did our ancestors say? Blood meant to be spilled won't stay in veins. Fear don't do death no good! You understand?"

"How can I let things be, Hasan? You say that we're living in war, but no one talks about it! They act as if there's no such thing, and they remain distant, as if the deaths were happening in another country! Whenever I bring up the war, everyone around me changes the subject and treats me as if I'm nuts! Then I say 'there is no war; this is all a nightmare caused by my anxieties,' and no one believes that either! I don't have a problem; we have a problem! Now, do you understand?"

"Ah, my poor sir! You're tiring yourself out too much, you're already weak as a bird!"

They boarded a service elevator and alighted two floors below the main level, then they passed through another corridor, took another elevator at the end of that labyrinth, went three floors up, and finally arrived at the ward. It was dim, and looked empty. Hasan the orderly laid him down on one of the bottom bunk beds, gave him a pill, and left him another one, instructing him to take it in an hour's time.

"I got to leave right away, sir. Look, I like you. You'se a brave man, but you got to take care of your mind! Now, don't think about a thing, stretch yerself out, and rest. You just try to gather strength 'cause you're going to need it pretty soon!"

"Alright Hasan, thank you," said Duna, smiling.

"Oh and don't you forget now," Hasan the orderly added as he was leaving, "those Anatolian saints know a thing or two… You let the water flow, let it reach the sea!"

Duna smiled.

"The water carries us all away, Hasan," he murmured. Hasan was long gone. "The water carries us all away…" He yawned.

Once again, he submitted to sleep.

THE FIRST NIGHT IS ALWAYS HARD

> "... *Fear and blood are not the end all be all. One thing, one single thing remains, despite all the destruction: man's encounter with man... There have been times when a stranger's glance, a single wink have saved us from the brink.*"

Cesare Pavese.
(L'unita Newspaper, Return to Man)

A man might become dumbstruck upon suddenly seeing someone he has loved and longed for stand before him. And that's what happened.

"Aras, is that you?" Duna called, but couldn't make a sound. "Aras?"

His voice was trapped. Then he realized he was still in the hospital ward, in the same nightmare.

"God damn it! When is this thing going to end?" he almost spat. He'd gotten his voice back.

"You idiot! You're still looking for Aras!" he scolded himself.

"Shhhh!" whispered the shadow by the bed. "Quiet down, there're people sleeping!"

Propping himself up on the bed, Duna tried to make out who the shadow was who stood in the yellow light seeping in through the small ward window, but could not succeed without his glasses.

By the time Duna realized he was wearing only an undershirt and drawers, the shadow, who was also walking around in his underwear, had already sat down on the edge of his bed.

"Who undressed me? When did it become nighttime? What else is going to happen in this goddamned nightmare?" he shouted.

"Relax. The first night is always hard, but then you get used to it," said the shadow. "You were sound asleep, the orderly came around, and gave you a medicine. He undressed you so you wouldn't die of heat in that sweatsuit."

"They're always drugging me!" Duna whispered angrily. "They're trying to get rid of me by keeping me asleep! Because I am aware!"

"You always used to make up stories like that!" the shadow said.

"Me? Who are you anyway?"

"Man, Duna, you still haven't recognized me?"

"The voice is familiar but…"

"How's it that you don't recognize your childhood friend Sefer, huh? Don't tell me you forgot Sefer the Baker, huh boy?" said Sefer, affecting his favorite Laz dialect.

"Sefer, is it really you?" Duna cried out joyfully.

"In flesh and blood! Ah dear teach, who we could never convert to Trabzonsport's side! How are you, my fellow Kuzguncukite?"

Duna embraced Sefer with the ardor of someone who'd struck gold. After grade school, Sefer had dropped out and started to work in his father's bakery. Thus his name had been put down in the minor league childhood friend category; someone with whom you'd share a single joke's worth of laughter, who you'd greet loudly from a distance, and whose absence you would only notice after a while. Yet now Duna embraced Sefer as if they had been bosom buddies.

Sefer was a bond to reality, and he needed even the slightest crumbs to get out of this nightmare. Sefer gave Duna a strong slap on the back, pleased at this unexpected reception.

"How the hell are ya, Duna? Do we have to enlist in the army to actually see you? I bet you still don't support a team!"

"Nah, I don't Sefer. I was never too interested in soccer, you know that. That was Aras' area of expertise."

"Buddy boy, you hardly ever left the mansion's garden… It was always the movie stars' daughter. You forgot about us once that girl moved into the neighborhood! Anyway, forget all that… Now, are there any kids on the horizon, you tell that to your brother Sefer?"

"What kids?" Duna was surprised.

"You know, kids, cubs, babes, lassies, that sort of thing."

"Ooh… No, no, it's too early yet."

"What do you mean early, my boys start junior high next year!"

"Are they really that old, Sefer?"

"You better believe it, teach! I'm already thirty-four years old, soon it'll be forty, and then forty feet under! Ha ha ha! Ay my little innocent!"

"Well, well, well, so you have kids that old, eh?"

"Sure, one of them's eleven and the other's ten, my joys, may God bless them... Don't be surprised if they show up in your class soon! See here, I'm going to send them to school, both of them... My dad didn't send me, but I'll make sure they go to school..."

They fell silent. Two childhood friends, sitting next to each other in a military ward, they fell silent.

"That's right, you didn't even have a big wedding, did you, Duna? Out of the blue, we hear that our neighborhood pal has quietly gotten married, and suddenly too...Boy, were we surprised. And to that lady doctor! That was another shocker... Anyhow... Is that the way to do it, man? It should have been big, with music and song and dancing girls, so that your brother Sefer could've fired his gun, and celebrated his friend's happiness! We should've toasted our rakis at Ismet' Baba's place!"

Duna laughed. "We can still do it, Sefer!"

Once again they fell silent.

"Sefer?" whispered Duna, "Sefer, is it true that there's a civil war? Do you think we are really sitting here in a military ward in our underwear because mobilization has been declared?"

Sefer, who loved to show-off to his friends his beloved Laz accent, put all his jocosity aside and carefully inspected Duna's face. He frowned.

"Are you kidding? Or could..." He stopped and continued to frown for a while. "Or could what they're saying about you be true? Have you lost your mind, man? If you're serious in what you just said you're either a maniac or a coward!"

"So it's true!" Duna collapsed once again. "If only someone would come along and agree that all these images are actually a dream, a nightmare... One person... Just one person! God, I'd be happy with one person!"

"Look here, Duna! Have you gone nuts, or are you just acting? What sort of man are you, buddy? Or are you afraid?"

"Yes, I'm afraid, Sefer. In fact, I'm terrified! If we really are living in a state of civil war, I'm afraid of why we're not talking about it, and why we're ignoring it. If, on the other hand, we're not living in war…then I'm afraid of the revenge this brain of mine will wreak on me, now that it has come up with this nightmare."

"Ah my poor man! What a waste!" Sefer pursed his lips, upset. "Is it all because of that girl? 'Cause, I don't know, yours was some sort of blind love… That's what they'd say."

"Don't be ridiculous, Sefer. I'm saying one thing, and your head is somewhere completely different. I don't give a damn what they say about me! I'm looking for the truth, that's all! Just the truth!"

He waited for his increasing anger to subside, and swallowed repeatedly.

"Look Sefer, you're a smart man, if you listen to me you'll understand that I'm not the one who's crazy around here. Will you hear me out?"

Sefer opened his hands to the sides, as if to say "what other choice do I have?"

"Now, Sefer, take a good look around you. Is there anyone left who's not been touched by or become utterly sick of violence, terrorism and oppression? Huh? Tell me? Civilians, soldiers, women, kids, babies… Aren't people dying every day? Yes. And aren't we keeping quiet as we watch it all happen? Yes. Look, you're quiet too right now, you too! There, you see? We're always silent. I was also, but the more I kept quiet, the more… now this happens!"

"Poor buddy, poor old buddy!" said Sefer sadly.

"I waited anxiously for months, years, for a civil war to erupt. I cannot describe to you the extent of my fear and vexation."

He stopped. He was surprised to realize that talking relieved him. Was the burden created by years of keeping these anxieties to himself slowly being relieved?

"And I awoke one morning. It was a Tuesday. The most monotonous of days! There was a knock on the door. Two soldiers were waiting on the doorstep. They enlisted me. Mobilization had been declared. The thing I'd been so fearfully expecting happened exactly the way I thought it would. Down to a 'T'! Do you understand Sefer?"

Sefer didn't make a sound.

"Do you think this could be real? Could war erupt just because I imagined it, in the way I pictured it, Sefer?"

Sefer, who was biting his lips in concern as he listened, kept his silence.

"I could've been living in another land that wasn't Turkey. For example in Bosnia, Sri-Lanka, Macedonia, or, I don't know, Rwanda. It wouldn't have made any difference, Sefer. Believe me, it would've made no difference! With these fears and anxieties, the same things would have happened to me there and my uneasy dreams would have been carried out exactly the same way!"

"Duna have you seen a doctor at all?"

"Hah ha! I see that you've joined the ranks of those who consider me crazy, Sefer!" Duna gave a tense laugh.

"Look Duna, you know I like you. Everyone in the neighborhood likes you. Your grandfather, Uncle Muharrem was one of the most respected people in Kuzguncuk, God rest his soul. Likewise, all your family are well-bred, honest, patriotic and religious folk. And of course Aras! Aras is a legendary name there…"

They both fell to thinking about Aras. For a while in that faint light they both quietly revisited the past.

"Alright, I understand, you've been through a very unfortunate experience, but you're a healthy young man. All that schooling, that education; get yourself together man! Forget these nightmare tales, open your eyes and be realistic for God's sake!"

"My eyes have been opened Sefer. Who knew it would take so long to realize that while someone is being murdered outside our houses, outside our own bodies, we too die a little with each person!"

Duna sighed. Sefer did the same.

"I began to relive this nightmare everytime I died. Violence and insanity was increasing, insensitivity was rampant. I was being eaten up by the worry that civil war would erupt, and this worry overshadowed all my hopes and joys. I couldn't open up to anyone. They either ran away or stuck their heads in the sand, claiming that I was exaggerating. There was only one person I could talk to and she…"

Sefer took a long deep breath and continued to stare at the floor, scratching his chin.

"Did you talk to that person?" he asked, not raising his head.

"I was afraid of boring her. She's had very hard days... You know..."

"You mean that girl? That actors' daughter?"

"Yes her, Ada!" said Duna in a voice that quivered and shone.

"And see what happens? That same morning, that Tuesday morning, the same day that this nightmare starts, another longtime fear of mine comes true. The newspapers declare Ada to be a killer! Not a single investigation or interrogation... Bang, just like that... So they can increase their sales... Completely arbitrary... And Ada disappears! God, one of the things I fear most in life is losing her! The whole world knows that!"

"Now, that really is a fact! You've been crazy about that girl ever since you were a kid!"

"You see, Sefer? The two events that have terrified me the most happen on the same day, in the same morning, and at the same time! So?"

"So?"

"So none of this is real, Sefer! It's a subconscious game, completely planned and executed by my brain! My inner balances were so weary, so exhausted that I guess my brain decided to teach me a lesson. Thus, my friend, the things happening here, and what we are experiencing right now are not real. Ada hasn't disappeared, and mobilization was not declared! You are not really here right now, you're back in Kuzguncuk. This is all a misunderstanding, a nightmare, a dream! It's all a trick of my brain!"

"Look Duna," Sefer angrily started to say, "Look, if you hadn't just returned from the hospital I wouldn't think twice about landing you such a punch that... I swear, would bring you to your senses and have you kissing my hand in no time, but your wounds are still fresh... Be a little tougher, buddy, is this any way for a man to behave? Tsk, tsk, tsk, you're going to drive me nuts too!"

"Leave the man alone, brother," came a deep voice. "Maybe reality is too heavy for him to handle. Who doesn't feel that from time to time?"

A shadow, sitting up on the bed behind Duna's, was addressing them in a somewhat drowsy voice.

"Don't bother the poor teacher, can't you see how depressed the man is already?"

"Sure, but, this is my childhood friend, should I just let him be so that he can end up in the loony bin? Where we come from, loving is looking out!

"It's true what you say, but don't you see that when looking out turns to pressure it backfires? If you ask me, loving is being able to look out without pressuring."

"Well said!" exclaimed Duna, turning to the man behind him. He was as relaxed as if he hadn't been the subject of their conversation. "Sefer isn't at all to blame. He's a good person. It's my brain that's making him talk like this. As you know, consciousness is dependent on proper brain function. At least, that's what I believe.... The fears that consciousness represses or denies become a part of the subconscious. And that is the reason for what I, and therefore you, are going through!"

"Well, it's impossible to disagree with the teacher here! I also believe what we are experiencing is an utterly despicable game. This is a shameless, ugly construct in which we are all being used as pawns!"

"Oh great, now we've really done it!" sighed Sefer.

"Allow me to introduce myself," said the other in voice heavy with irony and bitter humor. "My name is Mutlu. But contrary to my name, I'm not really happy, my friends. I practice law in Ankara. I'm what they call a Kurdish intellectual, unpopular with everyone. You know, the type whom both Turks and Kurds love to hate! They brought me here the other morning."

"Mr. Lawyer, you're not helping my friend here, you're making things worse... Those kinds of separatist words ruined us and apparently you still haven't learned your lesson! There's no such thing as a Kurd, brother, just a Turk. We won the War of Independence side by side, and that's how it's going to remain from now on!" Sefer dismissed him.

"See, see!" Duna cried out gleefully. "See, another proof has come up. In order for everything to fit the civil war scenario, my subconscious is putting very carefully selected people in my way. Sefer the Laz, Mutlu the Kurd, Hasan the Anatolian peasant, Kutlu the Caucasian, Musa the Islamist, and Birol, the enlightened Turkish Kemalist soldier! Do you see what elaborate plans my long de-graded brain is devising? Huh? Maybe now you'll believe me? This is a dream!"

"Well, after all, doesn't the geography of Turkey consist of these people, professor? But why not, perhaps all this really is a bad dream."

"Heey now! Hold on just a minute! Fine, I listened for conver-sation's, for friendship's sake, but you can't go around bad-mouthing such sacred things. I won't allow separatism! Don't you get on my nerves, or I swear I won't be responsible for what fol-lows!"

"Alright, alright, brother Sefer. I'm already sick of these games... What intrigues me more is the love story in this teacher's head. Brothers, in the end, what's real is life and love anyway! I ac-cidentally overheard you two talking just now, and you mentioned a missing woman named Ada. Well, it's tradition, you show com-passion for a lover in this land, no matter where or who he's from. If nothing else, that tradition still survives! Or have you never fallen in love, Sefer brother?

"That's something different!" said Sefer, trying to conceal his suddenly faltering voice. "You ever seen a real man not in love? Of course I suffered the fire of love, Mr. Attorney, but Duna here hap-pens to be married!"

"So what if he is? Should the heart be put in chains once one gets married? Besides, maybe he's in love with his wife. Isn't that possible?"

"Of course it is... But Ada is not my wife," said Duna, stand-ing up. He put on the glasses left by his bedside, in order to see Mutlu the lawyer even a little better in the dim light. "Ada... she is a very very special person in my life... Someone I tremble over, adore, and long for terribly... The person whose happiness I prize over my own, even to the destruction of my own... A gorgeous woman whom I admire, and whose hurt and disillusion I could not bear!"

He remained transfixed in the middle of the ward, surprised, but incredibly relieved at having been able to declare his thoughts about Ada to other people for the first time.

"What an amazing thing!" whispered Mutlu the lawyer in awe.

"Love! Heaven! Amour!"

There was a brief silence. It was not an uncomfortable one. All three of them were caught beneath a separate shower of light, one that varied according to their individual notions of love.

"Yes, perhaps," Duna murmured, "perhaps you could call this miraculous feeling I have for her love, but when Ada is the one in question, I think love is an insufficient word."

"You know Duna, these things you say sound a lot like the love I have for my sons. I love my boys so much, I feel so proud of them that, ay, I wouldn't trade them for the world!"

"Mine is more than paternal love, Sefer."

"How on earth would you know, Duna? You've never even gotten a taste of fatherhood."

"I, on the other hand, have," said Mutlu the lawyer. "I have two darling daughters. They're both sweet as honey, good as gold…. But our love is only a part of what teacher talks about… His is a fuller, more lively kind of love!"

"Well, there you go!" Sefer rejoined. "If you had a son you'd know about a fuller love, my boy! A son will change the lie of the land!"

"How can you differentiate between a son and a daughter, Sefer?" Duna scolded.

"Very easily. I have two sons and a daughter, the boys will keep my bloodline, the girl will serve some stranger's kin!"

"Master Sefer, is it because your mother was a man that you don't like women? Or did your mother love you less than her daughter because you were a boy?"

"You better be careful, I won't have anyone talking about my mother!" Sefer bristled.

"Hey, stop, cut that out! What are you two doing for God's sake? You're ruining a subject I haven't been able to discuss for years! Besides, who can weigh and measure love that you're arguing about its dimensions?"

"Sure, that's true…" said Sefer softly.

"Ada," whispered Duna, "Ada can, in a way, be my child, and maybe I am hers… She is my older or younger sister, my mother, my friend, my impossible love, and maybe even my 'self'… Ours must be a different kind of passion…"

He was struck by his own words. Was he saying all this? Did he know this all along

"Every love is different, none is like any other!" said Mutlu, laughing.

Just then a strong floodlight swept through the room. Dazzled, Duna saw in that brief instant that Mutlu the lawyer, despite his booming voice, was a skinny, gaunt young man. And that the ward was empty!

"Where are the others? Why are we only three people in this whole ward?" he cried out in panic.

"Yesterday," said Mutlu, lighting a cigarette, "there was a transfer; they all left."

"So are you telling me that hundreds of soldiers get sent to the front every day, without fail?" The anxiety had returned to his voice.

"I don't think it would be right to call it 'the front,' " said Mutlu, taking a deep drag of his cigarette. "They call it the campaign service station, and in my opinion it's more appropriate to the conditions we are in."

"Of course, I'd forgotten that you were a man of law," muttered Duna. "But whatever its name might be, hundreds of people go there and die, don't they?"

There was no answer.

"This is absurd! Who's the enemy? Where's the border, the front? Who're we fighting against? This is a self-destructive virus! No one's going to win in the end, no one! Do you understand? Because we're fighting against ourselves!" Duna yelled in escalating anger.

No one spoke.

"Fine, you just keep being quiet! Stay apathetic. But know that this is all absurd!"

"All wars are absurd," said Mutlu in a calm voice. "But civil wars are more absurd!"

"God damn this brain and subconscious of mine!" said Duna, and turning to his bed, threw himself upon it like a sack.

Dead silence.

"Don't you think there's anything strange about all this, huh?" Duna asked once again. His voice was slightly calmer now. "There are great logical and factual flaws in this scenario. Just think; during mobilization aren't the first draftees those who finished their military service most recently? Aren't they?"

Dead silence.

"Well then, how is it that as someone who was discharged six years ago after a four month short-term service, yours truly gets drafted with Sefer here, who finished his service years before that? Huh?"

Dead silence.

"Since when have they been putting college graduate soldiers in the same wards as those without a secondary education, tell me?"

Dead silence.

"You see, all this is extremely odd. Because it isn't real! My brain is introducing me to childhood friends so that I can keep some relation to the past, but it is too drunk with victory to notice that it is making logistical mistakes! Hah ha! You're not fooling me, Mr. Brain!"

"The situation is not odd, professor," said Mutlu. "The situation is dire. Because of the urgency pertaining, and in order to preserve the existent troops at full capacity while keeping a strong stand-by army, they've extended about six or seven years back for draftees."

"The lawyer's right," said Sefer. "It was such an emergency that most of us didn't even get draft notices. Whatever we heard from the radio or TV... It didn't even hit the papers until Wednesday."

"In summary, whilst an ecumenical decision has necessitated the augmentation of sanctions, the urgency heretofore has rendered deliberation infeasible, your honor!" said Mutlu in an exaggerated voice.

"Spoken like a true lawyer!" Sefer exclaimed.

"We still haven't been able to modernize our legalese," grumbled Duna. "That in itself could be reason for a civil war."

"You're really lost aren't you, teach? Here, have a smoke," offered Mutlu.

"Thanks, I don't smoke," said Duna.

"Did you quit?"

"No, I never started. I was just never into cigarettes... But those two, they used to smoke!"

"It's high time you forgot about them! Whoever they are, let them be, and you can breathe easier too! It's a double catastrophe to be caught in the middle of a civil war, or in the thick of a nightmare as you say, with your private life in such a mess! Here, have a cigarette!"

"Thanks, I'll pass."

"What do you teach, my friend?"

"Literature." Then, with all the tension of one who has barely avoided a trap, Duna thought, "My brain is testing me!"

"Do you not drink either?"

"Occasionally I have a few glasses of wine."

"Well, what do you do to relax, to unwind a little?"

"Let him sleep some, and he'll be fine, buddy!" Sefer interjected angrily.

"I read poetry," smiled Duna, ignoring him.

"Well, why didn't you say so!" said Mutlu, propping himself up on his bed. Then he went on with his deep voice, which seemed almost trapped in his puny frame:

> "One afternoon I sat by the side of the road
>   and thought
>   what will be left of us,
>   of the Balkan plains, the steppes
>   this cloud on its way to Neverland,
>   this earth and deep elm
>   browned by endless seasons
>   were all here before us."

He stopped. There was complete silence.

> "This final laughing torch of children
>   moonlight,
>   the sun that dries chilli peppers
>   and sad old people on the same clothesline
>   will leave shadows on the meadow
>   as it retires from this preoccupied world."

"Hear, hear! Man, you read that so well, with all that emotion! How can a guy not smoke right now?" said Sefer, lighting a cigarette.

"I've forgotten the parts in between, but I remember the ending, my friends," said Mutlu the lawyer, assuming a thick Kurdish accent. Then he went back to the poem he so obviously recited from the heart:

"The sound of our pipes,
    made from cherry and reed
    fades in the air.
    The wind of time, in her purple print dress
    grazes the mouth of a well.
    This lovely song will also be forgot
    among massacres, pain and blood
    and while our days are tossed around
    you will surely ask the question:
    what is left behind of us?"

"Did you write that poem, my dear lawyer?" asked Sefer.
"Ah, I wish I had poetry like that in my blood, brother Sefer. That's a poem by a poet who grew up around back where I live."
"Onat Kutlar," said Duna, almost to himself.
"Well, now it's your turn, teach!"
There was a short pause. Soon words started falling gently from Duna's lips:

"No one knows, I do not
    disclose this private truth,
    each escape from myself
    is a return
    to my frigid light.
    Dogs howl, thugs lie in wait,
    traitorous screams in foggy streets
    I am alone, I am afraid, but there's manhood
    I keep quiet
    I keep quiet, Ada
    You are there
    I know that you know, Ada."

He stopped. He felt the longing and rage growing inside him, attacking all his inner organs, and approaching him like a gigantic hurricane. Soon this pressure would cause his body to crack from the inside. First his ribcage would break, and then his inner organs would spill out, while he stood by and watched this last moment. He felt queasy. He closed his eyes.

"Isn't that a poem from Dogan Gokay's famous 'Brunette Ada?'" asked Mutlu.

"That's it!" said Sefer, rising from his bed. "That's the man, I'd forgotten his name. These guys used to call him Uncle Poet. That was the man who filled their heads with pipe dreams. He affects everyone he talks to. I forbade my daughter to listen to his talks on TV!"

"Do you know Dogan Gokay, professor? He's a superb man! Is he really your uncle? Man, what luck! So, tell us a little about him," Mutlu said excitedly.

"An apple carries the curse
    in its very seeds
    before and forevermore
    whatever he may do
    a man's
    greatest enemy
    is quietly
    inside his own skin.
    I keep quiet Ada
    You are there
    asking
    and where, where, where?"

"See, there you have it, there's betrayal and cynicism in that poem. Just like I told you, dear lawyer, that Poet Dogan Gokay didn't do Duna any good... He even prevented this kid from supporting a soccer team!"

"That's enough, Sefer!" cried Duna. "Shut up, that's enough! He is the first man who showed me the light of the mind, I don't want you talking badly of him!"

"The mind's light? Buddy there's no such thing, open your eyes and learn to act like a man, or-"

"Or what?" yelled Duna, and turning on Sefer, suddenly fell upon his friend, trembling with rage. "Get out of my way, Sefer! I'm, telling you, you're not here! These are tricks of my own brain, don't you get it? I'm sick of you and your brutish role in this dream!"

"Easy, go easy, buddy! Don't get all crazy like that, my Kuzguncukite friend!" said Sefer, trying to grab a hold of Duna's hands. "See, it wasn't so bad. With a little goading, you came back to your senses!"

"Take your hands off me!" Duna cried. "I don't want any of you, any of you! I want to get out of this logistically flawed nightmare, I want to get rid of all of you. Curse my brain! God damn it!"

He swung his arms around in anger, desperation, and panic, and when they hit a hard object, began to writhe in pain.

"Stop, gentlemen, what're you doing down there?" Mutlu said, running to their side. He tried to separate the two but Duna was attacking everything around him, raining blows on them or himself, one couldn't tell. Violently, violently, spreading violence…

"He's a spy! Yes, Sefer is a spy! He's the spy in this nightmare! He's the one my brain gave the role of being a spy in order to control me! I have to get rid of him!"

ALL GIRLS ARE WITCHES, ALL BOYS ARE PIGS!

"If I want to meet a butterfly I have to put up with a few caterpillars.(…) And if it weren't for the butterflies or the caterpillars, who would befriend me?"

Antione de St. Exupery
(Little Prince)

"You're too old to play with girls now!" said Aras in a resolute voice.

"You mean I can't ever play with girls anymore?" I asked, pouting. I could have died of grief.

"From now on, you'll play with boys!"

I could detect in his voice a hint of the grown-up manners he assumed when he wanted to protect me. I hadn't, until then, seen Aras act particularly sexist in terms of making friends, but the kids who wanted to play with him had always been boys. The girls usually preferred to play hopscotch or skip rope, games which Aras had never tried.

Once Ada showed up and started attracting attention in the neighborhood, Aras became uneasy, sensing that his own fame was being overshadowed. Only later would I realize that he was intimidated enough to take refuge in the preferential view granted towards his gender by society, which he was newly beginning to notice.

I never did care. I've always thought that the difference between the sexes is as unimportant as one's hair or eye color. What matters to me in any person, of either sex, is honesty, intelligence, and genuineness. There are values I care more strongly about than being a man or a woman. It was great fun to play with Ada, and I couldn't have cared less about power struggles between the sexes. However, those two were very much alike, and both were extremely concerned with such things.

"Who do you think you are, anyways? You don't even know how to read or count! You don't even know who Turkey's neighbors are... You're just a kid!"

The sense of victory that appeared on Ada's face as she said this had deeply affected Aras, and he had been badly wounded by the challenge of a girl his own age, who herself hadn't started school. For the first few seconds he looked dazed, as if a great rock had fallen on his head. But then he gathered himself, and played his greatest card:

"I'm going to learn those anyway, but you're never going to be a man, so there!"

"Who said I wanted to be a man, smartypants? Would I be that dumb? You guys have to be circumcised, and all that... And you know what they chop off in circumcision..."

Although Aras gulped down his fear and pretended to remain non-plussed, we both understood that he had met his match. The great race was on!

After I had fainted from disgust and overexcitement during the lizard tail adventure, I had stayed in bed for the next two days, feigning ilness to my mother. Stumped as to what might have happened to me, our neighborhood doctor, Uncle Etyen, had concluded that it must have been sunstroke or food poisoning, and had recommended a fat-free diet coupled with rest. Neither I or my brother, nor Ada, who came to visit the next day, had revealed the lizard affair to the grown-ups. That was the first secret the three of us shared!

First Ada's nanny, Aunt Cihan, sent word to my mother that they wanted to pay us a visit, and then, accompanied by the awed whispers of the entire neighborhood, they came over to say "get well soon." It was a day to be remembered. Ada was an unmistakable beauty in her red dress and matching shoes, with her chestnut hair made into a small bun at her neck. Every detail regarding her is stored fresh in the files of my memory.

"Oh what a lovely child! *Mashallah,* they've raised her very well!"

"Money and fame haven't spoiled her at all!"

"Well, she's going to be quite a heartbreaker when she grows up!"

They had laughed and looked over at me after this comment, and I had grown embarrassed.

"You wouldn't have come over if I hadn't drank that thing, huh?" I had whispered to Ada when she approached my supposed sick bed.

She had smiled sweetly, but had not replied.

My mother's excitement upon learning that a princess was to visit our house was so great that it caught us all by surprise. She bustled around, setting up a showy sickbed on the living room couch with the lavender-scented sheets, spreads, and pillow-covers from her dowry, which were reserved for special occasions. I suppose the thrill Ada and her family presented us with was similar to individually wrapped happiness tablets, with different dosages for every age; irresistibly attractive, mysterious, dreamy...

"Believe me, Mrs. Zubeyde, I'm always at their side. M'lady wants me to keep an eye on Ada, even from far away... When your son, who's very sweet and quiet by the way, came into the garden, I went away so that they could be at ease, but I swear to god I always watch them. They asked for water. I brought it. Then they disappeared for a while, but the garden is safe anyhow... In fact, this neighborhood, and the people here are all such trustworthy, such good people, no better than you, of course!"

Aunt Cihan was doing all she could to ingratiate herself to my mother, but she didn't have to try at all. Neither my mother, nor the other neighborhood women ever looked upon the people who worked at Ada's house as servants. They were accepted as part of Ada's family.

"So then, I heard this screaming and yelling, and when I ran over, what should I see but your son lying on the ground with Ada and another boy trying to revive him. I nearly lost my mind! Upon my word, I didn't know which one to run to... Just as I started thinking the other boy is older than these two, how did he get in the garden, did he do something to your boy, I found out that he was your older son! *Mashallah*, what a handsome boy he is, that one, Aras... he's your older one, isn't he? Oh, dear me! Thank goodness, nothing bad happened to the child, I was so relieved, it was a load off my heart, really."

Aunt Cihan took a small, burgundy-colored velvet box out of her bag. In it was a piece of gold tied with a blue ribbon.

"The master and m'lady sent this since they couldn't come personally to wish you well. Truly, they were very sorry... My lady said 'If Mrs. Zubeyde should accept this little gift we will have established a bridge between our families,' something like that. They want to meet you personally as soon as possible, with God's will. But they have very irregular working hours... It seems pleasant from the outside, yet I know what it's like first hand... Let me tell you, when they're filming a movie their family life gets completely disordered... They work day and night. It's hard work... Yet they are the most kind-hearted, humble people in the world, though no better than you of course. I've said it once, I'll say it again, they both have hearts of gold."

This was a miracle and my mother was in seventh heaven! That little piece of gold inscribed with *Mashallah* in Arabic lettering was, for my mother, the most precious gift in the world. Because the stars had sent it to her, personally!

As they chatted, Ada approached me silently and handed me a huge flat box.

"I brought you this myself, 'cause what're you supposed to do with gold anyway?" she whispered.

It was the biggest watercolor set I had ever seen. I stared at it, spellbound. The lid of the box, in which forty-eight colors were displayed magnificently, had the picture of a picnicking rabbit family. The mother rabbit wore a blue dress, and the four baby rabbits, dressed in red overalls, were eating carrots. The father rabbit had on a red vest with a pocket-watch and was smoking a pipe. They were all sitting on a red and white checkered sheet in a green meadow, smiling over their picnic basket. The sky was bright blue, and the few floating clouds looked as tasty as cotton candy.

"Do you want to have picnics like this when we grow up?" I asked Ada.

"Sure, but we're not bunnies, Mabel," she whispered in my ear. Looking at me with that secret sorrow in her eyes and that mischievous Ada smile on her face...

Once my time in bed ended and I got permission to go out again, I played in the mansion's garden with Ada every day. Occasionally, she would come over to our house with her nanny.

While all this went on, my mother was busy changing her hairstyle, into something younger and prettier, my father was watching quietly, and my grandfather was avidly trying to "normalize" Ada.

"Eh, they've raised this lass like a boy! She talks a lot, asks questions, and won't keep out of trouble, the pixie! Hah hah ha! Tell you the truth I like the little firecracker, she's sure confident... Her spirit reminds me of Rozita, may she rest in peace... Yet I say a girl has to be a little bit lady-like!"

As for Aras... After their initial meeting in the mansion's garden, my brother abruptly began to act like there was no such person named Ada, and had never been. He was in utter denial of a truth he could not handle. The day Ada first came to visit us he didn't once leave the bedroom. But as time went by and our collective interest in Ada increased, spreading all over the house, poor Aras had nowhere left to hide. Wherever he reached he found traces of Ada, she turned up under every rock, and his heretofore sole claim on the garden of admiration and attention grew steadily narrower. He had no problems with me since I never was a rival for him, but Ada was a true rival and she made Aras uncomfortable.

I was very happy. I had a great time playing with Ada. She was generous, just, and highly imaginative. She knew a lot of games, had knowledge beyond her years, not to mention toys, and was very beautiful. She was a chestnut colored, honey-girl! God, how sweetly her hazel eyes trickled into my soul!

She always invented new games, and we wandered together in our imaginary world, among countries and cultures I had never heard of. She reminded me of Aras with her confidence, intelligence and impressive personality, and made me think "if my brother had been a girl he would have been just like Ada."

When we played together she treated me more like her little baby than her friend, and sometimes became my mother. If I got tired of this and began to protest, she would allow me to play the father, but would still treat me as if I were a baby. In any case, I was so happy to be with her that I could not care less about the rest, and I never did!

On the days that we played in the mansion, we would also eat together. Before meals we would clean up in the downstairs bathroom, blowing soap suds into the air and washing each other's hands.

When Ada came over to our house she would have evening tea with us and sample my mother's scrumptious pastries. In other words, I lived with, and in admiration of Ada, and Aras was left alone.

As autumn approached, I began to hear alarm bells ringing. They were going to start school, and I still had two years to go... The desperate pleas I made my mother to enroll me in school were interpreted by them as my "love of reading" and a sign that I would "get ahead in life." Of course, "getting ahead" meant different things for everyone: for my mother it meant becoming an officer, for my grandfather, a tailor whose fame spread to the Balkans; for Aras, a submarine commander, and for Ada simply to be her poet uncle, Dogan Gokay! What my father thought, I don't know. I can only guess... Yet my only wish, which no one seemed to have noticed, was to stay close to Ada.

It was a short while before school started that Ada and Aunt Cihan came over for a visit. As usual, Ada had brought along her basket of toys. Also as usual, Aras had taken refuge in our room, and refused to come out. But things went differently on that day. Before Aras had a chance to leave the house, slamming all the doors behind him, Ada went over to him. She walked right into the room.

"Aras, I brought you something. You can give it back if you don't like it!"

Everything had happened so fast that I was just as surprised as Aras. Besides, what boy can resist a chestnut colored honey-girl standing at his doorway with a pretty package in her hands?

Aras, of course!

"Come on, open it!" said Ada, as she approached him. She didn't seem too ready to give up either. I was standing by the door, breathlessly watching the match between the two heavies in my life.

At first Aras did not even look over. Then he reluctantly lifted his head. He stared first at the present, and then at Ada. He frowned, sighed, and watched the ceiling. Even if he was proud and strong, Aras was still a child.

"No thanks! I don't need it!" he said half-heartedly.

Ada opened the present in her hand without a moment's hesitation. A colorful model ship set emerged from the torn package. 105 Aras leapt up from his seat in unmistakable joy:

"Wow! Where did you find this?"

"My dad bought it from the American Market. Of course, I ordered it for you."

That was it!

"Oh boy, this is gorgeous! Let's see how you make it," said Aras, pouncing on the box.

"I'm glad you like it," said Ada in a naughty voice. "I have lots of those. See, these are the games which we always play with Duna!"

Aras was stunned. Had he actually refused to play with models like this until now? Not at all… But I didn't say a word.

Ada had not played her trump card yet, but she was ready:

Before Aras was fully able to recover, she went over to him, put her arms around his neck, and kissed him on the cheek. Then, she grabbed me by the hand, and dragged me out to the living room where my mother and Aunt Cihan were sitting.

Aras was left standing in the middle of the room with the model ship in his hands, the regret of missed games on his mind, and a honeyed kiss on his cheek.

He was only seven years old, and going through his second Ada shock.

He was going to be much stronger for the following ones.

I never again saw Aras so bewildered.

OFF TO SCHOOL!

"It was just at this hour of our love that porcupines would descend upon the berries,
the season when lilac fell in Kuzguncuk's hair."

Erdal Alova
(Turn of Heart)

"Stars are exclusive people!" my mother had said.

I don't know about others, but the two that I knew were not so at all. At the time of their move into Kuzguncuk, and in the ten years following, Ada's mother and father were among the ten most popular film stars in Turkey (and if you ask me, they would make the all-time top ten list even today). Yet despite all the success and attention, they were both modest, genuine people.

They were not seen very often around the neighborhood. But when people spotted them and approached to shake their hands or kiss their cheek, they would greet everyone with candor, never acting artificial or spoilt. Their fame was not based on an, overnight success: they were both true stars! (My mother loved to use the word "star.")

A few months after they had settled in Kuzguncuk, Sureyya Mercan had entered the Chinaralti coffee house and saluted everyone with his famous "Fisherman Osman" line:

"Salaam aleikum my brother, my sisters!" Then he had bought coffee for everyone present. (Of course, when I was a kid, there was no such thing as filtered American coffee, or the instant kind that is so popular today... when one said coffee, it always meant strong Turkish coffee with a good head of foam.)

Ever since that day, Sureyya Mercan had made it a habit to drop by Chinaralti, have a cup of coffee, and play bezique with the neighborhood men. This act constituted his application towards becoming a Kuzguncukite, and it was accepted on account of his unmistakable sincerity. In later years, there were other famous or wealthy people who moved into our neighborhood, but none of them managed to be "from" here. Most of them left and the "otherness" of those who stayed behind has been forgotten. Common folk are the first to grasp the difference between truth and falsity, but they're also the last to react. And the greatest reaction is that of the people!

Pervin Gokay, who was a true star not only for her beauty but also for her grace and simplicity, was not as bold as her husband. She seemed rather shy and retiring, and I later found out that she came from a family which highly valued privacy. At first glance Pervin Gokay's sensitive silence gave the impression of coldness, especially in comparison to the boisterous character of Sureyya Mercan, who was quite a people's person. Her true warmth got a chance to shine during religious eves and holidays. In those days she would have halva, rolls, and fruit pudding sent out to the neighbors, would personally visit the elderly, and present gifts of candy, pencils and notebooks to the children. Kuzguncuk might be a poor neighborhood, but it is also a proud one. Had Pervin Gokay's sincerity been doubted, all the doors would have been closed in her face.

One thing I learned from their move into our neighborhood was that in order to be genuinely loved by the people, one had to be genuinely close to them.

I had seen them only once before in the mansion, and in such a private moment that I would never forget the lovely image. But I was officially introduced to them a short while after the lizard tail incident.

It was a hot afternoon. Ada and I were in the mansion's relatively cool living room, trying to build a city out of building blocks. Aunt Cihan was first to jump out of her seat, and then the maid, Aunt Hatice and her husband, Uncle Hasan the gardener started bustling about. I stopped playing on account of this wave of excitement running through the house.

"What happened, Ada?"

"Nothing, Mabel dear, either mom or dad must be home," she said, carrying on with the game.

The person whose arrival animated her was her uncle, Dogan Gokay. When Uncle Poet dropped by, Ada grew ecstatic with joy and ignored anyone else who might've been around. (I mean myself, of course…) Nonetheless, Ada was very attached to her parents, and her father especially spoiled her. But she kept her own interest hidden from whoever lavished attention upon her. Just like Aras.

Dogan Gokay had his share of fame, but being an intellectual celebrity means that one's contact with the masses is limited everywhere in the world. In this sense, there are very few writers and poets who are as famous as singers, or movie stars. Most writers are already aware of this from the start.

Pervin Gokay had her hair in a then-fashionable beehive, and was wearing a blue dress. Sleeveless, collarless, and knee-length. I would learn of her relationship to textiles and design later, thus discovering the source of her simple yet always elegant style. I notice only now that she wore mostly Chanel designs in those years.

"Ada, sweetie, aren't you going to give your mommy a welcome kiss?"

"Hi mommy, we were playing…"

The embrace between mother and daughter was just like in the movies. It had seemed theatrical to me, though I had envied it a little. Mom and I would never cuddle like that. Her mother stroked, smelled, and kissed Ada's chestnut hair. She traced her fingers over her daughter's cheek with small, circular motions, purring with affection. Ada had given herself over like a spoiled little kitten. They remained like that for a while, holding hands, looking into each other's eyes, and then they remembered me and turned around.

"Little fellow, you must be my daughter's famous Duna!" said Pervin Gokay.

I nodded shyly but enthusiastically.

"Oh, you're such a young little dear… What pretty baby blue eyes you have there."

"His grandpa calls him the Blue Danube," Ada joined in.

"Hmm, in that case, you two are the Brunette Ada and Blue Danube."

Then Pervin Gokay had reached over and stroked my hair. Her milky white hands felt soft on my cheeks, as I noticed her red nail polish. They smelled heavenly. They were not like my mother's dark hands which smelled of food. For this reason, I have always kept the secret childhood impression that a mother's and a woman's hands are different.

Sureyya Mercan was very noisy and cheerful. Upon our first meeting, he had lifted me up and tossed me in the air like a baby. I'd been embarrassed, but pleased.

"You little Casanova... Now that you found my cute daughter we can't get rid of you, can we? Hah hah hah!"

He was always laughing, hiding behind peals of laughter.

"Good for you, my lad, this is exactly the way I drew her mother in, if you know what I mean, hah hah ha!

Come on, let's play a round of backgammon, man to man."

"Daddy! He's still young, he doesn't know how to play backgammon, and besides, Duna's my friend, not yours!"

" Well, well, well... How about that, my little princess is already jealous of her admirer... Well done, young man, you know a thing or two... Hah ha ha! But come now, let me teach you backgammon, a man's gotta know how to play it!"

I still don't know backgammon, and never was too interested in learning. Later, Sureyya Mercan played backgammon, bezique, poker, and bridge with Aras, and generally ended up losing.

"Look here, Aras you little wizard! You'd better watch out! Stop beating Sureyya Mercan, for god's sakes! I'm old enough to be your dad... Poor Fisherman Osman is a country boy, spare him his pride why don't you?" he'd say, trying to win pity.

Even as a kid, Aras would keep playing with that serious face of his, as if he had not heard a thing.

When autumn came and school started, the news that Ada had been enrolled in the neighborhood public school spread joyously from ear to ear. She was to attend the modest public school, like all the other kids in Kuzguncuk. And that's what happened: Ada became a student just like the rest of us, but she never became one of us!

It wasn't her fault. Her nature, her character, and her upringing were different. Her posture, her walk, her laugh, and even her hand gestures reminded me of a princess (And I never lost this impression!). Seen from afar, it was immediately evident that she was a noble little lady mistakenly caught among us. Sure, her outfits were the kind we only wore on special occasions, always new, ironed, and pretty, but it wasn't just the clothes... When Ada's confidence, her assured, self-aware glances, her provocative pride and defiance were coupled with her honey colored beauty, one could not help but be impressed by the result.

No, don't think for a moment that I describe her like this due to my private infatuation with her. Certainly, I admit that I took a special interest in her from the day we first met, but it wasn't just me: Ada also made an impression on the other kids and as a result, they were too shy to make friends with her. Despite the fact that she never used her "daughter of the stars" status to her advantage, Ada had an aura of unattainability. Yet her friendship was warm and very colorful.

Ada and Aras ended up in Mrs. Nezihe's class, and they shared the same desk until they graduated from grade school. While at first I secretly mourned the loss of Ada and even suffered a loss of appetite, I soon realized that this was not the case. After Ada and Aras stopped feuding and became friends, Aras would accompany me to the mansion. I would play by myself while they did homework (keeping an eye on them, of course), and when they were done we would all play together, or eat the evening fare Aunt Cihan had prepared for us.

I had not lost Ada, but I was sharing her with someone else. My only consolation was that the person I was sharing her with was the first hero in my life: my older brother. Besides, what mattered to me was being together with Ada, knowing that she liked me. I never wanted anything more. I suppose everyone has their own way of loving, and that was mine.

In the first two years of grade school, there was only one candidate for class president, and he was always guaranteed to win: Aras Atacan! My brother: the bravest, smartest, strongest, and most daring boy in the neighborhood! But when they reached third grade (the year I started school) another candidate appeared: Ada Mercan! The neighborhood's graceful, well-mannered honey princess, and the top student of her class. That year Ada was chosen class president. I knew that although he did not let on, Aras had taken this rather hard. I also knew that my brother would never give up.

They both loved the adrenalin rush. They loved to challenge and compete, and thrived on constantly testing and outdoing themselves. Ada and Aras fed off this thrill; a safe, straightforward life would have starved them to death!

For this reason, their fourth year in school saw the beginning of a ruthless race for president. The race that got so serious as to involve a mini-election campaign, starred Ada as the brave, innovative candidate, and Aras as her conservative, traditional opponent.

"If you choose me," Ada declared, "I will give storybooks to everyone once a month. I will offer you soda and candy on your birthdays and have my picture taken with your family."

Then Aras climbed on the bust of Ataturk in the schoolyard and proclaimed:

"Choose me, and I'll make model ships for all of you. I'll pick fruit from the branches you can't reach on trees. Plus, I will help you with your math homework..."

Their rivalry, which was new to the school, grew so big that it extended as far as the neighborhood, and was talked about for days.

"That actors' daughter is running against Naim the Tailor's son! The girl is so smart, so sassy, I wonder how the boy's going to handle her!"

Finally, all the students gathered in Aras and Ada's classroom, and made such racket that Mrs. Nezihe, the most mild-mannered teacher in the school, lost her patience. Neither her affection for Ada, nor her attachment to Aras were enough to keep her from yelling at the top of her voice as she took control of the situation. Yet it only succeded in making the two of them continue their propaganda secretly.

Aras finally did manage to be re-elected class president, but he grew exhausted from having to do everyone's homework assignments all year long. Making the promised model ships, on the other hand, was no trouble at all since he loved to do it. However, the cost of cardboard, paint, and glue ended up being too much for him. He had to drop the pursuit when his allowance ran out, and it was apparent that it hurt his pride. Like most silent, introverted people, Aras was overly sensitive and proud. Being unable to fullfill his promise had saddened my brother a great deal.

In the final year of elementary school, Ada's campaign pledges included giving dancing and singing lessons. She had been taking private piano lessons for years, and although she wasn't particulary talented in music, she had whispered to me that she persisted mostly to please her mother. Her classmates, on the brink of pubescence at twelve years of age, chose her as class president partly due to the lure of dance and music, and partly because they were won over by Ada's person.

Either way was fine with me. Whichever one of them got elected, I was happy, and I preserved my coolness at school.

By the time they finished elementary school with straight A's and their teachers' praises, both of them were beginning to feel the preliminary hints of adolescence. Aras' voice had started to crack, and the first onset of pimples were on their way.

"Mom, my brother seems to have grown hoarse, is he sick?"

My mother would smile and say in a proud voice:

"Aras is becoming a man!"

My father would smile without raising his head from his work or his newspaper. My grandfather would gush:

"Eh, my precious foal is growing up to be a dark stallion, praise god!"

"But didn't we become men two years ago, mom?"

Following our circumcision two years earlier, when I was eight and Aras was ten, everyone had told us that we were now considered real men.

"Oh my little Duna, my great, good hearted son!"

The foremost guest of our circumcision party had doubtlessly been Ada. She had come with Aunt Cihan, and had looked pityingly at me and Aras as we lay on the festive bed. She had brought us each a wristwatch as a present, though my father had not been very pleased, saying they were too expensive. But the true reason for his disappointment was that he had also bought his sons wristwatches as circumcision gifts. Compared with Ada's high-tech, digital, waterproof watches, the ones from our dad, which were stylish in his youth, had not seemed very attractive, and we had not paid much attention to them. Since my poor father could neither express his joy, nor disappointments, none of us had been able to understand the hurt he felt that day. He exchanged the classical wristwatches for a large clock, and who knows, perhaps he remembered the defeat he suffered at his sons' circumcision party everytime he looked up at it. Nowadays, I wish we had taken my father's presents and put them away somewhere. But I'm only now learning that children begin to understand their parents in their thirties...

I remember very well the embarassment I felt when Ada approached our bed in a rare unattended moment, and lifted my circumcision gown to take a curious peek at my bandaged pee-pee. I recall just as vividly how Aras, moving swift as a hawk, grabbed Ada's hand and bit it fiercely to prevent himself from sharing my fate. Ada had cried out in pain, and although tears were streaming down her face, had gnashed her teeth and silenced herself, for fear of losing face before Aras. (Yet Ada, my honey princess, was never apprehensive of me in that way. She has always been comfortable enough to let herself go in front of me, to cry as much as she needs to!)

My parents were treating Ada's hand with ice cubes and oxygen water, and scolding Aras at the same time. None of us said a word about the reason for this strange behavior, further driving my already flustered mother and Aunt Cihan crazy.

"Eh, stop bothering them... There's surely a good reason for the boy's wrath," my grandfather said, grinning as if he had understod the entire situation.

"They didn't cut all of Duna's off, but they must have chopped yours off completely! They did too! Since you're so afraid of showing it..."

As much as I felt sorry for Ada's pain, which was apparent in her face, I was just as surprised to see her resolve to hide it. God, how alike those two were!

Poor Aras was stuck in quite a predicament, and sulking in his bed all day, he hadn't been able to take an interest in either the shadow-puppeteer, or the ice-cream man. He was only thinking of Ada. What if she really believed he had no pee-pee left? That night I had cried secretly, believing myself that he was left without a pee-pee.

A week later, in the mansion's garden, Aras took down his shorts and showed Ada that he had something left. Ada, whose hand wound had still not healed completely, had said in a very serious and convinced voice:

"Okay, now I feel relieved!"

All three of us had smiled, not certain of what this meant.

Now we were all relieved!

GENERAL TURHAN OZSOY

"Soldiers are not like other men… Since the culture of a war-ring class can not be the same as that of a civilized one the gap is never bridged. These people's lives are parallel to the daily lives of others, but show no relation whatsoever."

John Keegan
(A History of the Art of War)

"Intellectuals in particular have a tendency to characterize soldiers as crude and stupid," said the general.

After getting a haircut and a shave, Duna had put on his second lieutenant uniform, and been speedily taken, via military jeep, to the most impressive building in the garrison.

He believed that his chance to see clearly had been intentionally taken away with the weak lenses he was given. Nevertheless, while he was getting shaved, he had been able to distinguish that the face in the mirror was badly bruised. He had a black left eye, and a scar above his right brow. His nose was swollen, and awfully painful to touch, and a bump on his neck was constantly making its presence felt. The only familiar things about the shaved head and bruised face in the mirror were its blue eyes.

While waiting to be admitted into the general's office, he waited in the petty officer's room, which smelled heavily of soft soap. He was avidly trying and failing to ignore the face he saw in the mirror. Just then First Lieutenant Birol appeared with his hope colored eyes and bright smile. First, he stood to attention and gave a razor-sharp salute:

"Second Lieutenant!" he said.

Duna, who was at a complete loss as to what he should do, was not very quick to react. He remembered that lower ranking officers had to salute first, but since he was convinced of the surrealness of everything, he could only watch himself as if through a stupor. He stood up, inspected his hat, found the front part, put it on, and gave a sloppy salute. First Lieutenant Birol extended his left hand and shook Duna's hand eagerly, as if nothing had happened. They were like two close friends who met at a summer resort. Then Duna noticed something.

"Are you also left-handed?" he asked elatedly. "Because she's left-handed…"

"I hope you don't have any superstitions about lefties, lieutenant, "said First Lieutenant Birol.

"I think they're extremely intelligent, though that is also a prejudice. But she… she believes that being left-handed is unlucky."

"It is very fortunate that Brigade General Turhan Ozsoy wants to see you. You'll know what I mean when you meet him; he is an amazing man!" said First Lieutenant Birol, changing the subject.

Duna studied him carefully. His subject was healthy, natural, well-meaning and honest. There was such a clearly positive quality about him that whenever Duna reached the point of desperation, he appeared and momentarily dispelled the dark fearsome clouds. It seemed as if First Lieutenant Birol was not a suitable character for this nightmare, and that Duna's subconscious had created him accidentally.

"Please have a seat, lieutenant, don't mind me."

"Could he really be this polite and good-humored?" wondered Duna as he sat down worriedly.

"Our Brigade General is an enlightened, progressive, and sharp person. He does not deny the productive aspects of imagination, yet he is a realistic soldier. If we had been able to produce more people like him, we would not be in this situation today."

"By 'this situation' does he mean the civil war or the nightmare?" thought Duna.

"To tell you the truth," First Lieutenant Birol was saying, his gleaming brown eyes fixed on Duna, "I couldn't let them hassle you any further, since I was aware of your psychological troubles. Unlike them, I think that you are an extremely intelligent, intellectually responsible, and perhaps slightly hyper-sensitive person. And also… I might be giving you preferential treatment because I've taken a special liking to you."

"A special liking? Why's that?" asked Duna suspiciously.

"We'll talk about that when there's more time," said First Lieutenant Birol, averting his eyes with some embarrassment. "Our Brigade General loves me like his own son, and when I mentioned your story, he wanted to meet you in person. You'll see, he loves me like his own son…"

Maybe it was real. Maybe it wasn't his nightmare, but the civil war that was real. He was the one who was mistaken, not the others…

"That would be the worst," thought Duna. "The most painful wound is realizing that you are the one who's mistaken. The only permanent scar is caused by a betrayal of consciousness! The hardest wrongs to forgive are in fact those committed by one's own self…"

He had lost his sense of time, the most crucial determinant of his sense of reality. Maybe that was why his concept of reality had given way, and his present had been shattered. But what if his past?

"I couldn't bear that!" he said.

What if the contents of the nightmare were real, and everything else was an illusion? What if his inability to wake up no matter how hard he tried, to complete the breakfast on his pretty little balcony, to pet his cat Brunette, to read his students books and poetry, to drink coffee with his mother, to feel Merich's cool, calm presence, to live with Dogan Gokay's unparallelled friendship, and… and to see Ada, to esctatically watch her flow through life… What if, contrary to his belief, all these things were not a nightmare? What if a war was the true reason he had been apart from his loved ones for so long? *How* long?

Yet what was to be said for that strong voice inside him, urging him to "Wait! Wait and this will end!"

On the other hand, how could he now dismiss the civil war he had been so anxiously expecting as a nightmare and wait for it to be over?

He didn't know. He didn't know anything anymore. The only thing he knew was that all his past and present were imbued with a sense of intense expectancy.

"Please, lieutenant," First Lieutenant Birol was saying in a conciliatory voice, "Please control your nerves in there, when you're with the Brigade General!"

True, he had first jumped off the military vehicle, then caused scenes both in the infirmary and the ward, and had firmly denied the civil war which everyone else believed in. What's more, he had called anyone who came across his path a fake, and had treated them as if they were ghosts.

"There's no reason you should be uncomfortable, but I'm just asking you to have a little control, you understand, don't you lieutenant?"

· This young man was tactfully referring to them as "psychological troubles," but Duna had heard first-hand from Hasan the orderly that people thought he was nuts. Perhaps First Lieutenant Birol's terminology was an official version of "nuts."

A private appeared in the soap-scented quarters, and between two salutes, barked in a clear, sharp sentence, that the general was ready to receive the Second Lieutenant Duna Atacan. Meanwhile Duna noticed with surprise that he had stood up with the First Lieutenant and promptly returned the private's salute. Was he losing control of his body as well?

First Lieutenant Birol wished him good luck with a slightly apprehensive smile, and disappeared as swiftly as he came.

That was when Duna realized that the person he felt closest to in this nightmare, which he had waited fearfully to begin and now was waiting impatiently to end, was a young soldier.

The private led the way, knocked on the imposing door, entered, and standing firmly to attention announced with fervor:

"Second Lieutenant Duna Atacan is ready for your orders, Sir!"

Upon entering, the first thing that struck him was the vast dimensions of the room. The abundance of light and the spaciousness were very impressive. But the furniture was just as mighty as the dimensions. On the left there was a twelve-person mahogany conference table with a large crystal pitcher and glasses. Duna noticed that the pitcher was filled with water. Was there a meeting to be held soon?

The room had wall to wall carpeting of a light salmon color, and a magnificent Turkish rug lay in front of the general's desk.

"It must be hand-woven," mused Duna.

Behind the general's huge desk, on the right was a brigade banner with a single star, and a Turkish flag. An embroidered flag could be seen in the glass-windowed display case. A brass placard on the table read "Brigade General Turhan Ozsoy." Also on the table were a pennant of the Republic of Turkey, gold-plated twin fountain pen set and a burgundy leather portfolio. A huge black and white portrait of Ataturk was on the back wall, observing the room with thoughtful eyes.

Duna felt miniscule in this spacious room where everything was so enormous. "Don't you fall for this trick!" said his inner voice, but wasn't very effective. He stood to attention and gave a very exaggerated salute.

"General!" he cried. His voice gushed forth with the same devoted ardor as when he sang the national anthem in childhood.

"What is this?" he thought. "The game of playing the game by the rules? What am I doing?"

The general, without lifting his head from the papers in front of him, raised his eyes and looked him over carefully. Their eyes met. At that point the general left his papers and straightened up.

"At ease, Second Lieutenant, at ease! Come here, sit down," he said, pointing with one hand toward the chair in front of him.

Duna had begun to grow distrustful again, as he sat down in the indicated black leather chair. Even the chair was hefty, it sucked Duna in and swallowed him.

The general was a round-faced, portly man with a visible bald spot and hair thinning at the sides. Judging from the long fingers on his plump hands, Duna thought he must be quite tall. His long and thick eyebrows, like two jet-black arches, were the most prominent lines on his face. Yet his temples were beginning to turn gray. His beady eyes, which were dwarfed by his large round face, were bright black.

"Intellectuals tend to caricature soldiers as crude or stupid," began the general. "They never stop portraying us as dictators with decorated chests, stern faces, and empty expressions!"

"Oh dear!" moaned Duna. "He's going to take his hate of intellectuals out on me!"

That was not what happened. The general's voice was neither

angry nor condescending. It did not have the persuasive tone of priests or imams trying to show the Way to evil or ignorant masses. He was simply pointing out a generalization he found erroneous, and maybe even hurtful…

"Of course, there are soldiers who fit this stereotype,…but thousands of anonymous, honorable, and heroic officers are punished by this characterization, being found guilty by association."

"Why is he telling me this?" Duna wondered suspiciously.

"There have always been enlightened, progressive and humanistic officers with an appreciation for art in the Turkish armed forces, and there always will be."

"Certainly, sir!" Duna heard himself say.

"We know that you are a literature teacher," said the general, leaning his chin on his hand with a thoughtful look. "I was also informed that you are a 'well-read, erudite, and highly-sensitive' person."

"That must have been Birol," worried Duna. "Now we've really done it! He's going to rub my nose in how a man shouldn't be sensitive, and how being a tough man is necessary for being a soldier… Oh Birol, this is just what I needed, honestly!"

"Soldiers badly need people like yourself these days, lieutenant," said the general.

"He's testing me! Yes, he's testing me! If what I'm going through is real it's the general, and if it's a nightmare then it's my brain who's testing me!" Duna thought, growing restless.

"I do not agree with my colleagues who claim that this civil war, as you know we are being mobilized, was caused by an excess of democracy."

"Excuse me?"

Suddenly Duna had started to take an interest in what the general was saying. Nonetheless, he could not help but get snagged on the phrase "as you know we are being mobilized." The general was underlining "as you know," warning him that it was time he accepted this, and stopped acting like a loon or a child.

"In my opinion, Second Lieutenant, there cannot be a dirth or an excess of democracy. Either democracy exists, or it does not! Equality might not be widespread, justice might not be officialized, but democracy cannot be too little or too much! Democracy has its discipline and conditions too. Democracy is not a regime of infinitude and irresponsibility, but rather one of common sense and responsibility. Civil wars do not erupt in countries where it is applied fairly!"

"No, this is too much! This is going too far..." Duna sighed. "Taking a lesson in democracy from a soldier is going too far!"

"Throughout history, people have been ruled through the exploitation of two feelings: fear and hope," the general continued.

"Maybe he's caught up in the thrill of thinking he has found a young intellectual who will understand him, and he is relaying his heartfelt thoughts. In that case what I'm going through can't be a nightmare, and it is completely useless to wait for it to end."

He grew pale, his stomach ached, he began to feel light-headed, and his body, weakened by days or weeks of depression and wounds, trembled. Sharp whistles sounded in his ears.

"Are you alright, Second Lieutenant?" asked the general, hastily pressing the bell under his desk.

"Bring me a salty *ayran*, quick!" he barked at the private who appeared at the door.

"Yes sir, commander!"

The service private looked like a clone of the messenger private. Between all the salutes, atten-shuns and at-eases, a glass of the cold salty yogurt drink had been fetched, and its ingestion ordered. Soon colors and shapes started to return to Duna, who took long, deep breaths.

"Are you alright, son?"

Son? That anonymous tone had been replaced by a caring and personal voice.

"Look, Second Lieutenant," said the general, recovering his previous, distant manner, "as wrong as it is to trivialize all this, it is also erroneous to blow it out of proportion. How well our ancestors put it when they said a healthy mind belongs in a healthy body!"

"Yes, sir!"

"What society has gone through momentous changes without conflict? Our society is also experiencing a great change, that's all. Change is mandatory because change is inevitable! Otherwise the possibility of improvement does not exist!"

"What's holding me back?" Duna asked himself. "What's preventing me from liking this man?"

"Changes are dynamic, like waves. When waves collide they cause strong reverse currents. In order to understand this, Americans waited for a man named Toffler to write a book."

"A general who reads books, however popular," Duna continued his interior monologue.

"Actually, Second Lieutenant, the present day conflict did not arise from struggles between east and west, or north and south; what you would refer to in cliché terms as religious and ethnic causes."

At this point the general stood up. No, he was not as tall as Duna had supposed. He possessed a fair paunch, but he was hardly 5' 9". Yet his confidence and weight gave him an imposing appearance, like his office. He was one of the lucky people who looked taller and heftier than they were. On the whole, he was quite impressive.

"The heart of the matter lies in the fact that we are living through a great economic and strategic change. The cause of the problem is very simple: there exists a violent conflict between those who support this change and those who oppose it for purposes of preserving the advantages and gains they have held for centuries."

If he had been a family friend Duna met in another setting, say at the Kuzguncuk mansion, or at Ismet Baba's pub, dressed in civvies (a golf cap, cotton pants, and a polo shirt), and if he had been Turhan Ozsoy, a professor in "History of Civilization" at some university or another, then... then their relationship would be different. This is what Duna realized.

"How deeply conditions influence our relationships," he said in a mournful voice.

"Very true, Lieutenant!" the general replied. "But we shouldn't forget that humans are the only beings who, to a certain extent, can control conditions."

It was as if the general, caught up in his own words, and pacing his hefty self from one corner of his hefty room to another, was a lecturer in a military academy.

"Ever since the first transition from agrarian society into industrialization, mankind has endeavored to regulate his own shortcomings and environmental conditions. And to a certain extent, he succeeded. Observe, as a result of rural migration into cities, a number of new, courageous ideas emerged and took hold. Technology and democracy, which we call progress, have only been possible after the acceptance of ideas such as enlightenment, secularism, and the public election of rulers. Have you ever seen a scientific advance, a technological breakthrough, or an invention emerge from a country where fear and oppression dominate?"

"This can't possibly be real!" thought Duna, feeling depressed again.

"However, we must not forget that all these brave new ideas were greeted with violent and bloody opposition in Europe as well. Due to industry and trade, the Western civil wars took place between great land owners and the church. For everything new and progressive is first and foremost considered 'the devil's invention!'"

He paused, and circled his right index finger in the air, as if searching for something. The general then ponderously walked towards his imposing desk. He sat down on the comfortable, inviting looking leather chair, and Duna knew that he was hooked. The subject matter was not anything new but its narrator made it interesting.

"We are not, as the West claims, stuck between the hoe and the assembly industry, Second Lieutenant. True, we have not yet reached the information age, but our country has already made the transition into the production stage..." he said proudly. "The real formula for our liberation lies in our becoming a hardworking and very productive nation! We also have to uncover what it is that frightens us so terribly. Then we can eradicate fear, see the bogeymen for who they really are, shove them out of the way, and continue on our path. For the true cause of this civil war is the final cries of economic interest, as it tries to trip up progress and modernization!"

The general took a deep breath and returned to his desk. He sat down grandly, and leaned back in his chair. He even smiled with the proud expression of a problem solver.

Duna admittedly was impressed. First Lieutenant Birol had been correct; general Turhan Ozsoy was an intelligent man.

"You already know all this, young man. You'll say to yourself: 'Now why did my Brigade General tell it to me?' Let me explain why Second Lieutenant: because you are not aware that a soldier also knows or thinks about these things!"

By now, the general was regarding Duna with complete victory.

Duna smiled. He thought of his older uncle, Mustafa, who was an army officer, and his younger uncle, Kemal, an air-force officer. His mother's beaming face gazing in admiration at their uniforms when they came to visit their sister Zubeyde and their nephews in Kuzguncuk. The happiness with which she related to Duna her pure belief and pride in the Turkish soldier...

"We're a military nation, son," his mother would say. "The army saved us from two dark plagues in the past: ignorance, and invaders."

At that point his mother would turn her eyes lovingly toward the handsome picture of Ataturk, which hung right above the TV in the living room. The Ataturk in the picture was also in uniform. Born and raised in Igdir, with only a junior high school diploma, his mother was much more expert in determining the pulse of the people than a highly-educated Istanbulite. With a single sentence she could reach the heart of long and rambling discussions.

"This nation loves her soldiers because they are the ones who always bring us into the light!"

Yet Dogan Gokay approached the subject from a different angle:

"Anyone who has studied the art of war will admit to the military genius of Turks. Whether we like it or not, Turks have always been good fighters and soldiers."

The Poet Dogan Gokay did not like to display his own truths. He would throw out various truths and knowledge, together with their sources, in the appropriate time and place, and then withdraw. Those who came to him looking for prescriptions without any ideas or resources of their own were sorely disappointed, and always returned empty-handed.

When Duna returned his attention, the general was saying:

"I have two sons and a daughter. One of my sons chose his father's occupation, and became an officer. The other one is involved in tourism. The difference between those two is incredible. My officer son is a disciplined, serious, and responsible young man, whereas my younger son is a ne'er-do-well. He couldn't care less about national or international matters… Only money and girls… A man without ideals, a buffoon who laughs at everything… It is only animals who live for today!"

"Actually, Aret, my childhood friend, and grandson of our neighborhood doctor Uncle Etyen (may he rest in peace), is a very conscientious, consistent, and responsible person, working in the tourism industry. Work ethics and self-respect should exist in one's self, not in his uniform," Duna opened his mouth to say, but instead heard himself assent:

"I understand, sir."

"Of course there are hard-working and responsible people in every occupation, but I simply mean that some lines of work are more disciplined and responsible."

There was a brief silence. Then the general began his true speech in a soft, personal tone:

"Look, son, I know it is difficult to accept, yet we are living in a civil war and we need sanity now more than ever."

Another brief silence…

"If we remember that the true reason for all this lies in a struggle for change, for progress, and that the superficial images we see, or are shown, are only a game (which they always are in civil wars), then we will have greater power to retain our sanity."

A game? Can there be a secret relation between game and nightmare? Could there be a code hidden in these words?

The general stood up. His posture seemed to indicate that the meeting was over. Duna instantly jumped out of his seat, stood to attention, and waited.

"I like you, Second Lieutenant Duna Atacan!" said the general, squinting. "We believe that a patriotic and intellectual young man will not allow his mind to leave himself!"

He had hardly spoken at all, and had displayed a weakness unbefitting the image of a "soldier" and a "man" by suffering a fainting spell, but the general had liked him anyway. How could this be possible? Either he was being sucked into a pre-planned game, or… or none of this was real. (Thank goodness!)

But of course! Since everyone, beginning with his mother and including all his acquaintances, his grandfather, his teachers, his neighbors, publications and fairytales, had installed such a sense of military affection in him, the soldiers he saw in this nightmare would naturally all be bright, compassionate, affectionate, and very positive characters. Take First Lieutenant Birol, take Brigade General Turhan Ozsoy! Charitable, understanding, enlightened people...

"There is a soldier in all of our families, among all our relatives. The military has become a part of Turkey, just like a school or a mosque!" his mother used to say.

"But... but my brain, which is aware that there are mean and evil people in every occupation is giving in to my subconscious and failing to create a single evil soldier in this nightmare!" he thought.

He remembered Dogan Gokay who had an obsessive and violent hatred of General Pinochet.

"I wonder if a Chilean intellectual has had such a problem? Or, if I had been tortured during martial law, would I be able to think this way?"

While he was absorbed in his efforts to control his subconscious, sirens had begun to wash over them in waves. There was a pounding on the door, and a disheveled service private tumbled inside, without waiting for the "enter" command. He stood to attention:

"Fire, commander! A sabotage, near the arsenal, commander!" he cried.

The general picked up his hat, and remaining completely calm, ordered: "Understood private, go back to your post immediately!"

"Yes, sir!"

Then he turned to Duna. "Now, return to your unit, Second Lieutenant, and try to keep your wits about you!"

Duna gave a clumsy salute. While he debated whether to respond with, "Will do, commander!" or "As you wish, commander!" the sirens covered the entire garrison with bitter intensity.

Just as he was leaving, he thought he heard the general say:

"I love First Lieutenant Birol like my own son. Particularly since my older son was martyred in the Southeast..."

He froze in his tracks. He remained standing. He closed his eyes in sorrow. Then he turned around. The general was gone. When he found himself in the hallway, among bustling soldiers, he tried to understand how he got there. In order to solve the mystery of his predicament, he had to know every last detail. Like a good detective, he had to collect the incriminating evidence against his own treacherous brain. Only then would this nightmare end!

Since he had not re-emerged into the petty officer's room, there must have been two entrances into the general's room, and this did not seem unreasonable to him. But where was he headed now, as the mass of soldiers running every which way swept him down the corridor? His already weak sense of direction had deserted him entirely because of this nightmare. He felt like he was in one of those labyrinth puzzles he used to solve with Ada when they were kids.

"It's a little like Kafka's castle," he thought, unaware of his accompanying smile. "Everything is clear from a distance, and credible enough to seem real... But as it approaches it grows blurry, dreamy, and metamorphoses into an endless labyrinth within a labyrinth. Everything is a dead end, every exit is false... The more you want to leave this nightmare the more it smothers you, it chews and swallows you up..."

He stood before the two different exit doors in the hallway, and pondered. He shrugged:

"After all, isn't that what a nightmare is supposed to be?" he murmured. Randomly flinging open one of the doors, Second Lieutenant Duna Atacan stepped forth in that direction.

SLEIGHT OF WORD

"A writer is the loneliest one among the beast called man."

Lawrence Durrell

"I got my name from one of my uncle's best-loved poems."

I had never before heard of a child's name being inspired by a poem. Most of the kids I knew had been named after their grandparents, a historical or religious figure, or at best an admired celebrity (Barish, from the neighborhood owed his name not to the meaning of the word peace, but to the singer Barish Mancho). It was a wholly new and abstract notion for children's names to have their source in the heroes of novels, or poem titles. I was simply fascinated. But I could not remain outdone. I had to immediately create a myth about my own name.

"My grandpa gave me my name!" I said proudly. "A long time ago my grandpa lived in a place far away, where there was a beautiful river. It was so beautiful that people who saw it almost fainted. Mermaids swam in the river, and the king, who was their father, lived at the bottom... So my grandpa said, he said if I have a grandson whose eyes are blue like this river, his name should be Duna... Seee!"

"Mabel, my dear, first of all mermaids live in the sea, but actually they are not there either. 'Cause all this stuff is made up by grown-ups who think they're really smart, and who want to trick the children... And besides, rivers aren't blue, they're green!"

Actually, my parents had decided to name their children according to the names of the rivers that nourished the lands where they grew up. If their first child was a boy, it would be my mother's river, if it was a girl, then my father's. Aras and Duna! But when they ended up with two boys, and started racking their brains for a name for me, my grandfather intervened.

"What's the problem? Is the Duna male or female that it should matter, eh? Listen here, beauty and abundance don't belong to men or women, so you'd better name my grandson Duna. That's my will to you!"

Once my grandmother Mrs. Murshide also came out in support of her husband, my mother was convinced.

"Wait, don't get sad, Mabel, my dear! Look, if you want, we can make up a story about how the green nymphs who lived in the Duna had a blue-eyed sweet little brother, huh, d'you want to?"

I had hung my lower lip and grown tearful. Her name was from a poem, and mine from a river that wasn't even blue...

"One day this little river prince dreamt of Brunette Ada who lived in Kuzguncuk, and he came out of the river and lost his tail. Then he became a human being. Ever since that day, they have played very happy games in the Kuzguncuk mansion!"

Oh Ada, oh you little trickster! How did you always know to mend my brokeni reality-prone heart with your dreams and succeed?

"So, are you and me a prince and a princess?" I asked joyously.

"Of course!" she said, surprised that I had only now understood this.

"But what about Aras..."

"Is Aras a king?" I asked, knowing that the answer was yes, but afraid to hear it.

"You are each a river!" she said in an entirely different voice. As if she had not ever entered that fairytale world. "And me, I'm that island that sits all alone in the sea, like in my uncle's poem..." Those mysterious gleams in her voice, a pride I did not understand, and the usual Ada inflections...

I found out later that the poem called "Brunette Ada", was a well-loved work which had gained instant fame, and that its name had become synonymous with its author, Dogan Gokay.

This magnificent poem begins "No one knows, I do not/ disclose this private truth," and expertly, courageously expresses the inner weaknesses of a young man. With its frequent calls to a woman named Ada whose whereabouts and identity are never clarified, the poem had gained the admiration of women and given heart to men for years. "Brunette Ada", which was a favorite with the intellectuals and socialists of the generation before us, remained vital for our generation as well.

As for the river Duna, I was to learn with some sadness that it was neither green nor blue, but rather a dirty brown-gray color. However, just like my grandfather, the elder Strauss had found it befitting of the color blue.

"My mom and dad met while they were filming together. My dad was reading the poem called 'Brunette Ada' and my mother told him 'if you'd like, I can have my brother autograph that for you.'"

"Did she get the autograph?"

"Yup. Then, when they were reading that poem together my dad fell in love with my mom. And, the poem became their poem....And they never left each other."

"How nice!" I would think. Some kids had parents with poems and love stories, but the most romantic thing I ever witnessed between my parents were the looks following cryptic phrases like "really, dear, you're too much!" or "you naughty Naim, you." Every relationship had a story, but instead of letting it flow from one generation to the next, elaborated with delight, it was often concealed from children as if it were an impropriety, or a sin.

"What does it mean to fall in love, Ada?"

"You know…" she would giggle, cross her eyes, extend her lips almost out to her nose, and begin to make kissing noises. But when these sounds and her comical face were combined, she would look like a baby suckling enthusiastically, or a horse drinking water, and would remind me of the old steed of the milkman who still sold his product in open containers, defying the pasteurization age. By then we would both be crying from laughter, rolling around on the floor, and making those horse-feeding noises which we thought were the sounds of love. Aunt Cihan would immediately materialize at our side, give us a suspicious look, then laugh, shake her head, and sigh:

"Ah childhood! You just laugh at anything that comes you way! These are your best day, so keep on laughing!"

(All my life, whenever I've been elated, I have always come across some messenger of misery who reminds me that these are my happiest days. Either our culture breeds too many of these characters, and we have to put up with them because they can't be exported, or people who don't endeavor to overcome their past disappointments find consolation in checking other people's contentment!)

One day, after one of these laughing fits, Ada showed me a gorgeous album filled with black and white photographs of her parents. In most of the pictures, Sureyya Mercan was sporting a drink and a cigarette, and looking at his wife seductively. Pervin Gokay, slightly bashful of her slim beauty in the daring gowns, was nevertheless smiling in blissful languor by her husband's side. When we got to some romantic poses where they were holding hands, embracing, or gazing into each other's eyes, Ada started buzzing like a bee. I soon joined in, and we buzzed and giggled endlessly. (Why does every kissing scene witnessed by children newly discovering their sexuality make them laugh and grow slightly embarrassed? What is it that makes them so elated? The thrill of realizing that they have taken their first step into the garden of grown-ups, or the first hints of having begun the exploration of an amazing beauty?)

In one picture, Ada's parents were kissing. Perhaps it was a scene from a movie, or perhaps it was real, I can't say. But they both had their eyes shut and looked joyous.

"There, that's love," said Ada knowingly.

"Come on, we should do it too!" I said, excited.

We held hands, pressed our cheeks against one another, smiled and closed our eyes. She was seven, I was five, and in my opinion, we had fallen in love!

We opened our eyes to the sound of applause, and I felt terribly ashamed, as if I had been caught stealing.

"Wonderful, you're absolutely lovely, children!" clapped a rather tall, handsome young man with glasses, and wavy dark hair that was playfully tousled. He was wearing a tweed jacket and suede shoes (since he still has the same taste I don't doubt my memory).

"Uncle! Uncle Dogan!" cried the overjoyed Ada, and jumping into the smiling man's arms, she clambered up to his neck like a monkey (without a second thought about leaving me in the position of the forsaken lover!)

Naturally, while those two were rubbing noses and joking around, my heart was being strangled by jealousy.

"Come over here, young man! You must be the famed Duna. You also have an older brother named Aras, isn't that right?"

Ada's uncle knew everything. He extended his arm and shook hands with me like a grown-up.

"What fine names your family has given you two, I must admit I am impressed!"

I was glad that Ada's much loved Uncle Dogan had liked my name.

"Come on, uncle, juggle for us, pleeease! Come on, please!"

After watching him juggle three apples, retrieve a disappearing marble from behind my ear, and take a pen that he put in his coat pocket out of the curtains, I had developed a very good idea of what it was that a poet did: Hocus pocus!

To this day I still believe that good poets are verbal illusionists. But it took me years to realize what lonely people writers and poets are, and how they engage in this hocus-pocus business mostly to amuse themselves and to diminish the pain of their loneliness.

When, on the following day, I announced to my mother my intent of becoming a poet at a circus, I almost made the poor woman cry.

THEY BURN EVERYTHING THEY FEAR!

"Who can say, perhaps we have not died in quite a while…"

Ingeborg Bachmann

It all happened very quickly.

The fire's proximity to the arsenal and the possibility of a sabotage had created general panic, and the whole place was in an uproar. As the sirens blared, Duna suddenly found himself among soldiers who were hastily boarding jeeps and heading east, toward a dark, rising cloud of smoke.

He found it impressive that the soldiers were still able to operate under a strict chain of command despite the panic and mayhem ensuing all around them.

"Just like the scenes in Vietnam movies," he could not help thinking.

Someone his age could not be expected to remember World War II or Korean War movies. He was around ten during the Occupation of Cyprus, and had thought Cyprus was a very far off "ada."

He was not fond of war movies or war novels, but the wildly popular Vietnam movies of his youth were almost impossible to evade. These movies, which made good business for Americans, had become a mandatory craze worldwide and of course, had not escaped Turkey. There was a scenario for everyone. You could find anything you wanted in those movies, be it laughter, a good cry, violence, or affirmation of your anti-war sentiments. Even those who did not pay for tickets were bound to encounter the heartbreaking stories of crippled Vietnam veterans returning home to their wives and friends on TV, in commercials, or magazines. A bit of Vietnam had been relived in every part of the world with Jane Fonda and Jon Voight, or Robert de Niro and Meryl Streep; even Robin Williams.

"Hop on, lieutenant!"

Someone grabbed Duna by the arm and pulled him on to a moving jeep. Since he was unprepared, his body was delayed in responding, and his ankles were badly scraped against the fender of the vehicle. Once settled, Duna clenched his teeth in pain. When he leaned down to look, he saw that the pants on his right leg were torn and spied his right ankle bleeding through the tear. As the sight of blood made him sick, he quickly turned away.

"If it hurts so much, maybe this isn't a nightmare," he muttered through his teeth.

No one was about to hear him. They could not have cared less about his wound or the fact that it was bleeding. The soldiers in the jeep looked like bombs ready to explode. They all had machine guns and none of them spoke. It seemed as if they were no longer in this world, but in another dimension. They were wearing camouflage gear and their eyes were fixed on one point: the fire in the east!

Looking around, Duna realized that they were in the middle of a convoy. More jeeps filled with soldiers followed his own. Occasionally an announcement would come over the loudspeakers but just as in airports and bus terminals, it was unintelligible. Nonetheless, the stern and urgent quality of the male announcer's voice rang through the air.

As they approached the dark clouds rising in the east and the subsequent heatwave that would put a summer noon to shame, a burning smell also became noticeable. That was when Duna saw the human chain which soldiers had formed to help the firemen. The scene did not fail to make an impression on him even though he felt as removed from his surroundings as a reporter who was there to cover a story, or an audience member at a theater.

As they drew nearer to the smoke, the noises also increased. There were some explosions and the voices of many, trying to extinguish the fire....

"If we don't stop the fire before it reaches the arsenal we're toast!" a soldier with a blackened face was shouting, as he ran in panic.

"God damn those bastards! May their kind rot in both worlds, the traitors! The sons of bitches!"

"Is it definitely a sabotage?" asked Duna.

His voice melted, and disappeared in the air. "Sons of bitches, eh?" he said, not realizing he had been left alone in the jeep. "So nothing has changed! The murderer is always the butler, and the bad guys are always SOBs!"

The jeep had stopped and the soldiers had long alighted. Just ahead, the flames were rising among the skeletal silhouettes of buildings, hacking the ruins like red, burgundy, and black swords, and sometimes ascending coyly like a snake to the fakir's pipe, trailing smoke. It looked as if a drop of fire, sidling up lustfully to catch the other flames would suddenly turn into a pitch black monster and tip the balance of crimson from vital life force into lethal terror.

Duna was so struck by the hypnotic dance of the flames that he had forgotten where he was. Though truth be told, he would have been hard-pressed to give an idea of where he was in the first place.

The dance of the flames was very beautiful, and incredibly harmonious, but it did not give joy. On the contrary, it hurt...

"When does beauty stop giving pleasure?" he thought. What if this fire was in a fireplace? No, even contained flames were painful to him. For, in his dictionary, the concepts of fire and flame were primarily associated with burning.

Throughout history, tyrants had burned everything they feared and could not handle. Tyrants have always burned people, books, and buildings... Tyrants have always labeled people they feared as "witches" or "demons," and sent them up in flames!

"Yet thoughts and dreams are made of fire-proof material..." he murmured, covered in sweat.

Fire itself was not all that bad, but tyrants had a special affinity for it... Historically, destruction by fire has always been more appealing to tyrant murderers than any other method of death or torture.

"Maybe it's because fire also symbolizes the thing they fear most! The way murderers always return to the scene of the crime, maybe tyrants and fanatics have a subconscious fear of the relation between 'fire' and 'enlightenment?'"

Still unaware that he was soaked in sweat, Duna felt thirsty, but could not move. He was sweltering in the heat, but could not, or would not, tear himself away from the spell of the flames. There's a time when everyone feels they are nailed to the floor; now it was Duna's turn.

"Duna! Hey Dunaa!"

What? Was someone pronouncing his name?

"Duuna!"

If he was hearing correctly, this was the first time in a while that he was being referred to by his name. Not "sir," not "teach," and not "Second Lieutenant."… No, no, it was clear, someone was calling him Duna… Oh how good it feels for a person to be called by his own name, to have all those secret spices he associates with it suddenly released into the air.

"All right, my nightmare is coming to an end, someone is saying my name in order to wake me… But of course… I knew it, I knew from the start that this was a nightmare…"

"Duna! Duna man, over here!"

"It must be my mom who's waking me… Or maybe Merich … or her… Of course, it's her… she must have come back because she realized how much I worry about her, because she doesn't want to make me any more miserable… She can't bear to make me sad… But if it was her… She would have said 'Mabel'… 'Come on Mabel, the nightmare's over, time to wake up!'…or something. Hmm… this is a man's voice… Aras? Aras maybe? Aras, where are you?"

"Duna, why don't you watch out, for heaven's sake!" said someone who grabbed him by the arm and began dragging him away. "You were practically inside the fire… like you were waiting to be burned!"

Turning around, he saw a man in uniform, with close cropped red hair. A soldier who looked like all the other soldiers!

"Here, take this, I sneaked a little lemon cologne in my pocket, smell it, it'll help!"

The soldier rubbed a handful of lemon cologne on Duna's face. It was hot as hell but strong. Duna reeled, as if he had been smacked in the face. He took deep breaths. Only then did he notice his perspiration, and drew back reflexively. He surveyed his surroundings anew. Everything was the same. Tens, dozens of men in soldiers' and firemen's uniforms were dashing about, yelling, giving orders, carrying water, and risking their lives trying to extinguish the fire in nearby buildings.

"So I still wasn't able to wake up…" he murmured to himself.

"Are you alright, Duna?"

It took all his strength to take a close look at the soldier who continued to call him by his name, and who had saved him from certain death. Nevermind that lately, even "all his strength" had been insufficient in focusing his attention…

He located the eyes of the red-haired soldier and looked at them carefully, for a long time. The eyes of all soldiers, throughout the world, are different!

"Nesim?" he then heard himself exclaim joyfully. The other smiled.

"I'd begun to fear you would never recognize me," he said.

The two soldiers embraced in delight.

"Shalom, Nesim, my boy! How could I not recognize you? You're the keepsake of grandpa's great love, of his beloved Rozita… Though I hope grandma, god rest her soul, doesn't hear us!"

"Here, let me see, what happened to your ankles? Well, well, well… Hold on, let's rub some cologne there too… You've become a veteran away from the front, brother!"

Duna gnashed his teeth in pain, but did not dare look down for fear of seeing blood.

"The fire's under control! The fire's under control!" rose jubilant cries around him.

"The sons of bitches couldn't blow up the arsenal!" yelled Duna heatedly, forgetting his pain. Nesim, who knew that Duna was not in the habit of swearing at people's mothers and wives, stared at him in surprise. For his part, Duna tried to turn it into a joke by saying:

"You see, they've determined that the fire was started with people whose mothers were prostitutes," and gave a forced smile.

It was obvious that meeting Nesim and hearing the news about the fire had relaxed him, and put him at ease.

"Come over here a second," Nesim said, tugging at Duna and looking around anxiously. "They drafted me, but they won't give us weapons."

"Because you're Jewish? But they'd said that that was no longer in practice..."

"Don't worry about that now. Listen, I read an article about Ada in the papers Tuesday morning, the day they drafted me. I'm telling you because even if you haven't seen it you might hear about it and grow faint. She supposedly did this and that, and committed some murder years ago, and blah blah blah! Don't you worry about it, ok, buddy? I've known Ada since childhood, you know that. I don't think she can be a murderer! Are you listening to me Duna?"

"I have got to find her, Nesim!" Duna moaned. "This nightmare has to end, I have to wake up, and find her, do you understand?"

"How couldn't I, pal, how couldn't I! But do you think it is that easy to wake up?"

Wiping his face with the back of his hand, Duna looked hopefully at Nesim.

"Look Duna, the strife we are going through is the cost of this awakening! And you'll see, hopefully we'll all see together that after this civil war, this nation will not be put soundly to sleep anymore, thinking that every blackout is nightfall..."

"Civil war?" echoed Duna, feeling crushed. "I still believe that this is a nightmare, and one that has gone on far too long."

He repeated to Nesim the things he had already grown tired of saying, and added: "Oh Nesim! I would be so relieved if just one other person agreed that this is all a bad dream and told me it would end..."

Nesim looked at Duna, considered for a while, then put an arm over his friend's shoulder and patted his back.

"It will end, Duna. just wait! This nightmare will end someday. But guard your mind as you wait, and don't let it waste away in stasis."

"So you're telling me that this could be a nighmare?" Duna rejoiced.

"Well," answered Nesim, as if he was lecturing, "we all perceive civil wars in different ways. To some of us this is the real game, where all the cards are out in the open! Some of us believe that arms dealers are in dire straits, and those who share the great bloody profit of arms and drug trafficking are nestled in the government itself... To others, the entire problem rests in the fact that human beings are carnivores! And some suffer their inner war as a price of not having reconciled themselves with their past... Some talk of shady circles which cannot handle the information age... And you perceive it as a nightmare, who's to say, my man?"

"See now, you don't believe it... You tell me to wait and don't object to my convictions, but you don't believe yourself that this is a nightmare!" Duna said, crestfallen.

"When mobilization was declared," said Nesim, putting his hands on his hips, "I was busy writing an article on Camus who claims that the twentieth century is an 'age of fear,' and Beckett who counters that it is an 'age of expectation.' Its title was this: 'As the century of fearful expectation draws to a close.' In the subtitle I asked: 'Was Western philosophy of literature able to assess the twentieth century correctly?' I was thinking that among the people I would call to consult were a few writer friends and you... But then that Tuesday morning... It was in the books that we should meet here..."

Duna, who kept forgetting and remembering that the person he was talking to was Nesim, now forgot where they were, and asked:

"Nesim, you had some troubles with your doctorate thesis. Last time I saw you, you'd told me some things about your thesis, or the jury..."

"That business was settled long ago! Old boy, I transferred to Bosphorus University last year as a philosophy professor with a doctorate, don't you know?... Now I can die a Ph.D man, hah hah ha!"

Nesim's laugh sounded more like a scream. The sound hurt Duna.

"Would this conversation really take place between two childhood friends who meet as soldiers during mobilization?" he thought quickly. "Nonsense!" he said.

A voice was heard shouting "The fire is under control! Board the vehicles!"

A cheerful bustle replaced the preceding calamity. A quiet, relieved expectancy could be seen on the sweat and soot covered faces of the soldiers. The hectic and crowded surroundings suddenly became more orderly. Duna went over to the jeep Nesim had boarded, and sat down next to him. All at once he noticed that no one was giving him orders, and he was not receiving any. It was as if he was transparent or untouchable. No one was bothering him.

"This is solid proof that what I'm experiencing is not real," he muttered, smiling.

Nesim had suddenly grown silent, and was broodily turning over the plastic cologne bottle which was half empty from his recent efforts to revive his friend. For a moment Duna thought: "What if something terrible happens to him... What if Nesim dies?" He felt even worse when he considered how rare and difficult it was to raise such cultivated, fine people.

When he thought that he might never again see his friend, books in hand, writing, arguing, and talking excitedly... When memories passed before him like a movie reel, of climbing fig trees together in Kuzguncuk, and repressing their childish guffaws as they heard a hint of amourousness creep into his grandfather's account of Rozita... He suddenly had difficulty breathing.

Every person is, and should be valuable but (why hide it?) those we love, even from afar, even if we haven't met them, are more valuable! Particularly those we can love after having gotten to know them!

"Why didn't you leave, Nesim?" he cried all of a sudden.

The fear of losing him had turned into an uncontrollable rage.

"Leave for where?" asked Nesim, puzzled.

The anxiety smeared on our faces when we find ourselves on the verge of losing someone we love is always exacting revenge for our previous silences and ineptitudes.

"For Jerusalem, where your relatives are, of course..."

"And why should I go?" said Nesim, in a voice weary of answering the same question. Then he abruptly started shouting. Anger is the most contagious feeling!

"What did you just say to me? Huh? Do you realize what you said to me? I'm sure you said it to protect me, didn't you? Huh? Didn't you? Huh?"

Duna stared in amazement.

"Goddamn it! Then why didn't *you* leave? Or perhaps you'd prefer that I asked this way: If your royal heart so desires where will you go? Huh? Tell me! Come on, let's put our cards out in the open, pal... Even you think you're different from me, don't you? Even you're suggesting that I flee to Jerusalem just because our religions are different! Huh? Am I wrong? Come on, tell me!"

Duna, who had not expected such an outburst from the usually silent Nesim, was stunned. Surprise disrupts our regular behavior patterns.

"I didn't leave because, just like you, I'm from here, I was born here and I want to live here! Goddamn it! I didn't leave because I too work and pay taxes here, I too love this country! Do you hear me? I'm yelling at you in Turkish! Because I'm shouting my rage, my love, and my pain to you not in Hebrew but in Turkish, you ignoramus!"

He stopped, and took a deep breath. It was clear that he was forcing himself to calm down. After glancing at Duna who had shut his eyes and hung his head, he went on, more slowly, but tensely:

"Look, maybe if I explained this once more, in plain language, you could get it through your thick head! I didn't leave because: fish and raki in the Bosphorus, full moon at the Island, olive-oil dishes in the Aegean, Toros mountains in the Mediterrenean, houses in Safranbolu, Assos, and Kash, my mother tongue, these expressions, the women from around here who struggle to be smart while preserving their femininity, and the feelings particular to Mediterranean Anatolia... I didn't leave because all these things are only good when one is here... These values exist only if you live in your own culture... Call it cliché! Poke fun, say it's cheesy! Judge it as cornball! I don't give a damn! We're all of the same cloth, we all have the same feelings!"

He paused again. Having grown calmer, though his face still twisted in pain, he leaned toward the stock still Duna.

"Whenever all of us truly understand and accept the concept of being 'from Turkey,' then we shall be free!" he whispered.

Just then other soldiers boarded the jeep, and the vehicle took off. For a while, the two friends sat side by side without a word.

The silence dug into Duna's flesh like a sharp knife, causing him pain.

"Duna, have you read *Leviathan?*" asked Nesim.

He had gathered himself, and finally settled down. He was speaking in a soft, conciliatory voice.

"I've enjoyed all of Paul Auster's books," Duna replied, unable to look Nesim in the face.

"Oh no, he's still a kid. I meant that old Hobbes' *Leviathan.*"

"I've heard of Thomas Hobbes, but, admittedly, never read him."

"The philosopher who drew the wrath of his country's kings for analyzing the relationship between peace and power three hundred years ago! Hobbes fled to France to save his life, and published *Leviathan* there."

"Sounds like it's imperative to read this book," Duna remarked, trying to win his friend over.

"I can't say it's imperative, but Hobbes' *Leviathan* can be considered the first serious analysis of civil war. If we also keep in mind Thucydides, who wrote of the Peloponnesian War between the Athenians and the Spartans –" realizing suddenly that he was not in the lecture hall, he gave Duna a quick glance. "While in Cambridge for post-graduate studies, I had a teacher named Professor MacPherson. He would ask us in every class: 'Why, ladies and gentlemen, are we still reading Hobbes in this second half of the twentieth century?' We, as students of all races and genders convened at Cambridge from four corners of the world, were used to this question. Student psychology, what're you going to do… we would laugh and giggle. Mr. MacPherson would ignore us and always answer his own question with a sad expression: 'Thomas Hobbes was an authority analyst. And unfortunately, our world still falls prey to the passion for power, and the subsequent problems and bloodbaths it causes.' "

"I see," said Duna in a gentle voice.

"Hey man, what're you guys talking about over there? Hobbes or Shmobbes or something… Who're them guys supposed to be? And then there's some professor… What side is he on? I don't like the sound of his name one bit…" laughed the soldier sitting next to them.

"Everyone's got a different screw loose, brother... We're just gonna have to deal!" said another, grinning.

Then, twisting his finger in the air, he gestured "crazy," and burst into hysteric laughter. His face was covered in soot; he had obviously worked hard to extinguish the fire.

"You were right, Nesim," said Duna, ignoring the other soldiers. "Until a little while ago even I wasn't aware that I saw you as different. I must have been hiding this even from myself. You'll forgive me, but how can I forgive myself?" Not knowing how to hide his shy blue eyes, he awkwardly fidgeted with his glasses, and swallowed repeatedly, the way he always did when he felt nervous.

"And aren't we living through this nightmare in order to learn such things anyway, my Kuzguncukite countryman?" replied Nesim, trying to smile.

"My Turkish countryman!" said Duna, reaching for Nesim's hand but not daring to turn his head. Yet the hand he touched felt more like a frozen piece of metal than a human hand.

"He's afraid too!" thought Duna, crushed.

"Man, these two have gone off the deep end," said the soldier next to them, laughing.

The others started hooting and whistling. The inside of the military truck was filled with the dolorous laughter of soldiers relieving their recent tension.

"Leave the great lovers alone, hah hah hah!"

"Thanks Duna," whispered Nesim.

Just then they arrived at one of the garrison gates. All the vehicles approaching the gate were being halted and checked, orders were being given and received, and there was a general commotion. The first drop of evening had fallen into the air.

Suddenly they were taken off the jeep, and shuffled around. Duna was separated from the others, handed a machine gun, a sizeable backpack, and taken into a large military truck.

He turned around and looked for Nesim in panic. But Nesim wasn't there. He had disappeared without leaving a single trace, as if he'd never even been there. So quickly and instantly, without being able to say goodbye...

"Nesiim!" he called.

His voice melted in the crowd. As in all nightmares, his voice went completely unheard. His voice had collected and diminished between his mouth and ears. He looked at the heads of the soldiers around him to see if there were any with red hair. The soldiers had on camouflage and caps, and there was no hair color to be seen.

"The mind will surely triumph at the end!" someone said.

"Nesim?" he repeated.

That was Nesim's voice, but Nesim was not there.

Everything was happening too fast and too "much!" He kept skipping from one event to the next, from one thought or emotion to another without a chance to breathe, and was consequently growing more tired, depressed and incoherent.

He was going to pieces.

He looked at the machine gun he had been handed. He surveyed the heavy, metallic body.

"How we die, how much we kill!" he moaned. He sensed that he could not bear it much longer.

"You're still raw!" said the soldier next to him, in admonishment.

"I'm no expert!" answered Duna without looking over.

"If your lifelong neighbors slaughtered your family because they were of a different sect, you better believe you'd be an expert!"

The hatred latent in the voice washed over Duna.

That was when Duna turned around to stare intently at the bulky soldier at his side. His subject was sitting rock still, with set jaws, and staring at a point in space only he could see. This time Duna had difficulty recognizing him because he was clean shaven.

"Musa? Is that you?"

"There is no Musa anymore!" answered the other wrathfully, without looking.

If he had survived his jump from the military truck in one piece, he owed it in part to Musa. If he and First Lieutenant Birol had not held him by the arms he would have fallen much faster and...

Even in a nightmare, a person could not help but feel gratitude for someone who had saved his life.

"I got news yesterday that the godless bastards killed my wife and children... My son was still a babe, you heathens! If I let them get away with this may God strike me down, may I die a failed man!"

"How do you mean?" Duna asked, startled. "This massacre happened yesterday in our Kuzguncuk?"

"Those devil's seeds, don't they think I can give them the same pain?" groaned Musa with loathing.

"This can't be!" thought Duna. "This bad dream has really gone too far! Can so much evil be possible?"

Musa, without hearing him, was pouring forth the pain that had turned into rage through his teeth.

"The Thirty Years' War!" brightened Duna. "In the seventeenth century Germany lost two thirds of its population to sectarian wars that lasted thirty years," he continued, thinking it might calm Musa. "Revenge is the emotion which most fuels violence, Musa. Dissuasion's greatest enemy is revenge."

"Shut up you jerk! Can't you see, the man's in pain?" yelled another soldier at Duna.

"But this is just a nightmare!" said Duna, thinking it would cheer them up. "Soon I'll wake up and it will all be over! Don't you understand, all these are a terrible trick of my subconscious! It's all a trick!"

"Death plays no tricks, teach," said Musa, grinding his teeth.

And the military truck started moving. When Duna turned to look back for the last time, he saw Nesim in the evening gloom. They had left him behind in the garrison. The last thing he saw Nesim do was draw an "L" in the air. What did Leviathan mean, anyway?

"Where're we headed?" he asked blithely, as if they were going on a field trip.

"To your mother!" yelled an angry voice.

"To hell…" said Musa, "to the very depths of hell!"

HAPPY BIRTHDAY ADA!

> *"Fancying the sewer grates to be gigantic piggy banks I often tossed them my allowance.*
> *That is why the sea owes me more than anyone."*

Sunay Akin

"I'm bigger than you, so there!"

Actually, they were only born a day apart.

"In fact, you should call me ma'am!"

Ada was born on March 12th, and Aras on the following day of the same year. But they loved to bicker and tire out one another. What sort of personality did those two have, that even after I grew exhausted from watching them, they could continue to compete so ardently? I sensed that as much pleasure as they derived from surpassing each other, they derived a separate joy from the period of preparation that defeat necessitated. They were a perfect match!

"Nonsense! There's only twenty-four hours between us!"

Although that was what he said, I suspected that Aras was somewhat peeved at my mother for this twenty-four hour delay.

"Even if it's one hour, I'm older than you, Aras!"

Then she would look at Aras with that amazingly confident, eternally self-admiring smile of hers and offer a charity particular to victorious parties:

"I promise you that no one except us three will know. When we grow up you'll be taller than me anyway, and cross my heart, I won't tell our secret to anyone!"

Aras would not dwell on the subject, having received this secret message that they would stay together when they grew up.

"Alright, it's a deal, but don't ever ask me to call you ma'am again, okay?"

Ada would smile quietly. All three of us knew the meaning of that smile. Triumph was more important than anything for Ada! This always remained as one of her weaknesses.

They, like all childhood sweethearts, were rehearsing the life they would live together ever after, and assuming that reality would be a game similar to their present one. Who knows, maybe it was so. Already they were trying to establish the balances of power between them, often bumping into each other's admired strong points, bleeding their little heads and hurting themselves. Thankfully, children forget quickly!

When I thought of Ada and Aras getting married I grew very distressed, feeling the same pang as when my favorite toy got broken. Later I would console myself by thinking that I was not to lose her completely. At least the person I lost her to was my older brother, the born winner whom I could not even consider a rival, and I was reluctantly glad for that. However, I did not hesitate to utilize the subject when I came across an unfavorable food item or unpleasant situation.

"Mommy, I don't want to eat spinach! I don't have an appetite, mommy! And besides, if Ada is going to marry Aras when she grows up, why should I eat spinach mommy? Why should I become strong, huh? I can't even see a single iron in this spinach!"

Biting her lips to keep from laughing, my mother would immediately relent on the topic of spinach. After all, was not the girl whom her sons fought over the beloved child of her much admired stars?

"Pleease mommy, I don't wanna go to school today. They make you do the same thing every day, mommy, pleease!"

"Come on Duna, come on my sweet boy, put on your uniform and go to school! How can you already be sick of school, son?"

"Well of course I can… If I were in the same class with Ada, and got to sit next to her, I'd wanna go to school too…"

"Come here, my little, emotional Ferhat, come give your mother a hug," my mother would laugh.

Like all children who have found their mother's weak spot, I would immediately start abusing it. I say all children, but I must hold my brother to exception on this subject. I must have already mentioned that Aras was more of an adult trapped in a child's body than a child.

"When they get married I'll be all alone anyways. I won't have any friends… All alone and by myself…" I would whine.

My mother would fall for these guilt trips wilfully, like most mothers. She would cuddle me, stroke my hair, and laugh dreamily. Then, she would hold my hand and walk me to school herself, even though it was hardly a few blocks away.

In my mother's dreamy laughter, Aras, who already drew attention with his good looks, and Ada, lovely in a white wedding gown, would appear together and fly off to a happy eternity in the latest model convertible. I am utterly sure of it, because this was the dream package presented to women in those years. And women bought the package without really questioning it. My mother was the most typical of these women, yet she was so sincere, so naive in her belief that I could only love her the more for it, and feel a greater need to protect her. Every movie was a picture of everlasting love and one hundred percent happiness, but Sureyya Mercan and Pervin Gokay's movies were all the more so. Most of the movies in my childhood would conclude in marriage, and this would be called "a happy ending."

These were the dreams my mother's older son was worthy of. Aras was strong, intelligent, and decisive. He had all the important qualities looked for in a man (don't ask me "who looked for them?" I have always been afraid of the answer…) Furthermore, he was extremely handsome, knew what he wanted, and always achieved it. Just like his uncles (the maternal ones, that is…). Yes, maybe her son Aras did not come from a wealthy family, but they could not be called poor either… Besides, it was already clear that Aras would become very successful, and in those days it was generally believed that someone who was successful in his work would also be wealthy.

Whereas my mother's younger son was a different case.

According to her, I was more like my father's side of the family. Sweet, gentle, unambitious, sensitive, and a little coy. Coy? I wasn't coy or anything, but that is often the role deemed fit for the younger children of a house. Regardless of how much they might grow up and prove themselves, unfortunately the youngest kids always remain babies in their mothers' eyes!

Both me and my brother's birthdays were modest events, celebrated among family members with a home-made dessert, lemonade, and no fuss. My father would sew us a new pair of trousers or a shirt from the material he had left over, my mother would buy crackers, make raisin cookies, and prepare dessert, and my grandmother would give us pocket money wrapped in embroidered handkerchiefs, the same way she did for religious festivals. (Oh how precious those handkerchiefs, so boring to children, become with the grandmother's sudden death, how they are missed!)

On our birthdays grandpa would take us out on the ferry and introduce us to the large, historical mosques of Istanbul. While me and my brother stood in the courtyard of the mosque, munching on sweet wafers, he would perform two prayers of gratitude. When he came out of the mosque grandpa's face would be luminous, and as he looked at us through whispered blessings, we would sense how proud he was of us, and how much he thanked God for us. This feeling of security, which no one can buy, is vital nourishment for a child. We would then feed the pigeons in the courtyard. We had fun, great fun.

When the one day difference between his and Ada's birthdays was revealed, Aras cancelled his birthday. My brother could never be found on March 13th, and when he resurfaced he was a moody and irate child. It started when he turned eight, and continued until puberty. Unfortunately, this odd behaviour of his also affected my birthdays, which fell on September 12th, during the warm colors of Indian summer. Due to Aras' premature bout of manly pride, we were never able to recapture the old feeling of those mosque trips we made with my grandfather.

However, Ada's birthdays were something else. After they moved to Kuzguncuk, with the exception of one year, every March 12th was a festive day for the neighborhood children. On the table set for them there would be a birthday cake decorated with candles, and a dazzling array of pastries, tarts, pies, all kinds of sodas, fruit juices and colas. All the children would stuff themselves silly, receive the balloons and toys that were being handed out, dance, and be entertained by the clown and puppeteer. How ironic that all the

"March 12ths" except the year of the military coup have been imprinted as a day of celebration in the memories of our neighborhood children.

Years later, when Ada asked me:

"Do you think it's mere coincidence that a military coup has occurred on both our birthdays?" I knew that she was not joking... Other children, who were not from the neighborhood, would also attend Ada's birthday parties. Some were children of relatives, and some of friends. Most of them were spoilt, arrogant kids who were not like us. They would generally ignore us and play among themselves. Occasionally a few of them would join us, but on the whole we would complete the day as two separate groups. Ada did not much care for them, but I could tell that she liked the presents they brought. To be honest, we would all be spellbound by those huge, expensive, and unknown dolls in their large boxes, those electric trains, colorful cubes, legos and imported toys. Knowing that I would have the privilege of playing with them the following day, I could hardly contain myself.

On her birthdays I would buy Ada a box of the chewing gum labeled MABEL. This was the greatest secret between us, and it protected me from entering a gift-giving competition with the rich kids which I was bound to lose. Oh my dear Ada, my honey girl, my brunette beauty, how she would tactfully protect me from everyone... Her joy upon receiving that box every year was too warm and personal to be false. I would beam as gladly as if I had been the manufacturer of MABEL Chewing Gums, and let out a deep sigh of relief. Since they are no longer in the market, nowadays I can only obtain MABEL chewing gums like special collector's items from two stores in Kadikoy and Nishantashi. For her of course...

Among the friends and relatives who came to visit Ada from outside Kuzguncuk, the child she was most interested in was her older uncle's daughter. The Poet uncle was single and had no children but the daughter of Ada's older architect uncle, whom we had not once seen in Kuzguncuk, used to come over to Ada's house often and spend the weekends there.

The shy, sensitive, and extremely quiet cousin was nothing like Ada. Compared with Ada's incredible colors, confidence, and defiant wit, her cousin was rosy as a young peach, very blond, bashful, and introverted. Everyone would talk about how beautiful this girl was, about her silky shining hair, and shower her with praises but since I only had eyes for Ada, I would always remain neutral on the subject.

As an only child, Ada had a secret longing for a sibling, and would possessively drag her cousin around like a toy, declaring that she was her sister.

And the other would agree to being Ada's toy without a word of protest.

Anyone who saw the girl cousin would be immediately taken by her beauty and sing her praises. Leaving her poor cousin alone to squirm and grow hopelessly embarrassed, not knowing what to do with her beauty, Ada would grab a hold of me and whisper with little tremors in her confident, gorgeous voice:

"Do you also find her very beautiful, Mabel my dear?"

Unable to grasp how she could imagine such a thing, I would yell out so that everyone could hear "I think you're more beautiful than the whole world Ada!" (The next year I would learn about the universe, and announce that she was "more beautiful than the universe.")

Dismissing with a joyous look all the smiling faces turned in our direction, Ada would continue dragging her cousin around from where she left off.

Just then the "real boy" would appear, enter the room as if he had not seen anyone, conceal his tremendous shyness and distaste of crowds behind a serious face, and sit down sulkily in a chair. Even though us Kuzguncukite kids did not have outfits as fancy as the visiting boys with bowties, and girls with pom-pom socks and lace trimmed skirts, we were still meticulously and cleanly dressed for that day. But Aras had made it a habit to wear his oldest, most ragged clothes to Ada's birthday party, despite my mother's pleas. Then Ada would go up to her room, take off her princess dress, undo her angelic bun, and come back downstairs with one of her daily outfits. As always, she would tie her hair in two ponytails, one on each side.

Rather than Ada and Aras looking awkward in their daily wear, it was us who felt suddenly overdressed and superfluous, even grotesque in a way. There would be a transparent tension and the well dressed children would grow uncomfortable. Aras would not look at anyone, but sit by himself with the expression of someone guarding a very important and dangerous thing. Some of the visiting kids who were older and more striking resented him but still felt somehow intimidated. As the transparent tension began to grow darker Ada would quickly assess the situation, take the initiative, and walk Aras out into the garden. There Aras would present Ada with a model ship or airplane which he had bled his hands for days to prepare. During this episode I would not go near them but watch from the window, and wish I could be there. I would try to find solace in the fact that even if I felt excluded and rejected I was the brother of one, and the "Mabel" of the other. (What choice did I have?)

At precisely those moments when I felt orphaned, the sweet smelling blond cousin would sidle up to me, smile shyly, and wait for me to pay attention to her. I did greatly enjoy the attention of someone weaker than me when I felt lonely: it bolstered my pride. Besides, this girl was one whose beauty and "ladylike behavior" everyone extolled. Yes, I thought she was very pretty but still not as pretty as Ada... Furthermore, whatever "ladylike behavior" meant, I was not fond of it. In some way I sensed that Ada did not have this quality, and perhaps to protect her, I was rough toward her cousin.

When Ada and Aras were in the garden Ada's sweet-smelling cousin would bring me food and try desperately to please me. In the course of this well-meaning act she would simply smile at me like a mute, but the heat lying deep beneath her gaze would somehow reach my skin and almost burn me. I would not grow bored with her, but I did not at all like her silence.

It was one of those birthday parties, during the initial years when Aras had begun to grow taller than Ada. I think they were turning eleven, I must have been nine, and the girl cousin ten. Ada said in a know-it-all voice:

"So I guess my mommy and daddy must have made me exactly eleven years, nine months, and ten days ago."

Compared to my peers, I was relatively uninterested in sexual matters. Nevertheless, this captured my attention. I asked in amazement:

"How did they make you Ada?"

"We can't tell the children, can we Aras?"

I was neither aware of Ada's gradually developing breasts, nor of the pimples breaking little by little on Aras' face. I was very bothered by the way they excluded me.

"I wanna know too, Ada, how did your parents make you? Tell me, c'mon, tell me Ada!"

"Oh, but you're way to young Duna!"

Aras had left the room with an annoyed expression on his face, and the girl cousin had withdrawn into a corner with embarassment, rendering herself invisible as usual. I pursued the point relentlessly, because I had not understood that Ada's reluctance to explain was due to her own lack of knowledge. None of us knew! But those two were acting towards us and each other, *as if* they knew. Had Ada known of course, she would doubtlessly have been willing and eager to give us a lecture entitled "The Making of Children."

"You know, the mommy and daddy take off their clothes and um…they kiss,…and stuff."

"Whaaaat! You mean your mom and dad kissed completely naked, Ada?"

"Don't be ridiculous, Duna, your parents did the same thing!"

"No way, my mom and dad don't ever kiss on the lips, and they never take off their clothes, miss smartypants… My mom and dad have very good manners, so there!"

"Come on Duna, don't be a kid, this business can't happen with clothes on!"

"What business?"

"Business, eh?"

In order not to feel left out of things I pursued this "business" with such persistence, and pried into it so much that Ada finally gave up and decided to settle the "business" once and for all. (once she makes up her mind, no one can stop her!)

A few weeks later she took me to the bathroom of the mansion. After our own bathroom, which was more like a Turkish bath with its marble basins, the mansion's fresh smelling, carpeted bathroom, with its bathtub, urinal, and pink-tulled furnishings would always seem surreal to me. Previously we had always used the guest bathroom on the ground floor of the mansion, which was where I had encountered my first Western style toilet.

While I stared around at the bathroom, more in surprise than wonder, Ada had locked the door from the inside, and begun to undress with both a sisterly compassion and a sense of responsibility on her face. At first I had looked on, cluelessly, but Ada had soon convinced me to also undress so that I could learn a matter long overdue. We sat naked in the bathtub. The ceramic tile was freezing, I was cold, and my hair stood on end from excitement and shame. I felt as if I had swallowed a cane. You know the sense of unease that if you move everything around you will shatter into little pieces? Well, I was petrified just like that.

Dear God, all through my life, what choice did you leave me but to be grateful to her?

I was sitting in a miserable state of surprise and shame in the bathtub, and she, in order to educate me, to keep me from looking foolish, was doing something she wouldn't do for anyone else, i.e., not hesitating to show me her newly swelling breasts and still bald sexual organ! In the meantime, she was supposedly intensifying my dependence on her, being possessive, and whatnot... I would hear plenty of accusations such as these in the years to come, but who cares? Even if I had a choice, I would not abandon any of my experiences with her, including the most deadly ones. I always pitied those who criticized her. For they are people who are incapable of imagining that a woman with as rich and delicious a soul as Ada can even exist on this earth, let alone meet someone like her. (I can never understand how I get so worked up when it's a question of allegations against her!)

"See, mommies and daddies undress like this, stroke each other like this, and... kiss like this, my dear Mabel."

Her applied instructions had made me feel funny inside, and I began to giggle. But I grew instantly serious when a thought occurred to me.

"Are you teaching these to anyone else Ada?"

"Stop being ridiculous, Duna! You're my one and only Mabel!"

I had relaxed and smiled, but...

"What about Aras?"

"We're going to get married with him anyway, so we'll do this business then!"

"Are you going to get undressed then? I mean you two…"

"Mabel! Didn't I teach you everything just now?"

True! She had done everything she could, and had taught me everything she knew, so why was I asking?

"But Ada, if we did what parents do just now, does that mean we're going to have kids?"

"Oh my sweet little innocent Mabel! Of course not! We're not married, see?"

"Ohhh!"

The following year I saw Ada and Aras kissing for the first time. They didn't see me. At first I cried, and then I sulked for days. However, I took comfort in the fact that Ada's love and attention toward me had not changed. In time, I grew used to seeing them kiss frequently. No, I did not grow used to it, but rather, began to erase the image from my mind as if it had never happened. Soon I believed my lie, and like all cowards continued to live without facing it.

"But when you guys get married, what's going to happen to me?"

"You'll live with us, Mabel, my dear. What would I do without you?"

"Well, if you want me to… okay, then, I'll live with you…"

When we made plans concerning the future, we would always be alone with Ada. Aras grew edgy and embarrassed at the discussion of such topics, and always promptly fled the room. Ada, like all confident people, never insisted on the subject.

Toward the end of elementary school the nice smelling girl cousin had basically settled into the mansion. The girl cousin would always be there when Ada's family went to Koycegiz, then a relatively obscure site, for one month during summer vacations, or when they took us, with my mother's permission, to their summer house in Hereke on the weekends. After a while we became so accustomed to her that, like the other Kuzguncukites, we started to think of her as a member of the household.

Whenever all four of us played together, the nice smelling girl cousin would be as eager to pair up with me as I was to pair up with Ada. There was only one difference between us: while I yelled and struggled to be heard, that girl always accepted her fate with a quiet smile. The outcome never changed. If Aras was around Ada would inevitably choose him as a playing partner, and I would be left to the girl cousin.

The year Ada and Aras graduated from elementary school was an important one for all of us. Aras was signed up for a public middle school, and Ada, despite all of her poet uncle's protests, was registered to attend a private prep school. There were no kids in our neighborhood who attended Uskudar American Preparatory College, and we began to fret as if we had unexpectedly lost Ada. It was a melancholy period. Our order was disrupted, and our peace was lost. We had been told that the girl cousin was going to live with Ada's family because her mother had been taken ill, but the neighborhood was rife with whispers of how "the poor little girl" had been left alone because her parents were getting a divorce, and how her kind-hearted aunt and uncle had adopted her.

"See Naim, money doesn't bring happiness, look how that darling girl, pretty as Grace Kelly, got left out on the street because of a broken home. May god never wreck anyone's hearth… They say her mother is an alcoholic and her father a gambler…"

"What's it to us, Zubeyde, don't listen to those gossipmongers…"

"No really Naim,… Cursed be the devil!"

My mother loved to pull on her earlobe, knock on wood, and emit a wailing whistle like the one used to call dogs. When they heard this sound, demons would flee for their lives, and misfortune would be sent packing.

I had felt very sorry for the nice smelling cousin. So, her parents had thrown her out on the street, huh? It was a good thing that my and Ada's family never did such a thing. I too tugged on my earlobe, puckered my lips, gave a wailing dog-call whistle, and rapped my index finger on the window.

"If you don't knock on wood, you can't drive away the devil!" my mother warned.

To this day I discreetly make sure that the object I am knocking on is wood.

The fact that Ada was going to a preparatory school with rich kids saddened Aras more than anyone. Even though he tried to hide it, we all knew that his extreme quiescence was due as much to

Ada's preparatory school membership as it was to his being a junior high adolescent, and we all respected his suffering. We had taken this business so far that at times we treated Aras like a war veteran, a handicapped citizen, or the forlorn, luckless lover of a Turkish ballad.

Yet the older she grew the greater Ada's passion for Aras became, and she drew closer to him as her opportunities increased.

"I gathered these leaves for you from the schoolyard, Aras." Aras, who did not in the least enjoy having romantic scenes amidst a crowd, would grab the leaves with something of a grunt in the way of thanks, and cause a few of them to crumple and fall.

"The girls in my class said 'so, did you collect those leaves for your boyfriend?' and attempted to laugh. Naturally, they got their answer with a single blow: bam!"

At that point my brother, who thought he had for years carried the pride he felt from Ada's love covertly, would look at Ada in admiration and the two of them would get lost in each other's eyes. I was nine by then, and I would still anxiously interrupt:

"Didn't you collect leaves for me Ada?"

"Would I forget that Duna? Here, I gathered these little leaves for you from the courtyard."

I was always left with the little leaves...

The last time I asked if they would get married when they grew up, I was eleven and they were thirteen.

"Yes, my dear Mabel. I think Aras and I are going to get married when we grow up."

"But if your house is too small, where will I live then?"

"Mabel, dear, you're going to get married too!"

"Whaaat? Are you crazy? I can never leave you!"

"My sweet Mabel. I can't bear to be apart from you either. What would I do if I couldn't see you blue Danube eyes, and hear your voice saying 'what about me, what about me?' But there's another girl who really wants to marry you!"

I was stunned. So there was someone in this world who loved me very much.

"Who's that?"

"You mean you still don't know, Mabel, my dear? It's my cousin of course!"

Yes, that was possible. I was still slightly awed and slightly pleased to hear that I was loved so much. But I wasn't glad. Ada's cousin was pretty and smelled wonderful, but she was nothing like Ada.

"She's a really nice girl, Mabel, and she's adored you since the first day she saw you!"

We had exchanged glances with Ada.

"But she's nothing like you Ada!"

"And you're nothing like Aras, my sweet Mabel, but I still love you very much!"

She was right.

Ada was right.

All the kites inside me broke loose, and scattered into the air.

Ada's cousin is called Merich.

SELF DESTRUCTION

―――――→―――→――→――→――→――――

> *"Every discussion concerning civil war is an experiment on civil war."*
>
> Hans Magnus Enzensberger

It had been thirty-two hours since the military convoy had set out, headed for hell. There had been a few rest stops and a distribution of dry rations.

Duna, who, by the locations of their rest stops, figured that after first heading north, and then south, they were now going east, was cursing himself for having always been against purchasing those digital watches with dates, compasses, calculators, forks and knives. (Or was he confusing them with Swiss Army knives?) Wasn't he the one who used to boast about being a fan of classic watches with hour and minute hands? Well good for him! (Those speeches about how "my dear man, a watch should know its place after all!"… Why did he have to be so afraid of technology? Hadn't that chestnut girl tried her best to domesticate him for years on the subject of technology?…See what happened now?…) Now he had lost both his sense of direction and of the date, but not to worry because on his wrist he had a classic watch with and hour and minute hand, which kept spinning around inanely as if they were suspended at some strange point in time! In order to protect himself from his self-criticism, and to calm down, he opted to think that his already weak sense of direction was taking a revenge on him.

No one talked in the vehicle. Most of the soldiers dozed, or sat with thoughtful, narrowed eyes, while some murmured doleful folksongs.

As they had set out, all the soldiers had been given backpacks containing a blanket, canned food rations, a sewing kit, a pair of clean underwear, a commando knife, some rope, matches, a toothbrush, toothpaste, and thick socks. The other soldiers already had on their camouflage gear. Duna was given the same uniform at the first rest stop and having dressed just like everyone else he also began to act like them. Now he too had a dogtag around his neck, inscribed with a number. If he died, it would be placed between his teeth so he could be told apart from the other corpses.

After putting on the camouflage gear he had been taken into another vehicle and had consequetly even lost Musa. There was every indication that they had embarked on a long and difficult journey, and Duna translated this to mean that the nightmare would not be over soon. Yet there had to be a limit even to the dismay one feels at slowly uncovering the infinitude of a nightmare. Just like in real life.

He had only one reason not to let himself sink completely into misery; as always, a tiny little hope! He had placed his personal belongings into his army backpack. Perhaps all the other soldiers had also been handed their personal belongings, who knows? Or the "godsend" that always came to his aid when he was in trouble had once again created a little miracle (like all romantics, he chose to believe the latter).

Whatever the method, it had happened, and now, as he left on this dark journey, he had on him not just any book of poetry, but the book "Brunette Ada," personally autographed by the poet Dogan Gokay! Only soldiers who know that they are on their way to war can comprehend what a miracle this is… Everytime a man's hand touches the book, the words of love and deep yearning turn into warmth and physically spread through his body… The sensations and feelings of a soldier headed for war are highly altered from those of a soldier under everyday circumstances. It is a simplification of the matter to label this as merely the psychology of approaching death. War psychology is much more complicated, and it is nothing akin to, say, the psychology of awaiting execution.

Among Duna's personal belongings were the medication from Merich labelled "Physician's sample:not for retail," his familiar underwear, a bar of chocolate with pistachios, and the carbonated toothpaste which tasted so good to him. What else could there be? Since he was grateful for any proof validating his existence and his past, these items were now simply miracles! He needed even the smallest twig that could form a bridge between himself and reality. He would perservere! He would perservere and maintain his sanity until the end of this nightmare. Why should he give up so quickly?

"Why should I give three patties for five pennies?" Kosta the Fisherman's daughter Marika would say when they played in Kuzguncuk... What a pretty girl Marika had been, and how smitten by Aras... Nesim, for his part, had been after Marika, but was it that the Greeks and the Jews did not have a tradition of intermarriage? Or was it Armenians and Jews who couldn't marry? What did the Muslims do? How did it all go again? What were those traditions that allowed children of the same neighborhood to be friends, but rendered their love impossible? Where is Marika now? Are kids still running around and playing on the Icadiye hill? Should every good thing end with a person's childhood? What about Nesim...

"Hey pal, you dropped your letter!"

Duna was startled by the voice of a soldier sitting across from him. At first he thought he had misunderstood, but the other soldier bent down to pick up a piece of paper from the floor, and trying to keep his balance on the moving vehicle, handed it over to Duna.

"Did I drop this?" mumbled Duna.

He managed to mutter thanks, and the other, thinking this was a hidden letter from a fiancee, smiled knowingly. Unfolding the paper with curiosity, Duna came across a pearly handwriting.

Notes defying darkness:

"Wieland says 'what light means to our eyes, freedom (of thought and press) means to the human mind.'

"Yet is that what we do, oh no! We're still like 18 century Spain. At home, and in our private lives we investigate and inquire according to Newton, but at official places we still explain our findings in an Aristotelian manner so as to avoid trouble. We are two-faced and cowardly! We can't repeat in public what we discuss among family and friends, and yet there's still no one braver than us in the whole world!

"Is it Nesim?" Duna stopped to think. Had Nesim written these? Then how and when had this piece of paper gotten into his bag? Was Nesim's handwriting this beautiful? Quickly avoiding the thought of his own unruly script, he suddenly realized that he had no idea what Nesim's handwriting looked like. Rather thatn accept this as somewhat normal, he was filled with sadness. He didn't even know what Nesim's handwriting looked like, and he considered himself a close friend!

"A philosopher called Pilate said that fanatics want to preserve darkness, blindness and ignorance, and that they hate the emergence of light. I wonder why? Meanwhile, another man named Montesquieu did not hesitate to shower praises upon light, and woke up joyful at beholding light in the morning.

"You don't have a choice, you owls and moles! Now it's time for our enlightenment. As surely as you cannot stop a baby whose time has come to be born, so you shall not be able to prevent the people who have lived for centuries in this land from becoming enlightened! How can I be so sure? Especially in the middle of a war, drafted as I am without any weapons…"

"That's Nesim, definitely Nesim!" Duna cried.

When he raised his head he saw that all the soldiers in the military van were staring at him irately.

Producing an awkward smile, he pointed at the paper at his hands accusingly.

"How can I not be sure, you idiots? Does one have to be a doctor to know that a baby will be born on its day? I know, like I do my mother's name, the stories of societies running toward the light!"

"Oh Nesim, oh if only you were right!" Duna mused silently.

This time he had been more cautious, and simply moved his lips. Nevertheless, he knew that he was under the watchful gaze of some soldiers who found him strange.

He hid his head in the paper, trying not to attract anyone's attention.

"Don't get too happy yet!

Here's the first counter instance: the Germans!

How were the Nazis able to openly exterminate people of their choice in a country with such a tradition of enlightenment in philosophy, the arts, and the sciences?

According to Adorno's negative dialectic, the question is: 'Is this a failure of culture or of enlightenment?' "

Duna used to shy away from these as dangerous questions. Naturally it would be stupid, even heinous to accuse all Germans of being Nazis, but the most barbarous military ideology of recent human history had been born in Germany. Germany which had given rise to a highly developed civilization, in art, philosophy, and science. Why hadn't the Nazis grown out of cultures branded "underdeveloped," or "barbarian from birth," but rather out of... Where did the true error, the true problem lie, that...

He remembered fretting for days, with not a German in sight, that if he ever met one he might slip up and remind him that his was the culture which created Nazis. Since for some reason he had told "bald guy jokes" next to a friend with thinning hair... When he didn't even have the skill or habit of telling jokes...

"Next in line!

Second counter instance: The Soviet Union!

While the Soviet revolutions promised enlightenment, why was post-revolutionary oppression and terror increased by the enlighteners themselves?

The real question: Is violence a part of civilization? This must definitely be answered! A multi-faceted research must be conducted!"

"Oh Nesim, oh my dear friend!" Duna groaned in sorrow.

Just then another rest stop was reached, long-held needs were relieved, cramped bodies and hurting legs were stretched, the dry rations were consumed, water was drunk, cigarettes were lit, but still no one felt talkative.

When they boarded the vehicle again for the umpteenth time, Duna did not resist his heavy eyelids. Even in a dream, you had to know when to sleep. It did not matter how short/long, flimsy/sound, wet/dry, colorful or black and white the sleep was. When sleep called he did not resist anymore, he immediately ran towards it, knowing that in order to survive this nightmare he had to keep his strength. It was now a matter of life and death.

It was a long and uncomfortable sleep. Nudged awake by the soldier next to him, he saw that he had woken into the nightmare again, but did not wear himself out this time. This umpteenth waking, which he could now name, was like the Russian doll Matrushka, which produced more little dolls as you opened it. Again, again, and again… His own troubles on the other hand would grow larger as they went, and was called: "a waking nightmare."

They had stopped on hilly terrain. They must have been in a dry and arid land; the soil was baked into a color similar to that of a sick person's face. Despite this, there were patches of wildflowers defiantly sprouting in certain spots. Duna recognized the hyacinths, but did not know any of the other kinds. Here and there, a few slim trees stood lonely and sad. It was nearly evening, and chilly even though the season was summer. They were at quite a high altitude, which meant that…?

They were all taken off the vehicle. Orders were given, orders were received. Duna marvelled at how he was strictly obeying all orders, for he found himself extremely slow and unprepared in this fast-paced disciplinary system. But his youthful body and reflexes did not let him down, and he somehow managed. Right now, for example, he was standing to attention among two rows of soldiers.

"Are we in Central Anatolia, my friend?" he asked the soldier he had been paired with.

The soldier was silent as a rock, taut as steel, and looked as distant as if he had been in another world entirely. He looked too young.

"All these soldiers are actually extras in my dream!" mused Duna. "None of them are going to die! Thank god, none of them will die! When I wake up these terrifying scenes will end anyway!"

"This place looks more like Eastern Anatolia, sir!" whispered the stock still soldier next to him.

Duna leaned over and took a closer look at the young soldier. Did he know this youth? No. Staring carefully, he saw that there was a young, prematurely grown kid in that camouflage gear. You could smell his baby breath from under that blue beret.

"Tarkan? Oh my God, this can't be happening! It's not you, is it? Please tell me it's not you!" he groaned suddenly.

"It's me, sir!" Tarkan smiled broadly.

"But you're not even eighteen yet…"

"I'm a volunteer lieutenant!" Tarkan cried out with pride.

Duna bit his lips and stayed quiet. He remembered the summer nights when he ran into Tarkan, who walked around Ortaköy wearing his jet black hair in a long ponytail, sporting a single earring, and a book of poetry. There would be slim, graceful girls in dresses with long skirts and bare backs, swaying by his side like muses… Upon seeing Duna, he would give a salute that was part pride and part swagger, and would announce to Ortaköy in an audible voice that his literature teacher was passing by.

"He's a cool teacher!" he would say, laughing.

Then he would walk away, having done his teacher a favor near all those girls. When school started, he had made a great fuss, refusing to cut his hair, and the situation had only been settled with the interference of Duna, "the cool teacher," whereupon he had agreed to cut it off until the next summer. Tarkan was supposed to start his senior year of high school that year.

"Weren't you the one who got in trouble with the police for attending an anti-war demonstration, son?" Duna asked his student, confused.

"That's one thing, this is something else entirely, sir! I couldn't very well have sat at home because I was anti-war, while the country went to the dogs! My great grandfather carried the bullets he got in the War of Independence until the day he died, how about that? Our nation first, sir!"

"Dear god, have mercy on my mind! Son, this is a civil war, did you stop to think for one second who the enemy is in a civil war, huh?"

"Shh! Shut up you moron!" someone called angrily from the front of the line.

"Look Tarkan, this is nothing like the computer games you're always playing!" Duna continued to whisper without paying attention to anyone. "There's no return from here, the way you surf the Internet on your PC or your laptop, and then come back. This isn't virtual reality, son!"

"You're wrong sir, this time you're the one who doesn't know!"

The young soldier grinned with all the immature pleasure of having found his teacher's mistake. Mature people, on the other hand, become terribly depressed when they begin to detect their teachers' errors!

Just then a command rang out and they fell "at ease." There was a general excitement. Whispers and disconnected words flew between the soldiers. They went into a period of waiting.

"Second Lieutenant!" came a voice into Duna's ear. Duna sensed that he was the second lieutenant the disembodied voice was looking for. In fact, it turned out to be First Lieutenant Birol's voice.

"First Lieuteant Birol, I can't tell you how glad I am to see you!"

"I've been promoted to captain!" said Birol, smiling proudly.

"Has it been that long since I started this nightmare?" Duna mumbled uncomfortably. "Of course, in regular times, these things happen in August, don't they?" Pretending not to hear him, Captain Birol put his arm around Duna's shoulder, and pulled him away from the other soldiers. They began to walk together toward the few trees in the distance.

"The Brigadier General was very pleased with you. He's a difficult person to please, but as I had guessed, he understood you. I hope you liked him too."

"He liked me?" Duna repeated in surprise.

He was also perplexed as to what "he understood you" might mean.

"When the war's over… If we return alive and well, *inshallah*, the general will give a great celebratory dinner in his house. We are both invited to this dinner!"

Were Captain Birol's words a threat from his brain, or a warning from his subconscious as to how much longer this nightmare would last?

"But there is something else I want to say… I have a favor to ask of you…" Captain Birol changed the subject with some hesitance. "My fiancée," he said, stroking the engagement ring on his right hand lovingly.

Duna remembered that Birol was left-handed, but he had not noticed this ring before. He was not in the least interested in whether someone was married, single, or engaged, and he, in turn, did not feel any obligation to reveal his own private life. That's what an engagement ring meant to him. Merich, however, had worn a ring from the first, and placed a great importance on it. But she had neither hinted at him on the subject, nor pressured him emotionally.

"Merich is always silent, just like my father…" he thought.

"You'll remember I had told you that I had a special interest in you, lieutenant. My fiancée, Neshe, is a huge fan of Dogan Gokay.

Considering that you are married to the poet's niece... I was wondering if..."

"He means Merich," thought Duna.

"If we return unmartyred, I would really like to give Neshe a book autographed by the poet, as a gift... Especially that really famous book of his, you know..."

"Brunette Ada!" Duna said, finding solace in a deep sigh.

"Yes, that's the one...You'll do me this favor, won't you? You won't forget, I hope?"

Duna nodded "yes." He knew that if he attempted to speak he would start talking about Ada, and so he tried to bite his lips shut. Yet how much he had missed telling people about her...

Interpreting the complexity of emotions reflected on his face in a different manner, Captain Birol's eyes lit up dreamily.

"Maybe...By the Bosphorus...we can get together one evening, in that Kuzguncuk of yours, to eat fish and drink raki with our wives..."

His voice had wavered with the sexual tension of having unexpectedly referred to his fiancée as his wife, and he shyly averted his eyes.

"At Kuzguncuk, at Ismet Baba's restaurant-boat on the Bosphorus..." Duna murmured. "With the women we love..."

He also averted his look.

After a small break their eyes met once again. Two young men in camouflage gear, longing for the women they loved, Ismet Baba's restaurant in Kuzguncuk, the Bosphorus, fried savory fish with plenty of lemon and rocket, and tall steamed glasses of icy raki. They missed it awfully.

If one of them spoke the other would continue, but it was one of those moments when it's very difficult to speak. There was neither a joke to resort to, nor an excuse to take refuge in... At that point they flung open their arms and embraced as if for the last time.

As if?

"Just like in the movies..." Duna couldn't help thinking.

In the movies, soldiers who are about to embark on the road toward death, also think about the women they love in the last moment, in that very last moment when they feel the breath of mortality... He could not think of any names older than Vanessa Redgrave, Catherine Deneuve, Turkan Soray, and Liz Taylor. And of course the name that never left his mind... Even the thought of not being able to see her again was enough to drive him crazy. What makes death most unfair is that it tears one away from one's most dearly beloved!

He then drew in a deep breath, and thought "Thankfully, this is just a nightmare!"

"May you go in peace, Duna, my brother!" said Captain Birol. "Take good care of yourself!"

They parted. Duna looked around for Tarkan. He was there. He was simply standing there, waiting with all the other soldiers. Duna went next to him, and rejoined ranks.

"At ease!" a voice thundered. Hundreds of soldiers fell automatically "at ease."

"Atten-tion!"

They stood to it.

"Fellow soldiers! At this moment we are on sacred national land. Do not ask where we are. Due to the delicate nature of present conditions, it is our belief that that should remain undisclosed."

Was this Captain Birol's voice?

"Fellow soldiers, we are the Turkish Army. We are the children of an honored and diverse nation and we have gained the world's respect with our courage and strength. We are the Turkish Army, and we are here to terminate the war! We will be dissuasive, my friends! Not vengeful! Revenge does not befit a Turkish soldier! It will do us no good to encourage the war! Obeying the rules of humanity and war is a mighty deed befitting the soldiers of an honorable army. Only terrorists break these rules! They revel in chaos, anarchy, and violence!"

"Fellow Soldiers! Do not act with hatred and rage.

"May God help us all!

"I give you my blessing, and forfeit any claims I have on you, honest as my mother's milk! You too, give me your blessing, friends!"

There was a short, but very deep pause, and then the earth and the sky shook with the words "God Bless!" like a clap of thunder. These two words, which had fallen to the ground loaded with the electricity of human bodies, bore at the same time, the traces of a devastatingly peaceful hymn. Hundreds of male voices had formed an utterly unrehearsed chorus, and thundered the same notes. The surrounding rock and land had been unable to resist the heartfelt emotions packed into these two words, and had moaned in response. There was such an incredible weight of emotion on this sound, as can only be found in hymns and masterpieces composed with true love, that if it had hit anything by mistake, it could have caused a flood powerful enough to flatten everything in its path for days. Or conversely, it could have dazed a cold-hearted hero, undone his knees with fear, and brought him around to fairness. Death and hope, life and fear were all present in this sound. There was man in this sound: completely naked and alone. As in birth and death, everyone was equal in this sound!

Still unaware that his was one of the voices that cried out "God Bless!", Duna was stunned by the shock of the collective hypnosis that was being experienced. He found it difficult to collect himself, it was as if he was in a swoon, or in rapture… He had never taken part in the collective hysteria of soccer matches, but he sensed that that was nothing like what he was currently experiencing. He was trying to understand why he was affected to the point where his throat burned, and his hands and feet grew numb. He was forfeiting his claims on hundreds of young men he did not even know, that is, he was swearing that he bore no evil, hatred, or malice toward them, and declaring that whatever he might have born, he was forgiving entirely. But most important of all, he was doing this as a final duty before going to his death, and that's where the secret must have lied. These people, whom he was not yet aware he was a part of, were willingly choosing to die, without blinking an eyelid, for the sake of an ideal! (What if it isn't a dream?)

"Doing this, while thinking I am headed for death, must be working my nervous system at a five-alarm rate," he thought, discovering suddenly that he was included in everything. (No way, this is definitely a dream!)

When the words "God Bless!" which had turned light as life and heavy as death itself, poured forth from so many bodies simultaneously, they created their own power and almost intoxicated the owners of the bodies with the effect.

"Something like meditation…" Duna murmured, as he drew in a deep breath.

But what about the sacred musicality of those words? Was he making that up? Had not that earth shattering "God Bless!" a little while ago, filled him with the same cool tranquillity he had felt when as a child he listened to the Yunus Emre hymns his grandmother sang and got goosebumps? The way he used to start crying without knowing the reason, and his grandmother would stroke his hair, with a glowing smile of understanding, and say: "It's from love, my child, it's from the sacred love cleansing us inside."

So why did he have Wagner's Tannhauser stuck in his mind at the same time? In the overture to Tannhauser, was the spiritual refreshment provided by the gently ascending winds, and the accompanying strings a similar kind of peace? This circle he was hopelessly stuck in, at such a sensitive moment, was it also a sense of peace? Did not the deep satisfaction he felt while listening to Tannhauser contain as much praise for human idealism, passion, and beauty, as admiration for the honesty with which human weakness and brutality were depicted? Someone among us was stepping forward, with firm and passionate resolve, to tell of the filth, the evil, and the beauty within us…And we were more enraptured with self-love and self-pity than with what we were being told, or who was telling it… (Nearby, there is no Uncle Poet or Brunette Ada to whom he might ask "isn't that right?"… So he nods to himself…)

"It is said that in the music of Tannhauser, Wagner represents the madness of the human soul and its animalistic duality superbly," Uncle Poet had once remarked.

Then he remembered how he had abruptly stopped listening to Wagner upon learning that the composer was claimed by the Nazis.

"I'm not telling you to forget, children," Dogan Gokay had said, leaning on the sturdy trunk of his self confidence, which never made it necessary to raise his voice. "Forgetting is perilous in that it facilitates the repetition of mistakes. Idiots forget. Forgetting causes ignorance. Those who bear grudges do not forget, and use their knowledge in a self-destructive way. Wise people do not forget either, but are capable of converting their knowledge into positive energy for themselves and their ideals."

Duna, who was afraid to breathe lest he miss a single word of Uncle Poet's, would sometimes grow very annoyed with Ada who, thinking she was her uncle's peer, interrupted frequently and made know-it-all remarks. Yes, yes, he would grow annoyed with Ada. But he would not try to hinder her. Because that was Ada's role in this triangle, and it suited her very well.

"I am telling you to remember, children. However, attaining a certain level of aesthetic pleasure is a matter of maturity and education. Remember, without allowing your memories to obstruct your enjoyment of life! One never needs to drink to the point of unconsciousness in order to be drunk with pleasure! In fact, one can very well become drunk without having a single drop of alcohol."

"Sir, give me your blessing also, you put up with so much from us at school."

Tarkan had now abandoned the wild posturing, and had returned to his age. There was sorrow and longing in his eyes. His gaze was youthful, childish even. It was obvious that he would have flung his arms aroung Duna's neck if the situation had been appropritate, and he waited for his teacher to give him strength.

All of a sudden Duna felt very old. Yet he wasn't even old enough to be Tarkan's father. He was at most fifteen or sixteen years older than his student, but since school necessitated playing the part of the elder, sometimes one was compelled to age accordingly.

"My blessings, son!" he said in a fatherly voice that surprised even himself.

Was he stealing the role from Uncle Poet? Then, only to cheer up Tarkan, he gave in and whispered his secret:

"Actually, none of this is real, Tarkan. Everything we're experiencing is taking place within my dream. It's only a nightmare, thank goodness…" He paused, and added "I guess there are times in life when one feels glad to be having a nightmare…"

Then he turned to Tarkan, who was looking him over suspiciously, and continued his whispering.

"Naturally, I wish my blissful daydreams outnumbered my stronger fears, because then the images I have of happiness could turn into dreams… and maybe…maybe then we would be vacationing on a beach, instead of being at war…"

Immediately, a fresh, rosy smile spread over Tarkan's face. The tension he had felt just a moment ago had left him. Perhaps he was thinking of his sweetheart whom he would have at his side as he vacationed on the beach. Perhaps it was one of those poetic girls who sauntered by his side in Ortaköy... How lovely ne's sweetheart is oat seventeen! (Isn't he Ada?)

"When I wake up this nightmare will end, and you'll go back home. Don't be afraid at all, not the least bit, okay?"

"Who's afraid, sir?" Tarkan yelled.

"Alright, alright, quiet down, don't yell. I'm the one who's afraid, goddamn it, I must be the only one who's afraid, and that's why this nightmare is plaguing me."

Leaning slightly toward Duna, with a sympathetic smile, Tarkan said: "Thanks anyway, sir. I like that nightmare story of yours. A fine speculation... When you're in trouble you can think about it and relax. Well, your literature teacher's gotta be something else, of course."

"He didn't believe it either," sighed Duna. "No one believes me... God, so this is the greatest loneliness in the world!"

"Anyway, we'll see each other at school when this nightmare is over," he then mumbled, in order to save the situation.

"If we don't die, if we survive, professor!" said Tarkan, without hiding the knot of sadness in his throat this time.

The rest developed quickly. Orders were given, received. A calm submission, a silent feeling of acceptance had replaced that mystical excitement. With the onset of night, the security division Duna belonged to went into action. They began to descend down the hill in the dark, carrying backpacks and machine guns. He was not a person who exercised regularly but he discovered the advantages of being relatively active as he followed the soldier in front of him at his body's initiative. Only five minutes had elapsed when they heard a great explosion coming from below. Then they saw a light and began to hear voices. (No, please don't let them be screams!) They continued to descend the hill at a faster pace. Duna could hear his heart beat as if it had been hooked up to a powerful pair of loudspeakers.

After a long "little while" they entered a town. The streetlights were out, and the streets were empty. Following the burning smell, and using walls as shields, they advanced toward the light. When they arrived at the square with a monument of Ataturk, they found burning pieces of furniture strewn all over the ground, illuminating their surroundings. Stunned by the scene in front of him, Duna suddenly began to vomit. There were corpses with mangled arms and legs on the ground. Single shoes, children's clothes, scarves, large rocks, and sticks… There was a stench of burnt flesh all around.

His mind was rebelling against his eyes, and his nervous system, which could not bear to see blood, was seeking ways to deny what he saw. He leaned against a wall and waited for his stomach to empty out completely. He tried to calm down by swallowing repeatedly. Calm down? Ha! He didn't even know what it was to calm down anymore… If he could only close his eyes and wake up when he reopened them, if he could only wake up!

"Why do we relive this terror again and again, god?" he moaned and began to throw up once more.

Having nothing left in his stomach, he had started to retch repeatedly when he realized that he was doubled up from exhaustion and crouching by a wall.

He hastily muffled the voice that asked: "What if it's not a dream?" This *was* a nighmare.

As he was trying to stand up an awful clamor broke. He fell to the ground from the impact of an immense explosion nearby. First a heat wave licked his face. He immediately withdrew. One of his arms had automatically flown up to shield his face. Peeking through his stance he saw arms and legs flying in the air. Everything was red, utterly red… Blood was pouring! Then he heard the screams:

"They got me, ma!"

"Aargh, mama!"

"Help me for the love of God and Mohammed, I don't want to die!"

His initial reaction was to get out of there right away. If he couldn't escape by waking up, then he would escape this hell by running away. He had had enough of this goddamned nightmare!

His head had started to ache, and his ears were burning. Suddenly he realized that he had stopped hearing any of the screams around him. Neither those calling for help, nor those wailing in pain… Duna could not hear a single thing. His lines were cut off!

"I guess I've gone deaf!" he thought, surprised at his own composure.

Then he checked his eyes with his hands. They were in place. He hastily checked all his body parts and looked at his palms in fear. No, there was no blood on his hands yet. He rose to his feet. He watched the silent horror movie around him in stupor. It was as if he had fallen completely outside reality (which reality?). He was simply standing there in the twilight, frozen in a place full of fire, blood and human suffering.

Duna stood without being able to do anything, hear anything, or run anywhere.

Just then he spotted Musa. He stared. Yes, that was Musa. Musa from Kuzguncuk was lying on the ground a few feet away, pointing at his bloody leg and shouting. He stared as if watching a movie. He could not hear his friend's voice, but could deduce that the latter was screaming. All at once he revived with a sharp pain in his lip, where he must have buried his teeth. That's when he came to his senses. Suddenly he was able to move and hear the sounds around him. He ran over to Musa's side. He kneeled down and used a strip of cloth torn from his friend's good leg to bandage the injured one, just in case it prevented further loss of blood. At that point he realized that he could bear the sight of blood. It did not make him queasy anymore!

"I'm Musa. Musa from Kuzguncuk. I don't want to die! *Ya Allah, ya Bismillah!* I'm Musa. *Allahuakbar!*" Musa was rambling.

Duna wanted to load Musa on his back and take him to a quiet place where he could get help. But Musa was large and heavy, whereas he himself was skinny and extremely tired.

"Goddamned movies..." he muttered. "Are all the soldiers in those movies strong and brawny for heaven's sakes!"

He began to drag Musa along. First they left the Ataturk Square, and wandered around dark, narrow streets, moaning. Musa was half unconscious, and could Duna really be said to be in his senses? Occasionally he would halt, sit down, place Musa's head on his knees and wipe his forehead. Musa's bleeding had stopped but his fever had risen. He dripped water into Musa's mouth from his tureen at every rest.

"You're not going to die, Musa, never fear, my friend. This is a nightmare, just a nightmare! I'm going to wake up and it'll end! Believe me, it'll all get better…. Look I promise, I'll even drop by your grocery store. I'll drop by without worrying that you'll pressure me. I'll visit you until we learn to accept each other. Don't die now, Musa, don't you die… Oh Merich, where are you?"

Was he calling Merich's name because he needed a doctor?

Then he got back to his feet and straggled around the streets of the town, pulling Musa behind him. He did not know where he was going and who he might ask for help. He had not even realized that he was lost among the labyrinthine, cobblestone streets. He wanted to relax by thinking of good things, and the only things that occurred to him were Kuzguncuk, his childhood, Aras, Ada, his grandfather, and his mother. They were playing in the mansion's garden. Uncle Poet was telling them something; he was happy. He was very happy! They were happy then!

Finally he was too exhausted to move. He sank down next to a wall, and leaned Musa against it. They remained this way for a while. There was no sound, it was dark. The air was chilly. All of a sudden, before he realized what was going on, Duna found himself yelling at the top of his lungs. He was screaming like crazy:

"All you murderers, all you criminals in human costume! I'm talking to you, child-butchers! Bloodsuckers, bastards, vampires! You're not even human! What religion, what nation has been exalted through murder, huh? You're fucking rabid! God damn you! May you drown in the blood of dead babies, you hatemongers! You're killing my fucking friend! I hate you, see, I hate you too! Do you like that? Have you succeeded, huh?"

No sound. Only the angry echo of his voice came back to him. Not a sound.

"Why don't you talk! Come on, talk you baby-butchers! How do you slay babies right and left, huh? How can you waste people with bombs and fires, huh? How did you learn to kill for your beliefs, huh? God damn that kind of belief!

Not a sound. It was as if no one had ever lived in these lands, and Duna was doomed to remain alone here forever.

"Traitors! Cowards! Inhuman bastards!" he cried.

His voice had begun to crack.

Not a sound was to be heard.

That's when Duna began to unravel. He felt that he was going to pieces. His sweat-soaked body was splitting into its cells before his eyes. He started to sob uncontrollably. He was caught in a hopeless bombardment of tears, losing a piece of himself with every sob.

For a moment he thought he heard a voice say, "Psst, soldier! Soldier, lookee over here, soldier!"

"What do you want?" he snapped back.

"Psst soldier, I'm talkin to you son, lookee over here a bit!"

Raising his head, he could barely make out a door across from him cracked open. At first he thought he was hallucinating, but the silhouette of a woman wearing peasant's breeches detached itself from the open door. It motioned him hither with one hand. Duna bolted from his seat. Leaning Musa's body, which was now heavier than ever, upon his own tired frame, he dragged it along. They entered through the half-open door. As soon as they were inside, the door was firmly shut and bolted behind them.

POET'S WEDDING

"*Roaming from Maras to Mus*
I never left Istanbul.
How many yous have I loved on the way
Ayse, my ayse from head to toe."

Metin Eloglu

"My uncle Dogan's back from Paris, and he's going to have a shotgun wedding!"

"A shotgun wedding? Really? That's too bad!"

I had heard of people getting married, and had even been to my uncle Kemal's marriage ceremony at the officers' club, but this word "shotgun" had frightened me in conjunction with "wedding." How could I have guessed that years later I too would have a shotgun wedding?

"A shotgun wedding is kind of a bad thing, isn't it Ada?"

"Oh my sweet, angelic Mabel, it's not bad at all! People who love each other very very much have shotgun weddings. For example my mommie and daddy had it. I suppose I'll marry Aras that way too… I mean I guess…"

"Oh brother," I pouted.

Actually we were both upset by Uncle Poet's wedding. It does not matter in the least whether you are a child or an adult; it is sad to see someone you love get married (especially to someone you don't know at all). It means that most likely, you will lose the person you love, even if you live in the same city, even if they are right there in front of your eyes. Those who strive not to lose this person usually end up having to learn how to be friends with someone they did not choose. This is similar to a tailor trying to sew a new dress out of an old one. As might be presumed, the effort is more difficult than endeavoring to make a new dress out of brand new cloth, and its results are not always satisfactory. (That's what my father, Naim the modern tailor, used to say).

Ever since Ada's family moved to Kuzguncuk, the poet Dogan Gokay frequented the mansion almost every weekend, and always made time for us with his patient, wise, and cheerful countenance. We kids had understood upon first sight that he was very different from the other adults. His greatest difference was that he treated us like equals, and children love this. However, in so doing, he did not repeat the mistake that most grown-ups fell into by acting childish himself, by falsely sweetening his voice, or raising, elongating, and contorting it as if talking to a cat. The real secret of Dogan Gokay's excellent communication with kids and youth lay in his ability to create an environment free enough to encourage their creativity. In his own words, he could be a "partner in crime" to children and youth. Therein lies the magic behind his ongoing popularity with young people.

So the Poet Uncle who explained any issue that puzzled, pleased, or bothered us with an answer satisfactory for our age, and who with every question we asked led us to another mind-expanding query, was getting married! We would have to share him with someone else, or maybe even lose him... Maybe he would not come to the mansion anymore, and we would never see him again! My childish heart, which already filled with sorrow at the thought of Ada marrying my brother, was thoroughly broken with the news of this second wedding. (Sometimes I wonder "do traces of these initial experiences lie beneath my coldness toward the institution of marriage?").

Early in his youth, the poet Dogan Gokay had gone to Paris, which was then the mecca of writers and artists, and lived there for a few years. During this time an international campaign had been started in Paris to free Nazim Hikmet, who languished in prison because of his poetry and convictions, and the young Dogan Gokay had become one of the leading names of this campaign. Upon his return to Turkey, Uncle Poet, who had been blacklisted for demanding Nazim Hikmet's freedom, was thrown in prison, with his poems as an excuse. He never told us much about this part of his life. He did not like to discuss how long and where he had served time, but when it came up he would laugh bitterly and say:

"Oppression is a method that misfires most on youth. Oppression has never been the way toward dissuasion! But our fellows seem determined not to learn this. And that's why their weapons are always misfiring…"

On the other hand we knew a lot about his life in France. He would relate many interesting stories, marinated in his cheerful and energetic style, of writers and poets from various corners of the world. We would listen to tales of Parisian cafes, streets, cinemas and museums with our mouths open. In the end we had each constructed a Paris of our own and naturally, Ada had been deeply disappointed to visit Paris years later.

"Maybe my uncle Dogan's Paris never existed. I think he wrote and told us about his own Paris, Mabel…" she had said upon her return.

For our generation, Paris had never been that seductive invitation to passion, art and freedom. In our youth it was advanced technology, money and power that titillated, and our generation's gaze had been turned toward America. Perhaps because our characters were better suited to the former, but most probably because of our great admiration for Uncle Poet, Ada and I were exceptions who were still excited by the joys symbolized by Paris.

I did not care in the least. What mattered most was that Dogan Gokay had taken us seriously as children, whisked us off on a small tour of the world, and given us the awareness that there were other nations, races, and worldviews than our own. How can I forget the great fun we had in the meantime? After all, isn't it obvious from a single glance which adults have had a pleasant childhood?

He would tell us, among peals of laughter, that when he ran out of money he worked as a bartender and a newspaper boy. And sometimes he and a Spanish poet friend of his (who would go on to become famous), gave juggling performances on the streets of Paris to raise money for coffee and books… (Of course, my belief in the correlation between poetry and juggling was becoming thoroughly solidified.)

I was old enough to vaguely understand that waking up in the cold, dark Parisian mornings and going to work was not half as fun as enjoying romantic love affairs in Parisian boulevards, but I was a little too young to pick up the fact that he was someone who never cried about the past in front of other people, and who acted realistically in the present.

By the time I came around to it, I realized that Dogan Gokay was a pleasant, attractive man, and he was still young. He was neither classically strong and handsome, nor did he steal hearts with his hair, beard or gaze. Dogan Gokay is a graceful, clean-shaven man of slightly above average height and slim stature. Everything about him, from his hands to his skin, from his posture to his gaze, indicates at first glance that he is urbane and intellectual. In addition to being extremely sophisticated, his cheerful and energetic personality are his greatest charms. He is one of those exceptional people who never boast, but immediately draw respect and affection by virtue of their strong and generous nature. I suppose his colorful personality, which seemed brimming with a promise of adventure, and his eternally youthful looks rendered him more attractive than handsome men. Women have always liked him.

I was to learn later that, unlike now, he had been a very visible young man in his youth; and one whose name had been attached to a number of affairs. Ada's mother had whispered to her daughter, (who had, naturally, passed it on to me) that in Paris he was known as the "fast" Turkish poet.

A serious problem, the cause of which we were to find out later, had arisen between him and the owner of the newspaper where he worked as cultural editor. When we heard about it Uncle Poet had already quit the paper and returned to Paris. It was summer vacation, and at first I did not feel his absence greatly. In a month's time Ada and I had come to miss him, and to think of him often. But after a period of eight months, we became cross and extremely offended, thinking he had abandoned us.

"They met on the way to Turkey. You know, he still travels by boat. They returned to Istanbul on the same ferry from Italy. It must be lightning love!"

"Lightning love?"

I had not even gotten over the shotgun marriage bit and now there was a whole new category of amourousness... This "lightning" business had descended upon me with a bewitching and frightening splendor.

"My mom told me that this was love at first sight. Just like being hit by lightning, boom, and all of a sudden you're in love…" said Ada, fluttering her eyelashes and giving an exaggerated shudder to make me laugh.

I adored her little theatrics; she never tired of doing them and I never grew weary of watching. But when a third person joined us Ada's style would change, and she would continue to play in a less comical, more controlled manner. Just then Aras had joined us. Suddenly growing serious, Ada said:

"If you meet someone for the first time and feel like you've gotten an electric shock, if you're super affected, then that's lightning love!"

Then she turned and looked at Aras. How could I forget that look? It was if she had licked a sharp knife and bloodied her whole mouth…At first Aras was stunned, it seemed he was having difficulty breathing. Then he pursed his lips, frowned, and turned his head upwards as if he was thinking of some other very important matter, the way he always did when he grew embarrassed.

Ada, who had learned early on how to read him, knew the true meaning of this gesture, which would surely have gotten Aras into trouble with any other girl. Ada had realized long ago that Aras' verbal expression skills were underdeveloped, but she knew all the areas in which his wit and emotion thrived.

Aras was going to start high school that year. Ada had fallen a year behind Aras because she had spent a preparatory year learning English. Merich, who attended Uskudar American Preparatory College with her cousin, was in seventh grade. By that time she had completely moved into Ada's house, and been taken under her aunt and uncle's wings. I gradually, began to fancy that she never had had a family of her own, and that she truly was Ada's sister. I had seen Merich's mother only once, and knew her father from photographs. Though she was just one year older than me, I looked two sizes too small next to her. I would frequently overhear grown-ups say she would be tall like her mother. Merich, who looked old for her age, had become pretty enough to make people on the street turn around to stare after her. She had inherited her mother's rosy-white Macedonian hues, and did not in the least resemble her hazel colored, brunette cousin Ada. But if you ask me, these were not Merich's most important qualities. The thing I liked best about her was her smell. I have yet to meet someone who smelled as good as her. It's not a special perfume or anything, this smell is Merich's own smell: it is fresh and flowery. Ada loves fruity perfumes, but Merich never uses the stuff.

Merich could not enjoy her beauty and pleasant smell. She was turning from a shy, retiring child, into a quiet and indistinct young woman. She lived tentatively, like a foundling with her aunt and uncle who had taken her into their house and showed the utmost care not to treat her any different from Ada. Merich always lived like a guest in that gorgeous mansion where even I sometimes acted as if I were "the son of the house," and she never could forgive her father who paid her school tuition. She is still the same.

I think Merich had troubles about her existence, and she seemed to be crushed under its weight. I felt an interest akin to pity toward her; I wanted to protect her from herself, to prevent her from suffering any further. It bolstered my confidence to know that she liked me, because other boys' eyes would pop out when they saw Merich. My own eyes were fixed on a honey colored girl who had bewitched me all her life with her intelligence and courage. This girl, in love with my brother, struggled her whole life to conceal the mysterious sorrow which so complimented her lovely Mediterranean beauty with a jocosity that sometimes bordered on coarseness.

When she was fifteen, the year of that unfortunate incident, Merich stopped growing at 165cm; still tall for that age. I soon caught up with, and surpassed her. Years later, when she explained to me how the powerful trauma had affected her growth hormones, I was terrified to realize that she had been shaken more with the fear of losing me than the actual horrific event which had grieved us all. Sometimes the question of how we can remain blind to the tragedies or miracles that take place near us hangs over my head like a cursed riddle.

That was the year when I was pronounced to be short-sighted, and all of a sudden, at twelve, I became a "four-eyes." Besides the adolescent pimples that had slowly started to besiege my face, and my relatively weak, skinny physique, now I had this to deal with. As a grown man I have still never become someone who would be noticed out of his sheer presence, or whom girls would turn around to look at flirtatiously. (Even though my mother does not approve of it, the girls of my generation, no matter what their creed or background, look at the men they like flirtatiously, not languidly.)

Aras had the monopoly on good looks; as soon as he walked into a given location his handsomeness and masculine presence would immediately make an impression, and the atmosphere would practically alter. All girls, without exception, would turn their heads to look at my brother. As for him, like all attractive people, he had grown used to it. What's more, he would drive girls even crazier with his unconceited, calm manner. Aras was never a flirtatious youth. He had fallen for Ada from the very beginning. My brother was stuck on Ada's colorful personality and strong character, which were hard to parallel. How can I forget the glances he would sneak at Ada's hazel eyes when he thought no one was looking? In my opinion, the value he gave Ada has always been one of the extreme examples of how in love a man can be with a woman. Next to mine, of course…

"So is she a poet too?"

"Who, his wife?"

We had not seen Uncle Poet, who was to visit the mansion for the first time since he had gotten married, for almost a year.

"No, his wife is supposed to be a fashion artist."

"A fashion artist?"

Now, how on earth had Uncle Poet found such a strange professional woman…

"Actually, they call it stylist or designer or something, but I made up the name fashion artist. It's more Turkish, and super cool!" shrugged Ada.

As always, we were the only two talking. Merich was doing her homework with her incredibly neat handwriting: so uniform that it could have been a computer printout. Aras was browsing the gorgeous pictures in the National Geographic, which Ada had recently subscribed to. Both kept one ear on our conversation.

"She is supposed to be a stunning blonde, my parents met her!"

What I could not understand was how instead of getting mad at

Dogan Gokay who had abandoned us for a "stunning blonde," and instead of becoming jealous of that woman, Ada seemed positively animated.

"He won't be coming here as much anymore!" said Aras with a happiness he did not try at all to hide.

"Oh no!" I thought. "Here comes the hurricane!"

"He'll come!" said Ada, finally showing the stern reaction I had expected of her. "My uncle will still visit the mansion frequently, with his wife of course!"

Her voice had angry tremors that indicated the reverse could never be proven. Aras immediately withdrew, realizing that he intruded upon the sacred space between Ada and her poet uncle, and the hurricane was dodged.

As long as I have known them, the poet Dogan Gokay and Ada Mercan have had an incredibly beautiful relationship which they still miraculously preserve. After many years, when one of them began to age, and the other to mature, they continued to be able to travel together like two separate cars that accelarate at the same speed. This is not simply a coincidence. Those two are people who share a very similar sensitivity and approach to life. Both are vigilantly alert, have a vigorous intellectual capacity, nimble wit, and a sly sense of humor which they hide behind without even letting themselves know.

If you ask me Ada is neither like her mother nor like her father. Her personality is completely codified from her uncle's genes. Despite the traditional belief that a girl takes after her paternal aunt, a boy after his maternal uncle, Ada was, without a doubt, her uncle's girl.

In any case, it turned out that her prediction was right: Uncle Poet continued to visit the mansion frequently, just like always, he came back to us!

He had not changed at all. (So marriage was not as spooky as I had thought- was it?) With his wise smile that always seemed ready for mischief, his intelligent gaze which overflowed from the slightly increased prescription of his glasses, his thin ribbed corduroy trousers and his tweed jacket, he was still the same Uncle Poet. His wife was young, genuinely pretty, and deeply in awe of the poet. We could all see that, no matter what our age. She had not monopolized Uncle Poet the way we had feared, on the contrary she acted as casually and independently as if she had just dropped by the mansion because she was in the neighborhood. However she did not make the slightest effort to befriend us. She was an unusual woman. Her disinterest in anything around her bordered on indifference. What bothered me most was her name. She had a name which I had never heard before or afterwards, and which aroused uncomfortable associations within me. The battle I have fought to rid myself of my prejudices has been as hard as all my other efforts toward self-improvement, but I have never been able to transcend my problem with the name of Dogan Gokay's wife. God, how important people's names can be!

"Do you like his wife?" Ada whispered in my ear.

"I don't know...She's pretty I guess..."

"Oh, Mabel, that's not what I asked. Of course she's very pretty! I want to know what you think of her."

"I don't like her name! She's got a really ugly name!"

"Of course not, silly! For one thing, her name means 'volcano,' and besides there's only one name like that in the whole entire world... Just think, only one... And she's my uncle's wife!"

Her name was Burkan.

"Well, look how all of you have grown!" Uncle Poet had exclaimed elatedly. "A year is such a long time for children, and such a short one for adults!"

He was happy. His eyes flashed differently than before.

"Paris has changed immensely! That revolutionary, defiant air is nowhere to be found," he said, responsibly illuminating an important fact without betraying his disappointment.

"I've decided to become a naval engineer!" said Aras, out of the blue.

It seems he had wanted to express the fact that he had grown up in the most direct manner possible. In his rebellious voice, the determined yet still naive screams of a young man declaring he did not need Uncle Poet's wings anymore...

"Really?" Uncle Poet turned to him joyously. Perhaps he was hoping that a relationship could be established between them. "A very sound decision. Naval engineering is an occupation with a bright future, and it's very appropriate for you Aras."

Aras did not reply. This was the extent of their communication, and it would suffice Aras for the next few weeks.

"Well, have other occupations been decided?" he said, turning towards us.

"Personally, I am interested in social subjects, uncle Dogan," Ada said in a knowing voice.

"But of course!" laughed her uncle.

"So I suppose I'll become a sociologist or a psychologist or something..."

Dogan Gokay shook his head, trying not to laugh.

"Me," I offered, "I might become a poet when I grow up!"

"Hah ha! You're wonderful Duna! But you know, there's no school for becoming a poet."

"That's even better! Who likes going to school?" I grinned.

"I like it a lot," Merich said in a barely audible voice. "I feel very happy in school."

There was a deep silence. Although we were all still children, we were old enough to understand what Merich meant.

"Your father also has always loved school, Merich. Yet your Aunt Pervin and I weren't the most studious types," Dogan Gokay said, adopting a mischievous tone in order to lighten the situation.

The following year Merich convinced her aunt to send her to Uskudar Prep as a boarding student. We could only see her on the weekends. Did we feel her absence greatly? I don't know...

"So, tell me serious miss, what're you going to be when you grow up?"

"I am thinking of becoming a doctor, but I have to talk it over with my parents of course..." Merich said in a timid voice.

We all knew that she was lying. Her mother was in the hospital once again for treatment, and her father had not come by for months.

"Surely, my princess, that's a wise decision. Even at this age I cannot be as clever as you. You haven't taken after the rascally side of the family, thankfully!" he said.

In fact, Merich did go on to have a very successful, incredibly disciplined academic life, and graduated from every school she entered with honors. Unlike the qualities of leadership present in

Aras, who was just as successful as her, Merich always advanced silently and deeply.

I am certain that after we all left the salon that day, Ada managed to wheedle out of her uncle that she was the most special child in the family. Ada is a person who cannot go on unless she knows that the people she loves consider her to be their "most special" one. As for those people outside of the few she loves, they can come and go as they please.

"Wait, don't disperse yet, I have a surprise for all of you today," said the poet Dogan Gokay.

I recall it was a winter's day when the dry chills gnawing away at Kuzguncuk are merciless. Once again, the four of us had gathered in the mansion on a weekend.

"A surprise?" Ada cried cheerfully. "I love surprises…"

"Today, a friend of mine is going to come over and give us a very special presentation."

"Is it a juggler, Uncle Poet?" I asked eagerly.

"No children, it's not a juggler. My friend who will pay us a visit is a *Hayali*."

"A *Hayali?*"

That evening a tall, thin, middle aged (though to us, "old") man called *Hayali* Ismail came to the mansion. His almost melancholy seriousness gave away nothing. Uncle Poet's wife talked to him at length about how the costumes of Karagoz and Hacivat, the main characters in shadow puppet plays, could be modernized. Burkan's own outfits, which were always vastly different than regular women's clothes, scared me and I sometimes fancied she was an alien.

"Oh Mabel, dear, you're such a daydreamer, really… Besides, those alien dreams of yours aren't even original. Aliens walk around naked, but this Burkan, she wears haute couture!"

I guess I was the only one who enjoyed Ada's comments, and know-it-all behavior.

"What, she wears oat coater? Oh my god, how horrible!"

Our childhood years had not fallen within the era of Karagoz and Hacivat shows. We were more the TV and movie generation. Turkey did not have tens of local color channels and dozens of foreign channels via satellite, but we were the first TV generation.

By the time of our childhood, the atmosphere necessary for the shadow puppetry of Karagoz and Hacivat had long been spoiled. The concepts of dipping ink, being a bookworm, and coming from

a cultured family had been already replaced by solving tests, reading in your spare time, and being rich. Shadows had long lost their mystery by the 1970's...

While Karagoz and Hacivat had been superb childhood entertainment for my mother's generation, it was boring, slow and stale for us. Its humor and pace was not in step with our own. It was left behind for us only as an element of folklore.

But that night was different. That night we all enjoyed the Karagoz show, in fact we had uproarious fun. That night at the mansion, on a stage especially constructed for the poet Dogan Gokay and his friends, and with a shadow puppet set made of real camelskin, *Hayali* Ismail put on a show great enough to make me remember it for the rest of my life. His jokes were up-to-date, his language plain and nimble.

On some weekend evenings, guests would come to visit Dogan Gokay. Ada would whisper proudly to me that these were well-known writers, poets, musicians and painters.

When I chanced upon an actor or actress I recognized among them, I would run exuberantly to my mother and tell her all about it. My mother would make me describe particularly the female stars, over and over again. No questions would be posed to Aras on the subject because he was not interested in stars.

These guests were nothing like our Kuzguncukites. Some were men with goatees or strange hairdos who walked around in overalls or bowties. The women were even more odd. For one thing, most of the women had hair shorter than even the men. In terms of clothes they were divided into two camps, one wore dresses without sleeves or collars even in the winter, and the other never wore anything but pants. The lady with the shortest, eggplant colored hair always smoked a pipe. I didn't like her at all because the smell of her pipe tobacco would infiltrate my clothes and persist even after being washed.

During these crowded evenings Sureyya Mercan especially would show great care not to disturb the neighborhood. I would learn years later from my mother that there were those among the Kuzguncukites who were not fond of this avant-garde artist community, but that because of the affection felt towards Sureyya Mercan, the matter was met with understanding.

A few years ago, or maybe it was last year, Dogan Gokay turned to Ada, who was talking about the difficulty of trying to learn our true history by reading between the lines of the official version, and said:

"Look, my child, sometimes we have to remember to make use of symbols. Karagoz bears symbols that tell us a great deal about the Ottomans. This can be supported by written documents reaching as far back as the 1850's."

"There are truths which lie behind the characterizations of the Anatolian, the Pontic, the Kastamonian, the Kayserian, the Karamanlian, the Eginlian, the Harputian, the Kurd, and Baba Himmet, children. If you learn how to read these, you can decipher the codes more easily."

Hayali Ismail was extremely excited as he introduced us to these characters through his camelskin puppets, each a work of art in itself.

"Chelebi, Tiryaki, Beberuhi… these are Istanbul characters. As for the non-muslims: they are referred to as the Armenian, the Jew, and the Greek in Karagoz. There are also those who call them Agop, Nesimi, and Kirkor."

"And then, children, there are characters from outside Anatolia. If you'll forgive me, *Hayali*, I'm poking my nose in your business…"

"Far be it, sir, not in the least! We can only benefit from your vast knowledge!"

"Acem the Persian, the Arab, Arnavut the Albanian…" Uncle Poet started listing.

I had not been able to understand why *Hayali* Ismail had called him "sir." Besides juggling, did poets also pursue careers teaching Karagoz that I was not informed about?

"Now, don't forget about the hoodlum characters! You don't wanna be wronging the true boys after all, do you?" said Sureyya Mercan in his Fisherman Osman voice.

Sureyya Mercan was a warm, humble, carefree man, sweet as all the world. Ada had whispered to me that he too wrote poems and read them to his brother in law. In the years to come, some of Surey-

ya Mercan's poems inspired young composers of Turkish traditional art music. The poems of Ada's father are still alive in a few such
songs which became very famous.

"My father drinks for pleasure, he's not an alcoholic like Merich's
mother!" Ada had said in an irate manner. Yet Sureyya Mercan always drank. Not compulsively, but whenever he was in the mansion
he walked around with a raki glass in hand, the anise scented white
liquid and ice cubes clinking inside. There used to be wooden bowls
in all the corners of the salon, filled with roasted chickpeas, almonds,
and salted peanuts, which Aunt Cihan frequently replenished.

"Tuzsuz Crazy Bekir, Kulhanbey the hoodlum, Efe, Zeybek,
Matiz...plus Imam, Tablah, The Wizard, Cazuhan, Djinn, and the
Monster..." added *Hayali* Ismail, with pride, introducing each
character with the specific puppet.

"And actually *kochek* the boy dancer, *chengi* the dancing girl, the
clown, the *kanto* dancer, are all representatives of different ethnic
groups."

"There's the Ottoman genius, my friends!" Sureyya Mercan
jumped to his feet with a gregariousness fueled by raki.

"They would expertly piece together diverse elements, just like a
mosaic, and complete the picture!"

"You mean like a puzzle," Ada interjected.

She was glad to have gotten a chance to speak at long last.

"It's time you found a Turkish equivalent for this word pa-zul,
it won't do to be stealing other people's words all the time!"
laughed her uncle.

"Well, what do you know, this Karagoz show of ours is like the
United Nations! Ah, my gem of a country! Doesn't this call for listening to some *kurdihili hicazkar* with raki and feta on the side!"

"Sweetheart, maybe you shouldn't have any more to drink..."
Pervin Gokay cautioned her husband in her graceful voice.

"Last one, darling, believe me, this is the final one, my lovely
wife..." said Sureyya Mercan, and put his arm around her waist.

"They say that artists can't stay married but-god forbid the evil
eye- look at Pervin Gokay and Sureyya Mercan. *Mashallah*, they're
still like star-crossed lovers... May God preserve their happiness..." my mother would say at times, fixing her dreamy eyes on
my father.

My father, not knowing what to do, grew even more timid in these situations and acted as if he were not there. My poor mother was used to carrying on her monologue in between sighs.

"Look, not one person has ever seen Sureyya Mercan in any hardship. Pervin Gokay is a noble woman, that's for certain... Oh well!... Manners is something else, of course... People who've been brought up with manners are a different breed..."

I never knew who to feel sorry for. For my father, who fled my mother's passionate dreams and disillusion filled sighs, and took refuge in his tailor shop, or for my mother, who expected from him things beyond his capacity?

Aras was the smarter one. He would immediately withdraw to our room, and busy himself by constructing models, reading technical science magazines, or drawing pictures of planes and ships. That is, if he wasn't studying... Aras would never get involved in matters concerning my parents, he knew how to keep himself apart. I have always been the bleeding heart, naturally predisposed to getting himself into a fix. But always! Even if I hate myself for it, I sniff out trouble and immerse myself in it beautifully!... In other words, I am a virtual magnet for trouble.

"However, I would like to draw your attention to a certain point, gentlemen!" the piped woman artist joined in. "Everything was not as bright and sunny as you suppose in that picture. As a matter of fact, there were shadows, and very dark ones. We all know that even though it is diluted with humor, minorities are sometimes ridiculed and derogated in Karagoz shows."

"This is very natural," interrupted the actor Sureyya Mercan. "There's this duality in the nature of the business, a dialectical situation as my poet brother in law would say...Y'now what I mean..."

"Sweetheart, remember you promised not to drink..."

"I think you are overlooking an important point here," spoke the poet Dogan Gokay in a voice that encouraged everyone to listen. "The genius of Turks in military and strategic areas, and the success of Ottomans in establishing a state and managing to make it last for an extremely long period of time as a huge empire, should be praised, considering the economic situation of the time."

"Hear hear, my lion of a brother in law! I lift my final glass in his honor. Darling, look this is the last one, really my dear, my raisin eyed lovely wife…"

"The second matter is that what we call Anatolian Islam today. The religious culture that is dominant over a great part of the country, and harmonious with our traditions, was something the Ottomans won over for us. And as for the modern application of Islam, it will surely be accomplished by Mustafa Kemal Pasha's Turkey at one point or another."

The curtain rose and Hacivat descended upon the screen, chanting a *semai* verse.

"*Hai, hai, haak!*" he cried. "*Yaar,* I need a distraction! *Amaan,* I need an attraction!"

And Karagoz appeared on the screen.

"Soo, Karagoz my dear, you started school it does appear. Pray tell, have you dipped ink, have you torn paper from link to link? Can you draft a cursive hand?"

"I dipped the ink and shredded paper link to link. You bet I curse the draft! Try to bear the winter if you dare. There is no wood in the loft, not a piece of coal left. And as for the purse, well, that's all bare!"

On my way home, the verse that lingered most in my mind was:

"Hey, *Hai-Hai hak!* Wretched I the curtain, laid it in ruins, Better go 'fess up my wretched doin's.
Good friends, may you forgive any slips of our tongue!"

HOW MANY KINDS OF LOVE ARE THERE?

*"Lift your gaze
but do not look at
me…"*

Ingeborg Bachmann

"It causes pain!" she said.
"Every kind of love causes pain!"
She stopped.
I waited.
We both waited.
She must have been testing my patience.
Her lips moved after a long while.
"Says my uncle Dogan."

The bits of hazel that glittered in her brown eyes like tiny grains of sand were enough to illuminate my inner world. I do not know if there was anyone else who noticed the sorrow concealed beneath the joy of life that poured from that gaze… But I had my suspicions on the Poet Dogan Gokay!

"If you ask him…"

How can I not ask him, when Ada says so…

"If you ask him, the relationship between two men who've known each other since childhood, but who cannot get along for the life of them, who have always lived by making jabs at one another, is also a kind of love!"

I was somewhat confused, but wasn't that what Ada and her poet uncle loved to do anyway?

"These two friends, who have not been able to stand each other for years, finally age and become grumpy old retired men. And naturally, one of them dies. That's when the the other starts to feel the absence of someone to badger. Someone whom he has known since childhood, whose good and bad sides he is very familiar with. Someone he has trusted and looked out for, despite all the taunting, dogging and bickering. Another equally important point is the security which comes from knowing that the 'other one' is always there, in spite of all the immature horseplay. It is because love's nature is childish that the one who's left behind misses terribly the one who parted…"

She fell silent and looked at me longingly, as if she were the one left behind. (Or maybe I just imagined it.)

"You know Mabel, that is the true reason why no one wants to grow up!" she whispered.

Her voice shimmered like moonlight on Kuzguncuk's waters.

This girl's going to be the end of me! No matter how much she co-opted her uncle's words, both her and her uncle were born storytellers, and I had been assigned the part of listening to them in utter fascination! (It's not as if I never secretly wondered whether this was a misfortune that held back my own talents. For I have observed that living with people much more talented than himself can often stall the developments of someone with mediocre talents. But no, I prefer to follow this brunette path, not because I am submitting to fate or kismet, but because I am keenly aware of the pleasure it provides me.)

"So, my Uncle Dogan says that this relationship between the two old men, which certainly smells of acerbic vinegar from the outside, tastes like honey to their palettes, and is definitely a kind of love!"

"Definitely" no less! After all, does not the immediacy of Dogan Gokay's poem stem from the challenge posed by this boldness? And doesn't the defiant beauty Ada inherited from her uncle sway to the breeze of the same climate?

I had not liked this definition.

"Oh, so do all married couples who fight constantly and can't get a divorce also fall under the category of 'a kind of love?' Just because Uncle Poet said so…"

She knew very well that I was talking about Merich's parents.

She puckered her lips, opened her hands to the sides as if to say "it's not my fault," and shut her eyes. When she closed her eyes, all the greens, all the yellow and brown lights vanished off the face of the earth. Must have been because of the blue in green, because even the various shades of blue faded away.

"If you ask him, yes!" she said, reopening those gorgeous brown eyes, and reinstating all the lost colors back to the face of the earth.

"According to him, there are hundreds of different kinds of love. Every feeling, be it boring old habit, or passionate obsession, is a type of love…"

By then I was conscious of how she sometimes packaged her own thoughts in glittery words, and sold them to me as if they belonged to the poet Dogan Gokay. And whenever she saw it fit, she related her fantasies as things that actually happened to people. She was sharp enough to know that I was on to these brilliant tales, (I can't call them lies!), which as a child I believed in word for word, but this was only one of dozens of games between us. Furthermore, these games, which I knew she did not play with anyone else, had a clandestine taste for me.

"As you know, my dear Mabel, uncle Dogan always wants us to regard the world from a cosmic standpoint. When you look from above, with a bird's eye view, the relations between all things can be discerned much more clearly, of course…"

It was the middle of May, school was nearly over, and summer had begun to peek around the corner. The backyard garden of the Baylan Patisserie was opened, and there could be no better messenger of summer. The garden was almost dim from the overhanging vines, but this dimness worked like natural air conditioning during the summer heat.

It was Ada who had taught us about this hidden backyard garden, open only during the summer. The Kadikoy pier, which is the true naval entrance point into Istanbul's Asian side, and Bahariye shopping center has always struck me as depressing, uncared for, and unsightly. I still imagine that someday the overcrowded, noisy and poorly planned Kadikoy will be given a square with abundant greenery, parks, and patisseries… I've never found the Kadikoy square to be as appealing as our Uskudar.

Once the weather had begun to grow warmer, Ada and Aras

started meeting in Kadikoy after school, and occasionally, mom allowed me to go along with them. I was in junior high by then, but being the little kid of the house, I did not get to enjoy the rights Aras had at my age. Ada thought my mother was right, I was still too young, and they of course were all grown up!

Aunt Cihan and my mother only permitted our forays to Kadikoy under the accompaniment of a taxi driver they knew from Kuzguncuk. In two years, the third military coup of the Turkish Republic's fifty-seven year existence would take place, and there was an incredible feeling of unease in the air. Like all parents, mine were also very anxious. Turkey was once again unstable and restless. The tension emitted by Dogan Gokay and my officer uncles Mustafa and Kemal, was the sharpest indication I had of the effects of political turmoil, which seemed like a game to us. I was confused by the cryptic comments of grown-ups, such as "what's going to become of us, tsk,tsk,tsk," or "I swear, the army should just move in, and show them!" Newspaper headlines and TV broadcasts were filled with dreary, dismal words. I was still a child then, and I am now trying to recall those years exactly the way I experienced them at the time.

Despite all the cautionings of my parents, Aras, with a bit of cockiness, came home after dark, did not tell them where he was going, and basically scared them out of their wits. He was also late for our meeting at Baylan Patisserie that day. Taking advantage of the situation, I was enjoying the feeling of being alone with Ada at a patisserie. I imagined that when I showed up alone with Ada, everyone would assume I was her sweetheart, leaving me to experience this joy, however short-lived it might be. I have always detested the chasm between fact and fantasy!

While fancy is a multi-dimensional concept, harboring dreams, thrills, and promises of hope, fact only bears the three hard, solid, and angular dimensions of reality… Happy are those who have managed to weave their fancies into their facts… I suppose, you know me well enough by now that I don't need to repeat my admiration of the poet and his niece on this matter.

Ada had cajoled Aunt Cihan into sewing a hidden pocket in the backpack her mother had brought from abroad, and had started concealing her great secret in there. She now extracted a pack of

Maltepe cigarettes and a silver lighter from this hidden pocket. She had just turned sixteen and she was smoking like a chimney. I was annoyed at both her and my brother. I don't know which one had poisoned the other, but in the past few months they had both taken to smoking like age-old addicts. My grandfather used to smoke but he wasn't a heavy smoker. He used to say: "this damn thing is no good without coffee and a view on the side!"

Even now, whenever Ada smokes, I get overwhelmed with the worry that she is poisoning herself, that she might get cancer. But I keep it to myself, I can't tell her.

As we sat waiting for Aras, the waiter planted himself by our table and grew very insistent and aggressive that we order. Fearing his wrath, we decided to go ahead, and asked for Baylan's famous Kup Griye sundaes. Having taken our orders, the waiter continued to hover over and glare at us. Do waiters not like kids and youths? Years have gone by, but I still have not managed to become one of those heavy-tipping adults with bulging wallets whom waiters are fond of.

That was when we understood, the waiter was peeved at the fact that a girl "still in diapers" was puffing away nonchalantly. Although it did not seem that way to me, Ada must have "still been in diapers" to the waiter, who was in his thirties, but looked extremely old to us. He glared some more, and clicked his tongue in outrage. "Kids these days," are mostly irritating to the ones who preceded them.

Refusing to be put down, Ada immediately turned toward me and scolded me in a voice audible to the waiter:

"You're still way too young, Duna! You have to wait to grow up like me in order to start smoking!"

The waiter went away, mumbling.

Neither Merich nor I ever took up smoking. People who've never started strongly dislike the smell of cigarettes, and tobacco in particular.

By the time we began to spoon our sundaes enthusiastically, Aras was still nowhere to be seen, and Ada continued to think aloud.

"I think that the love uncle Dogan feels for Burkan is very different than the usual love between a man and a woman… Still, unfortunately theirs must also be one of the hundreds of different kinds of love..."

My god, she was only sixteen and she was lecturing me, a kid, on "the usual love between a man and a woman!" I sat, listening to her without knowing or comprehending much. Oh my dear little smug ruffian!

"Burkan is a beautiful lady, but she can't understand uncle Dogan!" she said, trying to lick the ice-cream off her lips, instead of wiping it with a napkin.

Ah-ha! Something had happened and Ada had begun to be jealous of Burkan.

"I think uncle should have married that woman, the French poet, who he can't stop talking about, the one called Brigitte... But it turned out that woman was a lesbian, so what could he do?"

"A lesbian? How do you mean..."

"Oh, you know, woman on woman..."

"Do women marry each other over there?" I cried in surprise, and of course everyone at the surrounding tables, including our waiter, stared in annoyance at the two kids who were discussing homosexuality.

Just then a very handsome youth entered the backyard patio of the Baylan Patisserie, his schoolbag tucked under one arm. He gave a luminous "Hello!" The whole patio brightened up. The girls sitting at other tables were either staring rapturously or nudging each other, giggling. I was used to this routine. Wherever my brother went, he would instantly attract the attention of all the women and the jealousy of all the men upon himself.

"Did you start?" he asked, as he sat down.

He had run because of his tardiness, and his cheeks were red. Pervin Gokay, who from the first had watched him admiringly as "our native James Dean," was right. Aras was as handsome as a James Dean picture printed a few shades darker. But my brother had another quality as impressive as the good looks and striking posture that made him appear older than his years. He had a maddeningly serious face expression, one that indicated defiance and unattainability. This was what rendered Aras supremely attractive! In my opinion girls were as aroused by his gravity as by his beauty. I suppose it goes without saying that since I was not very handsome and gave the feeling of an easy catch, I made no such impressions on girls.

Ada took a spoonful of her sundae and held it to Aras' mouth. Instead of eating the ice cream from Ada's hand, Aras took the spoon extended for him, and ate the ice cream himself. There are certain moments that can only be experienced between two people, in a split second. This was such a moment. (And I was condemned to live as a witness to many "such moments" between them!) Ada had wanted to show the surrounding girls that she was Aras' girl, and he had partially verified this. Like most people who are afraid of possessiveness, Ada was possessive of Aras secretly, but could not bring herself to make it known. And like all people who dislike being possessed, Aras was very wary, but strove to maintain a balance because he was scared to death of losing Ada. But most important of all, Aras was overly shy, and Ada a little too bold.

Aras lit a cigarette himself, and they sat facing each other, under a cloud of smoke. They smelled terrible.

"How was it?" asked Ada.

"Straight A!" my brother said dismissively.

"Ah!" Ada exclaimed in elation. "An 'A' in Algebra, 'A' in Chemistry, 'A' in Geometry, and now an 'A' in Physics as well…"

Then she reached over with a playful smile and stroked Aras' cheek. This must have been a warning to the girls of the other table who were still staring at Aras.

Aras, who I could tell enjoyed this caress, had regardless been unable to get over his shyness, and had turned his gaze on the ground, as if he'd dropped something. The sight of a serious and handsome young man remaining unresponsive to the touch of the honey drop brunette beside him was interpreted erroneously by outside observers but Ada had learned to read his soul a long time ago.

"The Physics teacher told me that if I manage to keep this grade point average next year, maybe they would be able to find me a scholarship in America," he said.

"Oh, that would be so wonderful! I'll come to America too, and we can go to college there together." Ada exclaimed.

"What about me?" I moaned in fear. My voice had the scream of a little boy who lost his parents in a crowded train station.

"Don't worry Duna, we'll come back when school is over!" Ada practically scolded me.

"But I don't want to go…" said Aras, completing his interrupted sentence.

Silence fell between us.

"So you're not going to go, even if you get a college scholarship in America?" asked a stunned Ada.

Aras hung his head and hid his eyes.

"I," he said gently, "I'm going to study naval production engineering at the technical university."

"America has first-rate naval engineering, stupid!" Ada snapped indignantly.

She was the quickest one to flare up among us, the one who showed her feelings most easily, and who forgave the fastest.

"I want to study as a naval cadet," said Aras in his gentlest voice, looking into Ada's eyes.

"You mean you're going to wear a uniform?" asked Ada, dumbfounded once again.

Aras nodded "yes." He was still looking into Ada's eyes.

You see, Aras had been this way since childhood. He would try to solve his problems by himself, to make his decisions and execute them on his own. Trying to give him advice meant accepting a fiasco from the very beginning. My grandfather could reach him through his parables, my mother through her praise, and so they managed to list their advice through covert means. With the exception of those two, Ada was the only one who could have her way with Aras. Ada does not have a special method for anyone. She is one of very rare, brave and lucky souls who can live as they are. Even this much of her uniqueness was enough to impress Aras, but most important of all, Aras admired Ada, Aras was in love with her.

The same thing had happened this time around. Aras had made his plans regarding the future, and arrived at his decisions. He was going to become a naval engineering officer and marry Ada. Was he driven by a longing for adventure, or our family's affection towards officers, I cannot say. But I think that the responsibility of being "the elder son of the house," and his realization that it was growing harder to live on my father's tailor income were the main reasons for his decision.

Aras had made his decision all right, but he was scared of Ada's reaction. Because the girl who adorned his future dreams was someone who loved her freedom just as much as him, who was just as independent and defiant, and who had just as strong a personality. My brother's period of making decisions alone was over. Just as we began to joke among family that he had met his match, and found another hardhead to toss heads with... that goddamned black disaster, that which never crossed our minds, was to fool us all.

"Then I'll go to America alone," said Ada in a hurt but challenging tone.

Aras had just started on his Kup Griye when he dropped his spoon.

"But you'd miss us there," he said with an earnest expression.

He spoke distantly, as if he were not included in this "us."

"Why does one of you have to go far away!" I whined.

"Youth is possessing wings to fly towards new lives and new worlds, says my uncle Dogan. He says, in a sense, life's dialectic makes this unavoidable!"

Ada had taken refuge in Dogan Gokay, the way she often did when she was in a fix. Really, sometimes Uncle Poet got on my nerves too...

"When we were kids it was so nice, none of us ever flew anywhere!" I whined again.

"You're still a kid, my sweet Duna," said Ada, turning towards me.

At that point she noticed me. When she did, an easy smile spread across her face. I had the effect of the happiness hormone on her. Aras, on the other hand, must have raised the level of her excitability and femininity hormones. Naturally she would not put it that way, but claim instead that "You are my seratonin, and Aras is my adrenalin and estrogen." It seems that since there is no single man who can produce the effects of all three on a woman, one man will always be left out, and women will continue to complain! Maybe someday a hormonal scientist will find a solution, or our code of ethics will experience a radical upheaval.

"Don't ever grow up, okay Duna?" she said, now openly lining her wounded voice with the sorrow she always carried around.

She leaned over and whispered in my ear:

"My only, darling Mabel!"

She was a young girl, sixteen years old, and she did not want me to grow up. Yet she was practically bounding towards adulthood and maturity. What made her seem older than her age was not only her naturally nimble wit, the speedy development of which Uncle Poet had contributed. The sexual aspect of Ada's relationship with my brother at the time had gone futher than I had imagined. Women are much more decisive and courageous than us men when it comes to matters of love and emotion. We men pretend to ignore it, but are in fact aware and secretly afraid.

"When school is over, we can go visit America together," said Aras as he started on his Kup.

This meant "I have thought it over and decided," in Arasian.

But my brother was still not a fluent speaker of Adaese.

Ada was silent for a while. The melancholy hazel lights glittering in her brown eyes were breaking my heart. I bitterly resented my brother when he caused Ada grief. Meanwhile, Aras, who knew that he had hurt her, but who was utterly clueless as to how he could make it up, was taking his frustration out on the ice cream. Never have I seen an ice cream eaten that fast.

Yet I knew. I knew very well how to calm Ada down, how to win her over. Not only Ada, but starting with my mother, I have always been able to win back the favors of every woman I have loved, and been loved by in return. I was not born as someone who cringes from apologies. There are hundreds of good ways to go about apologizing. (This sounds a little like it has been lifted from Uncle Poet's hundred ways of love, but if it is true, and if its close relationship with love is considered, is it not natural that apology too should have a plethora of different types?)

Nonetheless, my handsome brother, who was first in his school's karate and chess teams, whose genius in physics was often mentioned, who had managed to single-handedly decipher a foreign language enough to compete with Ada, and who was everycne's favorite, did not know how to win over Ada's heart. He did not have the skill!

Aras, who was so successful and strong, could not pull off something that to me was a piece of cake.

I could never understand this at the time. Children and people who never grow up believe in perfection!

"If you want, you can go to America, of course…" said Aras, biting his lips with the pain of having downed the huge sundae in a single breath.

Ada, who turned her wounded glance toward him replied:

"If I want to, yes!"

Oh Aras you fool, can't you see that the girl is crying out to be stopped? Who on earth believes the lie that women are hard to understand!

"If you want, of course…" mumbled my brother ineptly.

I was watching the two protagonists as if they were in a movie.

I was close to turning into Cyrano, writing out Aras' speech, and handing it over to him, but I still believed that my hero could overcome the difficulties on his own.

They looked at one another. They looked at each other with the still intact dreams of puppy love. They looked at each other beautifully. I must admit, I loved that look they exchanged enough to soar past jealousy…

"Don't go!" said Aras, straining as if he were accomplishing the hardest task in the world. Then he hung his head in regret, like a religious person who has sinned, and was thoroughly ashamed.

Ada did not reply, but it seemed that the subject was closed for the time being. Warm affection had replaced the cool sorrow on her face, which had been flaming with anger a short while ago. So, things were going to get rowdy after high school.

But nothing got rowdy after high school. A curse that had not crossed any of our minds descended upon us, and it altered all of our lives, even all of our futures. Every single one of ours!

It was time that I stepped on stage to save the moment.

"D'you know what uncle Dogan said, Aras?"

I will not ask anymore why some people are always assigned the role of "saving the moment."

"He hates my uncle!" said Ada, glad to have found a sheath for her hurt.

"Not at all, your relatives are all polite people," said Aras, making things worse.

"I don't understand, what did my uncle Dogan ever do to you?

He always says that you're a smart and proud young man, every-where he goes…"

"Dogan Gokay is a know-all, and an arrogant bastard!" Aras blurted out.

"Just like you!" Ada began to laugh.

Taking advantage of this miraculous laughter, I made another move:

"See, Uncle Dogan said that even if you get mad at him, the re-lationship between you two is a kind of love!"

"Whaaat?" yelled Aras. "You mean to say I'm in love with Do-gan Gokay?"

Ada grinned.

"No, silly… What my darling Duna means to say is that even if it contains hatred, every relationship that creates dependence or habit is, in a way, love!"

"Ridiculous! All this is ridiculous! And you guys believe this stuff… You two are really strange sometimes!"

Ada and I looked at each other. Enjoying the sense of being "us two," rare as it was, I took my fill of her brown eyes.

"Merich doesn't believe it either!" said Ada, trying to get on his nerves.

"Good for her!" said Aras, lighting another cigarette.

By now, the girls at the adjacent table, who had noticed our ar-gument, had fully green-lighted Aras, and were grinning at him overtly.

Aras did not like to play games on the subject of nearby tables and other girls. I do not at all think that this was because he was afraid of Ada, or feared losing her. Aras is a person of "black and white" phi-losophies, consistent, disciplined, and straighforward to a degree that would be considered conservative, or boring for some people. If he loves a girl, then all other girls are outside his area of interest.

"At school," he said in a vexed voice, "they're not too crazy about the poet Dogan Gokay. They say he's a 'communist lackey.' Be careful, both of you, when you're talking with others, there're all sorts of people walking around!"

"A lackey?" Ada bristled. "For one thing, my uncle Dogan is one of Turkey's most patriotic and realistic poets! He is one of the most fiery defendants of Turkish and the Republic!"

"It doesn't matter that I know, I just said to be careful. Because you two have a little difficulty crossing over from the world of dreams into the real world…"

"Let's go!" said Ada, leaping to her feet in anger.

The girls at the other table were making no scruples about their intentions on Aras. Ada could not have cared less. Aras had hit her where she was most vulnerable, and won this round with a knock-out. As she tried to stuff the cigarettes and lighter into her back-pack, it dropped to the floor and a book fell out.

"Are you reading *Aragon?*" he asked sweetly.

He had won the skirmish anyway.

"Yes sir, I am!" retorted Ada.

"I'd read Aragon's letters to Else," said Aras.

Aras went to an all-boys high school that was dominated by ex-tremely nationalist, fanatically right-wing views. His interest in the sciences was inborn. His interest towards literature, however, had sprouted entirely because of Ada. I only began to think my broth-er's interest in literature was not for show when Dogan Gokay told us that there was a serious relationship between mathematics and philosophy.

I was the true literature aficionado in the house. I used to read like hungry wolves. Initially my mother and my grandfather, and later Uncle Poet had encouraged me. Uncle Poet would give subtle advice as to what I should read. My love of books was an expensive one, but Ada shared all her books with me, and gave me some as presents. She was also the only one who knew I wrote poetry in secret.

Aras would occasionally look over my novels and books of poetry, and borrow them. But he returned them in such a short amount of time that even the possibility of his having read them would seem farfetched to me. I read slowly, underlining the sen-tences I liked, and writing notes in the margins. Later, when the time was right, Aras would suddenly make a casual reference and surprise me to no end. I have always admired people who read as fast as him and understood what they had read.

"Poems with a nice arithmetic and sound!" he said, as he held out the Aragon book.

That was it! Ada was hooked. She sat down in her chair. Her anger had already vanished.

"I'd made something for you," said Aras, taking out a dirty box from his pocket.

He gingerly opened the tiny little box, and what emerged was a little dog figurine made out of thin wire. It was very pretty. When inspected carefully, one could tell that it looked like Ada's Sivaskangal dog, Sivri.

Ada looked at Aras. Aras looked at Ada. Their eyes interlocked. I turned my head away, embarrassed. Thus I came upon the envious glares of the girls at the nearby table. I hid my eyes in the ivy that surrounded Baylan's backyard patio. The call to evening prayer begun.

"We should go, your parents will be worried," said Aras, as if our own parents would not.

As we were about to pool our money for the three sundaes, Aras, with a slight swagger, said "I got it!"

Aras was tutoring a freshman in physics. He was sixteen and he was earning money. We did not object.

We were leaving Baylan when I said: "So, that means my relationship with Ada is also a kind of love!"

They both laughed. I was the little brother of one, and the Mabel of the other, and I was never taken seriously.

Ada, who was holding hands with Aras, extended her free hand to me, and I took it.

"But that man says that love causes pain," giggled Ada, with the ease of someone who has never tasted that pain.

"Oh that know-all!" Aras teased.

"Maybe he's right?" I said, and they laughed at me once more.

We left Baylan, all three of us holding hands.

As soon as we got home I ran to the only Aragon book in my library and did no homework that night.

"You dream with your great
  eyes wide open
  I wonder what passes
  from your fancy, from your sight
  That country without a door
  without a permission for me to pass, is your kingdom."

I REMEMBER

"Death is the termination of the life force. If you unplug a radio, the music stops. That is just what death is like. Someday, in some place or another, a cord is unplugged and the energy current that was established at your birth is brought to an end. Life is terminated!"

"But that should not be all!" I said in angry protest.

My eyes were bloodshot from crying, and my face was swollen.

"My dear child, unfortunately that is all there is to it. We come and we go," said the poet Dogan Gokay, with a smile.

He was speaking as serenely as if he were immortal. That sage smile of his, which I had always admired, was beginning to get on my nerves for the first time. When that incredible understanding which comes with loving someone begins to wane, even trifles can be bothersome.

I got up from my seat to avoid seeing any more of the smile, went toward the window, turned my back to them, and hid my face in the garden beyond the glass.

"Just like theater," said Ada.

Her voice sounded distant and slow, like someone under hypnosis.

"We each have a part, be it small or large, short or long… We
might even have a leading role… But the play ends no matter what,
and then it's curtains…"

She stopped.

"And all our parts invariably come to an end."

I could not see them but I knew that they were nodding, the
way they always did when they agreed.

My grandfather's sudden death had affected me the most. I had
been unable to pull myself together for days. Even though he had
been having chest pains in the past few years, the fact that he had remained unailing and active had kept me from even the slightest
thought that he might die. A sudden heart attack, and he was gone in
a blink. Although at that point he did not hold as influential a position in my life as during my childhood, my grandfather was important to me. He had a special place in my heart. He was the first person
with whom I experienced the childish over-indulgence of knowing I
was always, under all conditions, right. There were even times when
he defended me against my mother. He was a talented storyteller
who sent me to lands of fantasy with the way he expertly fashioned
fact and fiction into memories. When he looked at me he rejoiced for
the future of the world which he had never lost faith in, and pined for
the long lost relatives whom I reminded him of. Despite a great fondness for Istanbul and Kuzguncuk, this romantic Plevnian tailor, like
most aging immigrants who've spent their childhood elsewhere,
missed his native land and settled on me as his "Blue Danube." He
was a person who knew to enjoy life, who could preserve the past
without burdening the present. Anyway, why am I recounting all
this? What's the need for so many words? That old man with the generous heart was my grandfather and now he was gone.

"You're talking like textbooks!" I yelled. "But I'm not a page in
a book, don't you see!"

"That's because, my child, a fire burns the place where it falls!"
said Dogan Gokay in a soft voice.

He got up from his usual easy chair in the mansion's living
room, and approached me.

"Death is like a *mucerret* scent which cannot be detected unless it is released in one's proximity. Of course now you're going to ask me what *mucerret* is... Oh if only we could have modernized our language without impoverishing it... Anyhow, *mucerret* means abstract, intangible... Whenever the time comes and it befalls someone close by, that's when one can sense death's smell. It is a thick, dusty, heavy smell like that of a room which has not been aired out for a while, and it afflicts a person... until..."

"Until what?" I swivelled around.

Even I was surprised at the hostility of my voice. Uncle Poet went on, without losing any of his politeness or composure:

"Until the human brain takes charge of the situation. By then it is time to return to life and convert pain into sorrow. The human brain releases chemicals that cause one to forget the pain, and it even makes a person happy enough to laugh out loud. This is the only way to retain one's sanity. The saying, 'you can't die with the dead', is so true because it expresses what I have just told you."

"But this is unfair!" I protested. "How can you expect me to forget my grandpa? I can't stop thinking about him. I even remember little incidents and details about him that I had not thought about for years, everything I had forgotten, I remember it all, all over again!"

I had gotten out of breath. I stopped.

"I'm always remembering!" I moaned.

I was the one who was really being unfair. Ada and her family had been as close and helpful to us as if it had been their own grandfather who died. Sureyya Mercan had personally attended the funeral prayer and the burial. They had had *helva* sent to all the neighbors and provided a reading of the Qoran. Both Pervin Gokay and Sureyya Mercan had come over to our house to offer my parents their condolences, and to have a cup of our coffee.

"In some situations, the ability to forget is a blessing, my child! Yet unfortunately some of us have not had their share of it... Those of us... we always remember!"

He fell silent and the brown eyes behind his glasses were lost in thought. I tried not to wonder who he was remembering.

"Your grandfather, the Plevnian tailor Muharrem, was a venerable man. He was a tolerant, intelligent, educated person," he said soon afterwards, quickly concealing his recollections.

He had only met my grandfather twice. In one of these, the conversation, music, and overall good time emanating from a gathering my grandfather held with what few peers he had left had reached the mansion. Sureyya Mercan, who had a weakness for the sound of the tambur, for Turkish classical music and for a table of meze, had dragged his brother-in-law over to our house and been immediately embraced by the elderly group. Even though Dogan Gokay, bearing an amiable smile, had remained slightly left out of things, he had managed to win over my grandfather after I went to sleep. The next morning my grandfather declared:

"Well, the artist father of that wily girl is a fine fellow. He's a man of the people, upon my word! But now, that girl's uncle, it turns out, is a very learned gentleman. I didn't even know the half of it... Bah, he almost knows my Plevna down to the very streets! He's never even been there, m'lad! He tells history, but as if he's been there himself, such a story he makes, pine honey drips from his lips, god bless him! And he's so modest that I grew embarrassed myself, believe it or not! He's a patriot, admirer of Ghazi Pasha. He's nothing like what they said, good for that poet!"

In the days following, my grandfather asked me to read Dogan Gokay's poetry. He was very pleased with the ones about the War of Independence, and about folk legends.

"Anyhow, your grandfather did not forget to leave us fond traces of himself as he left..." said Uncle Poet to me, and smiled.

Ada had also come over to my side. All three of us had gathered before the window of the mansion's living room. It was summer vacation, the heat had begun to grow oppressive, Ada's family was soon to leave for their summer house and Aras was to enter the college entrance exams that summer.

"My father," said Dogan Gokay, letting out a sudden laugh, "The story goes that my father was unable to resist the famous buttercream of Marash, where he was sent as an inspector of the Ministry of Education. He downed an entire pound of it in one sitting. A pound of buttercream, and what with baklava and borek at the side, naturally he keeled over on the spot! Hah hah ha!"

Now this was going too far... Was this man entertaining himself with his father's death?

"You are so insensitive, Uncle Poet!" I heard myself shout.

Insensitive?

Dear god, what did I say? Was it the poet Dogan Gokay, whose poems had touched thousands of people, whose fine, emotion-laden metaphors had been popularized in song, who was insensitive? Suddenly I grew very ashamed. I grew incredibly ashamed. I felt weak and hopeless. The more I brooded on it, the more miserable and frustrated I became. Everything was closing down on me. I was not able to stand it any longer, and began to cry.

Ada, who was waiting by my side as if for an emergency, immediately took me in her arms. I, in turn, hugged her tightly, the way I had wanted to ever since the day I first saw her, and drenched her cheeks and arms with tears I somewhat enjoyed shedding. Embracing her fueled the torrents within me rather than calm them. Embracing her did not pacify me, hugging her did not tranquillize me. If she had been a queen, she would have sent the king who returned to her, drunk with his own victory, right back on the road for new conquests. She was one of those people who arouse, allure and elude, and whose charm is partially mired in this mystery. Capturing her was not only difficult, but also merciless, for it was absolutely clear that she would wilt and disappear as soon as she was caught. Brunette Ada was never meant for men who seek relaxing, soft, and calm breezes in a woman. I myself was too young to be certain of what it was I sought.

When I raised my head, I met Ada's melancholy brown eyes. Large hazel eyes that looked on with love… She never looked at me piteously, or protectively. In her gaze I always read the subtitles: "I will remain by your side, I will understand you, but I will not belong to you."

"My darling Mabel!" she said. "This will all pass, we will all get through it together, believe me, together."

Together meant: you, me, Aras, and the poet Dogan Gokay. Maybe that was not what it meant, and I had misunderstood things from the start…

Since she had called me Mabel, I gathered that we were alone in the living room. Uncle Poet had left us by ourselves. Perhaps in hurt or anger.

"I have to find him, I was being absurd! What have I done?" I said, as I wiped my face with the paper napkin Ada handed me.

"Don't worry, he doesn't take things like this seriously. He knows how sad you are."

"It was like he was making a farce out of it... like he wasn't at all sorry..."

"Yet it was Uncle Dogan who is said to have been the one most devoted to his father. He was unable to pull himself together for months after his father's death. Plus my grandfather did not die from eating buttercream or baklava or anything like that. My mother says it must have been stomach cancer. He was taken ill while on an inspection to Marash, and was returned to Istanbul. He was admitted into a hospital, and died there two months later."

She stopped and bit her lips for a while.

"He's trying not to take his fears and sorrows seriously, Mabel, try to understand! In the end he's a human being like the rest of us... He hides his fears and pain in books... He writes and places them on a shelf. My mother says he is a 'man like a saint,' but... would Burkan agree, I really don't know. Burkan must be the one who knows him better than all of us..."

I could not figure out whether she had uttered this last sentence in envy. If she wants to, Ada can also conceal herself very well.

"My grandfather knew he was ill, but he refused to be treated," I said, as if in a trance.

"That stubborn old Plevnian grandpa!" said Ada, smiling.

She was trying to prevent me from breaking into tears again.

She put her hands on her hips just like my grandfather, (I cannot bring myself to say dear departed grandfather) and she mimicked his voice:

"Look here my gentle girl, you wouldn't know yet, but when the water is spoiled, every wittle thing is spoiled, see... Here the water is spoiled, the sea is spoiled, the rain is spoiled. We poisoned our waters, my girl... 'ow can water be sold in bottles, I ask you? You see what a state we've fallen to my wittle one! Bah, they say that even the Danube is spoiled, but this heart can't bear to believe it! Ah, ye great River Danube! Bah, bah, bah!..."

She was funny. Ada is still funny. She can still make anyone laugh whenever she wants to. I laughed. Smiling, we looked at each other. We were alone in the living room. Suddenly I saw us as two adults who, years later, were looking at one another in the same living room. Ada had grown up into a young woman and I had become a young man. We were mournful. I could not understand the reason, but I was seeing us both distressed, years from then. She was trying to make me laugh, once again, but we were sinking back into sadness. Her face had not changed much, her eyes were the same. A shiver came over me. I was more unsettled by the frightening, heavy charge of emotion in that scene than having glimpsed a picture so clearly snatched from the future. I closed my eyes in order to avoid seeing any more. I reopened them to the voice of Ada saying:

"Hey, look over there!" It was still the beginning of that summer. She was seventeen, and I was fifteen. It was a long time before that future which had appeared so suddenly before me. I breathed a deep sigh of relief.

When I looked over, I first saw Dogan Gokay, who was in the midst of a very merry chat with Uncle Hasan the gardener. Then I caught sight of my brother, who had sworn not to enter the mansion from the garden gate, jumping over the garden wall with a model airplane in hand. Before you could say "this can't be happening!" Aras made a smooth landing right next to Uncle Poet. I could not hear them but I was able to see how uncomfortable Aras was in the situation. There was someone else who saw it as well:

"Come on, hurry, let's save Aras!" said Ada, as she dashed off to the garden.

Save Aras? Nothing could be worse! This had to be the worst excuse someone who was Aras' sweetheart could give to run to his side! (Ada is a human being too after all…) Even during the time of my grandfather's death, Aras had not revealed his sadness, or as Ada said, "he'd suffered alone, like a wild beast."

Now I was left all by myself behind the window. There they were! My smart, handsome, strong brother Aras, ready to conquer the future… Dogan Gokay, still attractive, confident, famous intellectual poet, favorite among women, and a great figure of envy in literary circles…

And of course her…

It would be unfair to use words such as "beautiful", "cool", "dizzying" or "gorgeous" to describe her. You might only come close if you said that she was as different as something out of this world, striking as a comet, addictive as well brewed coffee, defiant as a silkworm, and unique because she was sent alone to this planet. Hers is a thoroughly steeped and pervasive beauty. But most important of all is her charm, which attracts me like a strong magnetic field, and her colors: the contrast between her fair skin and dark hair, the lovely Mediterranean warmth in her eyes. There is Ada between her uncle and her boyfriend, utterly aware of being loved, assured of her magnetism, wearing flourescent lingerie made out of happiness… shimering…

They were standing only a few feet away from me. Very close by. Aras, uneasy at having been caught jumping over the garden wall, Dogan Gokay enjoying himself at having taken "the young stud" prisoner, Ada endeavoring to reconcile two men she loves dearly. They were standing very close to me, only a glass wall between us. A very thin, glass wall. Nonetheless they, those three, on the other side of the glass wall, having long forgotten me, and I on the other side of the glass wall, all alone… And without even a grandpa…

My first vivid moment of utter loneliness and pain coincides with that particular day. It was the first time I had caught those three so far away and myself so alone. My initial reaction was very natural: a desire to run away from them all! Why should I stay there any longer? I had to run away, hide, and experience the feeling of desertion, which was compounded by my grandfather's pain, on my own. I turned around sharply, prepared to dash off. But I was unable to run. When I turned around sharply I bumped into something solid and that thing fell to the floor.

"Merich, I'm sorry… I didn't know you were here…Are you okay?"

She was holding her bleeding nose and smiling at me from where she had fallen. During the time I was thinking of my vast loneliness, Merich had been standing right behind me…

I helped her up, we went to the bathroom, washed her face, pinched her nose until it stopped bleeding and waited. While doing this we had perched on the side of the bathtub. All of a sudden Merichch leaned her head on my chest and closed her eyes. I hugged her, thinking it was the natural thing to do. (Why natural? Do you hug everyone who leans on your chest?) Then, out of the blue, she started to cry. I was puzzled as to why she had started crying when I hugged her, and not when her nose bled, or when she got hurt. Some of my girl friends at school were cry-babies, but I was completely unaccustomed to a calm, quiet girl like Merich crying this fervently. In order to console her, I began to stroke her hair. Her hair was blonde and soft as silk. This pleased me greatly and I continued to run my fingers through it. What's more, this was the first time I was stroking and consoling someone rather than being the one who was being petted and put at ease. This also pleased me. Just then another utterly unexpected thing happened. Throwing her arms around me in a flash, that shy, retiring Merich kissed me on the lips. Her lips were soft and delicious, and she smelled wonderful. My face started to burn and throb, and the fire spread across my entire body. There was a girl at school who flirted with me, but since my mind had always been on a certain brunette girl, I had never laid a hand on anyone else. The rotten part of it was that since the girl was my brother's sweetheart, I could not lay a hand on anywhere but her hand. So, Merich was the first girl I'd ever kissed. (I suppose I should say the first one who kissed me…)

Since I had never considered her a potential catch, I was surprised, but also excited by the way her breasts stiffly pressed against my body. I responded to Merich's kiss with a sexual awakening which was late compared to my brother. She was biting and kissing me like there was no tomorrow, and crying intermittently. She was excited, agitated, impassioned.

We were kissing in the bathroom of the mansion with an enthusiasm that stemmed as much from my discovery of sexual arousal as from the fiery aspect of Merich's character which was so at odds with her usual timid, pale demeanor. Then Merich stopped abruptly. She grew embarrassed, hung her head, and hid her eyes.

"They're not right for us!" she whispered.

Her voice contained the joyful relief of having finally revealed a long kept secret.

I could not believe that the shy, quiet Merich had caused my first awareness of sexuality, in the form of a stiffened organ between my legs, and a fire drenched body. Perhaps I had subconsciously refused to experience this awakening as an affront to Ada. I don't know.

"Where the hell are you guys!" said Ada, rashly entering the bathroom. She was considerably shaken at discovering us sitting on the rim of the bathtub, practically glued together, with a somewhat guilty expression. She was shaken! She staggered, as if she had received a slap in the face.

"What're you two doing here?" she scolded.

Ada had never scolded me before.

She was still scolding Merich as she dragged her out of the bathroom:

"He's still a kid, don't you dare touch him!"

While I simply stood there not knowing what to do, I could hear Merich's sobs coming from inside.

Merich was crying, Ada was raging.

This is how I always remember my grandfather's death.

I remember.

EVEN IN MY DREAMS I AM MYSELF!

"Self-awareness is the only true proof of our existence."

René Descartes

"This soldier's dead!" said the old woman.

"No! No, Musa hasn't died!" cried Duna. "He can't die! He can't die because none of these goddamned things are real! Don't you get it? It's not real! Everything, but everything is a nightmare, a dream!"

The violence and fury in his voice was so terrifying and unstoppable that it made one's blood run cold. Even worse, he had begun not to hear his own voice. His face was pale yellow, his eyes were popping out of his head, and his body was extremely tense. He was tense enough to have jumped a few feet in the air or killed whoever stood in his way at the slightest noise. His glasses were covered in dust, his uniform was soiled.

"I'm sick of explaining it, but you still insist on not understanding! How many more times do I have to tell you? Look, there's nothing to fear, alright? I said, alright?" he yelled.

Frightened, the old woman took a step back.

"Don't you worry, this goddamned war, this violence and hatred is wholly a revenge of my cursed subconscious! Okay? You understand, don't you? Wait, have a little more patience... People born in this country are always waiting and enduring anyways... For centuries... God is Almighty! You know! God's will be done! Don't you move a finger, just keep silent and wait! Almighty God! Mother Nature, Father State! Great! You just keep on waiting! You understand, don't you? Well, keep waiting... This time just wait a bit until I wake up... We've all been waiting for centuries anyway!"

He was out of breath. He paused and then whispered as if to himself:

"If I could wake up, oh if I could just wake up from this godforsaken sleep... If I could wake up right now... We'll all make it through this nightmare. Every one of us... You, me, and all the other characters in this nightmare."

Then he turned to the old woman:

"You understand, don't you?" he chided.

He was met with incomprehensive but piteous eyes.

"If you understand, then why're you looking at me like that? Huuuh?"

He leaned toward the woman menacingly, but she did not seem to be very intimidated.

"Ah, my poor boy! They got you bad, child!" she said, slapping her knees, and moving her lips fast in inaudible prayers, after which she would blow into the air.

At that moment, hearing a child's voice coming up behind him, Duna noticed the presence of a hard object pressed against his back.

"Ma, this soldier's nuts!"

Turning around, he saw a dark, clever looking boy of about ten with unkempt and unruly hair.

"Stick 'em up! I'll waste you right here!" yelled the boy in panic.

The boy was holding a gun, and it was not a toy.

"Alright, alright, relax! We're not watching cartoons here, okay? Don't you start being Robocop or anything! Drop that gun, you might get injured or something... For God's sake, don't make me have to deal with you too! I don't like guns, even in a dream... Come on, drop that gun little guy!"

"Shut up, soldier! I'm not little, okay? This gun ain't no dream, it's loaded. Now start marching!"

Duna winced with exasperation.

"So, I guess we're starting all over again..."

"Cut the crap, drop your gun and walk inside... Don't dillydally, I won't take no pity, I'll waste you!"

That was when Duna noticed that his rifle was slung over his shoulder. He took it off, placed it on the ground and, walking through a nearly dark courtyard, entered the house.

"You must watch a lot of movies. Action movies, of course... I wonder if TV brought anything else to Anatolia?"

"Cut the crap soldier, march!"

"Yeah, I know. You won't take no pity, you'll waste me!"

He took off his boots in a small entrance, and entered a room covered with a kilim. The boy stood behind, watching and training a real, loaded gun upon him.

"Get over there and sit on that sofa!"

"Hold up boy, hold up my Ali. Leave that poor soldier be. Can't you see, his mind's flown away to other places, poor wretch." said the old woman, catching up to them.

"Here, soldier, you lie down on this here sofa. God will grant us speedy deliverance, *inshallah!* Don't you ever lose your faith in God's unity, my son, come here, lie down just so..."

Duna anointed his wounds with handfuls of the compassion in the woman's voice. He obeyed meekly. He stretched out on the sofa which bore a cotton flower print cover, and immediately passed out.

When he woke up, he found himself in the same house, lying on the same sofa. Furthermore, the light was still dim.

"Goddamnit!" he shouted.

"Maa, the loony soldier's awake, and he's cussing!"

A table had been set on the floor, peasant-style, and a red teflon pot in the middle was emitting tantalizing vapors.

"They still eat on the ground. I guess the Anatolian peasant still hasn't managed to rise up to table level!" he grumbled as he rose from his seat.

Then he saw the gas lamp which spread a dull glow, and which was covered with a hand-made doily.

"Are there still villages without electricity in Turkey? Where the hell am I?" he yelled, frustrated.

"Maaa, the loony soldier don't know where he is!"

The old woman entered the room, holding three aluminum spoons and steaming flatbread.

"Don't worry, child, you're among good people. No harm's gonna come to you from us," she said, and sat down cross-legged at the head of the table.

"But where am I? What's the name of this town, where does it fall on the Earth's geography? Where are my glasses?"

"Come here, soldier child, come and have a bite to eat. Look, you're all skin and bones. You should eat a little so you can get strength. You'll find your place, your land, your way, your geography when you gain strength... First we tend to life... Here's your glasses, I took them off so they didn't bother you while you slept, and I cleaned 'em. So you can see better."

"See better?" Duna gave a small, mocking laugh. "Are you kidding? He had defective lenses fitted into my glasses specifically so that I could not see better."

"What kind of rogue did that?" the woman asked in indignation.

"Who else, my subconscious of course...My subconscious, that is, the thing that organized this nightmare... A part of my brain." he said, and put on his glasses.

The woman, now very saddened, shook from side to side and beat her knees.

"Ah, my poor child! What's this here war done to all of us... Oh my poor child!"

"Pain and fear keep growing, hate and anger snowball... And of course as a result, violence rears its head even higher," muttered Duna.

"It looks like you were an educated fellow too... I don't get some of the things you say but you speak well... Ah dear child! Come here, sit down, have a bit of soup. Here, son... Don't you lose your faith, my boy, these hard days are gonna come to an end, with the blessed creator's permission, they'll end soon."

Duna felt dizzy when he got up, and stumbled. Then he quickly sank down at the table. But he could not sit comfortably. There had to be a way to sit at the low table. He observed. The woman had crossed her legs. He tried to do the same, but his legs, which through generations had become used to eating at a table, were not very skillful in executing this maneuver.

"I wonder if my mother's folks also used to eat on the floor?"

"Come again?" the woman asked.

"Oh, nothing... I'm talking to myself..."

"It'll pass my boy, *inshallah* you'll recover soon..."

Ali also joined them. He tore a piece off the flat bread and began to munch away. The warm smell of the bread quickly spread across the room.

Even though he suffered physical difficulty in filling his stomach, which sat cramped in his contorted body, Duna's hunger proved victorious, and he practically attacked the homemade porridge which was eaten from a communal pot in the middle of the table.

"You'll forgive us, there's not much provisions left in the house, so whatever God granted us…"

"No really, it's very delicious. I haven't had homemade food in broth for a long time."

"Good for you! May it cure your ills, dear boy!" said the woman in a friendly voice.

"Maaa…" cried a boy from the other room.

Duna froze. For the boy was drinking soup right next to him.

"Ma, this soldier's moaning! Looks like he's waking up, ma, quick, c'mere!"

"Musa?" said Duna, leaping to his feet in excitement.

He had long forgotten his friend.

Upon entering the adjacent room, he first came across another boy who looked like a twin of the little Ali. He also held a gun and was standing guard before a window tightly covered with a black curtain. This boy was two sizes smaller than Ali, he must have been around seven or eight years old. He might have been older, but since Duna's glasses made it impossible to see clearly, this was his best guess. Then he saw Musa. Lying half naked on a wide bed, Musa was missing half a leg! The knee on his amputated leg was tied with a white, bloodstained bedsheet. He was semi-conscious, and moaning.

"What did you do to Musa?" cried Duna. "Where's Musa's leg? Murderers, butchers, monsters! How did you cut off the man's leg?" Then, violently biting his own hand, he began to cry.

"My god, what's this torture for? Why do you let this nightmare go on? Why can people be so cruel to each other?"

The old woman attempted to hold Duna by the arm and calm him down. But her attempt triggered an unexpectedly harsh reaction. This time Duna flew into violent rage, started to threaten the woman and scream like a madman.

"With what right, what authority? Who are you? Surgeon, judge, or God? What do you think you are, huh? Would you muti-

late your own son like that, huh? I want an answer! I want an answer to all my questions! I want justice! Goddamned fools, I'm sick
of all of you, understand? Sick!"

Ali's younger brother, who had raised his gun toward Duna, was struggling to protect his mother. Yet the woman did not seem to be much affected.

"Hold on, son, don't go gettin all crazy 'gain... Alii, quick son, bring some water for your uncle soldier, hurry my Ali!"

The woman seemed completely calm, composed, and certain that she would succeed in pacifying Duna. Pulling on his arm with a strength wholly unexpected from her small frame, she forcefully sat Duna down on the sofa and almost poured the harsh, tasteless water brought by Ali down his throat. She pulled off his glasses, and splashing handfuls of lemon cologne on the still trembling young soldier's face, revived him with her large peasant hands. Her hands, which had raised who knows how many children brought forth by a womb unacquainted with contraception, which had stroked and battled the soil for years, exuded a sense of healing that both surprised and soothed Duna, who felt as helpless as a motherless child.

Duna came to his senses when the sharp alcohol of the cologne burned his eyes. The scent of lemon reminded him of someone.

"Nesim!" he wailed.

"Oh Nesim! Where are you Nesim? Where are the philosophies we thought would improve the world, where's the new, brave, civilized world? They silenced you, and they're making me into someone else Nesim! I'm disappearing Nesim!...Nesim...They're numbing me... They're going to continue this nightmare until I become an insensitive, accustomed, apathetic being... Nesim!"

"Don't you fret, son, dearie!" said the old woman. "Every night has its dawn. Providence won't arrive until the subject despairs!"

Then, sitting down next to Duna, she patted his back and began to sing a hymn. Was it Yunus Emre? How doleful, how soothing her voice was... She stopped and quietly began to recite prayers. Actually she was whispering something with fast moving lips. It was impossible to hear the words. Yet, judging by the peaceful expression on her face and the mystic, barely detectable sway of her torso, Duna supposed that she was praying. He remembered the prayers his grandmother Mrs. Murshide, and his grandfather Master Muharrem recited, believing that they would protect him from any harm. The safe and happy childhood days… Isn't that the port one takes refuge in at any moment of strife? Only if one has been fortunate enough to experience such a childhood, of course.

They remained this way for what seemed to him a long time. Duna was appeased. He noticed that he did not feel as helpless as before.

He turned around and looked at the woman with a critical eye. The woman was not at all as old as he had thought. She gave the impression of an old woman because she was unkempt, tired, and covered with layers of clothes. She was dark skinned, plump, and had hazel eyes. Duna decided that she would look no older than forty-five if she lost a little weight, put on a woman's outfit, had her eyebrows slightly trimmed, and had her white hair, which poked out from underneath the carelessly placed floral print gauze on her head, dyed and combed.

"Forty-eight, tops!"

She must have been a strong, able, level-headed and smart woman who was only stuck in the identity of "ma." Since there was no one else in the house besides her two sons, she must have been the one who cut off Musa's leg.

"This must be a characterization of the 'Anatolian Woman' whom my grandfather called 'the Ottoman Woman,' and my grandmother called 'the Turkish Woman,' " he thought.

Suddenly he became aware of what he was thinking.

"Were you the one who cut off Musa's leg?" he jumped up in bewilderment.

"I began cutting when my man went into the army…" said the woman in a voice resigned to its fate. "At first 'twas chickens and roosters, then even sheep. I took a look at that friend of yours, that fine soldier strong as an ox, he was almost a goner… that leg would do him no good… I sharpened our sheep knife, and calling God's name, I cut it off. The leg was rotten, all torn up anyway."

In order to cheer up Duna, who, mouth agape, was watching her in amazement as if listening to a science-fiction story, she added: "Don't you worry, now! I buried the leg in the garden, in the appropriate manner…"

"This is really too much…" whispered Duna. "An incredible imagination… My subconscious is exceeding my powers of imagination, I can't cope with it anymore." he added in stupor.

"And yet, the poor wretch burns like the devil… If his fever don't drop, this brave old Mehmet won't make it… I did all a subject can do, the rest is up to God!"

She stopped. Once again she said prayers through rapidly moving lips and blew in the air.

"Who knows where his mother might be, what prayers she says for her son… Curse this war and whoever started it… Is there any medicine left that we can give the poor soldier… To ease his pain and lower his fever."

"Where's my bag? Find me my bag!" Duna brightened suddenly.

"Give me my bag! There's medicine in my bag!"

His voice was trembling with joy.

"Alii, run and get your uncle soldier's bag… c'mon Ali, my tiger!"

Ali dragged with difficulty the backpack which almost equalled him in size, and left it in front of Duna. Then, lifting his gun, he said: "No games, or I won't take pity on you!"

"I know Ali, you won't take no pity, you'll waste me!"

He took out the antibiotics and painkillers Merich had left for him out of his backpack.

"Maybe we can save him! Maybe Musa won't die!" he said out loud. "In order to prove that this is a nightmare, he has got to live!"

Lifting up the feverish Musa with the woman's help, Duna tried to make him swallow one extra-strength antibiotic and two painkillers. He had never before considered how difficult it might be to get an unconscious person to swallow something. He had to wrestle Musa for a while. For years he had been under the impression that swallowing was a reflex, but swallowing and gulping were separate functions… Finally, by crushing and dissolving the pills in water, the woman succeeded in feeding them to Musa by the spoonful. Both they and the bed had gotten soaked from the water that dripped from Musa's mouth.

"God bless you, my precious son! Do you know what a good deed it is to save a life? God has commanded: 'thou shalt not kill!' That means he has said 'keep alive!' See, this here world is still afloat thanks to the goodness of souls like your own! Our country will be saved and salvaged, with first God's, then your help!"

Once again she closed her eyes, recited prayers with rapidly moving lips, and quietly rocked from side to side.

Duna discreetly extracted a white, elliptical little stone from his bag, stroked it, and deposited it in his pocket. He then returned to the other room, in the hopes of drinking the rest of the soup, but discovered that Ali's younger brother had made quick work of it. When their eyes met, he sensed that the boy was slightly embarrassed. He gave a huge smile, in order to put his little companion at ease. The jaw muscles of people who have not smiled in a while become strained in the course of this forgotten act. Duna's jaw grew taut and painful.

"What's your name?" he asked in an affable voice.

"Lutfu!" said the boy, chewing on his last mouthful.

Duna thought of how young Lutfu was. Then he tried to remember himself in Kuzguncuk, at that age. What a happy, lovely chilhood his had been... Ada, Aras, Uncle Poet, his grandfather, his mother, Aunt Cihan... The initial characters of his boyhood, the real strokes behind the development of his character... Yet these kids were not even going to have a youth to remember fondly, or to take refuge in during periods of strife.

Lutfu wiped his mouth on the tablecloth.

"Thanks be to God," he said as he rose, and went over to Ali who was keeping guard by the window covered with pitch black curtains. The two brothers exchanged vigils without a single word. Ali lay down on the sofa and quickly fell into a deep, childlike sleep. He had hid his gun beneath the cushion which he used as a pillow. Duna thought that he could make a good guess as to what he was dreaming about. When he lifted his head, he saw a portrait and a saz hanging above the sofa. The portrait was of the prophet Ali, and the saz next to it was hung on a nail by a fancy embroidered strap. The woman was clearing the table, when a great clatter was heard coming from upstairs. It was as if a heavy object had fallen to the ground. Footsteps followed. Duna, who had just sat down on the sofa leapt up.

"My rifle, quick, bring me my rifle!" he shouted. then he stopped and froze for a little while. "My god, is that me?" he asked sadly.

"Do I need a gun to protect myself as well?"

"We hid her!" said little Lutfu, and grinned, as if to say "so there!"

"Don't worry, it must be cats or somethin'," he then said, pointing upstairs.

"Oh, oh yeah, don't worry son, must be cats or something!" dismissed the old woman.

Ali, who had woken up from the noise, turned over on his side and fell back to sleep as if nothing happened.

"They're hiding something upstairs. There's someone, or some people who're hiding in his house," thought Duna.

"If that's the case, fine, I'll play by the rules…" he murmured.

He adjusted his wet uniform, cleared his throat, threw back his shoulders, and pushed back his glasses.

"The cycle of armament is a part of the civil war dynamic!" he said, finding his lecture voice.

Mother and son looked at each other in bewilderment.

"At first everyone becomes armed, the buyers and the sellers are both satisfied. In fact, this transaction is encouraged with official policies!"

Lutfu raised his free hand and turning it in the air, made a "crazy" sign. His hand was tiny. There was a mischievous grin on his face. Now he looked exactly his age.

"That is what a man called Hans Enzenserberger says, who wrote good books on civil war," continued Duna in a calm voice.

He knew by now that the role assigned to him in this nightmare was that of "dream lunatic."

"My name is Duna. I am a teacher. I am from Istanbul. I was born and raised in Kuzguncuk, which is a village on the Bosphorus. What is your name?"

The woman must have noticed that Duna, who suddenly began speaking like a "normal" person, addressed her in the polite form, so that she lost her self-confidence for the first time, and grew befuddled. Her existence, stuck solely in the identity of "ma" had abruptly emerged from anonymity, becoming personalized, and she was completely unprepared and defenseless on the subject.

"Our name is Hatice," she said bashfully.

"Pleased to meet you, Mrs. Hatice. Forgive me, I only got to introduce myself now because of the conditions we find ourselves in… I was wondering, if it's not too much of a luxury, could I have some coffee, a nice frothy, sweet cup of Turkish coffee? I don't know if it's asking too much?"

This time, with the unease of having been referred to as "Mrs.," the woman adjusted her head scarf, and straightened out the breeches she wore under her skirt.

"What luggusury, a guest's place is at the head of the house, my dear Mr. teacher son, but damn this war, we can't find any coffee…"

Duna noticed that he had suddenly leapt from the status of a crazy soldier into that of a guest teacher in the eyes of the woman.

"Hold on, now!" said the woman, her eyes flashing. "Let me fix you a quick chick-pea coffee…"

"Chick-pea coffee?" Duna made a face.

The woman laughed. Some of her lower teeth were golden.

"You won't even know it, Mr. teacher!"

"Are these people fake coffee merchants or something?" wondered Duna.

Duna had not noticed that the huge box covered with lace handiwork was a TV, and it was from within the closet on which it stood that the woman now produced a jar. The jar contained a blond flour that suddenly reminded Duna of the roasted chick pea powder his mother ground on winter nights and mixed together with sugar. That mystical flavored roasted chick pea powder, the crunchy taste of which Ada's nanny had tried to imitate, but never quite succeeded because she used powdered instead of granulated sugar.

The foamy mixture that Mrs. Hatice soon served in kilim patterned Sumerbank cups, highly resembled coffee. However it necessarily lacked the most crucial charm. It did not carry the smell of coffee; that greatest of smells, which entices, maddens with delight, and paints whatever environment it is introduced to with the color of pleasure.

He could not bear to hurt the feelings of the woman who waited without taking her eyes off him for his approval.

"God bless your hands, Mrs. Hatice. I guess it all depends on what you take it to be…" he said.

"Yea, that's right... What are you gonna do..." the woman sighed. "Well enjoy it, and may it be blessed as your mother's milk, my good hearted child. *Inshallah,* when this war's over you'll bring your betrothed and have some of my real coffee, and kiss my hand. You won't forget your Aunt Hatice my soldier son."

"When this nightmare's over...To explore these parts with Ada..." murmured Duna.

Suddenly he jumped up from his seat. He dumped all the medicine out of his backpack on the sofa. He was greatly agitated.

"I have to go, Mrs. Hatice! Make sure Musa takes these every six hours. He should drink some meat broth or something, he must have lost a lot of blood. Here, these vitamin pills contain iron, give him some of these also. I must leave right away!"

"Hold on, son, hold up a bit! Just when I thought you'd gotten better and everything... come on now, don't get all crazy again, child!"

"This nightmare has to have a point of exit, my subconscious must have a weak spot! It must! Who can know that better than me, huh? No one! I have to get out of this labyrinth, at once... I have to go and find Ada. The newspapers have declared her a murderer... You must have heard it already! The paparazzi undoubtedly are hounding her... Oh I absolutely have to find her!"

"I don't know what you're saying soldier, but know that I won't let you go nowhere before the other soldier gets better!" warned the woman sternly.

"But this can last forever, and I can't bear to wait any longer! I have to go back to Kuzguncuk, there're people there who need me!"

The woman laughed bitterly. Her gold teeth flashed once again.

"There's need for you here too, teacher."

She unwound the black floral print gauze which was plazed haphazardly on her head. Her gray hair, together with her long braid, was completely exposed. She then re-tied it around her head calmly, without the slightest hurry. She had wanted to show in this way that she considered Duna a member of the household, that is, the member with responsibilities: the man of the house.

"Now you too have to learn, Mr. Teacher son! You have to learn to wait, patiently, without falling into any black abyss. Like all the rest of us. You too."

"I wasn't able to call anyone…" said Duna, letting his arms fall to his side. "Who knows where and for how long I have been sleeping? They must be worried about me. Ada, Merich, Uncle Poet… And of course my mother… My mother can't bear another blow!"

The woman gave a deep sigh.

"Mothers," she said, as naturally as if she were talking of the wind, rain, sun, or soil, "mothers are the strongest souls God created in the world. The mother of every creature is the strongest among those creatures! That is God Almighty's law. Heaven is not under the feet of mothers for nothing!"

The tears that suddenly streamed down her face had begun to fall like rain on her skin which was dried from neglect.

"The greatest pain is that of one's child, may God keep it from my worst enemy! But, what can you do… Even if you have only one child left, you live, and take him under your wings."

The woman sobbed silently for a while, then sniffling, she spoke again: "In our creed, God does not approve of someone who doesn't protect other people's children like his own, my son… God says, 'do not come before me with mortal injustice.'"

Duna kept standing, not knowing what to do. He had no choice but to be soft-hearted in front of a crying person.

"Who knows how many sons she lost?" he thought tenderly.

"Stay here my soldier son. Stay, there's need for you in this quarter. If your friend gets better you can take him with you, if he dies you can bury him in the garden, next to all the others."

"Bury the dead? Next to the others? Oh dear god, what's happening to me? Why can't my dreams be like everyone else's?" he cried and sank down on the sofa.

Would he have felt the same responsibility if he had brought another wounded soldier to this house, a stranger, instead of Musa? Did a person bear responsibility for the lives of complete strangers? Ought he? If he did, then was this acquired, learned, civilized human conduct? Or were some born with this feeling of responsibility coded into their genes?

"God damn it, I'm no good," he cried.

"Even in my dreams, even in the utter fabrications of my own subconscious, I'm the same bleeding heart, the same responsibility laden blithering fool who holds other people's well-being above his own! God damn me to hell! And he did… he sure did! What else could He do."

"Hush, son, God will resent you if you keep talkin' bad about yourself. What is it that troubles you, child? Are you stuck on someone? Are you parted from your beloved? Why do you tear yourself up, this way? Why can't your golden heart find peace?"

Duna did not even hear her.

"If I just took off now, maybe this nightmare would end. Maybe I'll make it out of this cursed incubus… And not just me, you who have gotten stuck in my nightmare, you too will be rescued… Do you understand, Mrs. Hatice?"

The woman shook her head, to indicate it was hopeless.

"But what am I doing? Huh? What am I doing? Instead of getting the hell out, I'm staying here until Musa recovers! You know, Mrs. Hatice, Aras would never have done this! Ever! Aras would have found a way out of this nightmare long ago. He would have rescued both himself and Ada already. Aras has always been one of those people who know from birth when they need to get away! He would never have allowed pity to sway him from his path! For his name is Aras, and people always admire the likes of him!"

Lutfu, who was standing guard by the window oversized gun in hand, was staring at Duna and gesturing the "loony" signal, while Mrs. Hatice looked on with mournful eyes, and recited prayers.

"There, you've seen it yourself, you're witnesses! Even in my dreams, I cannot manage to be strong like Aras! Even in my dreams I'm a responsible, romantic, bleeding heart! Even in my dreams, I am myself!"

"Don't abuse yourself this way, my brave Mehmet. No soul can bear this torture you put yourself through, son!"

"You understand now, don't you?" Duna murmured.

"Do you also understand, Lutfu?"

Little Lutfu gave a fiendish laugh.

"Even in my dreams…"

Duna clenched his teeth. He took a deep breath. He was exhausted. He gently stretched out on the sofa, and closed his eyes.

Duna escaped in to sleep.

WHERE TO, ARAS?

"Dear brother, when are we going to build ourselves a raft and set sail across the sky?"

Ingeborg Bachmann

By the time I came along, he was living in our house like all the others; just like my mother, father, and grandfather.

By the time I arrived, Aras was already living in our house. I was the last one to join the family, and I had accepted the existence of the others like a natural inheritance, without giving it any further thought. The same way I had naturally expected them to love, protect and feed me... I was a child, and children have no idea of how the things they possess are earned. Childhood is beautiful when it is experienced in this manner!

Aras was one of them. He was, and would always be. I did not know what it was like to live without him, the thought had never crossed my mind. Why would it? He had come before me, he was there. He was stable, trustworthy, smart. He used to love me and look out for me. He was my older brother, and he would stay my older brother.

But that is not what happened.

Aras left one day.

All of a sudden, just like that, without giving us any notice, or at all preparing us for his absence...

Aras simply took off one day. For good.

Even his departure was befitting of his legend. Aras left in the exact manner of heroes. Handsome, young, and brave! Clever, talented and successful! He had done it again: even in his departure my brother had managed to be a hero.

Yet Ada was the one who had wanted to leave, while Aras desired to stay. And there were no signs to show that it was Aras who would leave for good.

Aras spent that summer trying to pass his exams. He had graduated from high school as valedictorian. He had earned degrees in inter-collegiate karate and swimming, and had become district champion in chess. He had won the military student examinations of the Naval Academy, entered the nationwide college placement exam, and was waiting for the results. His first choice in the college placement exams was the Istanbul Technical University Division of Naval Engineering. It was also his only choice.

Naturally, he could not stay idle while waiting for the exam results... He wrote to the student union of engineering at Michigan University, which is esteemed for its naval engineering department, slavishly read whatever he could find on the topics of sailing, battleship technology, and navigation, and did not, at times, know how to direct his intelligence which overflowed from his eyes and hands.

And of course Ada...

He and Ada had started to disappear more frequently and for longer periods of time. Ada seemed completely smitten by Aras, and Aras was ready to do anything to keep her admiration. Was this love, I don't know? Yet with a certain childish intuition, I had sensed all along that they both loved themselves more than each other. I have never been able to believe that Aras loved Ada the way I loved her.

Aras loved the interest and admiration of a girl who was difficult to please and capture.

Ada, for her part, was drunk with the attentions of a talented, courageous, and superbly handsome young man who had managed to win the adulation of a bright and lovely girl like herself. They, like all people whose egos are over-developed, mistook the reflection of their self-love as love itself. As I was to learn later, this was in fact the love experienced between equals.

Yet I loved Ada because she was Ada, exactly the way she was. I was born with the knowledge that loving someone means being able to accept their most terrible aspects, and even their shittiest, most frustrating qualities! In other words, one of those fools with under-developed egos! One of those born losers!

Anyhow... A person has to live with his character one way or another... That is why I still love Ada in my own way.

As for my mother and father, their pride in Aras was not voiced as in the old days. Even success can become a habit.

Whatever he tried his hand at, Aras was triumphant anyway. If he was entering a chess championship, he was bound to receive a degree, if he was going to take part in swimming meets, there was no doubt he would return home with out a medal. When I, who had never signed my name on any significant accomplishment completed a schoolyear with all passing grades it caused a celebratory air in the house, while the fact that models my brother assembled in a week found buyers for sizeable sums was greeted as casually as the air you breathe.

"Guess what name the Ottomans gave two British made Nordenfelt submarines after purchasing them?"

"Oh Aras, as if there were any submarines during Ottoman times..."

"Well, good for you Miss Ada, such fine ignorance at this age! The concept of submarines has been around since Leonardo's times, you know! Let's see, how long is that? Something like four hundred and fifty years... And then there's the Narval of 1899, and of course that was a very advanced submarine, decked with two boats..."

"Alright Aras, fine, I give up! God, I'm about to pass out, I swear! I don't want any technical details, just tell me what the name of the first Ottoman submarine was."

"Let me first remind you that the submarine assumed its true identity after the invention of the periscope, and was consequently begun to be used with military purposes during World War I."

"Aras, I swear, you're doing this on purpose! You're going to drive me crazy, aren't you? Just tell me the name of the submarine, you pest!"

"Among the submarines that were shipped to Istanbul for assembly, only one of them was completed. The nickname of that craft was Whale, but its real names were..."

"Fine Aras, I'm going to stop asking, and I am depriving you the pleasure of torturing me like this!"

"Wait, don't go, I'll tell you. Ada, hold on! Look, the names of the first Ottoman submarines were Abdulmecit and Abdulhamit!"

After he tutored a notoriously lazy high school student in physics for a handsome fee one semester, the kid had passed his examinations with a B+, and his family had roused the neighborhood by coming over with expensive presents and grateful words. My parents had sufficed by indicating their happiness with a modest smile on their faces. His name was Aras, and it was already worth a signature.

I, on the other hand, only two months shy of fifteen and constantly pronounced fourteen by both Ada and my mother, was still treated like a child– a fact that embarrassed me particularly when I was around Ada.

Perhaps I did not fit a traditional "male child" profile that would make my parents proud, but the traditional male profile had already started to change, starting from the cities. The usually traditionalist doormen pushing baby-strollers, and prototypes of the "socio-realist tough guys" who did not shy away from falling in love had all begun to appear in Istanbul during my time, although they were not in such profusion as today.

True, my avid interest in literature, books, and details were qualities not frequently found in the traditional male child. I loved to read poetry, and wrote some on the sly. I dreamt that one day I would gather up the courage to show my poems to the poet Dogan Gokay. I had no taste for sports, except for bicycling. And to me, bicycling was not a sport but a game.

I never sensed that my mother was dissatisfied with me. I was a healthy boy, I was interested in girls- and though this was the same girl my brother loved, it was greeted with sympathy because it gave my family a clue as to my virility. Plus, I enjoyed reading. These were sufficient for my mother.

I have to admit that even though she never hinted at anything of the sort, I suspect my mother of having loved me as the daughter she longed for after her first son. Perhaps I am being unfair, since I am ignorant of what they call the most harrowing of affections: filial love, and incapable of comprehending the maternal ability to love one's child no matter how talentless or how much of a failure he may be. I don't know! I still cannot say. In the end, I was much more different than an "Aras project" for my family.

Who knows, maybe it was all in my head... Maybe, just like

Franz's father Hermann Kafka, my own father (and mother) never nursed great expectations of me because they thought I lacked certain important qualities.

Meanwhile, the question of where I got my alarmism rests in my personal DNA archives as another region of my genetic blueprint that has not been brought to light.

Aras' gleaming future looked to me like the wide, neon-lit avenue of a North American city. No one doubted that he would be able to accomplish his goals. Success gains importance when it is attained in the direction of one's desires. We looked at Aras and were able to see that he would become the successful naval engineering officer he wanted to be. My mother had taken to calling him "sweet Jordan almond" after the nickname given to naval cadets in their white uniforms.

No one, save for three people, had any reservations about the future of Ada and Aras. Ada's mother was one of these people, and another was her younger uncle. Pervin Gokay, who knew her daughter very well, was aware that she had not grown up with the aspiration of being a wife who accompanied her officer husband to various seaside towns in order to attend social events and raise children. Ada had never been a girl who dreamed of passing under outstretched swords in her bridal gown, or of six storied wedding cakes that released a flock of doves. I would learn later that Merich was the one who had grown up with such fantasies.

Pervin Gokay had always been sympathetic to her daughter's interest in Aras, and had never once dwelled on the fact that he came from a lower social class. We were all certain of that, since her husband was the same way. Pervin Gokay is a confident, educated, and genuine enough person not to be bothered by things such as social status. Her qualm was that the future Aras planned might be too narrow and constricting for Ada.

The poet Dogan Gokay, on the other hand, entertained different worries, probably because he knew Ada's independent and defiant character as much as his own. According to him, Aras presented a traditionally conservative male profile despite all his fine qualities, and therefore inherently lacked the ability to love a free-spirited, modern woman for a long period of time, and to share his life with her.

When I came in from the garden to pick up something from the mansion's living room, the two siblings continued their discussion without a pause, perhaps because they still considered me a child, or due to another reason I was too young to understand at the time. These talks had begun after Aras' graduation, and the adult laughter that followed cute tales of puppy love had by then been replaced by the anxious overtones of serious discussion.

I was the third person who had doubts about Ada and Aras' future. Mine was mostly personal. Typical Duna worries like what would I do if those two left my life, and the like.

Except for these three people, everyone else was caught up in a fairytale. Sureyya Mercan, who was an incorrigible romantic, had already begun penning the speech he would give at his "honeygirl" Brunette Ada's wedding. My mother, who was not to be outdone, was dizzy with not only the joy of expecting happiness and success for her elder son, who was her greatest achievement, but also with the fact that her in-laws would be great stars of Turkish Cinema. Merich was silent, but I was sure that she eagerly awaited their marriage. Merich waited silently.

As for my father… My father did not know how to express his joys, or his sorrows, and he made no effort to learn. My father worked, slept, read the newspaper, ate, and watched TV. Whether he did anything besides these my mother must have known, but when I tried to read her body language, I began to doubt this as well. For many years I could not decide which one to feel sorry for, my mother or my father.

In fact, that was to be the last summer of our childhood. Aras, who was going to be a college student, would not hang around with us much any longer. Next year it would be Ada's turn to go to college, then Merich, and finally it would be my turn, and the gate of childhood would be closed behind us forever. I had surmised that that summer would occupy an important place in our lives, but I had not expected it to change our lives completely. No one had!

In those years Sureyya Mercan's "Fisherman Osman" movies had been converted into a TV series, and were being filmed overseas. His wife and daughter sometimes accompanied the actor who frequently went abroad for the shoots. Upon their return to Kuzguncuk they would bring us presents and photographs from countries like Egypt and Morocco which sounded far away, mysterious and exotic. Those were the final years of Turkish Cinema, when the venerable institution struggled in its death throes.

In contrast to Sureyya Mercan who was experiencing a rejuvenation of his artistic life with the popular character of "Fisherman Osman," Pervin Gokay had returned to her initial pursuit of stage acting. If she had accepted the offers of mainstream theaters she could have lined her purse with the seats her famous name would help fill. But she preferred to perform Chekhov in repertory playhouses and at the same time manage a textile studio she co-owned with Burkan.

It was hot. That day… It was hot the day Aras left. Because the heat in the garden was oppressive, we were in the cool living room of the mansion. Sureyya Mercan had just returned from a movie shoot in Athens. He was telling us about how he got along with the Greeks.

"The only difference between Greek and Turkish cuisine is that they have a twentieth of the variety our dishes have! Other than that, everything else is the same, my dear fellow! Wondrous flavors! Honestly, their ouzo is simply a sugary kin to our raki!…Ha hah ha!"

Dogan Gokay was sitting in the easy chair, watching his brother in law as if he were a movie, and inserting historical footnotes where he deemed necessary, with the modesty of someone who has just recently, and by coincidence learned the facts regarding Greco-Ottoman relations.

Burkan and Pervin Gokay were discussing new clothing designs on plans they had spread out over the twelve-seat dining table in the further end of the living room.

Merich was in a corner, playing guitar as timidly as if she were committing a misdemeanor, Ada was standing by the phone, waiting for Aras to call, and I was standing by Ada, trying to keep her from growing too anxious.

Aunt Cihan frequently entered the living room to serve either cold, fresh lemonade or homemade ice cream.

At one point Merich came up to me and whispered something in my ear. I did not understand.

"Can you c'mere a minute, please..." she said, tugging at my hand.

Aras had gone to a Galatasaray soccer match at Ali Sami Yen stadium, and had promised to telephone Ada when it was over, but he still had not called. Ada was restless, I did not want to leave her alone and pay attention to Merich.

"Instead of being a whiner, I should have gone myself," Ada was grumbling.

They had attended some soccer games together, but it could not be called their favorite activity.

"Duna, c'mere, I want to tell you something."

I could not go with Merich because I was unwilling to desert Ada.

Just then Aunt Cihan, her eyes wide with terror, ran into the room.

"Anarchists have set off a bomb near Gayrettepe! Ma'am, is the game in that area, God forbid?"

We all froze for an instant. The poet Dogan Gokay was first to recover.

"Did you listen to the news, Nanny Cihan? Where and when exactly did this bomb explode?" he said, rising from his seat.

Ada had grown deathly pale, I immediately grabbed her shoulder with one arm.

"Don't be afraid, nothing will happen to my brother!" I said, afraid.

Sureyya Mercan turned on the TV, cursing at the anarchists, and Pervin Gokay, with a maternal instinct, ran over to console her daughter. I was thinking of my mother. Dogan Gokay first called the Milliyet newspaper to obtain information. Then he called Cumhuriyet and Hurriyet.

"He's here, look, there he is!" cried Merich, taking us all by surprise.

And looking out, we saw Aras, as he jumped over the garden wall and made his way toward the mansion. Aras was alive. Nothing had happened to my brother. Everyone let out a deep sigh.

"God must have evened his debts!" said Aunt Cihan, her eyes filled with tears.

"God spared my son-in-law for his loved ones!" gushed Sureyya Mercan in his most exaggerated theatrical voice.

Aras, who was none too pleased with the attention lavished on him, had not even heard of the explosion. He had left his friends in order to call Ada, but seeing the long lines for the public phones he had jumped on a bus and headed straight to Uskudar. Then he had run all the way to Kuzguncuk from Uskudar, and he was completely out of breath.

"Have your friends also arrived at their homes safely, I wonder?" inquired Pervin Gokay.

"Musa the grocer and Sefer the baker's son…I'll go see right away if they're home."

Ada, now calm, as if it had not been her who just a minute ago lost pallor from grief, was asking Aras about the final score of the game.

"Duna, come here a minute, I have something to tell you!"

Now I had time to listen to Merich. Now that Ada did not need me anymore… Now that Aras was with her.

"My mom has fully recovered, Duna. She's going to be discharged from the hospital next week," whispered Merich elatedly as she ushered me out of the living room.

Merich's mother had been initially treated for depression, then for alcoholism, but these treatments had been stopping and starting for years. I knew nothing about her mother except for the fact that she was a former Turkish Airlines hostess named Merih. Also Merich had once showed me a photograph. In the picture a very pretty woman and what then seemed to me an old man with unruly hair were sitting next to one another. The woman was holding a very blond baby in her arms.

"My mom has finally accepted that my dad won't come back to her. This time she's getting better!" she said.

I was not so convinced, but I did not want to hurt her feelings.

"I'm very glad," I said politely.

"She wants to live with me once she gets out of the hospital, but I don't want to leave Kuzguncuk."

"But your mother needs you, I think you should move in with her."

"Yes, but… if I don't live in Kuzguncuk, I won't be able to see you…" she said, lowering her head and almost pulling her fingers out of their sockets.

"You go to a boarding school anyway, Merich. You can visit the mansion on weekends, like now…You should help your mother!"

I did not know whether I said this to get rid of Merich, or out of genuine compassion.

"Hey, what's goin' on here?" said Ada who, having long ago regained her usual naughty, know-all emotional state, had appeared by our side.

"We were talking," said Merich.

"Forget about talking, let's go take a walk by the seashore. The summer's almost over, we won't be able to find evenings like this anymore… So don't come complaining to me later! Alright?" Then she added in English: "Let's go folks!"

"I don't want to walk, you guys can go," said Merich in a wounded voice.

"Oh, give me a break Merich, liven up a little! Come on, stop acting!" said Ada, shutting her up even more.

Well, it would take Merich a few days to get over that.

"Aren't you coming yet?" said Aras, also materializing by our side.

"Aras, you should tell mom you're back or she'll be worried about you."

"No problem, bro! On my way here, I whistled while passing our house."

Aras had a particular six-note whistle. This whistle was known throughout the neighborhood, and communicated special messages between his friends. Ever since he was a boy, my mother has always followed my brother's location by this whistle.

"Oh yeah, Duna, I bumped into our Rozita's Nesim on the way. He sends you his regards. His first choice is Bosphorus University Social Sciences… He said 'let's meet one day and remember Grandpa Muharrem.' I wanted to tell you before I forgot," said Aras.

"Come on, Atacan brothers, you can talk on the way. Let's move, people! Mom, we're going to tour around a little! We'll be around Ismet Baba's place. We'll be back for dinner. We'll eat here, won't we kids? Alright alright, let's get out of this 'mature folks' home!' "

It was nearing evening. It had not grown dark yet, but colors had gently begun to fade, and the sun was making preparations to set. Merich must have hidden in some corner, having judged that joining us to be another unfulfillable task. Aras and Ada were too difficult for her, and I was in orbit around those two.

The three of us set off. The weather had cooled down. Since almost everyone in the neighborhood regarded Ada and Aras as "betrotheds," they walked around hand in hand without the slightest hesitation, enjoying the opportunity to exhibit their love. As for my existence, it legitimized their relationship and added a moral dimension.

We were telling ridiculous jokes and laughing. After a while we found ourselves by the Fethi Pasha grove. We sat underneath the trees and chatted some more. Aras was talking about a Playboy magazine they had found in a boy's desk last year. While they were looking at the naked women in the magazine, the assistant principal had busted them, and given them all a good smacking, but as he left he had taken the Playboy and placed it neatly in his briefcase. My brother related this event with guffaws. Ada must have found it very funny too, for she was also laughing. They were sitting hand to hand, knee to knee, and sharing their laughter. I felt like getting up and taking a stroll. I stuck my hands in the pockets of the corduroy pants my father made, pulled back my shoulders, and walked away. They did not even notice I was leaving.

When I returned they were not there. I called out but received no reply. It had grown darker and colder. Suddenly I felt afraid. They would not have taken off without me. True, we were not very far from home, but mine was not a shiver of fear. It was a shiver of loneliness!

I entered the grove and trod on the leaves which had slowly begun to fall. Soon I heard soft murmurs. After a concerted effort, I recognized them. They were right there and they were making love. I sank to the ground. I stayed, not knowing what to do. I wanted to run away, but could not. Suddenly I thought of how Ada's naked body was touching Aras' naked body, how they were kissing each other's ears and putting their tongues into each other's mouths.

Perhaps my brother was touching Ada's breasts, smelling her neck, stroking her back, kissing her knees, biting her feet and perhaps... No, no, they can't go that far, I thought, trying to console myself. Because that would cause Ada to become pregnant and... Oh my god, then I would be the uncle of Ada's baby!

A person should either correct a painful situation or get away from it. Unable to do either, I was writhing in pain. I was just like Merich. I strongly desired the mutual love of the person I loved, but I did not think myself worthy of her. And the person I loved loved someone else more than me!

It was for this reason that while my brother and my imaginary lover were making love, I sat frozen nearby. All of a sudden I grew cold, overcome by a violent shiver. It was not very cold, but I was trembling like I had been left naked in the Arctic Circle. My teeth were chattering and I was shivering furiously. Turning around in the hopes that they would not hear me, I saw a pair of cat's eyes in the dark. It was an incredible scene. Ada had seen me in that gloom, and the flash in her eyes was more wildcat than human.

She came over to my side, tugging at her clothes, trying to get dressed, and gave me a hug.

"Are you alright Blue Danube?" she asked.

Just then Aras appeared at our side, grumbling. He was also trying to get dressed.

"I think he has a fever," said Ada, looking at me anxiously.

"Duna, man, have a little resilience forgodsake! You're supposed to be a guy!" Aras chided. I already knew that I could not be the kind of brother he wanted.

"C'mon, let's go home so Duna doesn't get sick," pressed Ada.

"Look little brother, you have to fight fire with fire! Why don't you and I jump into the sea over there aways, take a quick swim-you'll be better in no time!"

"Let's go home!" I said, shivering. "Who'd think of swimming in this weather, Aras?"

"Don't be so lily-livered, man, girls like strong boys, don't they Ada?"

"Oh Aras, cut it out..."

"If I jumped into the sea from here, wouldn't you like it?...Huh?" grinned Aras.

We started to walk, I was still shivering, Ada had taken my arm. We had descended down to Pasha Pier.

"I can dive in right here, and swim back!" said Aras once again.

There was a challenging, territorial tone to his voice, yet all the territory was his anyway. I simply did not understand it. I was not even fully conscious because of that goddamned shivering fit.

"You can do it, Aras, dear!" said Ada proudly.

Aras immediately began to undress. He gave me his t-shirt, and tying his sneakers, the famous "Converses," by their laces, he hung them over Ada's shoulder.

"Aras, don't jump!" I cried.

Aras pinched Ada's cheek. Ada smiled at him flirtatiously, and my brother ran towards the sea. He took a blind dive.

"THUMP!" was the sound we heard.

That's it! We did not hear anything else.

THUMP!

The sound of a hard object hitting another hard object.

That's all!

Aras was never again!

Aras jumped and ended.

"He died quickly!" said Doctor Aret. "Painlessly."

Afterwards, they said Ada was "in shock," and took her to the hospital.

Aras had departed painlessly at eighteen.

Ada stayed in the hospital for days.

I was left holding Aras' t-shirt.

My mother did not cry at all. She first let out long, high pitched screams, and then began beating herself.

When three large men were unable to restrain her, the doctor gave her a tranquilizer injection. Thus slowing down, my mother started to wail in a language I had never heard before. None of us had known that my mother had learned Georgian from my grandmother. The neighbor women crowded around my mother.

Ada's parents spent the night by their daughter's bedside in the hospital.

From that day on, my father never talked again. My father fell completely silent and his hair turned gray overnight.

I was left standing around, holding Aras' t-shirt.

After leaving the hospital, Ada went into seclusion in the mansion for months. I was not able to see her for a very, very long time.

I sat next to my father for a while. He had fixed his eyes on a point in the rug, and simply stood there. The neighbor women were holding a vigil over my mother in the bedroom, and cooking the ceremonial helva in the kitchen. Our door was open, the whole neighborhood was walking in and out of the house, bringing food, and conversing in whispers.

There were police cars parked outside. They were inquiring and investigating, whether it was a suicide or homicide that had lead to Aras'…

Ada dropped out of school the following year.

Everything was like a bad movie. Or a nightmare. Either the movie would end, and the lights would come on, or I would wake up. I was watching the people moving around me like a character in slow motion. I was dazed. I was numb. It was my own body that moved, but I was not really inside. I had been stripped of my body, walking around as an observer.

I went to our room, still clutching the t-shirt Aras had entrusted me. I handled the books on the desk. He had left the one called "Submarine Boats" open. I touched the model ships. I rifled through his notebooks. I waited. I waited for him to come up behind me, give me a powerful punch on the shoulder and say, "Hey bro, have you quit reading poetry and taken a shine to mechanics?"

"You can never understand someone else's pain!" the poet Dogan Gokay had said.

Feeling a hand on my shoulder, I swivelled around elatedly. Merich threw her arms around my neck, buried her sweet smelling head in my shoulder, and began to sob.

At last! Someone was crying at last.

I hugged her and also began to cry.

As the pain inside me turned into tears and flowed out I felt somewhat relieved, and revived. But Merich was still crying floods. It was as if Aras had been her brother, and not mine.

I wiped her face and massaged her hand with lemon cologne. I brought her a roll of toilet paper to blow her nose. Soon we laid down on Aras' bed with our clothes on, and hugging each other, escaped into sleep. It could not be called sleep. We just passed out intermittently, that's all.

I frequently woke up to Merich sobbing. I would hold her and kiss her cheek to calm her down, but she only wept harder. Why was Merich weeping? Because she would lose me entirely to Ada who was left alone after Aras' departure? Was Merich crying for her future or for my brother's passing? I still can't say why the sweet smelling Merich, leaning her wet nose on my chest, was crying.

That night, Kuzguncuk did not sleep.

That night, a part of me left together with Aras, disappeared completely.

That night we all lost something.

A piece of our future, a huge chunk of our hopes and cheer.

After that night, nothing was ever as good as it had been.

Nothing!

Oh, where to, Aras, where to, in this way?

A week later the college examination results arrived. Aras had won his first and only choice.

TEMPORARY MIRACLES

"Regard yourself with love, for once; you are the essence of the universe; you are man, the apple of creatures' eyes."

Sheik Galip

"He's not strong enough to live, and he doesn't want to die!" said Duna in a melancholy voice.

"You must be patient, son. An impatient man either ruins his own head or becomes a clown!"

"How much more patience can one have, Mrs. Hatice? I've practically turned into a well of patience. My whole life has passed, waiting in patience... See, I have been waiting in this house for three whole days."

They were eating flatbread and drinking unsweetened tea. There was no cheese, jam, or honey left to roll inside the bread, nor sugar to add to their tea.

"For five days," corrected the woman. "You've been passed out for the last two days, child. How weary you must've been, to sleep so soundly... And I kept quiet, so that souls might find peace..."

"Five days?" mocked Duna. "You don't say? You're pulling my leg Mrs. Hatice, aren't you, thinking 'this one's already weak in the head?' Oh my god, keep me sane!"

"God forbid! Why would I do a thing like that... But see 'ere, when you said 'my God, keep me sane,' that was a smart word or two, Mr. teacher! Your mind's sure grown bigger than your size, and believe me, it keeps gnawing away at the other... 'Course, that much brain for a man all skin'n'bones like yerself is too much, and they keep squabbling away... And you're the one gets wasted in the process, child! Stop worryin' yourself like this, and let things take their course a little. In the end, God's will be done, anyhow!"

"I see you've gotten into the mood of this nightmare, and begun to talk like all the others Mrs. Hatice, huh?"

"God forbid… God forgive us!"

"So it's been exactly five days and five nights since I arrived at this house, and I've just been sleeping here for forty-eight hours, is that what you're telling me now?"

"O would I do that to you, dear child? Would I let you go hungry? We dripped soup and water and the like down your throat, and lemme see, my Ali took your arm and now and then took you to relieve yerself. Don't you remember nothin'?"

"If I did, I wouldn't be asking, would I?" snapped Duna.

"You spoke and you struggled so much…you're even troubled in your dreams, son. Should we have you blessed or somethin'? There's no believing in spells and djinns in our creed, but what's befallen you? I just don't know!"

"That's very true that I am even troubled in my sleep, because right now we're in one of my dreams!"

"Tsk, tsk, God forgive you… Don't, child. Think of those who love you, those you love… Try a little to get better for that Ada or Adalet, whatever she's called, your wife or your betrothed or somethin'…"

"Ada's not my wife!" Duna retorted once again.

"It's no business o' mine, but… you seem real sweet on that girl."

"Yes, so I am!" said Duna, getting up in an attempt to pace around the room, exhibiting nervous tics. But he grew dizzy from the sudden movement and leaned against the wall.

Averting her eyes, the woman pronounced more prayers and blew in the air. Then she got to her feet and cleared the teacups. Heading into the kitchen, she left him alone.

After some time she called out from the adjacent room:

"Get over here, teacher son, come an' help out your good friend a bit!"

They had done this several times since Duna had woken from what the woman claimed to be his forty-eight hour long sleep.

Duna would lift Musa up by the arms, prop him up against a pillow, and the woman would spoon feed him soup, like an infant.

"He's not strong enough to live, but he doesn't want to die..." Duna repeated.

On the whole, Musa was responding positively. His fever had receded, yet he could not manage to regain consciousness or pallor. He would occasionally open his eyes, look at Duna, and produce a half-smile. Duna was doubtful that the smile was meant for him.

During the process of feeding Musa, the soup that dribbled down the corners of his mouth fell on the bed and on the under-shirt he was wearing. Presumably with the contribution of summer heat, the house stank of sour soup, urine, and sickness, but it did not seem to bother anyone except Duna. The woman and children had accepted the situation, as if they had always lived under such conditions, and had even grown indifferent to it.

According to Duna their lives consisted of only three elements: to live in fear, to make do with what they had, and to wait! To assert oneself, to show one's differences, and to ask for something more, something better, were still considered forbidden and sinful... And of course, above all: waiting! They waited, forgetting the reason and purpose of their wait... So long had they been waiting that if they were given a life of abundance, freedom, and fearless-ness, they would not have known what to do with it.

"A human society that has not erased terror and quiet passiveness from its genes cannot thrive, Mrs. Hatice!" Duna blurted out, suddenly. "How can a person be productive who has not learned self-confidence? Huh?"

"Now you stop your babbling an' listen to me," said the woman, who did not seem the least bit taken aback by Duna's words. "Look, this Musa friend o' yours is near good a son of mine, but since it's inappropriate for me to do, you're gonna take care of his toilet, cause he's started eating food now."

The bed where Musa lay was covered with an oilcloth from the waist down. No matter how revolted or nauseous he might become, it was up to Duna to attend Musa's bathroom needs. When he realized that the woman, who was waiting with her eyes turned away, had assumed the harder part of the task by washing the soiled sheets, he felt awed once again by her courage and self-sacrifice. Ever since he arrived at their house, he had wondered what had happened to this woman's husband and other children, but had been too hesitant to ask.

Just then he thought he heard music. It sounded as if someone was playing the saz and singing in a doleful voice.

"How nice it would be... I'm eager for any music, no matter what kind," he mused, and tried to forget the voice he thought he heard.

Yet he continued to hear the music. He turned to the woman, who was busy spreading a clean sheet and oilcloth under Musa, and asked animatedly:

"Do you hear it too Mrs. Hatice? Isn't someone singing a folksong upstairs?"

For the first time the woman grew angry, very angry. She frowned and began to yell:

"What folksong, what tune? I don't hear nothing! I'm sick o' your craziness!"

Duna, who did not at all expect such a violent reaction from the woman, was taken aback. The music was openly going on, the voice was very clear, and it belonged to a woman.

"But I hear it!" repeated Duna cheerfully.

He practically ran into the adjacent room.

"See, it isn't there! The saz that was hanging here, right here on the wall, is missing. Someone upstairs is playing the saz and singing songs, or folksongs, or whatever it is!"

Ali was sleeping and little Lutfu was standing guard.

"There ain't no saz or anythin' else! Who's gonna play it? You've lost your marbles again, you're makin' things up!" admonished the woman.

She had placed her hands on her hips and furrowed her brow.

She was as fierce as a cornered cat.

"But there's someone upstairs!" said Duna, starting in that direction.

Leaping up the wooden staircase in twos and threes, he made his way to the second floor. The woman followed him, screaming madly.

"I said hold on, stop you scoundrel... There ain't nobody, stop you cursed fool! God, have we fed a snake in our house, hold on you miserable wretch, stop!"

Once upstairs, Duna flung open the first door he found, and came face to face with a young girl, frozen in terror. The girl was not older than seventeen. Her long black hair hung down to her shoulders. It would have been hard to find a picture in which naturalness, freshness, and innocence were better portrayed.

"If the Renaissance masters had drawn their blond angels in the Eastern Meditteranean, they would have produced this girl," thought Duna in a flash.

The simultaneous impact of hundreds of violent stories she had heard, and perhaps witnessed, created an abyssal fear in the girl's eyes. Duna, having never before met a woman who was afraid of him, became terribly depressed. As he was searching for words to comfort the girl, she broke down and started crying and trembling.

At that moment the woman entered the room like a furious beast, and throwing herself in front of the young girl, made a shield of her own body. She was out of breath, her eyes were aflame. It was clear at that point that she was ready to do anything.

"You can't touch my girl without takin' my life! Know that I won't let you put a hand on my doe, you monster!"

Duna could see the feelings of threat and fear being transmitted from the mother's body to the daughter's, and vice versa, as clear as electric waves. Threat was blood red, and fear was a bitter yellow color. These two emotions grew with every further communication, spreading throughout the room, and crushing all other emotions and colors. In the end threat and fear surrounded them entirely, and the air became difficult to breathe. As blood red and bitter yellow spread further, their eyes and nervous systems were the first to be irritated, and the room became rife with aggression. That calm, understanding, unpretentious, and fortitudinous woman had given way to some other savage person, who was prepared at any moment to mutilate Duna as if he had been a chicken, cow, or Musa's leg.

"This is unbelievable…I'm so sorry… really, so sorry…" Duna mumbled, devastated. "I'd just wanted to listen to music…"

Then he turned around, and muttering to himself, began descending down the stairs, with stooped shoulders and mournful steps.

"My god!" he moaned. "How did we all go collectively insane? Where did we lose our common sense? Why are we constantly afraid… from one another and from God?"

"Stick 'em up soldier!"

Ali had woken up, and planted himself before Duna, pointing Duna's own gun against him. Trembling like a leaf from fear and agitation, he was waiting for Duna to raise his hands. Little Lutfu also looked on with fright and curiosity. What really surprised Duna at this point was that Ali's puny child arms could carry such a heavy machine gun.

"I'll nail anyone who touches my sister! Awright, soldier? I'll blast you off this earth, I warn you! I have the power!"

Duna lifted his arms, surrendering to Ali. He could have died of grief.

"I'd just wanted to listen to music." he said.

All the letters that spilled from his mouth were a bitter black.

Using words to describe a scene imprints the picture into one's memory with a strength that the mere sense of sight cannot muster. Duna did this once more.

"You're part of Generation extra-X that has grown up with action movies. Your generation has nothing to do with the previous ones who loved Indians and hated Cowboys… But you should've been receiving an education on computers in school, or playing with your friends."

"What're you sayin' man? You nuts or what, God forbid."

Animated by his brother's words, little Lutfu was making a "crazy" gesture by turning one hand in the air, and reciting the rhyme: "loony loon, mad as moon, loony loon, mad as moon!"

"What I mean to say, Ali, is that," Duna started to explain.

Then he gave up.

"Forget it, this is all a nightmare anyhow."

At that moment Mrs. Hatice came down the stairs holding a long rope, and sitting Duna down in a chair, began to tie him up.

Duna was watching the woman tying his hands and feet to the chair, and the armed boy standing across from him, without the slightest resistance.

"You've gone out of your minds!" he said in a controlled voice. "You, who call me crazy, you're the ones who've really gone mad…

You think I'm going to attack a little girl, young enough to be my student, and you tie me up this way. This much fear is insanity!"

"Maa, is it true this soldier's a teacher, or does he make that up out of his head too?"

"How'm I to know, my Ali. One minute he talks all smart'n' proper, an upstanding man, the next he starts talkin' all sorts nonsense, throws himself around, denies everywhich thing, an' raves away…"

Then she raised her head and shouted, "Girl, c'mere! Both o' them are harmless now!"

She turned to Ali again, and said, "See, it's these types who change from one moment to the next, that I don't trust one little bit!"

"What kinda teacher are you, mister?" asked Ali, without wavering the gun he had trained on Duna.

"Literature," replied Duna, sitting with his hands and feet tied to the chair.

"What's that mean?"

"Stories, novels, poems, plays, and even fairytales. You could also call it the science of words."

"You mean you teach fairytales at school?" said Ali, laughing in surprise. He had smiled for the first time, two dimples appeared on his cheeks.

"Yea, it figures!" said the woman who had grown calm by then.

The young girl who came timidly down the stairs, was now inspecting Duna with a curiousity that had replaced the previous terror in her gaze.

"This one's real skinny," she whispered to her mother. "He ain't so big as the other one."

"She's seen Musa, she knows him," thought Duna.

Looking at the girl, he spoke in a friendly voice:

"The thought of harming you never crossed my mind in any way. I haven't heard the sound of music in a long, very long time… I've missed it so much… The music reminded me that I was human… I got very excited. It was like a miracle…"

He stopped and tried to move around in the thick grip of the rope that had begun to hurt his wrists.

"Just like life…" he said. "Life is a temporary miracle of our common sense that whispers to us when, where, and who to trust."

He stopped. He cleared his throat.

"Nevertheless, I'm sorry I scared you."

The girl was perplexed.

"I told you so, he's an odd one... Maybe not bad – tho I can't say now! But he sure is odd... All of a sudden he gets riled up, talks nonsense and rubbish, then he quiets down and turns into a good sort. You can't trust people like this, my girl."

Sensing that if he continued to say things the woman found "proper," he could manage to get out of this comical situation and the injurious rope, Duna forced himself to speak.

"My wife also sings, and plays the guitar," he said.

Yet he could not recollect any of the songs Merich used to sing.

"What's your name?" he asked, in order to gain some time.

"Sulari," said the girl shyly.

"Merich, my wife that is, has a beautiful voice. Since she's kind of a shy type, I can only get her to sing when we're alone, or in the company of a few relatives."

At the same time, he was cursing himself and thinking, "Damn! What did Merich used to sing?"

He was about to say "Beatles, Suzanne Vega, and Tracy Chapman tunes," but he stopped himself. He had to find Turkish songs. Honestly, did they not sing or listen to any Turkish songs?

"No, no..." he murmured. "For instance, she sings and plays Yeni Turku, Timur Seljuk, Livaneli, Sezen Aksu..."

"I sing Pir Sultan... We like folksongs, but I know of the ones you speak," said the girl smiling bashfully.

Her complexion, grown sallow from lack of sunlight, brightened up in pastel colors with this fleeting smile.

"There's a song," Duna immediately took up the conversation, "There's a song that my mother listens to with great sadness. The one that goes something like 'I miss my mother, my father, and my village...' Do you know it? When she came as a bride to Kuzguncuk, she says she used to miss her family a lot. Merich would play that with my mother on the guitar."

"Isn't your ma from Istanbul?" asked the woman, her interest roused.

"My mother's from Igdir. Around the region of the Aras river. My father's supposed to have fallen for my mother when he was on military duty in Kars. If you ask me, my mother is still a beautiful woman. She also has some Georgian blood, dark hair, dark eyes, and she's tall."

"So, an Anatolian woman," said the woman in a proud voice. "What's your ma's name?"

"Zubeyde."

"That's a nice name," said the woman, with deference, as if she were saying "nice to meet you."

"If you meet her someday, she'll thank you for feeding her son in your home," said Duna, taking the opportunity.

"No matter, anyone would do the same," replied the woman, and then lowered her head in embarrassment, so as not to see Mrs. Zubeyde's son, whom she had bound tightly with rope.

Before the woman lost her change of heart, Duna jumped at his chance, "Oh Mrs. Hatice, when're you going to untie these hands of mine, for god's sake? Look, my arms and legs are all numb! And my back hurts. Besides, what did I ever do to you that you tied me up this way?"

"Go on ma, untie this soldier! See, he don't look like a bad sort…"

"Hush girl! What d'you know of menfolk? They're all the same! They think of nothin' but flesh!"

"Flesh?" Duna exclaimed, his face contorting in disgust.

He felt like he was watching raw meat hung from the hooks at a butcher shop window.

"If you swear on your mother's head…" said the woman in an indecisive voice, "If you swear you won't touch my daughter on your mother's head…"

They were startled by little Lutfu's voice crying out desperately, "Maa, c'mere girl! Somethin's happenin' to this wounded soldier, girl!"

All except Duna ran into the room where Musa lay.

"Girl, bring me some water!" shrieked the woman in panic.

"Hold on, child, hold up, son…" she was saying over and over again.

"Quick, sister! Gimme that bottle. Hold that end, hold tight, now pull!"

"What's going on in there? What's wrong with Musa?" shouted Duna.

No one heard him.

"Why don't you speak? Come untie me! I said untie me!" he screamed.

"Don't let go, hold on tight!" the woman yelled.

"What're you doing to my friend? What part of him are you butchering now? Quick, untie me you barbarians!" Duna bellowed.

His voice sounded like the roar of a wild beast. He would have been shocked to hear his own voice. He didn't.

Suddenly the cries stopped, and a deep silence fell over the house.

"Now what? Is Musa dead? Speak, you fools!"

Not a sound could be heard.

"Untie me, I have to get out of this nightmare! I'm sick of this house, of this nightmare, and of you! I have to get away from all of you, do you understand me, you goddamned people!"

Then he threw himself on the ground together with the chair. He fell down heavily on his right arm. His arm hurt terribly, but he continued to crawl on the floor in anger. More correctly, he endeavored to drag himself and the chair. Just when he thought he'd soon arrive at the room where Musa lay, he bumped his head against a hard object. Everything went dark.

Not a sound was to be heard.

NEW LIFE

"*The new life is beginning. Alas, from now on I will hardly be free of trouble!*"

Alighieri DANTE
(New Life)

"Do you want sugar in your coffee?"

She shook her sideways to indicate "no." In Turkey we throw our head back in order to say a wordless "no," and shake it once backwards. In the process we usually lift our eyebrows and click our tongues. The gesture she had used to the same effect was a Western one, and to us meant "too bad!" She had recently acquired this gesture.

"What about milk?"

That pretty head shook sideways once more: no!

"You have to watch out for your stomach, Ada. You drink I don't know how many hundreds of cups of strong, black coffee a day. And you've increased your smoking."

She smiled wearily scattering sorrow all over the room.

It got on my clothes. I touched it. It was of a chestnut color.

"Thank god you're not the one studying medicine instead of Merich." she said in a tired voice.

"Your jibes don't hurt me."

The coffee cup was once more raised to her lips and its contents gulped down thirstily.

"Of course, Merich is too calm and untroubled to make jibes!"

"Thanks a lot," I grumbled.

Another melancholy smile. But a little more genuine this time, since she had succeeded in annoying me!

"When I was a kid I thought you'd become a poet, and Merich a cellist in a symphony orchestra…"

She drifted off.

"But…everything's changed so much…"

Merich had never played anything besides the guitar, and she'd decided very early on to become a doctor.

As for me, I am what they call a "closet" poet. It has been said for centuries that everyone born in this land is something of a poet anyway. That fall I was to start attending college as a literature student. Ada was so deeply lost in thought that the coffee cup had tipped in her grasp, and was dripping on the gorgeous Kayseri rug. I went over to her side. I took the cup gently from her hands and placed it on the table. I sat down beside her, put an arm around her shoulders, and stroked her hair. She leaned her head meekly on my shoulder. We stayed in this manner for a while.

"It's so hard to forget, Mabel!" she moaned.

"We won't forget, Ada. We'll learn to live without forgetting… We have no other chance. And what's more, we…"

Silence.

"We always remember!" she sniffed.

She could not afford to weep any more.

Suddenly she turned and looked carefully at my face. It was as if she were trying to recapture something she had glimpsed a moment ago.

"What is it? Why are you staring that way?" I asked.

"You've grown up, Duna," she said, smiling.

All at once I felt embarrassed.

Ada had been one of the two people who were most damaged by the loss of Aras. She remained in the hospital for days after that horrible accident, and did not leave the mansion all winter; she had sentenced herself to confinement. She did not socialize with anyone except her parents, her uncle poet, and myself. If you could call that socializing… She had dropped out of school. Everything she had previously delighted in was left out of her area of interest, which had been washed and shrunk in her tears. That winter, watching her sit beside me without a word, mutely holding my hand, I was terrified into thinking that after Aras I had lost her as well. And at that point I would have done anything not to lose her. Anything!

In early spring her mother took Ada to stay with a second cousin of theirs who had emigrated to North America. When Ada returned to Kuzguncuk a year later she began to see people once again, but she was melancholic and distant. My naughty, mischievous honeygirl who illuminated every road she walked on, had vanished. I suppose she had gone away with Aras. As for the Ada who returned from North America, she was almost a stranger.

I have to admit that after Aras left nothing ever fully regained its appeal. None of us were able to laugh to our heart's content, and the sun in our skies always remained eclipsed.

Her honey colored hair, which for years had hung down to her shoulders in a carefree manner, and which she used to brush back with her fingers, was cropped to ear-length. The relaxed bangs that accompanied her new hairstyle shadowed her forehead, making her look older and more mysterious. She had trimmed her brows and begun to wear earrings. She seemed to prefer black clothes for the most part. She wore tight pants, boots, and half-sleeved turtlenecks which had no resemblance to her mother's classic Dior taste.

For a few years she stuck to this style like a uniform, whether it was summer or winter, wool or cotton, black, gray or burgundy. Her neck was covered, her arms exposed.

Uncle Poet took one look at her and dismissed it by saying:

"Very avant-garde!" I did not care what it was, I had been bewitched again the second time I first saw her.

Ada had made an effort to alter herself completely, and had succeeded in her outward appearance. Even though I could not grow accustomed to her cool and serious manner which did not suit her at all, I was hopeful·because she was at least smiling and socially interacting.

In the beginning we were like newly acquainted youths. We talked of this and that and North America, trying to stay away from the letter A, let alone mention Aras' name. The only subject that cheered her up slightly, and even made her grow somewhat exuberant was photography. She had signed up for a private photography class in North America, and had dedicated herself entirely to the pursuit. Not only had she finally discovered a talent unknown to the rest of us, but that talent had saved her life.

First the private course had been completed, then photography journals had been contacted. From the vast quantity of samples she brought with her, one could see that she had been taking photographs madly, without time out for eating or drinking. By the end of the year three of her pictures had been accepted by a well known North American magazine, and had been published in two consecutive issues in the "amateurs" section.

When she said, "Just imagine, Mabel, I made money from pictures I took!" a gleam of joy flickered in her eyes for the first time since that accident.

Pervin Gokay wanted her daughter to receive a college education in photography, and strove with maternal ardor to convince Ada to this end. But high school had to be completed first. On the other hand, the poet Dogan Gokay argued:

"There can be no school or diploma in art. If the artist does not possess talent and work discipline, the rest is simply self-deception. Let her be. If she really wants to, and if she has the talent, then she will complete her own education!"

Sureyya Mercan's sole wish was that his "one and only Brunette Ada" should be by his side, and content. He would hug her and read her poems of longing in his emotional, overwrought voice, while both his eyes and his liquor glass always remained full.

Ada did have talent.

It was as if she was born with a microchip in her eyes, designed to capture the true, overlooked beauties and tragedies crammed into the nooks and crannies of everyday life. The microchip was called talent, and who knows in what branches of the family tree it had been planted.

"Can I have another look at those?" I asked.

It was nice to sit next to her on the sofa and stroke her hair, but the layer of mourning and grief covering us was suffocating. I had asked to look at her published pictures in order to change the subject and direct it towards her area of interest. She did not resist. She got up ponderously, and picked out the ones she wanted out of a pile of magazines lying on the coffee table. (Dear God, what torture it is to watch her "get up ponderously!" Ada did not used to get up. She would leap out of her seat and fly to her destination. Always leaving behind a rainbow, and feelings of admiration or envy...)

· · ·

First Photograph: The Hole in Love (black and white)

A major city avenue, lined with glittering billboards, where evening gloom is descending. A young couple, kissing passionately on the stairs leading down to a subway station. The girl's head is shaved, whereas the boy has hair down to his back. They are both wearing grunge. Jeans riddled with holes, patched, messy, dirty sweaters, ankle socks in high-heels, and combat boots. The young man has grasped the girl's head in his large hand, which sports the tattoo of a eagle with spread wings. The girl has one knee bent, and lifted backwards, exposing a little hole in the sole of her shoe.

She's scribbled a note in Turkish in the corner of the magazine: "'The Hole of Love,' or 'Love riddled with Holes?'" On the side, it says, f:2 8 1/15 min.

Second Photograph: The Guitar Case (color)

A bustling, sunlit avenue with towering skyscrapers in the background, where South American musicians clad in hats and colorful ponchos, their long black hair hanging down to their shoulders, are giving a concert. A crowd of people have gathered around them, and are listening contently. In the middle is an open guitar case containing change and a few bills. In front of the case a boy of ten, having noticed Ada's camera while in the process of throwing change into the case, has turned toward the lens with a startled expression, and a clumsy smile. As a result of this "awareness" the boy has become completely dissociated from the sounds and people surrounding him, has almost entered another dimension. The coin, caught in midflight on its way to the guitar case, looks like a blurry UFO image.

Under the page where the picture appears, she has jotted down in Turkish: "Oh, kiddo!" And next to it 100 ISO.

This picture had rattled us all, caused us to clench our teeth, swallow, and remain utterly transfixed. The boy in the picture bore a striking resemblance to *his* childhood! The boy was a spitting image of Aras!

Third Photograph: Harborfront Series (black and white)

The photographs which she had named harborfront series were three in number, and had appeared in the last issue of the same magazine, in a two page spread. These were pictures of a middle-aged woman with a white apron tied around her waist, tending to her hot-dog cart, taken at different hours of the day.

The day and time had been recorded at the bottom of the three pictures, which looked rather similar at first glance.

Monday morning, 11:23 a.m.

The vendor woman is serving four customers who have formed a short line in front of her. On one side of her cart hangs a sign in crude handwriting, which reads: HOT DOG $1.99. The front of the cart, which looks like out *kokorec* stands, is jam packed with plastic, economy-size ketchup and mustard bottles and boxes of various pickles and onions.

Monday afternoon, 2:45 p.m.

The vendor, hands in the pockets of her apron, is gazing at a cruise ship docked nearby. Seen from the side, she has stooped shoulders and a hunched back. Her head is slightly inclined toward the left, and she displays a glum half profile. Weary! She has stepped clear of the stand, leaving the hot-dogs a few paces behind her. She is wearing clogs... No customers.

The cruise ship, which is bedecked with merry flags and pennants, bears elaborately inscribed calls to adventure. Tourists, with their tell-tale cameras and camcorders slung around their necks, are strolling about the pier.

Monday evening, 5:50 p.m.

The hot-dog stand is still in the same location, at the same pier. In one corner of the photograph two young girls are skateboarding past a young man in a wheelchair. The docked cruise ship and the vendor woman are not in the picture.

She's written another Turkish memo in pencil, under the final photograph:

"Gone!"

(Ilford 200 ISO)

For a long time, I was left holding the journals in which the pictures had been published. She had sat down across from me, and was waiting patiently. (Good god, I would not have believed, even in a dream, that she could wait patiently.)

"Do you really like them, Mabel?" she finally asked.

"Yes," I said, not taking my eyes off the pictures.

The pictures she had taken were good, their straightforward language affected me as much as the stories they told, but the layer of lavender-scented sorrow that covered all of them broke my heart.

"I'm going to take better ones, Mabel! I have to take better pictures, do you understand me?"

"I know, Ada."

Ada spent the next four years in Northern America as well. She earned a high school and an art school diploma, but most important of all, Ada began to make herself accepted as a photographer in the region. She succeeded in having pictures of gold, orange, and red autumns and white winters printed as postcards and sold at local bookstores. She proudly wrote to me that in the last two years she had made her living without any assistance from her family.

Her letters were news heavy. It was not at all difficult to realize that she took pains not to write about anything personal or emotional. Her heart was shut tight, and even approaching it was prohibited. I don't know what she experienced during those four years, and in which relationships she sought consolation. She never related them, never touched upon them. I never was able to ask. Since I did not notice any marks made upon her, I presumed that the relationships she must have lived were fleeting, necessary ones, and comforted myself. I endeavored to keep from even thinking that she might have taken great care to erase these imprints. Nevertheless, I suffered palpitations each year thinking that she might show up with a handsome, healthy Mr. Orient-lover by her side.

Every summer vacation she returned to Kuzguncuk for three months, and we spent most of that time together. She was close, friendly, and warm, but she was not the same old Ada. She had wrenched away the spirit, animation, and mischief within her to keep them from interfering with her grief; boxed them up, and buried them beneath a tree known only to herself. Although it was not hard to guess the location of the tree, I was by then "grown up" enough to have learnt that one needs to personally desire to bring back a part of themselves they have done away with.

She made no promises but knew I had not given up hope. I strongly believed that Ada strove to keep me from despairing, and that she was ready to do more. I even thought that I was the real reason behind her struggle to gather herself together and stand firm despite her internal quibbles. I always felt I was important to her, more important than anyone... For I was her Mabel, and would always remain that way.

"Thanks Mabel!" she was saying. "Thanks for being compassionate, and for not deserting me."

This was what I read in the eyes of the lovely girl who resembled Ada, every summer she returned to Kuzguncuk.

During those four years, which I consider to be the gloomiest of my life, it was not only the loss of Ada and Aras that I suffered. The poet Dogan Gokay, who, fixing his intelligent gaze upon me, used to enrich me with his conversation and life experiences, had also slipped back into the shadows. I was only able to see him during the summer when Ada came back to Kuzguncuk and I missed him terribly.

The only heroine of those years was someone who had not been given a large role until that point. The problem was hidden not in the distribution of parts, but rather in the existence of other candidates. However, now the stage was set for her, and she had without the slightest hesitation stepped up to the leading role.

The only person left was Merich. Every weekend, after dropping off her belongings at the mansion, she would come over to our house to dine and keep us company. We were not at all averse to her warm presence, the way she quietly snuggled up to us and spread a scent of blonde, fresh baked sesame rolls into the rooms and curtains of our house, which had suddenly fallen silent with the stench of death. I suppose we were even somewhat grateful to Merich.

She was always the same. Silent, tame, and industrious. Her presence was not arresting, or even noticeable. However contradictory it might seem that these qualities should coexist in a remarkably pretty young girl, men like myself, who are partial to the charm that liveliness, confidence, and humor bequest upon a woman, will comprehend my meaning.

My mother was the one who was most pleased with Merich's "virtual" relocation into our house. At the approach of the weekend she had begun to cook the food Merich liked, and to watch for her arrival. Whenever Merich returned to the mansion or to her boarding school for the night, my mother would grow sad and stand gazing after her. For my mother Merich must have held the place of the daughter she could never have, and the elder son who had taken off so suddenly. And Merich did not disappoint her. She helped out in the kitchen, around the house, and could not praise mom's pastries and teas enough. In my opinion Merich sought and found in our house the long overdue pleasure of family life and maternal love, which she had never possessed. Once in a while I would witness her and my mother standing next to one another in the kitchen, working for minutes without speaking, and I would grow rather depressed.

Another change that had taken place around the house was that my mother, who I had assumed would go mad after the loss of my brother, suddenly devoted herself to worshipping five times a day, handling prayer beads ceaselessly, and reciting the *yasin*. Until then she had been someone who only fasted during Ramadan and listened to the mevlit services on religious eves. Having discovered the strength to bear Aras' loss in God, my mother hardly raised her head from the prayer mat for years, but she never altered either her dress or her lifestyle.

Merich had never concealed her interest towards me. Whenever we were left alone she would sidle up next to me, lean her head on my shoulder, and occasionally kiss me on the cheek. I had no doubt that if I reciprocated in the slightest, I would embark upon an exhilirating journey down the desirous curves of a whole other passionate Merich; I had not forgotten our first kiss. But the spark necessary for my reciprocation was never struck!

Although I was willing to concede that Merich was easier, and classically more beautiful than Ada, her pastel beauty did not sweep me off my feet or cause hurricanes in my heart. Moreover, her resigned, submissive demeanor always aroused feelings of pity and protectiveness within me. On the other hand, I found Ada, whose eyes radiated gleams of intelligence, and whose lips dispersed naughty, heart-stopping smiles, to be extremely sexy. Forget spark, Ada was one of those passionate females who can keep a man under a constant state of vigil between dangerous lightning bolts and rainbows!

Merich and Ada are still the same, and I am still of the same opinion!

The other person who was most affected by Aras' departure was my father. Since his relation with the world was already weak, my father could never recover after that accident. He took offense at the world, and fell silent. It was as if his tongue became paralyzed, as if that night he turned mute. He never spoke again. He did not read the paper, nor did he watch television. He declined to look at my mother's face, and failed to recognize me. His heart, which could not bear injustice, took it as the greatest and final grievance that his firstborn son, who pleased him in every possible way, should leave as the result of a shitty accident. His business faltered, and he became unable to work. Life had turned into an utter burden for him. Two years later, as I was finishing high school, he suffered a stroke to his right side. And a year later he died quietly.

Everyone in the neighborhood consoled themselves that my father who had "died due to the sorrow of his son" had "been saved!"

On our way back from the funeral, my mother leaned on my arm and sighed:

"Naim's finally been reunited with his son and his father!"

I wanted there to be the smallest hint of relief in this sigh…I truly did.

"You're right, mom," I said.

My mother gave my hand a barely perceptible squeeze. (Or I wanted to think she did.)

Certain people who increase their production of gossip in times of disaster and misery (of whom thankfully Kuzguncuk has only a few!), had already begun to whisper that it was a sign of misfortune that three men's funerals had departed from our house in four years. Since movies and images are considered sinful in Islam, they trembled with pleasure in furthering the fallacy that the devilish daughter of the stars had brought a curse upon our heads. Each time we heard these merciless rumours, I and my mother were wounded anew, as with another death. They did not even notice that we knew they would never have been so cruel had they had a genuine concern for us.

I was very glad when my mother, whose large, strong hands had weakened and almost shrunk in the last few years, did in fact squeeze my hand. Everybody was leaving but here was my mother, right by my side, struggling to keep a hold on life.

I turned around to look as we entered the house: Sureyya Mercan and Pervin Gokay were accompanying us, as always.

But Ada was not there. It was as though Ada had left together with Aras.

"Aras isn't alone anymore," I said, to cheer up my mother.

"Neither are you, son," replied my mother, forcing an exhausted smile.

She slowly turned her head to the other side. On her other arm was a very pretty blond girl, whose eyes were swollen from crying. Merich and my mother embraced, and consoled one another. I stood nearby and watched them.

Everything was happening without my participation, independent of me.

I looked at my mother and Merich.

I watched them.

RAIN GIRL, REBELLIOUS ROMANTIC AND
CRYSTAL WATERS

> *"Tomorrow advances slowly,*
> *its eyes are blind still."*
>
> John Berger

"What you just did is called P.I., Uncle Dogan!"

"Well then…" laughed the poet Dogan Gokay.

He uttered this exclamation whenever someone he loved or respected too much to grow cross with made an offensive remark, and he smiled according to the degree of affection or respect he felt for them.

"I mean, the opposite of what they call P.C. in the West!"

"Well what do you know!" said Uncle Poet, and burst out laughing.

His laughter dispersed across the living room, floated around, and settled in various corners, reminiscent of the soap bubbles we loved to blow through metal hoops when we were kids. The soap bubbles, which gleamed and burst upon whoever they fell, released a pine scented coolness all around. I wished that I could have been ambling through a grove perfumed with pine cones.

"Uncle, you shouldn't say 'man of science,' but rather, 'scientist!' 'Political incorrectness' should not be a weak spot for people who are sensitive on issues of human rights and freedom!"

Ada had returned to Turkey for good, and we had gathered for dinner in the mansion to celebrate the occasion. Those of us who were "left behind" were all there, including my mother, and we were rejoicing at the fact that Ada had resumed her old antics. As always, our fondness for the past had to do with the people we missed.

"When we, as a nation, recognize that this country requires artists, thinkers, and men of science as much as it does engineers, doctors, economists, and techicians, we will already have taken the next great step. Given that mankind is a whole of body and soul, the spirit is also included in the materialist area of interest," the poet Dogan Gokay had remarked just a moment ago.

"Besides," Ada continued, looking around for a cigarette, which she had claimed to have quit completely, "it's high time we got past this era of 'mankind.' While womankind is busy rapidly proving to mankind, in a language he can understand, that she too is human, we have to learn to unify under the word 'humanity' in light of 'political correctness!'"

I do not think anyone except myself sensed that she was scouting for a cigarette. Since I knew that she did nothing more than harm herself during these bouts of self-denial, I grew uneasy.

"If we evaluate these terms politically, and not as being such and such -ist or so and so -ism, then it will not get on anyone's nerves."

"Well, well, well! Will you look at that rascal... She's grown up enough to lecture her old uncle... Hah Hah ha!.... Crazy girl, Brunette Ada, Honeygirl! Come, let me give your wisecracking head a kiss!"

Sureyya Mercan was already tipsy after two drinks, although the real reason for his exuberance was that he was reunited with his daughter. He got up from the table and, swaying slightly, approached Ada. He gave his daughter an ostentatious hug and kiss.

"You're right, my child!" said Dogan Gokay in a cheerful voice. "Language is as vibrant an environment as a living organism, and it develops the more civilized we become, the more we learn!"

He could not rest without having filtered and properly settled a new situation through his own words. He had to be in control!

"Let us drink to the new gain of our language and our civilization!" Sureyya Mercan declared, raising his glass.

We, in turn, downed whatever we had been drinking in our glasses.

He was drinking water.

Three years ago, the poet Dogan Gokay had quit alcohol and tobacco entirely, although he had not been an avid consumer of either, and he was now drinking water. As far as I know, he did not
have an ailment or any serious health problem. However, due to
his "talent" for imposing self-inflicted torture through willpower,
just like Ada, he had made a promise himself that "if I live to be fifty, I won't touch alcohol or tobacco!" Not only did he stay away
from the stuff: the words themselves had been erased from his vocabulary.

It was difficult to believe that he was fifty three years old. In my
opinion he was still a handsome, attractive man, not past his mid-
forties. And not just in my opinion… High school students num-
bered among his female readers and admirers, and although Burkan was not a jealous woman, one could easily sense that she was
tired of the attention directed towards her husband.

The poet Dogan Gokay had caused an uproar in our literary
world as much for the publication of his tenth collection of poetry
"Rain Girl" a year earlier, as for his latest novel, "Suddenly the
Clocks Stopped," which had debuted on bookstore shelves a few
months ago. Naturally, he could not have been more pleased.

Meanwhile Sureyya Mercan was still drinking an increasing
amount.

"Really, my dear Dogan, it's easier said than done, I mean, let's
assume I started the stuff when I was seventeen,- 'course there's no
definitive records on the time, but anyhow…let's just assume,
huh?.. Look, if we suppose that I drank a liter per day, as a reasona-
ble measurement, don't you wonder how much that makes in thirty five years? Hah hah ha!"

Dogan Gokay, who, in order not to hurt his brother in law's
feelings, maintained a forced smile whenever this alcohol arithmetic came up, once again did the same and, pushing back his glasses
which had slipped down his nose, continued to listen reluctantly.

"If we say that I drank approximately three hundred liters a
year, it totals up to twelve thousand liters, my dear fellow! A whole
twelve thousand liters, hah hah ha! Now if we bottle this amount,
then we get sixteen thousand bottles. If we lined up those bottles
one next to each other, do you know how many kilometers that
would make, my friend?"

"Just look at the things you brag about in front of the young people, Sureyya! It really doesn't suit you at all! Besides, the doctors want you to quit drinking completely."

"Forget about the doctors, my love! I'm telling all this so that the young people don't start drinking, my lamb, my beautiful wife, my graceful princess! Anyway, now that my lovely niece is about to become a doctor... There's no need to go to any others! All right, Merich, sweetheart?"

Turkish Cinema, which had ceased to exist, had left many such as these two talented performers out in the cold, and had also played a part in the increased interest Sureyya Mercan, one of Turkey's most popular actors, took in alcohol. Pervin Gokay was more sensible. Upon observing that cinema was plagued with economic and creative troubles, she had first turned to theater, and then to parts in TV movies and dramas. However, she spent most of her time in the concept and design department of the small textile company she had established with Burkan. As far as I knew, the company neither made the fortunes of its two co-owners, nor left them wanting.

Pervin Gokay was eight or nine years older than my mother, but my mother looked like her older sister. Pervin Gokay's view of womanhood differed greatly from my mother's. She was not fatalistic, she found it just as necessary to use her mind and intellect as her body, and she enjoyed more favorable conditions. Furthermore she took care of herself, exercised, and came from a generally younger looking family tree. Plus, she had not experienced the death of a child. (And she never ought to!)

Burkan was still sexy and very attractive. She had never endeavored to tear Uncle Poet away from us the way we had feared, on the contrary, she had remained distanced from us herself. I cannot say to this day whether this was a matter of choice or obligation. Burkan did not like to talk. I have often thought that sexuality was what she and Dogan Gokay had in common. Only later was I to realize that the two of them were good friends.

"Our Blue Danube: the Rebellious Romantic is going to be a literary historian, our Brunette Ada: the Rain Girl will become a photography artist, and our Golden Merich: Crystal Waters herself is soon to be a medical doctor! I give you the youths who are the pride and joy of our nation. I now raise my glass in honor of these young people! To our children!"

Having found a new and excellent excuse to drink, Sureyya Mercan cheerfully downed another glass. If I remember correctly he was drinking raki, as he usually did. Burkan, Ada, her mother, and I drank rosé wine, while my mother and Merich preferred fruit juice. Ada's nanny Aunt Cihan, who was now employed as cook, Uncle Shakir the gardener, and his wife, the mansion's veteran laborer Yashar Kalfa, were also dining with us that evening.

Whoever the woman had been whom Dogan Gokay had loved and had in mind while he wrote his first book of poetry, he had not complained when his sister and brother in law had all of a sudden co-opted the name "Brunette Ada" for his niece. But he tried for years, in his own gentle and gracious manner, to institute a "nominal revolution" and change Ada's nickname to "Rain Girl." It was not exactly unsuccessful, but Ada remained as "Brunette Ada" for the most part, and preserved "Rain Girl" as her middle name.

"Crystal Waters" was a moniker Uncle Poet had coined for Merich, his other niece, and, like all the rest, it was extremely appropriate. As for the missing member of the squad, he had been named "Captain Dean." Yet Aras grew uneasy and embarrassed by such games.

If that night "Captain Dean" could have been at that table, I thought of how he would have shone bright in his naval uniform. He would have been a budding naval engineer, a young officer, and in all likelihood, Ada's husband. This thought caused my eyes to burn, and my throat to grow parched. I tried to shoo away that handsome naval engineer from where he was imprinted in my brain. But ever since he had left, this was something I had never managed to accomplish.

"It's hard to be a literary historian or an academician," I said in my usual soft-spoken way. "The conditions are unfavorable!"

"Well, what d'you know!" said Uncle Poet, bursting into laughter.

"C'mon Duna, most literary failures are cropping up as historians all over the place, and you're saying that after four years of training the conditions are unfavorable?" Ada scolded.

"And he graduated with flying colors!" Merich said in a proud, barely audible voice.

"I'm going to teach," I said.

I had graduated recently, and there were certain things I wanted to do, but the most pressing problem was finding a way out of the financial straits we had fallen into after my father's death. I did not have the luxury of occupational frivolity. I felt a responsibility toward my mother. When my father had become unable to work, we had been able to get by for a while on pending orders which my mother completed. After my father left for good, we had sold the three-story wooden building where my grandfather had lived and where our tailor shop had been located, and lived frugally on the interest for a few years. At the same time, Pervin Gokay had been gracious enough to let me work at the design studio on weekends, so that I had been able to contribute a small amount to the household income during my college years. In fact, I seemed to have a knack for designing clothes, but I knew I was not as good as my grandfather. Besides, I have never been an ambitious person. I neither dreamed of being a famous designer, nor a poet whose words were remembered forever. My dreams had only one heroine... My poems were middling, and my designs adept, but I was no genius! Only when talent is convincing enough to be coupled with a desire for success can roads filled with obstacles be surmounted. You know by now that Ada and Aras fit the description perfectly.

"Are you serious?" asked Ada.

"Yes, he already applied to some schools," said Merich, as if to emphasize that she was closer to me than anyone else.

Uncle Poet smiled affectionately:

"A very fine choice, congratulations Duna. Teaching is difficult, but it is also a most important job. I am sure that your students will be very fortunate, son."

He had called me "son" for the first time. Until then he had always called us "child."

"I'll second that!" cried Ada's father merrily. "When we were in middle school we had a class called natural science, who knows what it's called nowadays... Anyhow, our nature teacher Mrs. Lamia was a tiny little old lady, may God grant her a long life if she is alive, and bless her soul if she's dead. You'd think that she'd fallen into our classroom while telling her grandson a fairytale, or dropped in through the kitchen while she was washing dishes. And oh boy, what rascals we were!..Hah hah hah. Forty rowdy so-called men of the Men's college! Well, if you so much as blew in the direction of Mrs. Lamia she'd topple over. A miniature of a woman, my dear Dogan! So of course there's no fun left in rowdiness or practical jokery…"

Whatever Sureyya Mercan related, in that improvisatory talent particular to people who are born actors, that thing or person would leap into life and appear before us. If he put it into his mind to describe a rock, his body would become the rock, his voice would take on the voice of a rock, and his pleasure would increase proportionately to the success of his mimicry. Now he had gotten to his feet and was bringing Mrs. Lamia to life, and we could imagine the Natural Science teacher as if she had been there in person:

"Number 156 Sureyya Mercan, you're not prepared, of course…"

"Ma'am, our clock broke down, my mother fell ill, my father's aunt died, my sister got the measles, and so of course I couldn't study…"

"Sit down. You get an "F"!"

"Have you no mercy, Ma'am, I mean, look, I've been plagued by every trouble God ever gave! I don't feel too good, ma'am…"

(Naturally, the whole class is cracking up with laughter, and I'm still holding out.)

"You never did feel good in class, you little miscreant! This is not the theater, this is a school!"

(Naturally, I flunk, my dear fellow! hah hah ha!..)

An image of the unruly fifteen year old Sureyya Mercan appears before my eyes, his face covered with pimples. A real rogue!

"Well, after all that flunking they finally gave me the boot. So, only years later was I able to complete middle and high school, through outside graduation exams… Soo, moral of the story: love your teacher, pass without failure! Hah Hah ha!.."

"But your teacher was right when she said 'this place is not a theater,' Uncle Sureyya. If you'd gone to a conservatory, you would have succeeded."

Poor Merich always thinks that she is obliged to run to everyone's assistance. This time she was trying to save her uncle. But having started out as the fourth and naughtiest child of an indigent family, Sureyya Mercan was extremely proud of his current position in life, and never stopped mentioning how there was an opportunity for everyone in this country.

"It is imperative to receive a specific education for certain occupations. For instance, attending medical school in order to become a doctor... however, not only is this not true for every occupation, but sometimes it is not enough to just graduate from a school. What matters is being able to succeed in life!" dismissed the poet Dogan Gokay.

"He's a euphemist!" Ada whispered in my ear.

My eyes met those of Merich, who was looking at us curiously. I smiled.

"Well Ada, so you managed to make yourself somewhat accepted over there, but what are you to do in these parts? Who are you, who do you belong to, who is going to appear in your pictures?" asked the poet Dogan Gokay.

Ada kept silent and smiled imperceptibly- I sensed that she was still searching for a cigarette.

"I asked myself for days why there isn't a female Ara Guler in our country."

"Come now, we have women photographers too, don't be unfair to them," her mother objected.

"How many international photographers have we produced since Ara Guler, and how many of them are women? Can you list them off the top of your head?"

Names were mentioned, attempts at recollecting surnames were made. Rather than people under examination, we resembled children playing bingo on New Year's Eve. We had missed playing a game in which we could all participate cheerfully.

"The people you've listed are fashion or commercial photographers, that is, the good girls of the studios... Is there anyone who tackles nature or landscape photography? I don't mean for trendy reasons, I mean someone who just says 'by God, I'm going to pull this off!'"

"Alright, I get it... Our rain girl is going to be something of a journalist, and a moviemaker, and she'll set out on the road with cameras strapped to her back!"

"So, my daughter shoots photographs, my wife and I shoot pictures...well we used to shoot pictures... once upon a time... those days are long gone... Anyway, I was saying: I should be especially grateful to the individuals who invented this camera business, brothers and sisters! What was the infidel's name: Graham Bell?"

"Oh, now really!" we all protested.

"Well why not? While everyone we look down on as infidels were busy inventing everything beneficial to humanity, we non-infidels were simply looking on, yawning lazily..."

"Well, that much is correct but the unbeliever's name is what's wrong, you've been drinking too much again, darling..."

"Now look my sweet wife, even if I don't have such fancy diplomas as you all, being a native son, I know all about those fellows Thomas Edison and Lumiere, my sultan! I'd just wanted to test the rest of you, that's all, hah hah ha!"

"Really Sureyya, a critic might hear you and declare you an ignoramus right away. There's no humor, fantasy or jest in this country, there're only irrefutable truths..."

"What impresses me as much as Ara Guler are the photographs of the American Dorothae Lange. I suppose I'm seduced by the idea of documenting the opposition between humanity and nature, of human landscapes and the struggle to domesticate nature."

"You mean pictures with storylines..." said Dogan Gokay.

"Absolutely," rejoined Ada, flushed with excitement.

"I've inspected many of Dorothae Lange's photographs. There is something in that woman's frames that is incredibly interesting and compelling to me. She lived during the same period and in the same locale as Steinbeck. But mostly because of the similarity in their worldviews, one can say that Dorothrea Lange's pictures are a kind of visual translation of Steinbeck's novels!"

"Bravo! If she can speak that much on one picture, it goes to show she's more your daughter than mine, dear Dogan! Oh well, every rose has its thorn, doesn't it now, hah hah ha!.."

"Mrs. Zubeyde, this visual translation business must be what we'd call 'photographic rendition', wouldn't you say?" Uncle Poet asked my mother, who was quietly sitting at the table, casting frequent, loving glances at Merich.

"I would s'pose so, I don't really understand much about these things... But it makes my heart rejoice to see the youngsters so excited."

"As for me, my heart rejoices at your mince-meat pastries, Mrs. Zubeyde. They are absolutely delicious, I must say!" Pervin Gokay interjected.

"Thank you, I'm glad you enjoyed it, but what is my cooking compared to Mrs. Cihan's..." said my mother, embarrassed.

"I swear, these dolmas of Nanny Cihan are nothing short of magical, kids! The more you eat, the greater your appetite grows! That flavor, that celestial burst of yogurt laced stuffing through sour leaves, must be a gift from God. Here, pass me another plate for god's sakes!"

"Sureyya dear, maybe you shouldn't eat anymore, you'll overdo it and not let me sleep again at night."

"Look Dogan, see what my wife complains of! She's making a connection between dolmas and sex, you understand, hah hah ha!"

"I don't know about that, but I have never tasted anything better than Yashar Kalfa's sour okras, anywhere else. An amazing talent, you have my admiration!"

"Thank 'ee Mr. Uncle, I can cook it again, just you ask!"

"I don't know who made the *ezogelin* soup, but it deserves the greatest praise. Out of this world," said Merich.

"Good for my pretty doctor girl," said Aunt Cihan, smiling.

Ada was not even listening to them. "In the 1940's, Dorothae Lange applied for a Guggenheim scholarship to photograph American farm life. When I read what she wrote in the application forms, I discovered what really struck me in that woman's pictures."

"What's that?"

"Lange said: 'Documenting man's relationship with land and with one another will provide a key resource for future research in our industrialized society.' "

She was so animated that her beautiful eyes emitted a brunette energy high-voltaged enough to illuminate Kuzguncuk in its entirety. That was when I realized how crucial photography was to her. My god, how much I had missed it! A child who had fallen asleep within me stirred, and even if he did not dare to open his eyes, he smiled. I shut my eyes in order to see that boy more clearly. It was a wondrous meeting. When I reopened my eyes I ran into Merich's gaze. She was fearfully searching my face for a sign that I was there. Ah, why do we all spend our lives waiting in fear of something?

"In her pictures the misery of immigrants, the doubts of farmers, and the expressions, the postures of hunger and unhappiness during the Great Depression are retold with an incredible clarity and poise, without being overshadowed by social exploitation, ideological propaganda, or personal anxiety."

"So the woman was not a merchant of poverty, eh... You kids would not know what poor quality the revolutionary novels and photographs had in our day, you were still babies then."

"But Dogan, there are humane and aesthetic elements in the pictures of Ara Guler and Fikret Otyam during those very years..." protested Pervin Gokay.

"That's exactly what I'm saying! If Steinbeck had pursued photography he would have been Dorothae Lange, and if Sait Faik or Sabahattin Ali had become photographers they would have been Ara Guler."

"Well, sure, you gotta have male photographers for a society of real men, you know what I mean brothers and sisters, hah hah ha!" laughed Sureyya Mercan.

All at once Ada rose from her seat and harriedly left the living room.

"What's the matter with her now? Did I say something wrong?"

"No, Sureyya, my dear, something occurred to her and she'll show it to us momentarily. She won't rest until she does!" smiled Dogan Gokay.

"Mr. Uncle's right, she was like that even as a girl, my hazel doe," said Aunt Cihan with an affectionate smile.

"Our little miss is always quick and spry," added Yashar Kalfa.

"*Mashallah, Mashallah!...*" sighed Uncle Shakir.

Just then I heard myself say:

"Ada is a free brown bird who only herself knows where and when she will fly next. Her wings must never be broken, her direction must never be asked. How well that would suit her!"

My voice was idiotic and sticky with awe. Who knows what

look registered upon my face at the time? Perhaps the asinine expression of a foolish lover. A deep silence ensued. One could have heard a fly buzz. None did. Trying to avoid both Merich's and my mother's eyes, I hid my own in the scarlet of the Kayseri rug on the floor until the silence was broken.

"I'd better make the coffees now, how would everyone like theirs?"

"What a good idea, Nanny Cihan. I want the blackest one. Just like Ataturk!"

"Didn't Ataturk have his coffee fairly sweet Sureyya?"

Burkan had spoken for the first time.

As the coffees went on their way, Ada rushed into the room. She was holding a large album in her hands. Without looking around at anyone, she continued her speech from where she had left off- oh the charm of that confidence!

"Look at this picture! The year: 1936, the place: California. An immigrant woman is suckling her baby in front of a tattered tent. Before her is an empty metal bowl and a dilapidated gas lamp. The baby's hand-knit shoes are grimy and riddled with holes. The woman's clothes are tired of growing old. That year's pea crop has frozen on the fields and the family has been left famished. I don't know if you'll believe it but the woman is only thirty-three years old!"

The album was passed around the table. The wrinkled face of the woman in the photograph was completely covered with anxiety. There was no room left for any other emotion on her face. A poetic rendition of anxiety and grief had been masterfully placed within that picture frame.

On the facing page the same immigrant woman had averted her worried gaze away from the lens and fixed it on some far off point. A boy of around eight who had hid himself by burying his head on her shoulder, reflected his discomfort through his stance. The woman had one arm propped on her knee, leaning her chin in her hand, and held on her lap the baby who slumbered after having been breastfed. Between her two children the woman gazed off into space, waiting.

"Even in that state she was a fine looking woman…" sighed Sureyya Mercan sadly.

"Stop your rakishness and think about why your daughter is affected by these pictures, Sureyya, my dear."

"There's that famous French photographer, the one who has become popular with his black and white shots of kissing couples. Isn't his name Doisneau?"

"Yes uncle, that's right."

"For a while there was talk that his pictures were staged. Naturally, it disillusioned many people."

"Now the same can never be said of Dorothae Lange. Look at the woman in this picture, in my opinion she's a Steinbeck protagonist, and what interests me most is the language that the photographer uses. See, this picture does not arouse feelings of pity or disgust is us. We become moved and saddened by the aesthetic poeticism of a skilful poet who tells of pain, anxiety and loneliness. And this is much more lasting and effective than pity!"

"I think I saw these pictures somewhere before." said Merich.

"Certainly doc, these are very famous photographs!" replied Ada.

"Raingirl, you have understood this business!" the poet Dogan Gokay rejoiced. "From now on we know what you will be photographing."

Having been commended by her true idol, Ada glowed with pleasure and bestowed upon us that brilliant smile of hers which lightens up my soul. A shimmering light spread through me, a little spoilt, a tiny bit coy, and somewhat shy. She was extraordinarily beautiful, and a stunning brunette. In that miniscule amount of time I was transformed into the happiest person on earth. That's all!

"If you'll excuse me, I'd better head home," said my mother as she got up from the table.

She was going to go back home, perform the belated evening worship, count her prayer beads, and say her prayers. She had had a fine night and in her prayers for better ones to come, she would include mine and Merich's names.

"Won't you have your coffee, neighbor?" asked Yashar Kalfa.

"I can't drink coffee at night, I don't know if it's caffeine, but something won't let me sleep afterwards."

"I'll see you to the door Mrs. Zubeyde. We're honored that you came. From now on, we'll be expecting you more often, alright? We're old friends, old neighors, and almost relatives by now! We should meet more frequently in this fleeting, mortal world, and enjoy ourselves… See, we're already growing old…"

"Come Sureyya darling, is this the time for such melancholy speeches? I mean, what is the use of saying things like that? Don't you mind him, Mrs. Zubeyde. He already has a sensitive constitution, and after a few drinks he just turns into a big baby. As you know, he has a heart of gold. We're always glad to see you. Goodbye."

After I returned from accompanying my mother home, the table had been cleared, Burkan and Pervin Gokay had settled down to talking business in one corner, Merich had started a game of backgammon with Uncle Hasan the gardener, and Sureyya Mercan, Dogan Gokay, and Ada were still peering at Dorothea Lange's album and conversing. I joined them passively. I listened to them and watched Ada.

Ada had come back to us, yes, she was here with her old spirit, liveliness, and passion for the first time in years, but how much of it was real and how much of it was my wishful thinking?

Soon, I learned that Ada had rented a separate studio-apartment and would henceforth live in Beyoglu. Her parents, who were prepared to make any sacrifice for their daughter's return to life, had not opposed the idea even though they were not very fond of it. I remember turning stone cold. Ada was ready to embark on a new life, and she had already started on her way. I was the one who was marching in place, who was waiting around in an indecisive and bewildered state. I was always waiting. I felt clumsy and useless. But what was I waiting for, after all? I decided for the thousandth time that I was a prize fool. I said goodnight to everyone and quickly left in order to go and hide in our house which was directly across the street.

A pale yellow light was emanating from window of my mother's room, on the second floor of our house. My mother must have been sitting on her prayer rug, reciting the *yasin*. My mother. The only family I had left. My mother. The woman who still held out and defended life. My mother. The strong woman who embraced the only hope she had left with all her might. Her only hope and source of life, her litle son, her Blue Danube, who is still indecisive and awkward.

Aras, oh Aras, why did you dive into that dark sea? Why did you leave Aras? Why were you powerful, like you would always be by my side, and why did you leave in such a hurry? Why did you deceive me?

I felt like running up to my mother, throwing my arms around her neck the way I did when I was a boy, burying my head in her shoulder and finding peace in her soothing touch. How restless I was, how tense!

So, what would have been different if Aras had stayed anyway?

What would have been different? Ada would have always been close by, I would have seen her happy, and would never have had to part with her… Probably!

Now I was losing her once again. She was fleeing from me, from the mansion, from the neighborhood, from Kuzguncuk, from her family, and from everything that reminded her of Aras. Perhaps most of all from me. My eyes were itching, and my nose was beginning to run, but I tried to resist the urge to cry.

Perhaps those who found Ada arrogant, cold and selfish were right. This raingirl, this brunette sorrow, this honeygirl was in simple fact an egoist and did not even deserve my love!

Yes, yes, she was spoilt, she was vain, and even when she was a tiny little kid she would talk to rocks. She used to talk to a small white marbled stone, that was the day I met her. How beautiful she had been, how colorful and warm! She was one like no other in the world!

"Duna!"

I turned around expectantly.

"My mom wants to get married," said Merich.

I could not make out her face in the darkness but I could tell from her coffee-breath that she was standing very close to me.

Instead of yelling "What do I care!" I held myself back and mumbled:

"Oh, that's great!"

"I guess they've been together for a long time but now the man has divorced his wife and wants to marry my mom. When they do, my mom wants me to live with them."

At that moment what Merich was telling me seemed as distant and irrelevant as the wedding tale of a couple of aliens discovered in outer space. She must have waited for me in the mansion's garden. Perhaps she had also been nearby as I talked to myself and missed Ada's marbled stone, and she had heard everything.

"You should support your mother Merich," I said without any further consideration.

"But I don't want to live with them...I can't leave Kuzguncuk. Don't you get it Duna! Besides, I only have a year left before I finish school!"

She was on the verge of tears, only an ass could overlook the pleading tone of her voice.

"You'll find a dorm!" I said with the voice of an ass.

That was when Merich started to run toward the mansion in tears.

Now, what was it I said?

Merich was one of the last people I could have wanted to hurt, and I did not like hurting people anyhow. Or was it true that there is always someone one can hurt? I stood frozen for a while.

I knew very well what Merich had meant to say, but I had preferred to play dumb. God, why did everything always have to be so complicated and difficult?

I would have gone after her, won her over, and told her that she was not all alone, that she could stay with us. She had practically been living in our house for the past few years anyway, save for sleeping there. Meanwhile, it was not as if her aunt and uncle were not putting her out on the street or anything...

I was petrified. My feet were stuck to the ground. I was left stranded in the mansion's garden on a pitch black summer night. I felt heavy as an anvil, and sick of life's resistance.

After quite a long time, I turned my back to the mansion and walked, dragging my feet toward the light in my mother's room.

I walked.

WHEN NOW BECOMES THEN

"What is a lover, whence is heaven; if he knew these, not one would trade today for tomorrow."

Sheik Galip

"I don't agree with anyone anymore, not even myself," said Duna.

"This 'ere teacher of yours is talkin' in his sleep again, Musa son. Wake up the poor wretch so his soul may find some little bit of peace."

"Have you ever seen a man talk so sensible in his sleep, ma? Can't you see that this charmed teacher lives in a state of half-sleep?"

"I have been feeling threatened for years. I have always lived under threats as a person, as a man, as a lover, as a political…"

"See, didn't I tell you so ma, dear," Musa repeated. "Even when he goes to bed he can't quite fall asleep, the poor fellow. Demons and goblins bar his way. In his dreams, he's washed and drowned in poisoned waters."

"Ma, is the teacher possessed by djinns?" asked little Lutfu sympathetically.

"There ain't no such thing as djinns, idiot!" grinned Ali.

"His lack of belief is killing him, ma. When people like him, who've read and learned a little too much, have weak beliefs, they go out of their minds, just like this, may God preserve us…"

Musa tugged on his ear and rapped the knuckle of his index finger three times against the wood of the sofa.

"They try to save the world, but either they end up as smartasses, all alone in the world, or they unravel, like him, and can't even save themselves! See here, I'm a merchant man, and as god's my witness, I can tell right away a dupe from a sly man. God bless him, Duna is a fine lad, and he comes from a very devout family, and yet…"

"I took a likin' to this 'ere four-eyed dark boy, but what we gonna do? Shoo girl, go bring us cologne or whatever's left. Boil some mint water… I'll pray a little, an' it'll do good for the man… He's his own mother's pet after all…"

Finding himself in the same old house, everytime he awoke, stuck with the same family in a place of scarcity had pushed Duna's disappointment well beyond the limit. He was suspended in an unknown geography, an uncertain time, and an indefinite waiting place. Musa was his only connection to the real world, and he held on to his friend for all he was worth. If he could awake, oh if he could only awake, he knew that he could be completely rid of this nightmare, but god damn it, he just could not do it. Was waking up really this hard? Is awaking always a difficult and painful process?

He had been glad to have bumped his head as he crawled around on the floor with his hands and feet tied to a chair. This time when he awoke, he would be sure to have exited the nightmare. Because his grandfather used to say "if you want something really bad, it will happen" But once again that was not how things turned out. When he awoke he was lying across from Musa's bed in the inner room, with hands and feet untied.

Musa had shaved, his face was livened up with color and he was sitting by Duna's side, wearing civvies which were slightly too small for him. He was missing one leg, but there was such a hopeful light glimmering in his face that the lost leg was left behind in some unimaginably distant, gloomy past. Only in two cases does such happiness register in a person's face: when he is in love, and when his love is returned by the object of his affections! Duna had not seen Musa so lively and blithe ever since their boyhood days. He checked his eyes, unable to believe what he was seeing. Sure enough, his glasses were missing.

"Where're my glasses?" he panicked.

"Here, son of mine, I'd put 'em away so they didn't get broke."

"Thank you, good brother, may God be pleased with you. Ma Hatice says I was saved thanks to yourself. There have been times when I've nursed unfavorable thoughts about you. God forgive me. Will you forgive me too, teacher, so there is no bad blood between us?"

Musa the grocer, who in the last few years had come to despise anyone who did not visit the mosque, and whose eyes had not exuded a single glimmer of hope, had been replaced by the affectionate Musa, Duna's childhood friend. His face, bathed in compassion, did not bear a trace of hostility.

"Please Musa, what did I do…"

Duna stiffened and grew uneasy, like all people who become terribly embarrassed upon being thanked.

"Ma Hatice says I wouldn't have made it if it had not been for the medicine in your bag. May God turn all you touch into gold, Duna my brother."

"If it hadn't been for Mrs. Hatice, neither of us would be around. Even within a nightmare you must remain healthy, otherwise you will not have any chance of waking up…"

"Come again?"

"I was saying that they're the ones we should really be thanking."

"God himself placed them in our path. All of them, every single one of them is a beloved subject of god."

"Now, now son, anyone woulda done the same. Our creed is love of man, dear sons. God has proclaimed 'I will love he who lovest thou.'"

"Would you like some water, Musa?"

Then Duna saw the girl again. It was as if the angel faced girl who played the saz had blossomed from a child into a beautiful young woman during the time he was asleep. She had gathered her long black hair in a ponytail, dolled herself up in her own way, and was swaying about with flirtatious overtones in her voice.

"May you be as saintly as the water, may your hands never suffer trouble Sulari," said Musa, somehow coming up with the voice of a shy young lad.

"You're most welcome!" giggled Sulari.

"Great, this is all we needed!" sighed Duna.

He sat up on the sofa. He wiped the inefficient lenses of his glasses with his camouflage gear which had by that time grown filthy. He began to inspect Musa and the young girl carefully. Their eyes had long become blind to those of anyone but each other.

"When did this happen? Musa, have I been asleep for a long time?"

His voice bore the quizzical calmness of someone who has not quite grasped the situation at hand.

"Yours cannot be called sleeping, esteemed brother. You have been passing out for days," said Musa, his eyes locked to Sulari's in bashful affection.

"I get it. Same old story... This time the scenario has been spiced up with a little romance. You're not as sharp a screenwriter as I had thought, my dear subconscious!"

"Scuse me brother?"

"See, there he goes again, son!"

All of a sudden Duna leapt up from his seat and elatedly cried out:

"Of course, I've got it! Now I've got it cornered!"

"Got who cornered? What're you saying brother?"

"Now I've found a way out Musa! Since you're all better now, we can leave this town right away. Then we can retrace our steps back to the first nightmare and escape this curse! Do you understand me?"

"God forbid... Don't call it a curse brother. Hold on a minute, relax, will you?"

"Look, they didn't let me leave before you recovered, and I didn't want to run away, but now, now we can leave... Besides, my escape from this nightmare will mean the salvation of you all, I swear to you Musa!"

Musa, taken off guard, protested: "But I haven't recovered yet!"

"Musa isn't well enough yet..." Sulari piped up.

"Besides, if he leaves, who's gonna protect us?"

"You shut your mouth girl!" Sulari's mother scolded her.

"Great, this is just great!" said Duna through his teeth, as his arms fell to his side.

He sensed a mounting indignation. Musa, who had recounted the slaughter of his family and vowed revenge while driving to this very town, just a short time ago - though Duna could not say how short was now talking about defending the people of the other sect, who were resisting death due to the same factional differences.

"Fine, but who're you going to protect them against Musa? Huh?"

Their eyes met. Musa averted his gaze and hid his eyes from Duna.

"You'll defend us against the enemy, won't you Musa?" said Sulari in a voice filled with admiration.

"I wonder which enemy?" sighed Duna tersely.

"Which one of us is a foe, and which one of us is a friend? Who's going to protect whom against who? How're we going to tell each other apart?"

Suddenly Duna felt twenty years older. Helpless and weary, and angry at the same time. His cheek muscles were twitching, his teeth were grinding into each other in desperation and rage. Once again, he sat down on the sofa. Actually, he collapsed. Fatigue is the most telling sign of ageing.

All at once he noticed that of the black cloths which tightly sealed the windows overlooking the courtyard had been undraped. The sky was growing dark. He was overcome with the melancholy loneliness of afternoons. He felt extremely foreign and alone. Mrs. Hatice entered the room with a gas lamp, the short wick of which had been lit. Little Lutfu must have been sleeping, and Ali must have been standing guard in the adjacent room. Everything was always the same. They were always waiting under temporary and dangerous conditions. With fear and doubt, with resignation and habit.

"C'mon girl, do as I say!" whispered the woman as she served tea on a plastic tray.

The tea had been carefully steeped and came with sugar and durum, rolls of flatbread filled with cheese.

"Where did all this come from, I thought you were out of sugar, flour, and cheese!" exclaimed Duna in surprise.

The smell of the freshly brewed tea and the steaming flatbread was so appetizing that Duna remembered having once known the joy of life.

"Oh, nowhere… I'd just put it away for some kinda joyful, auspicious occasion. You enjoy it, son!"

"So what happened that's so special? If my nightmare, which you call war, is over, then what're we still doing here? If it hasn't, then what're you celebrating?"

Mother and daughter exchanged a meaningful look, and smiled.

The fact that Mrs. Hatice was capable of smiling surprised Duna.

"Go on girl, why don't you start it right away!"

As they drank their tea and ate their rolls, Sulari reached for her saz with an arch smile and painted the room the color of longing with her tender soprano voice.

"Let them not build houses on tall tall steppes
   Let them not send daughters to far far lands
   Let them not mistreat her mother's pet
   Lo even the birds know I've missed my ma
   My ma and my pa, I've missed my village.

"If pa had a steed he could ride it here
   If ma had a sail she could steer it here
   If my brothers knew the way they'd make it here,
   Lo even the birds know I've missed my ma
   My ma and my pa, I've missed my village."

The sudden flow of music soothed Duna, but Sulari's thin voice and the memories conjured up by the song made him feel infinitely blue. Longing grabbed him by the collar, started to shake and painfully abuse him. He put down the durum and the tea. He imprisoned the longing within his eyes by swallowing repeatedly. But he was overwhelmed by its scent: the faint smoky scent of sawdust on city streets, sprinkled in order to prevent mud after a rainfall. Realizing he could not evade it, he took in a deep breath. As with most feelings which are postponed for fear of pain, this one did not hurt as much as he had thought, in fact, it refreshed him for a short while. He posed a question to Musa, thinking that if he spoke he could alter his state of emotion and mask the sense of longing.

"Musa, when we were kids, you, Sefer, and I used to sing a song in Kuzguncuk, and then laugh our heads off, do you remember the one I mean?"

"'O, remember love that blissful night!'" chuckled Musa.

"There was that plump woman, her older brother would play the violin and she would sing that song in the garden. We would imitate the woman and split our sides laughing. Hah ha! And you were such a whiner Duna... And the woman, what's her name... you know, that old maid aunt of our Hovik..."

"Of course," said Duna with a smile, "Madame Terzian... Agop the Tiemaker's daughter. She had a beautiful voice. She would get mad at us and threaten to tell our mothers."

Their eyes met. Once more, Duna grew abruptly grew serious.

"You're right Musa," he said, feeling hurt, "that woman, Madame Terzian was our, yes, OUR Hovik's aunt..."

He stopped. He had grown sad again.

"And she would never complain to our mothers."

Musa averted his eyes. Duna stubbornly waited for him.

There was a visible tension between the two men and it spread throughout the room, the color of electricity. Like most women who possess sharp instincts toward male conflict, Mrs. Hatice stepped in immediately and refreshed the teas, while Sulari began another *koshma*, or folk ballad.

"If I were a nightingale and came to stand
  Before the mercy of my Maker
  If I were a false apple flowering upon your branch,
  What would you say

If you were a false apple
  Come to flower upon my branch
  If I were a silver staff to snap you off
  What would you say

If you were a silver staff
  That came to snap me off
  If I were a handful of millet, gathered one by one
  What would you say

If you were a handful of millet
  come to scatter on the ground
  If I were a baby hawk that swooped and snatched
  What would you say?"

Sulari's youthfulness and innocence combined with the beauty of her voice to disperse peace across the room, and illuminated the setting as if the gas lamp had suddenly been turned on full power.

"Praise be to your hands and voice Sulari. How well you sang!"

"Thank you Musa, if it pleases you, I'll always sing!" smiled the girl coyly.

They smiled.

"Thankfully, beauty and goodness don't unite in one single race or gender, and surely not in one religion and sect..." whispered Duna jubilantly. "Now you know, Musa!"

Musa did not know what to say. He was irritated by Duna's needling comments, but he sensed himself melt and dissolve under Sulari's admiring gaze, in a manner he had never felt before.

"If you'll excuse me, I need to visit the outhouse. Duna teacher, c'mere, help me out a minute."

Duna stood staring, puzzled as to how he could help, and uneasy about the amputated leg.

"When I first learned that I would be half a man I wished that I had been killed, but then... I became grateful for what I have, thinking that the Almighty has wished it so, and that this must have been my fate. It's a sin to complain, it offends God. And besides, umm... here, hand me that crutch..."

That was when Duna saw the rudimentary crutch fashioned out of a thick tree branch. It was awkward and crude, but it did the job.

"Come, take my arm, teacher, the loo's in the garden."

When they stepped out into the garden on a starlit summer night, Duna first halted in amazement. He had forgotten that stars were suspended from the earth's ceiling at nighttime. Immediately afterwards, he felt that he might grow crazy with joy.

"Musa, we're still alive! Look, clean air, stars, soil, the tree in the garden! Musa, if we run away from here and make it back to the initial nightmare, I can wake up! I swear I can wake up!"

"Tut, brother, hold on, don't let go of me or I'll fall! I'm not used to walking on one leg yet, for heaven's sake! And cut that out, will you? Don't, for God's sake! This isn't a joke, we're at war, if somebody heard you..."

Duna's sudden joy turned suddenly into sorrow. The broken pieces of joy stabbed his body like sinister shards.

"Look esteemed brother, I brought you out here for a reason. For I have something to tell you. Listen Duna, I'm going to stay here and God willing, with His permission and our prophet's – much adored and exalted– leave, I am going to marry Sulari, according to their traditions."

"Whaat? Musa, have you gone crazy?" cried Duna. "Man, you are a grown, married man, the father of three children... Besides, Sulari's young enough to be your daughter... She's still a child!"

Musa hung his head. He spoke with a timid voice:

"A young woman's more unrefined, you know how it is..."

"You mean it's easier to impress them! Oh God, I've never ever been able to comprehend this convenience mentality."

His sudden anger was once more replaced by an abrupt melancholy. Burning inside, he turned his head heavenwards, as if reciting a poem:

"Yet love... love reaches its zenith only when it is the triumph of the impossible!"

Musa interrupted Duna with a trembling voice: "They've slaughtered my family ruthlessly, I have no one else left in Kuzguncuk."

"Musa, no such thing would happen in Kuzguncuk! Don't you understand still, all these are the fears of my goddamned brain, its curse colored fantasies... All these things are parts of a nightmare!"

"God forgive us... Don't curse, brother..." said Musa without raising his head.

His voice was soft, even compassionate.

"I don't get mad at you anymore. This's just the way you save yourself... I know, you've suffered a lot... Both your strapping older brother, and your father... It's not easy, you're right. At the same time... The girl you loved... When a person falls in love... Well, now I know that when a person falls in love theirs is a whole other predicament..."

They fell silent. On a gorgeous summer night, resplendent with stars, two childhood buddies were left standing quietly in a blacked-out town located in a certain part of Anatolia. Only the crickets spoke.

"This girl pulls me toward life," said Musa shyly. "Never before have I entertained such feelings for a member of that gender. My wife, may she rest in peace, was mine by arrangement, and she was a well mannered, wholly devout lady... But this girl... She's dropped such a fire inside me that... It's not right for me to talk before she's rightfully mine..."

"Love!" said Duna, continuing to look up at the stars. "How love inflames a person... At first from joy, then from pain...How lovely it is, and how much it hurts!"

"Something funny has happened to me Duna... I've fallen to childish ways. I can't sit still, I can't hold anything inside."

"Love should not be a luxury for anyone, Musa."

"When I see her, lights shower down upon my face..."

"Love is the joy of being reborn, each time you see your beloved."

"It's as if she's a fairy, an angel! A tree in heaven, nectar Sulari..."

"Love is suffering a long bloody death each time she so much as flicks a finger."

"What tribulations I went through, thinking she would not fancy or want me, I almost died."

"Love has slackened when it does not keep you in a state of vigilance."

"From now forth, it is a duty as holy as life itself to keep her content, to preserve a smile upon her face."

"Love is the most exquisite of torments, the deepest of joys."

"Ah, Duna, if you only knew!.." sighed Musa.

"I wonder, had I not believed in love, would love have played such a prominent role even in my dreams?"

Duna asked himself.

Just then a dog howled far away.

"Well, what about the difference between you two, Musa? What about that difference, the wrath that's been kept fresh for centuries, and for the sake of which blood is being shed, huh?"

"But they're not like that!" Musa protested. "Her late father-he was killed in this war, was a Cem Dede. He is supposedly descended from the line of Imam Zeynel Abidin. In short, a very respectable person, one whose path was toward God... What's more, we're all Moslems, praise God, we're children of the same faith."

"Aah!" Duna sighed deeply. "You say they're not like that Musa. If none of us are like that, if we're all good and well, then why are we all killing each other Musa?"

Musa kept quiet. They did not speak at all for a time being.

"If you don't mind, I'll just relieve myself, now that we're out in the garden," said Musa finally.

Duna turned his back to Musa and supported his weight. Musa unzipped the trousers that were too small for him, and urinated in the middle of the garden.

"If you'll excuse me Duna," he said, as he finished his business," you know what your real problem is? You think too much, brother. Quit thinking deeply. Just concentrate on living the war, if you're at war, and living in peace, if you're at peace. You're in fantasy land, and you're always dreaming! Your never have your feet solidly in the ground. Look, no offense, but you were this way even as a boy, you were nothing like your brother! You know what you need?"

"What do I need Musa?" asked Duna in an exasperated voice, having perceived it as an insult that Musa had peed out in the open, right next to him, and on such a lovely night too.

"You need faith and love, brother. Mark my words, you'll recover and be cured straight away."

He closed his zipper with difficulty, leaning his weight both on Duna and the crutch. He was done.

"I tasted the greatest of loves before you even knew what it was called," said Duna with a bittersweet smile, "The greatest of loves and friendships."

"That girl again?"

"Yes Musa, my love always resides at the address of that brunette girl."

"What about your wife?"

"That must also be some kind of love, Musa… You know how they say there are a thousand various types of love…"

"Wait, isn't the order you keep a monogamous one Duna?" pressed Musa.

"Yes, that's right. A person can love many people at the same time, but can only be in love with one of them Musa," whispered Duna.

Myriad colored balloons floated dreamily in his voice. Musa was surprised to see the balloons, and began watching them dance in the air. A bewildered smile had appeared on his face.

"Yet a man only loves one woman throughout his whole life. Those before and afterwards are a search, an escape and a deception!"

All the colorful balloons floating in his voice burst noisily and fell softly to the ground.

"I was unable to make either myself or Ada happy, Musa. I married Merich, and started living with her so that I could at least make someone who loved me happy. Besides I'm someone who enjoys making other people happy, and who by birth feels obliged to be 'good'. Don't act like you don't know."

He stopped.

"You can also call me an idiot, a moron… It's said behind my back anyway."

"Don't, brother… Don't ruin yourself… God Almighty has decreed: 'Do not Lose Thy Faith.' If you want, interpret that as 'don't lose hope,' but just don't let yourself go… Besides Ada…"

"She's a whole other subject!" Duna cut off Musa. "Ada is a ray of light, a mirage, an abstract concept like a miracle… Ada is, by now, under my skin, within my soul Musa!"

"It's hard, brother!" sighed Musa. "Love is the greatest gift God has granted us, second only to the gift of life."

This time it was Duna's turn to be startled. "Is that you talking, Musa? Is that really you, huh?" he said, bending down to look Musa in the face.

Musa continued to speak undeterred: "Our God Almighty has ordered: 'Free Thyself of Malice and Hatred!' See, we're in a civil war, who knows who'll live or die… Or become martyred… I just thought that I might as well wash and cleanse my soul before the inevitable end."

"But of course!" smiled Duna bitterly. "As if I'd fall for this… I'm supposed to believe that everything changed so quickly and incredibly, that all of a sudden I'm hearing what for years I've wanted to hear from you, and that all of this is real? Forget it! This is all fictional, all parts of a dream... Even if everything seems well organized the true defining factor fails in practice!"

Musa looked at him sadly.

"Time!" said Duna. "Have you realized that there's no concept of time in all of this, huh?"

"God have mercy!"

"Time is defined as a setting in which events follow one another, or as the continuous motion which causes the present to turn into the past, is it not? Fine. But have you ever thought about why physics and philosophy define 'time' differently?"

"No."

"Because, Musa, because there are actually two types of time. One marks events in consecutive order, while the other, having appeared after the creation of the soul, becomes unintelligible when the soul is inactive, as, for example, during sleep!"

"You've started to talk like a book again," complained Musa.

"True, I've learned what I say from philosophers. And since time is 'practically the definition of an active concept,' i.e., the place where every kind of truth is verified, then why is there no such thing as time here, huh?"

Musa sighed with growing irritation.

"Because Musa, I am asleep right now and the concept of time has disappeared ever since this nightmare began!"

"Alright Duna, alright esteemed brother, that's just so, don't worry about it anymore..." said Musa, patting Duna on the shoulder with his free hand.

"I'm going to leave Musa. I'm going to get out of here and back to the first nightmare and from there I'll switch into the real world. You have to stay here and experience this love affair. In the end, we'll see each other in Kuzguncuk anyway!"

"*Inshallah,* Duna brother. May God provide us with those days of peace, whole mindedness, and contentment, *Inshallah!*"

"See, for those to happen I have to wake up first Musa!"

"God, great God, grant sanity to this poor subject of yours!"

"That's okay, don't believe me Musa, I'm used to it."

"Duna brother, you have my blessings. Watch out for yourself. May God protect us all!"

They embraced.

"Just like in the movies," thought Duna.

"Farewell Musa. I want you to know that even if it was a dream, it gave me great joy to see you recognize love and compassion for those who are different from you."

Musa laughed. "Man is made in the image of God, Duna. I have not read as much as you, I'm rather ignorant, but I know, brother, that no one can run away from himself."

Duna smiled a broken acknowledgement. He hated farewells.

"For god's sake Duna, stop running away!"

"Musa, give my regards to Mrs. Hatice, Lutfu, Ali, and Sulari, tell them that I had to leave urgently."

"Don't worry, they already know that."

As he walked towards the garden gate, he was holding the small white elliptical stone tightly in his hand. Just as he went out he turned around and whispered:

"Tell Ali that my gun was not loaded."

"Neither was Ali's," said Musa laughing. "Their ma had unloaded all their guns!"

THE SIGNS ARE INNOCENT AT FIRST

"and why do the children shiver when a whole city has burned down?"

Huseyin Yurttas
(XX. Century Laments)

"Hands up! Don't turn around!"

He had been wandering around the narrow, cobblestone streets, losing his way under a starry sky, and enjoying the bewilderment of an unexpectedly recovered freedom. His body was weak but he felt better then he had in a long time. Should the hope that escape is near enter a person's blood, even the most foreboding signs will bear inexplicable crumbs of joy!

Soon he would return to Kuzguncuk. For starters, he would polish off that scrumptious breakfast he had set out on the balcony. No, no, before that he would find Ada and bandage the wounds that that "execution without trial" in the newspapers must have caused her. They would go to Baylan and have a kup griye on the back patio before it was closed down for the season. Ada would show him her new prints and update him on her exhibits. Then she would take his arm and say "Boy, did I miss you Mabel!" With that, all his troubles would vanish, and he would be reborn. He knew, this was the way it always turned out, and the way it always would, until the day he…

"Put your hands behind your head!"

Just when he had set aside this civil war business and this nightmare… Just when he had been able to dream of reaching Ada… Just when he had put his hands in his pockets, with neither a backpack nor a rifle… Yes, the book of poetry had also been left behind together with his backpack, but so what? He already knew all the poems by heart. And besides, the way he was going, maybe Musa would even start reading the poet Dogan Gokay's poems. Most important of all, however, he had that white elliptical stone with him, in his pocket.

"Don't try to pull any smart stuff soldier, or I'll nail you!"

The massive, rigid object which had been dug into the lower part of his back, already hurt his flesh. Duna could tell that the person behind him was a short, young man from the positioning of the gun at his back, and from the latter's tone of voice.

"Now march!"

With his hands locked behind his neck, he set off marching at gunpoint, into a starry summer night. During this long walk through identical winding streets, which he suspected was designed to make him lose his sense of direction, Duna realized that the town was larger than he had thought. And yet his sense of direction was already weak, and he had no idea as to their whereabouts. As they walked on, they came to a place outside of town where houses began to grow more scarce. Duna guessed that the few buildings around them were shanties. Did there always have to be a band of shantytowns around every settlement?

"Was it Hegel who said humiliation is a cause for civil war?" asked Duna.

"Shut up!" ordered the short, young male voice behind him.

Duna shut up. They came to a halt in a desolate area, in front of a ramshackle hut. The hut looked like it had been thrown together just a few hours ago with rocks and planks scavenged from here and there. The armed man who shoved him toward the door, rapped four times on the entrance.

"Oh no, here comes another episode of inner-nightmares!" groaned Duna.

The opened door revealed a second man, whose flashing eyes popped out of his black ski mask, and who was holding a machine gun. He looked at Duna, grabbed him by the shoulder, as if handling a vermin, and wrathfully hauled him inside. Then, throwing him to the floor, he began to beat the daylights out of his prisoner. Duna first heard his glasses fall and crack under someone's boots

Before he knew it, kicks were raining down on his head, back, and groin. He felt dizzy with pain as he tried to shield himself. The person beating him had ten or fifteen legs, feet, and arms, and was cursing through dozens of mouths simultaneously. Insults hailed down upon Duna's mother and wife from all the different mouths, and his entire lineage was violated thousands of times. He was not in a condition to wonder what he had done to draw these people into such rage and fury, he was having trouble breathing, and felt he might go mad from the pain.

"You're insane!" he yelled. "You're inhuman!"

When he felt he was being struck on the arms and chest with a hard object, he thought that perhaps he had stopped feeling pain. Upon realizing that the warm liquid flowing from his mouth was blood, he remembered that the sight of it did not make him queasy any longer.

"I am dying in my dream," he thought. He was nauseous and his vision had blacked out.

"How can so much hatred and violence fit in a human body?" he screamed. But he could not make a sound. He lost consciousness just as he was thinking:

"But what if it isn't a dream..."

When he opened his eyes the first thing he sensed was a putrid smell, and the first thing he saw was the dried blood stains on his uniform. He did not, by then, have the slightest idea as to what the hour was, or how much time had elapsed.

He found himself in a rather large room, sitting next to a wall with his hands tied behind his back. The room was almost completely empty and it smelled absolutely, positively disgusting. His stomach heaved a few times. Since he was missing his glasses, everything seemed blurry. When he tried to make the slightest movement, he felt his body ache violently. He first discovered that his arms hurt a great deal, then that his neck hurt more, next that his back and chest caused even further pain, and finally that his head hurt above everything else. Every new organ he sensed hurt more than the previous one. He felt a stabbing pain in his back when he breathed.

"They must have broken my ribs, my arms and my skull!" he thought, shivering in fear.

A few feet away lay a stack of objects, and that was where the terrible smell emanated from. He squinted in order to see more clearly but he still could not make out what he was seeing. His face smarted when he tried to strain his eye muscles. He decided he must have had sores even on his face. Straining himself to the utmost, he tried to focus his vision of the stack, and unable to believe what he finally saw, he cried out:

"But these are corpses!"

That was when he began to vomit. Over and over and over again. Finally having nothing left to disgorge, he began to retch.

"They're going to kill us too!" said a voice.

There was someone else alive in the room. Someone alive!

Another living person! Someone else with hope for living! Duna fervidly swerved his head in the direction of the voice.

"They've thrashed you pretty bad, lieutenant," said the voice.

The voice was familiar but he could not quite make out its owner, who was partially blocked from his sight by the stack of corpses. Though, of course, even if he had seen the man fully, he would not have been able to recognize him without his glasses.

"I thought you'd been rescued, lieutenant?"

"Captain Birol? Is that you?" cried Duna, overjoyed.

"Yes, even though I might not look much like myself after all this torture… Forget about me, how did you come to fall into their hands?"

"I was hiding in a house," said Duna, "but in order to get out of this nightmare I had to leave and return to the first nightmare. As you know, I don't belong here, this is only a…"

"Ah, of course…" sighed Captain Birol. "How could I forget, all this is simply a segment of your nightmare, it's not real!"

"Yes."

"Ah, my dear teacher! You've been saying the same thing ever since that day I picked you up from Kuzguncuk. You have lived through and suffered so much, yet you still insist on the same thing! Take a look at yourself. You've been taken prisoner, you're lying here covered in blood, but you still claim that you're inside a Kafkaesque novel. They're going to kill us soon."

"That's even better!" said Duna, thinking he might faint from the stench of rotting human flesh, "Let them kill me, let them do it right away so all this can come to an end! Because I'm really sick of this nightmare!"

"Do you actually have some sort of belief in reincarnation, sir?"

"Certainly not!" Duna retorted. "I have such extensive proof of the falsity of my predicament that I would start doubting my sanity if in fact I believed all this was real!"

"Even now, lieutenant?"

"Of course. See here Captain Birol, just look at yourself for a minute. What do you see? Huh? A young, intellectual, positive, productive, and modern soldier. You are a shining example of the national synthesis the poet Dogan Gokay envisioned. A young Turk of European standards! You are not a bigot or a fanatic. You are confident, educated, and intelligent. A progressive model officer! I always wished that there were such soldiers in the Turkish forces, and that is why my subconscious created you for this dream… Does that make sense?"

"Well, honestly, lieutenant!" smiled Captain Birol bitterly. "Thank you, I appreciate your good opinion, but the officers in the army are for the most part comprised of soldiers like myself anyway. So you see, reality does not always have to be horrific, professor! And no matter how constructive and modern a soldier may be, he is a battle tactician who has been trained with an "enemy" target. If there is no enemy, there can be no soldier, can you understand this?"

"It's difficult to comprehend such a thing," said Duna, "when we could raise our kids for a world without enemies…"

"Ah but lieutenant, this thing we call reality is not something that was created by humans, and is not particular to our world. We are actually prisoners of nature, while at the same time being its component, its product. You'd know better than me, literature and mankind are your field of study."

"Evil is accumulating slowly, silently…" whispered Duna. "Social fragmentation, the encouragement of spying, the mafia, secret organizations, terrorists, cultist merchants are starting to become part of the settled order everywhere, in every country. Neighborhood men, who walk around in regular human costumes during the day, turn into frenzied, murderous hooligans after a match one night… While we go about believing that Nazi atrocities cannot be relived, European fascists slaughter babies in Bosnia! In Orwell's novel, these..."

Just then they heard the sound of a machine gun outside. Once again, Duna felt nauseous by the odor of rotting human flesh, which he managed to forget while speaking. Male voices were heard near the door of their room. It was impossible to tell what language they were speaking, but one could hear occasional Turkish words. Rapid, crude, and harsh voices.

"They're going to kill us soon!" said Captain Birol through his teeth. "Second Lieutenant Duna, have courage, have faith! Never show that you are afraid, and never beg mercy from your executioner! Don't give them that pleasure, die with your honor!"

"What use is a dead man's honor?" asked Duna.

"Recite the testimony of faith, lieutenant!"

The door crashed open and two men with pitch black ski masks and machine guns entered the room. Duna guessed that the shorter of the two was the one who had captured him.

They walked up to Captain Birol and stopped. They were wearing black t-shirts and baggy black pants, and had combat boots on their feet. The taller one, whose arms were carpeted with black hair, kicked, and spat on Captain Birol. Then they talked between themselves. The language in which they spoke must have been an amalgam of several others, and it was immediately apparent that the speakers abused it. Every once in a while it was possible to discern Turkish words as well. They were arguing. Just then a man's scream, followed by a gunshot was heard from the backyard. the masked and armed men dashed outside.

"I guess this type of calm and helpless wait for one's execution doesn't only happen in movies," thought Duna.

"Who are these? Why are they killing us?" he then asked.

His voice resembled that of an academician who has just ran into his professor at the library while doing research.

"They call themselves U.T.F," said Captain Birol, in a pained tone. "United Terrorist Front. A huge new group that joins terrorists and anarchists of every creed and political leaning. Their rules are an absolute remission of rules, their aim is the destruction of this country and system. Their method is murder!"

"Fine, but such an alliance can't have a future..."

"Ah, dear teacher! This is utter annihilation, a final self-destruction! Their belligerence and hatred is not only directed at people unlike themselves! At this point they are sabotaging their own lives. I mean look, they've bombed the factories that produced their bread, the hospitals that treated their children, and the schools that educated their families. They smashed and burned the medicines, operating equipment, and school desks. And just yesterday they killed their own peer due to 'betrayal of the cause.' They're a gang which has lost sight of the reasons for its sacrifices!"

"This is collective madness!" said Duna, wincing, as if his brain had been scalded with boiling water.

"This is what I mean when I say indications already existed. In the beginning, signs are bloodless and innocent," said Captain Birol.

Then he suddenly began to moan. "God damn it, I can't bear this pain any longer… They broke my left arm, the pain is killing me… Aah!… The tears on my face are not from sorrow but from pain…"

Duna checked his own arms and lags. They were completely numb. He did not feel anything. No, wait… He did feel a pain but this was the pain and stink of rotten flesh that had spread throughout his body.

"Greed, alcoholism, rampant comsumption, politicians who support ruthless get-rich-quick schemes, media groups, racism, and the increase in domestic violence…" Captain Birol rattled off this list with the desperation of a person running to catch the last train, "These were innocent signs…"

"Are you alright Birol?"

He did not even hear Duna.

"These were the causes that fed and fueled violence and aggression… You know, lieutenant! You know these so… Aaah my arm… so well that… because of this nightmare you have been living through for years…"

"How strange…" said Duna. "I would not have thought that these were the things two young men about to die would talk about…"

"Two soldiers!" corrected Captain Birol.

Duna understood then that Birol still retained his consciousness.

"Besides, what does it matter…"

"It does matter!" he interjected. "It matters because this conversation cannot be real in such an environment! This can only take place between two intellectuals who are enjoying fish and raki, or cheese and wine on the Bosphorus, on a starlit summer night. You see, Birol, every instance serves to disprove the argument that what we are experiencing is real, and I end up being right everytime!"

"I guess you're going to die, thinking that this is all a dream, professor!" sighed Captain Birol.

"A man said that perceptions are just like optical illusions, they can be reversed in an instant," Duna muttered absent mindedly.

His voice was deep, calm, and distant, like a man talking in his sleep.

"If… if we survive and don't die," said Captain Birol, "I want to ask something of you, teacher… I mean even if I am martyred…" his voice choked up, "I would be very happy if you presented an autographed book of poetry by Dogan Gokay to my fiancee Neshe for me…"

They fell silent. They let loose the pains tormenting their bodies, the stench nauseating their stomachs, the violence deranging their heads, and the longing scorching their souls. Without uttering a single word, they simply looked on.

"Also…"

"Also?"

"Also… look, if you survive this… hold on tight to that woman for whom you are willing to face death, hold on to her that she might know your love…"

A terrible clamor drowned out his words. This time, there were three people who kicked the door open, the third one being a masked woman. Upon seeing them, Captain Birol calmly began to recite the testimony of Faith, but he was cut short. As soon as they entered the room, the masked individuals, without speaking, immediately took up positions facing Captain Birol, and scourged him in chorus with their machine guns. The young soldier flailed about, blood gushing out of his body. The assassins, aware that their victim had been killed, still continued to fire transcendantly, prolonging the duration of the murder, still they continued to fire.

Stupified with fear and terror, Duna felt his ears ringing, his stomach aching violently, and his knees knocking against each other.

"My god, they're enjoying the violence!" he sobbed. Then he hung his head and waited for his turn.

He was amazed that at such a moment he could still wonder whether or not Quentin Tarantino felt the same pleasure while writing "Natural Born Killers," or directing "Pulp Fiction." But all the same, just before he died, this was the only thing that came to his mind!

He heard a single noise. He held his breath and waited.

When he opened his tear soaked eyes, he realized that he was the only person alive in the room. The murderers had slammed the door and left.

"They saved me for the next feast." he moaned.

He raised his head. He could see the bloodied, doubled up body of Captain Birol across the room perfectly clearly, as if the nearsightedness of his eyes had been cured without glasses.

His own body, drenched in blood, sweat and tears, began to rock with sobs.

"My god, oh my god, I am so ashamed to be glad that I will live a little longer!"

He was not yet aware that he had wet himself.

SEX LIES

"Most people will agree that sex is pleasurable. Yet you must be aware that if you do not convert your sexual energy and allow it to trickle out, your liveliness will be exhausted. This exhaustion will gradually cause psychological pains such as fatigue and depression, and physical ones such as back and kidney aches."

Chia &Chia
(Taoist Sex Secrets for Women)

"People should have at least one reason for living in a certain neighborhood!" I said.

"We no longer have any reason to live in Kuzguncuk."

My mother was sitting on the prayer rug with a radiant smile on her face, barely moving her lips as she counted prayer beads. She had placed an embroidered, ivory colored gauze cloth gingerly upon her hair, allowing its corners to fall on her shoulders. By that time her luminous black hair, the sheen and thickness of which she had always been proud, had turned quite gray and she gathered it all in a bun at her neck, just like my grandmother. Also, like my grandmother, she had taken to wearing long dresses with close fitting skirts. I was glad that my mother wanted so much to resemble my grandmother, and that she succeeded in her effort. I liked my grandmother.

"We're stuck here... Memories are everywhere... We can't breathe..." I said, averting my eyes, "Let's move somewhere else and start a new life, mom."

My mother continued to count her prayer beads. The silence

between us was very peaceful but I myself felt extremely restless, and brimming with anxiety.

"Why do you men act so sneaky and cowardly on certain subjects, son?" asked my mother in the gentlest of voices.

"What did I do, mom?"

"What more could you do, dear son? This girl came to you and said I have nowhere to go, lend me a hand... And you just turned away."

"Mo-om...What was I supposed to say? Come and stay with us, or something? Huh?"

"But of course," replied my mother in a perfectly calm manner, as she got up and began to gather her prayer rug. "There isn't a person left who hasn't heard that this girl has been after you ever since you two were children, and you still act like you don't know, son. Are you going to find anyone better than her? She's very pretty, educated, has a profession, and she's very ladylike. Furthermore, she's not capricious or vain!"

"Mom!"

Obviously I was aware that after Aras and my father passed away Merich had been a remarkable source of support for my mother, and to a certain extent had saved her. And I did not hide my gratitude to her on this account, but was this not more of a feeling of indebtedness?

Meanwhile, my mother was of course alluding to Ada who was both capricious and vain, who neither possessed an occupation nor the slightest ladylike manner, and showed no hope for future reform. My mother was the product of a generation and environment which only considered officers, tailors, teachers, doctors and engineers to have a profession. Photography was not a career in her eyes.

Yet during the years when Ada and Aras seemed certain to have a future together, there had been no girl more intelligent, classy, or noble than Ada. Was it Ada who had altered so drastically after that "disaster," or my mother? Perhaps in her view, the same Ada who had seemed like an ideal bride in light of Aras' strong personality and a thousand and one talents, did not appear appropriate next to me.

"Look, dear child, I won't be a burden to you two. You can

build you own home, your own nest, and furnish it as you like. I can have a toilet and bath added to the small room downstairs, and move in there. I won't bother you at all. After all, in this mortal world…Life hangs only by a thread, son…"

The two room apartment downstairs had been converted into a stockroom, because she had not wanted any tenants, and the toilet had been closed down. So, my mother was even willing to live down there…

Her voice trembled but she immediately gathered herself. I too, pretended not to have heard. We were both weary of suffering and weeping.

"Mom, look at all the things you've devised when there's no plan or pretext! Don't, for God's sakes! Besides, it's too early yet."

"Too early for what?"

She rolled her prayer rug into a long, slender cylinder and stored it behind the door. Walking up to me, she raised me from my seat, took my arm, and dragged me into the living room.

"It's been a while since you and I had a nice cup of coffee, just mother and son. Now, sit down here and I'll bring two medium sweet cofees. I'm going to make them the way Mrs. Murshide, may she rest in peace, used to make them!"

There were cheerful and even mischievous undertones in her voice. I grew elated and frightened at the same time.

"Wait here, don't run off anywhere!"

I went to the window and drew open the tulle curtains. I looked out into Uryanizade Street. It was nighttime in mid-winter. I searched for the glittering mansion across the street. Now, only a single light glowed wanly in the structure. With the death of Uncle Shakir the gardener from cancer, the garden too had lost its liveliness and had turned into a haphazard, messy, insignificant place. The small fountain was as depressing as a ragged, snot-nosed street urchin. The vine covered arbor, under which so many fine conversations and discoveries of childhood and youth had been lived, had wilted away, taking with it all the truths it had known and witnessed. None of Sivri's successors had been able to adapt to its environment. Sometimes, even when all the ingredients and measurements are correct, the meal can turn out to be tasteless! Finally, the mansion's garden had been left without a dog. Despite seasonal gardeners and workers, the mansion's garden had never been able to regain the glorious beauty it possessed during Uncle Shakir's period.

Sureyya Mercan was very ill. Ada, who had rented a studio-apartment in Cihangir, often came to visit the mansion and stayed in Kuzguncuk. Therefore, I also dropped by two or three times a week, in order to see both her and the poet Dogan Gokay. Merich's mother had gotten married and Merich had moved into a student dormitory.

"Mrs. Murshide used to add the sugar to Turkish coffee after the water had boiled, let's see if I can make it as good as her!" called my mother from the kitchen.

How I had missed my mother calling cheerfully from the kitchen. I smiled.

It was the first semester of my teaching career and, as I was doing more studying than the students themselves, I was constantly exhausted. After having passed the aptitude test, I had applied to a number of schools for employment, and accepted the first serious offer that proposed a salary surpassing my expectations I had begun work right away.

I was teaching literature, composition, and substitute philosophy at Atacanli Private High School, and monitoring oral examinations for college preparatory courses. There was a great pressure, a heavy load upon my shoulders. I would panic, then tense up in order to hide it, and the tenser I grew, the more I turned into a stuffy person very much unlike myself. There were numerous youths before me, staring at me, some with bright, some with weary, and some with mocking gazes, waiting to fling my inexperience in my face like a rotten egg at any moment. For the most part, they considered literature and social sciences to be "pretend" classes, and plodded on, convinced that the only true guide in life was mathematics and physics. At that time I regarded them as potential threats, and did not sense any camaraderie between us.

The rumor that I was one of the institution's owners, due to the similarity of my name to that of the school's, had already reached my ears. My attempts at trying to explain that this resemblance was pure co-incidence would inevitably backfire and I would end up being teased by students who declared "Oh yeah, sure, teach, they also say that I'm related to the millionaire Sabanci!" After a few months, I gave up trying.

"Here it is: splendid Turkish coffee I wouldn't exchange for the world with that so-called Nescafe of yours!"

Ever since I had graduated and entered the workforce, my mother had begun to smile like before, to hold phone conversations, to make neighborhood visits, and to read the paper for the first time. Despite all that had happened, there was one thing that still went well, and my mother clung to it dearly. I can't speak for every man who has had a strong mother, but perhaps because of her, I have always admired women who are strong and devoted to life.

"Here, let me take a good look at my Blue Danube for a second!"

"Oh no!" I thought in alarm. It was not at all difficult to guess what direction our conversation would take after such an opening. Remember, I was one of those casualties, who, being the youngest in the house are never considered to be an adult by their mothers. After "that disaster" my mother, who had first been left without a son and then a husband, had somewhat reluctantly placed me in the most important position of life according to her: that of "the man of the house." Nevertheless, she would immediately transform me into her little son, the one she petted with nonsensical syllables, whenever she saw fit. In the past I would have been extremely upset with all these mannerisms and tactics, and would have become surly, but living through pain changes a person... My mother was still on her feet, and she was the last person left of my family. Perhaps my change in attitude was due to an instinct to fortify the shaky foundations of my existence, rather than simple gratitude. And of course I was born as one obliged to assume "the role of goodness" in this world, and could not do otherwise.

"Is the coffee good?"

"Naturally, your coffee is always good Mrs. Zubeyde."

"Good, anything for my son!"

"Oh no!" I shuddered once again. It was clear that a terribly sentimental mother-child chat was on its way.

"Duna, I was thinking..."

"Mo-oom!"

"What is it? Why're you looking at me like that? I didn't even open my mouth yet."

"I know what you're going to say, Mrs. Zubeyde!"

"Oh, and what's that?"

"That whole Merich business of course…"

"It's not like you think!"

"How do you mean?"

"Sexuality is not as important as you think, son. A person's sexual desires might increase with time and affection."

Excuse me?… My mouth fell open. I must have heard it wrong. Coffee spilled from the cup in my hand onto my trousers. I tried to wipe it off clumsily. No, there are certain things that are possible, and other things that are not… My mother, of the Eastern Anatolian heritage, a middle school graduate and a housewife, my timid and sometimes even conservative mother was giving her twenty-three year old son sex advice, and I was supposed to believe that?

I had not once seen my mother and father hold hands or display public affection. I had never heard them call each other "honey" or "sweetheart." Was my bashful mother, who averted her eyes at even kissing scenes on screen, now giving me sex lessons? Had I been left so far behind, trailing after my mother? Or had my mother changed without my noticing it?

So, sex was not as important as I had thought!

But how on earth did my mother know how much significance I actually assigned to sex? Oh, so sex was not as important as I made it out to be, huh? Bah! Humbug! Is that so? What rubbish!

"Now, why are eating, drinking, sleeping, defecating and urinating important, and sex isn't? So one can live without sex, huh? Ridiculous! We've seen the misery, perversion and violence of those who experience sexual poverty, who have sexual problems…" This was what I wanted to shout at my mother, but I restrained myself and kept silent. Besides, what would be the use of discussing sex with my mother?

"Certainly, sexuality is important, but not as much as you think. Furthermore, sexuality grows with mutual affection, son. Love that is one-sided does not bring peace, dear!"

My bewilderment must have been written all over my face, and

I suppose I was the one who was embarrassed to talk about sexuality with his mother.

"We don't need to talk about this mom... Besides, I'm not as awkward as you might think on the subject," I said.

My voice could have been likened to that of a child whose toy has been taken away from him. My mother laughed.

"No one is, Duna."

When I looked up, I saw unfamiliar gleams in my mother's eyes. She was right, perhaps I was the one with the outdated opinions.

"The world is rapidly changing, son, and that ruthless thing called time flees by so fast once you're past twenty-five, god help us! All of a sudden you realize you've grown old. Things you don't hold tight just slip through your fingers. And sometimes... even those you do hold tight..."

She stopped. We both stole a glance at our hands.

"A youth that is spent with vanity and indecision never brought anyone joy."

She stopped again. Apparently, my mother had her mind set on surprising me.

"You're not like Aras, Duna. He..." she took a deep breath.

This was the first time that she was able to talk about Aras, and to utter his name so calmly.

"Aras is a very decisive boy, sometimes too much so."

Barely moving her lips, she said a very quick prayer for my brother.

"You... even when you were a boy, you would remain indecisive for long periods of time, and when you did make up your mind you would grow miserable for having missed your chance. You'd remain sorry for days on end, and drive me crazy. You take a little after your late father."

I kept silent. I was heartbroken, but my mother was right, and she was not telling me this as a reproach. Perhaps my real problem stemmed from my inability to accept myself the way I was. I wonder what the average age is when a person embraces himself for all that he dislikes about his character?

"In real life, male-female relationships do not turn out the way they do in movies, son."

Wait a minute… honestly, who is it that's speaking?

The first page of my sexual education was actually written by Ada's parents, long before movies, comic books, TV, and novels. I was around five years old, and I had just started to visit the mansion. While I was playing with Ada in the garden, a taxi had stopped in front of the gate and from it had alighted a slender princess of a beauty I would never be able to forget, wearing a black print dress with large white and lilac flowers. The cab driver had felt the need to run over to her side like a private chauffeur, and hold the door open her. The gardener and nanny who suddenly appeared at the door, had greeted the princess in excitement, and even Sivri the puppy had been unable to hide his adoration. Just then, Sureyya Mercan had dashed out of the mansion with glowing animation, and after kissing the princess' hand, had taken her arm. Their eyes had locked into one another's, without seeing anyone else.

The princess had many suitcases and she had also brought some cake-shaped boxes. The gardener was carrying these into the mansion.

"My mother was in Rome for a movie shoot…" said Ada, trying to attract my attention.

So, Ada's mother was this princess!

Just when they were about to enter the mansion, the princess remembered her daughter. She ran over to Ada and hugged her daughter with a guilty face. She presented her with fancy wrapped chocolates which she produced from her handbag. She announced that there were a great deal of toys in her suitcases. Perhaps she would have stayed longer and noticed me, but Sureyya Mercan swept her off into the mansion, almost tugging at her with jealousy. I was charmed!

"Lovebirds!" Ada had said slyly, as she unwrapped her gifts.

As Ada parroted the epiphet Uncle Poet had given her parents, her face registered a mixture of the jealousy of a child who feels excluded by her parents' love towards each other, and the tenderness of a mother who forgives her children.

That same day I entered the mansion for a reason which I now cannot quite recall. Perhaps I was pursuing a lost toy, or was simply curious. I don't know, I can't say…

At the time I was not aware of the rule that we kids were allowed to play anywhere we wanted on the ground floor of the mansion, but that we were prohibited from going upstairs, where the bedrooms were located. I had started to climb the stairs, mesmerized by the soft, sweet giggles and whispers coming from the second floor. As I approached, almost magnetically drawn to those tender, soothing whispers, my little boy's heart practically thundered out of my chest. Finally, I stopped in front of the bathroom where the foor was left ajar, and stood nailed to the spot.

For starters, the bathroom had seemed incredibly dazzling to my eyes. The walls were covered with mirrors, and the floors with plush white rugs. The sink and bathtub were yellow, and then... And then I had seen them in the bubble-filled bathtub. Ada's mother and father were stark naked, they were stroking each other, and laughing. Her father was biting her mother's breasts, and her mother was smiling instead of crying. Clasped in an embrace, they were rocking back and forth in the bathtub and moaning with pleasure. As for the way they licked one another, I could not make head or tail of it, because the only thing I enjoyed licking was mastic ice-cream.

A five year old child can somewhat sense what these things are, but he cannot name or comprehend it, and therefore feels uneasy. My first glimpse had been that of a joyful and pleasurable lovemaking, and it had left a positive impression upon me. Nevertheless, I have to admit that I had found the adult world to be different, and slightly intimidating compared to the world of children. Thankfully my own parents did not know how to do such things, they were different.

The next episode of my sexual history is marked by little Ada's interactive instruction session in that very same bathtub, when, taking pity on my "ignorance" on the subject of baby-making, she had showed me her naked body and informed me of the impossibility of conceiving until one was legally married.

After that I had frequently witnessed Aras and Ada kissing in various locations. However, I had experienced my first sexual arousal when, following my grandfather's death, Merich had suddenly hugged and kissed me with unexpected passion as we sat on the edge of, once again, the same bathtub, and I administered to her nosebleed. That kiss had caused a true sexual awakening within me, and Merich's fiery overtures had made me feel that I too could be desired by a girl.

The brief touches and feverish kisses I exchanged with Merich never ceased to arouse strange feelings in me. The transformation of such a seemingly quiet and timid girl into a wholly other, impulsive and desirious female both excited and frightened me. Later on, I was to learn that conversely, women who look assured and healthy can be troubled and repressed in bed.

I never refused Merich's desire to corner me here and there and to kiss me with her whole trembling body, though I always avoided taking things any farther than a few brief strokes. First, because I am too stupid to ever learn how to say "no,"; second, because of the love combined with pity I felt for Merich, and third, because there is no man who can resist being so desired by a beautiful girl. So, it's all very complicated.

The fourth and genuine reason was the wretched, idiotic, and childish notion of saving myself for someone. As if someday Ada would notice that I too was a man, and I would go to her, having never cheated on her with anybody else! A miracle, a magic, a mystery! Dear god, is it only fools who believe in miracles, or do miracles only reveal themselves to those who believe in them?

During my college years, I had sexual affairs with three girls. One of them was the sister of a classmate, and she was three years my senior. She had just divorced her husband, who had cheated on her with her best friend; she was heartbroken and terribly hurt. One day, when she had stopped by school to meet her brother for a movie, she had invited me to come along. It was winter; a chilly Istanbul day, hostile with fog and wind. Exactly the weather that makes one's demons come alive. After the movie, we had gone out for a cup of *salep* at a cafe.

She had looked into my eyes and asked:

"Is there a man, a single one in this world who won't cheat on women?"

Her voice contained the pain of those who have been betrayed, the grief of those whose innocence has been slain, and the bewilderment of children who have matured early. She was all aflame, with her dark olive skin and thick, tousled hair. Her coal black eyes were misty with sorrow, and her nervous, jittery fingers seemed ready to strangle her own neck at any moment. Oh how she needed a loving touch, a bit of peace…

"I will never betray the woman I love!" I said gently. "She will never ask, but always know."

That was when she started to cry. She held my hand and sobbed loudly. If it had been any other time, I would have been embarrassed to be seen at a cafe with a young woman holding my hand and crying profusely. That day I was not the least bit bothered. We left together and went to her house. The Uskudar ferryboats were not running due to the fog. I called my mother to let her know, and stayed the night there.

I made love to a woman for the first time in the true sense that night. Before me was a young, hurt woman who had suffered greatly, and she made love to every inch of my body, alternately as a fierce lioness and as a hopeless little girl. At first I thought I was kissing and stroking her in order to make her happy, but soon I realized that I took great pleasure in kissing and nibbling on her full breasts, in grasping and squeezing her fleshy thighs and entering inside her to wander for long periods at a time. Once she caught on, we made love until the morning, not counting brief sleeping and snacking breaks. That night I learned that satisfying a woman during sex is intensely pleasurable for the man as well. And that was also when I understood how deeply a woman was wounded by infidelity.

Our relationship lasted for about six months, as a series of tempestuous afternoon lovemaking sessions. She was healing, and starting to see herself as someone who maintained her self-respect instead of "the dumb woman who has been made a fool of." She returned to the old job which she had quit upon getting married. A mature and sexy smile began to replace the green pain of betrayal on her face. The more we made love the prettier and more confidant she grew. I liked her. She was the one who had saved me from all my small, petty sexual experiences and made a man out of me, and I had emphatically wanted to tell her so. This did her good.

"Duna, you're the most romantic miracle I've ever had!" she would say, peeling off my glasses, taking my head in her hands and kissing me long and full on the lips.

"But darling, I know that I'm not your miracle!" she would add, without the slightest resentment. She was not resentful because she was not in love with me. We had taken a liking to one another, and we both badly needed to touch, kiss, and be kissed. Nevertheless, anyone who knows me will attest to the fact that I cannot be involved in even the most sexual relationships without the existence of emotional fulfilment.

We were not at all alike, with hardly anything in common. Neither of us nursed any expectations other than being together "for a while." I was too naive for her, and she, for me, was...

At the start of summer, Ada had returned to Turkey for vacation, and I had once again been ensnared in the magnetic field of the Kuzguncukite Honeygirl. Women are incredibly gifted at sensing "the other woman!" But she never reproached me. (Perhaps Ada was not quite a rival for her!)

She called at the end of the summer to say that she had met someone else.

"I did not cheat on you Duna. We just started dating. I like him a lot."

That winter she got married. I was invited to her wedding, and I went.

"Let me introduce you to Duna," she said to her husband. "A genuine person whose favors I will remember gratefully even if I never see him again!"

We never saw each other again.

The second one was Aliye.

It was during the time Ada used to come back for summer vacations, when she was gradually becoming acquainted with the photography circles in Turkey, and showing slides of North America to small interest groups. A girl who worked in an amateur photography club in Beyoglu practically latched on to us, popping up wherever we went and trying her hardest to become friends. At first, we had taken kindly to her. She had emigrated to Istanbul from a "distant eastern town," the name of which she guarded for dear life, and had completed night school. While working at a firm, she was also trying to learn a foreign language and photography. She was desperately holding on to life, determined not to fall at any cost.

Her personal struggle had made an impression on Ada.

"What if this girl ran away from home? What if she's being followed by gun-toting, honor-defending older brothers or something?"

Ada introduced Aliye to her own friends, helped her expand her circle of acquaintances, and contributed to her income by conjuring up various tasks to be done for her own pictures. Aliye idolized Ada and was not indifferent to me.

"This girl has talent, Duna. She can turn out to be a good artist if she uses her mind a little," Ada said.

I realized that Aliye was troubled, but at the outset, I had no idea of the extent of these problems. She felt that she had been wronged and slighted from birth, and expelled the rage of this injustice on everyone who crossed her path. She was capable of upsetting everyone, including herself, by abruptly turning grave in the middle of a joke, or by switching from a highly emotional state into one of cold sarcasm. Out of the blue, she would start singing loudly in the most inappropriate situations and burst out laughing in response to a tragic event. The indignance of not having been raised in a big city with wealthy means had turned into a self-destructive hatred.

She had a different physique. She was thin and tall. Her cheekbones, which were pronounced enough to draw attention, and her slightly slanted eyes which had imparted on her a hint of the Far East, combined to make her considerably sexy. She would attract attention wherever she made an entrance. However, her violent restlessness, which she seemed to have accepted as her lifelong burden and which she actually enjoyed, kept her from enjoying life as a young, attractive, independent and self-made woman. She could destroy everything, even the things she had accomplished with difficulty, with a fanatical fury and then became all the more furious upon being left empty-handed.

The tight trousers and cheap sweaters she could barely afford in the beginning turned into leather pants and stretch blouses as soon as she came into some money. But the colors always remained the same. Aliye wears only black and paints her lips burgundy. She has condemned herself to a life sentence of mourning!

Men who found her attractive would grow intimidated and flee when they saw that she travelled frequently and violently between

sharp edges. Nothing is more fr...
tional outbursts of women.

By the time Ada returned ...
America, Merich was busy with ...
a heavy course load. My old ...
with her new husband. Right ...
me frequently and to show ...
which I visited between class ...
Gokay who once said: "natu...
diately fills them!"

I was always startled to find ...
might, I could not figure out how ...
what kind of job she had, but this was no...
joy her attention. Men of every age enjoy being seen wi...
woman at their side. Some will not admit to this, some will conceal
it, and others will vehemently deny it. But the result is the same.

At first she was calm and stable. She had hooked me on my
weakest point, and proceeded with slow but sure steps.

"Man, that Ada is such an superb creature! I never seen a woman like that in my life!"

"That she is!"

"An incredible woman, I swear! For one thing, she's way obser-
vant… When she's talking to you she scans everything in the area
with her third eye and third ear, and then she pulls the trigger!"

"She's got talent."

"Professor Semih couldn't stop praising the attention she
showed to details. 'Course, he's hitting on Ada… Well, she's a pretty girl, real cool, and educated… Even in her plainest, most ratty
state Ada's far from pretty, she's, I dunno… umm… you know
how she has this princess-like manner, well that drives guys crazy."

I was peeved at this Professor Semih business. Who was this
guy, and how dare he hit on Ada? Then, as usual, I immediately began upbraiding myself for getting angry on the subject.

"What's it to you? Is it your business who Ada chooses or lives
with? She's an independent young woman and has made no promises to you! You are just a couple of childhood friends! Know
your place, Duna! And I hope you're not thinking that during
those cold winters in that large, glamorous, crowded North Ameri-

...e all by herself, watching TV and eating
... she simply went to and from school like a
...es, would you be happy if that were the case?"

...Aliye and I began to attend symphony concerts
...gether. She read like a madwoman, endeavoring to
...cover her weaknesses. I commended her determina-
...if one does not experience the pleasurable aspects of
...g the only thing left behind is a series of obligations, of
...n school troubles and dreaded classes are a direct result. Aliye
...s not interested in learning anything to become enriched or to
take greater pleasure out of life. She was equipping herself with
knowledge in order to exact revenge. Even her learning ambition
was bitter, her enthusiasm black.

"We've become a society without oskigen, look around, everyone's stealing each other's air!"

I knew that she was studying to develop her vocabulary and dic-
tion, but she could never say "oxygen." Although she succeeded in
correcting this afterwards, whenever she gets angry she cannot help
but say "oskigen."

"You're head over heels in love with Ada!" she cried.

We were in the Emek movie theater. "Days of Cinema" had not
yet adopted the name "Istanbul Film Festival," and we were watching a Spanish movie. I can't quite recall its name, but it was the
adult version of a fairytale, about the doomed love of a king, re-
worked with black humor. I *think* it was a Spanish film.

"Shhh! Quiet…"

I had not understood what happened.

"But she doesn't love you! You're just a toy to her!" her voice
was blissful, like someone moaning with pleasure.

I was annoyed. What had hurt me was not that all the other mo-
viegoers had learned of my love toward Ada, but rather that they
had been given the false impression that my love was unrequited.

"That's ridiculous Aliye. Quiet down!"

She did not. She acted even more belligerent and pernicious. As
a result, we were forced out of the theater with the sshh's of other
audience members.

"Look, there're a thousand various kinds of love," I said, as we
walked on Istiklal Avenue, toward the Tunnel.

"And every single kind hurts! That's one of Dogan Gokay's poems, isn't it?"

"Yes. It's not a secret or anything!"

"You and people like you annoy the hell outta me Duna!"

She came to an abrupt halt and began yelling in the middle of the street.

"You experience every minute of your life first-hand, and you think that's completely natural! You spoiled, arrogant bastards! You guys were growing up chatting with Dogan Gokay before I even knew his name! You guys always complained of too much oskigen while I could hardly breathe! Why doesn't God damn you all?"

Passersby stopped and stared at this young woman who, with full burgundy lips and tight black clothes, was screaming at the youth next to her in the middle of the street. At first glance she did not seem hysterical or fond of attention.

"Quit playing these games Aliye. Either we keep walking, or I'm out of here! You get your kicks out of hurting other people and making yourself suffer, instead of really living! I'm sick of your absurdities!"

Aggressiveness is definitely contagious. In the end I too had stood in the middle of the street, bellowing back at her. So I turned around and strode away in a huff. I was admonishing myself. Aliye was making me nervous. She ran after me, and took my arm.

"Did you mention getting kicks? Come with me!"

From that day on we made frequent love in her small, decrepit, two-bedroom apartment, which always smelled of the greasy cooking of next door neighbors. Aliye was brimming with an incredible sex drive and energy. She did not know satisfaction or fatigue, and she constantly aroused me. As in her daily life, her tastes in bed were also masochistic. I could not fulfill some of her desires, because they struck me as barbaric. It shattered my emotional equilibrium to bite a woman I was making love to until she bled, or to hit her, and I simply could not do it. Meanwhile, my mother had embarked on a mission to feed me better, attributing my weight loss at the time to the difficulty of my coursework.

Aliye was twenty-six, (once again, an older woman) and she knew what seemed to me an extraordinary amount on the subject of lovemaking. She knew every overt and covert sex technique from that of the Taoists to the Persians, from the art of the Japanese to native Amazon practices, and she practiced them with me. But what was truly impressive was her talent and experience on the matter of oral sex. Indeed, I was losing weight.

Since Aliye was terrified of any serene, enjoyable period of time, she was always pursuing tension and discomfort. Everything one experienced with her was stormy, with strong gusts of wind, hail, and showers. She never failed to curse the day she was born into her family as a fourth, unwanted and unloved daughter, yet she had never tried to get drunk off the joy of her own successes. Aliye was afraid. Of loneliness, humiliation, ridicule, desertion, of loving, and establishing a stable relationship, or life. She ran away from all the beauty that makes life what it is, and in the process she levelled everything in her way.

Whenever I made the slightest attempt to reach out and help her she attacked me and tore me to shreds. I was never able to get close to her in the course of our relationship, which lasted almost a year. After our incredibly fierce and animated lovemaking, in that room which reeked of frying oil, I would try talking to her. If, taken off guard for a few seconds, she displayed her broken, love-starved heart, she would immediately regret it and start showering insults upon me until I lost all humor. I had come to understand that in fact, her every attack bore a self-destructive urge.

She would throw away the posters, colorful bedsheets and patterned coffee cups I bought in order to enliven her room, and remark that in her classroom, only her rules applied. Yet all her struggles were toward surpassing her class, and these contradictions wore her down, consumed her.

"You know, I've never had an orgasm with anyone!" she said one day, as we lay on the bed.

She could not have expected me to believe this. She made such active, passionate love that I was simply stupefied, as if I had suddenly been dropped from a great height.

"I've never met a guy who can get so close to me! They're all gonna leave anyway."

Desertion-phobia! I could not claim to be unfamiliar with that feeling.

When Ada returned to Kuzguncuk that summer the four of us,

including Merich, went on a tour of the Bosphorus. During the trip Aliye had devoted her exaggerated attention to Ada alone, as if there had been no one else in the party, and Merich remarked:

"I'm scared of that girl, Duna."

"I suppose she feels guilty toward me for liking you..." ventured Ada.

Later, I forgot all about her, and also spent that summer caught on the trail of Ada's magic Milky Way. This was not something I had done against Aliye specifically. When it came to Ada, my interest toward all other living beings decreased. To be honest, I was already backing out of this painfully tidal affair which, for me, held no promise of a relationship. During that time period we would occasionally bump into each other in Beyoğlu, where she strove to attract everyone's attention with her loud laughter and the outrageously dressed youths at her side.

"This girl's going to wreck herself. We should give her a hand," said Ada.

I had not been able to understand whether she had said that to herself or directed it at me, because she was scheduled to return to North America soon. And she did.

I met Aliye a few more times. At each encounter she increased the level of insults thrown at me and estranged me even more. Sexuality, caught in this crossfire, could only grow mechanic, and ceased to function. I decided to break it off, or rather, rid myself of her completely. She grew more infuriated than ever.

I had purposely stopped calling her. As a result, she began to follow me. I did not answer her calls and changed my way when I saw her on the street. Apparently she once came to Kuzguncuk and made a scene. My mother was not home that day, having gone to Karacaahmet for prayers. Musa the grocer and Sefer the baker had put her in a taxi and sent her back home.

She exhausted me, and brought out a cross, ill-tempered side of myself to which I was not at all accustomed. It was at the height of finals period, and I hardly had a moment to spare. As for her, she not only suspected that I had another lover, but was utterly convinced of it. In fact, she had gone to seek out Merich at the Medical School, and had left her alone after learning that we had not seen each other for weeks.

"What kind of relationship could you have with this girl that she can come to school to interrogate me?" Merich had asked, on the verge of tears. "You wouldn't even hold hands with a girl like that!"

I had taken refuge in the lie that all men tell in similar situations. "Oh, she's just exaggerating, making things up in her head!"

And like all women who assume their beloved to be perfect, Merich believed me.

I did not know how to rid myself of Aliye, and was frankly rather intimidated by her. I nursed no hopes whatsoever about the limits of her instability. But everything ended much more swiftly than I expected. I met her one last time, in order to explain that "it was all over." I had resolved to act politely and amiably. Just as I was lecturing her about the unhealthiness of some relationships, struggling not to sound hurtful, she cut me short: "Fine, fine, don't bother. I'm used to being abandoned. Life never misses a single opportunity to slap me in the face!"

She got up and left. She did not even say goodbye. (Did she have to, anyway?)

Afterwards, we did not see each other for a long time, but the reports I heard of her were terribly saddening. It was said that she had been actively involved with drugs for a long time. All that about her job at a company was a lie. She was taken into custody, but released due to lack of evidence. I heard that she was saved from committing suicide at the last moment. I'm not going to lie; none of these incidents made me want to go to her side and hold her hand. I neither felt the inclination, nor the courage. I dreaded, and even feared her vicissitudes. Aliye needed to be treated before she destroyed herself.

Years later, when Ada showed up with her, she seemed recovered and calm. I did not understand at the time that this was just an optical illusion.

The third was a model whom I had met at Burkan's fashion design studio, where I worked on some weekends with Pervin Gokay. She was cute and attractive. She was only doing small shows for the time being, but had her sights set on becoming a famous model in the future. I thought that she was too emotional and affable to fit the role of her dreams. Her lively, vivacious manner during our brief conversations always imbued me with small enchantments. One day, out of the blue, she invited me to coffee, and I accepted. At first we simply dined and had fun together. Little kisses and hugs. When we began making love at a common friend's house one day, she said:

"Let's do it without spoiling my virginity!"

I stood gaping in surprise.

"My dad allowed me to be a model, but only on the condition that I would take virginity tests whenever he wanted…"

I felt crushed with sadness. The double standard of these ethics, this two-faced honesty had overwhelmed me. I immediately put my clothes back on and got her dressed. She was apologizing through her tears, and reiterating how much she liked me. We met and talked a few more times. Then she married a wealthy business-man, whom her father approved of. Recently, Pervin Gokay whispered in my ear, with a sly smile, that she had born twins.

"What do you say, Duna?"

"Huh?"

My mother was looking at me and smiling with a contentment only mothers can find in looking into the faces of their children. I could not gauge how long she had been waiting for my inner dialogues to come to an end.

"Would you like some water, son?" she asked gently, with a voice full of patience.

"No thanks," I replied, trying to recover.

"Look son, Ada has pretty much established her own life. And as far as I know, there is no one else you are that attached to. Now, as for Merich … I was thinking, before Merich unwillingly marries someone else due to the conditions…"

"Mom! Please, stop pressuring me. Fine, you may be right, but marriage is so… Well, it just can't be made-to order. Besides…"

"Besides, what?"

"Besides, marriage frightens me. Giving a vow of devotion, re-maining loyal to the same person for the rest of your life… Who has ever been able to keep this promise? Have you ever been con-vinced that you never deceived and were never deceived, Mrs. Zu-beyde?"

I had thought that by changing the subject I would throw my

mother off the track, but she remained resolved. Not upset in the least, she gazed at me with a knowing smile.

"If it's a matter of someone you love dearly, you can't bear to hurt them, Duna. One goes out of her way for her beloved. Anyway, you have been doing this for years, son."

I sighed.

"And yet…"

Her voice suddenly trembled and grew darker:

"Ever since Aras, who most deserved to live in this world, departed, I have been sick of those 'lifelong vows,' son. You embark on something, you strive to set it right, you try various approaches, you act honestly, and if it still does not work out, then you cannot force it, child. You can never force it!"

Her voice faltered but recovered just as it was about to fall and shatter completely. My mother had gotten to know pain well enough to handle it.

"As much as you love Ada, Merich loves you just as desperately Duna. If you want to be cruel like Ada, then keep going, but you're a loving, adaptable person. It's time to stop tormenting this girl."

"Mom! You're being unfair. Ada's only obliged to act that way because of Aras' memory!"

She got up and briefly stroked my hair with one hand. "I'm going to bed, may God grant you rest, calm, and peace of mind. May God grant us whatever He deems auspicious, son. My prayers are with you, my Blue Danube."

Then she left. My mother really left the living room, after ensnaring me in a cycle of hundreds of questions. I felt like a sacrificial lamb; I was about to be forced into an arranged marriage. I could suffocate from the pressure. Sure, my mother was right, but still…

I got up, paced around the room, and planted myself in front of the window, straining to see a light in the darkened mansion. There was none. I resumed my restless pacing. Then I suddenly stopped dead in front of the glass display case made of walnut wood, and left to us from my grandfather. A small silver candlestick, wrapped with a greeen ribbon, had been placed in the very forefront. Someone had given us a silver candlestick and interestingly enough my mother had been able to keep herself from telling me the news. The devil prodded me, I opened the case, and picked up the candlestick. It was a fine, elegant piece of work. When the candlestick was removed, the card that had been propped up behind it fell to the floor. I bent down and picked up the card.

"Dear Auntie Zubeyde,

I have not received my salary yet, but I wanted to purchase something for you with my first paycheck. You have always understood how much I wished I could have had a mother like yourself. In the end, come what may, I will be a daughter to you. With my eternal love and respect,

Your daughter: Merich."

An affectionate smile impressed itself on my lips, and a lump that I simply could not swallow, got stuck in my throat. Absentmindedly stroking the silver candlestick, I heard myself groan: "Oh Merich!"

Having closed the display case, I was just about to retire for the night when that stone caught my eye. That small white stone she was speaking to years ago, when I first saw her. That talking stone which was Ada's first gift to me.

I left my eyes on the stone and returned blind to my room.

KEEP ME FROM YOU!

"An eyestone in my hands/ I walk on with empty eyes
How was I supposed to know/ one drop would turn into a sea
I marvelled/ when it bloomed like a blue fortune before me."

Can Yucel

"Just like the old days Ada. Eating kup griye at Baylan... The back patio might even be open."

"Oh Mabel dear, oh that incorrigible romanticism, that nostalgia of yours. And my own..."

"Your what?"

A tiny sigh rose at the other end of the receiver, remained suspended for a moment, and fell back down after a brief resistance.

"Oh your own what, Ada?" I asked irately.

"My own incorrigible weakness for you, of course!"

"Fine, then tomorrow at ten I'll be waiting for you at Baylan. I'll be wearing a corduroy coat, nearsighted glasses, and I have curly black hair. However, closer inspection will reveal that I have shy blue eyes. I do hope you'll recognize me."

"No way Duna, you must be crazy, how am I supposed to get to Kadikoy by ten in the morning? It takes at least an hour and a half to cross over to Asia from Taksim during rush hour. Have some mercy!"

"Then let me wear a coat of a different color, one that you might prefer, so you may be able to recognize me."

"Can't it be in the afternoon, Mabel, pleease, huh?"

"I have two hours of class in the afternoon, and if you'll remember teachers can't cut classes! Besides, I don't have an afternoon colored coat..."

"Eleven, okay?"

"Alright."

"I'll see you, teach. You just wear your brown corduroy coat, it always goes well with your baby blues."

"Farewell Brunette Ada.

"Later, Blue Danube."

I must simply be nuts! Whenever this woman calls me "My dear Mabel" I melt with pleasure, and start emitting joyful screams like a boy lost in a chocolate factory. My adrenalin increases, my day becomes more lovely, and I experience the bittersweet sorrow of never having grown up. Everytime I'm about to see her, I get butterflies in my stomach, like a young man about to meet his sweetheart for the first time, and whirr, whirr, whirr… The enchantment of the five year old boy, when I first laid eyes on her: man alive!

"There, you see!" she said, as she kissed me on the cheek.

She was wearing a black beret, a black angora cloak, and a burgundy scarf, which was an exact duplicate of the one her poet uncle sported. Her peach scented perfume made me feel warm inside, and her nose felt icy on my cheek.

"There, you see, Baylan's back patio isn't open yet. And I don't like this dusty, cramped inner room one bit."

With the crankiness of those who are not early risers, her voice and face reflected a hunger for sleep which the tiniest spark could ignite into irascibility. Since I knew better than to bother her during such moments, I simply watched this gorgeous woman. She took off her cloak and placed it on an empty chair. Then she flung her satchel-like bag on top of it. She was wearing a black sport coat with brown chamois lapels. This was a model which I had designed for her, and which her mother had had tailored. Underneath, she wore a pistachio green turtleneck, and I was certain that it was short sleeved. She was going to wear this style like a colorful uniform for years to come, depleting the resources of a North American store in the process. If monotony in clothes is a consciously chosen route, I cannot help but seek a motive of self-chastisement behind it.

"Besides, whoever heard of eating ice cream at this hour of the morning, Mabel?" she grumbled.

I was gazing at her with a smile, an hour before noon. My god, how empty, lacking and lonely my (and the) world would be if it were not for this woman! Could I even conceive of a Kuzguncuk, Uskudar, an Istanbul, a Turkey, a world, or even a universe without her? Had I been able to, even for once? Had I ever existed in her absence? The intricate and delightful joy she gave me, the heart-in-your-throat excitement, the condition of vigilance for fear of losing her… A constant state of madness… The fatigue of infinite altitude… The beatitude of knowing its permanence… The innocence of knowing you will not be betrayed… The anxiety of being left alone… And the assurance of returning to her… What woman has been able to put a man through all these feelings for such a long period of time? Is not the fact that a miracle can remain so close and constant, material for a whole other legend?

"If you're just going to sit there grinning and staring at me then I'm leaving Mabel!" she said in a temperemental child's voice. She was deprived of sleep, and she meant it.

"I am just as happy as I used to be, right here, at this very moment," I whispered.

"You rebellious romantic," she said, immediately disarmed.

When she smiled, Baylan's gloomy inner room became illumined. We ordered two esspressos and got rid of the waiter.

"Now tell me Mabel, what's your hurry? Why did you call me here, screaming at the top of your lungs, at this hour of the morning, right in the midst of my busy winter schedule? What is this 'crucial business'?"

"A most urgent, pressing, and important topic!"

"Well, I hope so. Or else, you're really in for it! Honestly, Mabel, the only thing on my mind right now are my interrupted dreams! Besides, I have to hand in the agency's photographs by tomorrow. And there's not much time left until the exhibition. Boy, there's so much to do! But of course, when right in the middle of all this the Blue Danube calls, and says 'Help Ada!', everything stops in its tracks. Why? Because… because that's just the way it is! You know how everyone has their weaknesses…"

"Keep me from you Ada!" I said all of a sudden.

I had appropriated her style, something she had not expected from me in the least. She sat there, startled.

I waited for her to recover. She took out a pack of Camels. Ever since her permanent return to Turkey she had resumed the tobacco habit which she had quit in North America. She stared at the picture of the camel on her left hand, as if watching the pack itself. Then she turned towards me suspiciously. She looked me over.

"A nice shot, Mabel!" she said, smiling.

"'Scuse me, can I smoke in here?"

The waiter, who was approaching our table with espresso cups in hand, stared with the surprise of having heard such a question for the first time in his life.

"Why, sure!" he replied, thinking he was being mocked.

Then he rushed to light Ada's cigarette with a wildly exaggerated gesture, and smiled rakishly.

"Is it Merich?" asked Ada, as she smoked her cigarrete.

"Her, my mother, but mostly me."

She reached over and took my hand. Her hands were freezing.

"Duna," she said in a mournful voice, "Duna, you know that…"

I waited to hear whatever it was that I knew. She pinched her cigarette furiously with her free hand. She inhaled the smoke hungrily, like a suckling child.

"You are much more important and valuable to me than you think! That is how it's always been, and how its will always be!" she said.

I was holding her hand in mine, trying to imbue it with some warmth. I could not look her in the face. Then she spoke, haltingly, as if extracting the words from other sentences, and stringing them together:

"You are more things to me than anyone could ever be… The place reserved for you in my soul is greater than anyone else's. You're not only a friend, a blood brother, a confidant, and a very close pal, but you're also a great love. The only person with whom I can be as spoiled as I want and not be afraid of losing. You're, partly my mom, a bit my dad, in fact, the grandfather I never knew, and maybe even the son I will never have… Also my eternal fan and of course, my untouched lover. You are my innocence Duna; the closest person I've got! Actually, maybe you're my other half? Do you understand what all this means? Huh?"

I closed my eyes. I gulped down every word she said, but I was still thirsty. Because the word I had wanted to hear was not among the ones she had listed. Upon reopening my eyes, I saw that she was crying.

"I never told you this, but…"

I waited timidly. The tears that were hurriedly spilling out of her hazel eyes were rolling down her fair cheeks.

"You… even though you've always thought Aras was a great barrier between us, you are many things to me that he never was, and never could be. If not for you…You have to know this… If not for you, I would diminish greatly, and I could never handle that Duna!"

She retracted her hand. She wiped her face. She was tired.

Then she hung her head and murmured, "If the whole world betrayed me, if everyone on earth lied to each other, and even if there was an intergalactic, collective depression; if everyone was shaken, brought to their knees, and thrown to the ground, I would remain standing. Because I have my Blue Danube, I have my Mabel, and he's different!"

She sighed. She played with the cigarette pack bearing the picture of the camel: "And of course, I'm the most selfish girl the world has ever known!"

She stopped. I realized that she would not speak any more. Contrary to my expectations, I felt awful. I had asked the poor girl to come here first thing in the morning and then I had upset her. Or had I actually planned to do this?

"It really hurts to realize after waiting for years to start a life together with someone and thinking that finally there's nothing left in your way, that you yourself are the true obstacle!" I said, and almost swallowed my tongue in surprise.

This was a very carefully thought out sentence which had been planned a long time ago, but I swear on everyone I love that I had not been aware of it until just then.

"Remember what that man had said: love hurts in every form. God damn it, does this Dogan Gokay always have to be right?"

Just then, our waiter had materialized out of nowhere, and there he stood, glaring wrathfully at me, the cruel man who was making the woman next to him cry.

"Would you care for another cup of coffee?" he asked Ada in a compassionate, macho voice.

Noticing that she had not even touched the cup in front of her, Ada sniffed and wiped her face with a paper napkin. "Oh yes, that'd be wonderful. Could you bring us a couple of fresh, hot espressos?"

The waiter grinned, attributing Ada's public display of emotion to a sense of personal camaraderie she might have felt with him, and replied: "Right away, ma'am."

"I thought about you often Duna. Especially when I was abroad. Where, and how far things could go with you. And yet…"

"And yet, what?"

"And yet, I was always afraid!"

"You're insane. What were you afraid of, what *are* you afraid of?"

"Of losing you, Mabel! Everything I lay a hand on slips through my fingers. If I get close to something I love, I lose it."

"Here's your coffee! I hope you like it. Allow me to light your cigarette."

Not only had the waiter failed to replace my coffee, he had also succeeded in throwing me extremely dirty glances. Fine, so I had gotten on the guy's nerves, what was I supposed to do?

"No I never took the 'cursed girl' rumors to heart but I was very young and therefore terribly affected by them. There were such times, Mabel, that… I started to believe that I had killed Aras, and tormented myself. I really believed that. In fact, I'd even gone so nuts as to actually obsess over my left-handedness. These episodes still come and go."

"Come on Ada, don't do this," I mumbled.

"That night… that last night… if you only knew Duna…" once again, she started to cry.

"Ada, I… Ada, I love you more than you can know, more than you can guess or, even imagine. And I don't want you to cry anymore, alright?" I said, holding her hand.

"Would you like anything else?"

The waiter-in-shining-armor was back.

"The bill!" I yelled.

He pointed to the bill on the table, as if dealing with an idiot, and said: "The bill is paid at the cash register here!"

True, I had forgotten that.

"Our love is an impossible one, Duna," said Ada, in a voice that was unaware of the inane exchange going on between me and the waiter, and in fact, of the waiter's presence in general.

"There is only one condition on which this love can continue."

The waiter would not leave our table, and I felt capable of drowning him in a spoonful of water.

"We should not come together Mabel!"

"That's preposterous, Ada!" I protested, also having stopped caring about the fact that the waiter was listening to our conversation by inventing chores nearby.

"What you say only happens in movies and novels, but we're real. See, I'm a real life young man, in flesh and blood, and I can hardly breathe in your absence!"

"If I said to you now, come on, let's make love, do you think we could succeed Duna? Huh?" Ada cried out heatedly, and that was when the waiter took his leave.

I was stunned. True, I knew the girl before me quite well, and she was capable of saying such a thing, but now, like this, and to me?

"If we reduce love to daily life, we'll destroy it. We'll ruin everything. We'll be like everyone else. We'll start getting mad and incensed at each other, and worse, we'll wear each other down and start taking the other person for granted. Aras... If he had lived... Perhaps we would have long been separated or divorced. Or maybe..."

"Maybe what? Don't drive a person crazy Ada!"

"I don't know. I was always fascinated by his extreme decisiveness, his single-mindedness, and maybe we would not have broken up, just for obstinacy's sake."

"You were always in love with him;" I said, with a wounded but understanding voice. (Why understanding?)

"A woman loves a man differently, and every woman loves many men at once in her lifetime. You know, women have no other chance, Duna. Because men..."

She reached for another cigarette. I took it out of her hand. The last things she had said were sprawled out before me like a great sea in which I would wander long and thoughtfully, but my fate was locked in that final word.

"Because men what?" I asked.

"Because men are without surprises!"

I was surprised.

"Even the most diverse of men is monotonous, therefore it's women who really need polygamy! Because the need for sexual diversity never killed anyone, but emotional deficiency does!"

I felt depressed. Only those who have experienced it will know what an awful burden it is to be included among "all men." Even though I have been extensively educated to rise above universal male handicaps such as immaturity, brute force, misogyny, and libidinal obsession, everytime I am included in the same category with them I feel crushed and heartbroken.

"Oh sweetie! My one and only Mabel, you're different of course."

"Yeah, I'm very different, and that's why you love being my impossible lover."

"Alright, let's go! Right now. We're going to my place!"

"Hold on, stay calm Ada, I have class in two hours."

"You'll be on time for class. But we have to do this right now, today!"

"Do what Ada?" My voice trembled in anticipation and fear of the answer I was about to hear.

"We're going to go and make love Duna!"

Dear god, was this my madly beating heart, or had it left my body to become a body of its own? I fell in step behind her without a word of protest as she left a wad of cash at the counter, grabbed me by the arm and dragged me out before the jealous looks of the waiter. I do not know how and where we got into her used domestic car, when we put on our seatbelts, and how we arrived in Cihangir. It is also unclear what she told me on the way, or how I managed to suffer through Madonna yelling "Like a Virgin" from the car stereo. As we ascended the neglected stairway to the fifth floor of an old building, and as we entered the freezing studio, I felt that I was not there, but rather, watching another Duna from behind frosted glass, in a sped up movie reel.

I had calmed down by the time I began watching Ada dash around the house like a well-programmed and efficient robot. First she switched on the electric radiator. I let my eyes rest on the transparent switch which immediately glowed red. Then she turned on the already prepped coffee machine. I turned my gaze in the direction of that red switch, and the scrumptious coffee smell that emanated from it. Next, she turned on the stereo and Mozart wafted into the room. The switch on the stereo system also glowed red. I became entranced with this bright appliance as well. When I realized that she was somewhere else, I followed her. She had turned on the electric water heater which now also glowed red.

"There are so many red switches," I said.

"I hope the water supply isn't cut off. The pressure tank is a joke in this neighborhood," she said.

"Ada, we don't have to do this," I said, grasping her arm and pulling her toward me.

That was when I realized how tense Ada was, and I reeled back in surprise. The tension she gave off made me shudder, as if I'd received an electric shock.

"No, Duna, we have to give it a try! I don't want to keep you from starting your own life any longer!" She spoke indignantly, as if she were miffed at someone. Could that person be me? Or did Aras still wander around here somewhere, visible to no one except Ada?

"But this isn't the way to go about it," I protested.

"Did we ever manage to do it any other way Duna?"

She dragged me into the studio, which was slowly beginning to grow warm, and sat me down on the edge of the couch. And she started to undress. My god, I felt horrible. I have never been to a brothel or lusted after love for sale, but now, it was as if...

"Ada, sweetheart. Stop for god's sake! Don't do it, don't depress us."

She was left with only a white lace brassiere and panties. She was very beautiful.

"Ada, this might be the only thing that can't be forced and you know it... Please don't, don't hurt yourself."

Try as she might she could not unhook her bra, and it made her even angrier. It was (was it?) as if she were trying to exact revenge on something. Then she gave up, and her arms suddenly fell limp to her sides. She was extremely angry. I approached and put my arms around her. She had grown cold as ice. I wrapped around her the plaid blanket that was on the couch. She curled up and nestled in my lap. I smelled and kissed her hair. She whimpered like a young child. My god, how much I loved this woman! Preserve my mind, o god!

We simply sat there without speaking, listening to Mozart and inhaling the coffee aroma. All of a sudden, I bent over and kissed her. She did not participate, but merely responded. Her lips were more delectable than I had imagined. Slowly, I started stroking her shoulders, and caressing her ears and neck. Once again she responded without enthusiasm. I thought that I would die of excitement when my hands touched her breasts. Because she too had become aroused, and had begun to breathe faster. But suddenly she burst into tears. Like one being killed during an orgasm, I first cracked before I died.

"It's as if I'm committing a crime... This is a great sin, a terrible crime against humanity! I can't, no, I can't!" she cried.

Suddenly I also grew ashamed. I was left sitting there like a naive boy who had tried to make love to an elder sister. Or a cheap scoundrel who had attempted to take advantage of his older brother's wife. Yet I had not felt that way a moment ago, and if she had only said the word... But she was screaming so loudly, and shaking so uncontrollably that I grew frightened. Very frightened.

"It's alright dear, it's okay sweetheart. You're right!" I said, hugging her once more.

This time I embraced her tight with a true brotherly warmth. I was terrified that she might lose her mind, that she might go back to that hospital or overseas, and that she might not return for months or even years. I was petrified that her emotional frame, which she had just recently been able to reconstitute, might break and shatter. I was scared, scared, scared!

If maturity is being able to make informed choices between priorities, then I had matured there, on that day. In any case, had I not been sworn from birth to do anything not to lose Ada? No, since this was going to upset her so greatly I was willing to remain once again, and perhaps forever, as her asexual love Mabel!

Soon I had managed to pacify and clothe her, and we stood gazing at the distant view of the Bosphorus from the window, sipping coffee. Actually, I was in no state to enjoy any views. I kept looking at her, grieved and gladdened at the same time. I had both lost and found her. Goddamn it, I was sick of all these dualities.

"We have to leave right away to get you to school on time," she said, ever so gently.

"I can't find my coat."

"Look in the back room Duna."

The small room in the back was her bedroom, I went in and searched for my coat but could not find it. Just as I was about to leave, a silver frame on the commode caught my attention. In an old color photograph, two boys were standing awkwardly staring at the camera. I suddenly remembered that the picture, in which I must have been twelve and Aras fourteen, was taken by Ada. Aras, like all people who hate pictures, had grown very rigid, while I with my pimpled face grinned behind the glasses which I hated at the time, but which now seemed rather cute. Aras, even in that boyish phase was strikingly handsome, while I was always "extremely" cute.

Then it hit me once more, and I was compelled to sit down on the bed due to the force of the blow. Dear god, this grown woman was still living with a photograph of two kids on her bedstand! It was because of two boys, one of whom had long been dead, and the other who wandered about awkwardly, that Ada could not carry on with her life! Aras' ghost and my own indecisiveness prevented this girl from maturing, and what's more, kept her from being free. Ada had locked her heart into the year of Aras' death, and could not undo it. My god, this was how much the girl loved us, and it was because of this love that none of us could go on with our lives! Why had the three of us' lives interlocked so firmly? Why had a love become such a burden on our young, budding lives?

That was when I remembered Merich. She was the fourth wretch whose name was not even considered in this picture. We were all selfishly excluding her. Yet Merich had been with us from the first. I felt a sharp, almost bleeding pain inside. My stomach burned terribly. "Am I hemorrhaging internally?" I wondered, growing suspicious. I took off my fogged-up glasses. Picking up the silver frame, I took a closer look at those two kids. If... if I moved out of her way, would Ada perhaps find the strength to continue her life unhindered? If I stepped away from Ada's path, Merich would be happy. My mother would be pleased. I suppose I would have been doing everyone a favor if…

"That last night…" said Ada, touching my shoulder, and standing directly behind me.

"That last night… When you caught us under those trees, Aras and I had truly made love for the first time. Not counting small, fleeting things, it was on that last night that we had really become each other's for the first time."

I gulped. I had not known that. I mean, actually, I had never thought that they had really made love.

"Maybe he dove to his death so foolishly with that joyful intoxication."

Her voice trembled but she recovered herself.

"Because Aras was so very happy that night. He was finally convinced that I would marry him. If I had only been able to stop him…"

She sighed.

"If I had told him 'don't jump,' if I had just stood in his way, and yelled and screamed…"

I turned around and covered her mouth.

"At least," I said," At least my brother didn't die a virgin, at least just before he died he was able to become the man of the girl he loved most on this earth. Ada, stop mourning the past, at least my brother managed to be a very happy young man before he died!"

Ada stared at me to see if I was joking. But I was utterly sincere in what I had said. Taking her by the hand, I led her out of the bedroom and out of her studio-apartment. It turned out my coat had been in her car all along.

That day in class I set aside the official syllabus and talked to my students about the most beautiful love poems, and the most unforgettable love stories in the world. I taught my students that love was nature's greatest gift to us, and that a life without love meant death.

At first there were some who hooted and made wisecracks. Shortly afterwards I had delved into love's thousand and one types and biochemistries, and had verbalized love with my whole being. There was dead silence in the classroom. All the youths including the girls, the boys, the misbehaved, the lazy, the spoiled rich, the well-behaved, the intelligent, and the hard working, were listening to me with rapt attention. It was on that day that I began to love them.

That day I had succeeded in doing what had evaded me for months: I had managed to impress my students and become a role model for them. When the bell rang, not one of them moved. They all sat and stared, their mouths watering at love, which I had rendered an almost visibly gorgeous creature.

Soon my fame spread among the students into the halls. Walking across the schoolyard, I had begun to respond animatedly at the dreamy looks of the girls and the admiring looks of the boys.

The following day I called Merich. I proposed to her.

I don't remember ever making anyone happier. It felt good to make her happy.

We got married that summer, before school ended, with a shotgun wedding.

Merich was the happiest bride in the world.

Whenever I see the red switch of an appliance that is turned on, I remember the tasty lips of Ada, whom I kissed as she sat half naked on my lap.

THE FAMILIARIZATION OF EVIL

> "speak, little prince /
> is despair being stranded /
> one thousand miles from any town /
> will you touch down /
> from your tiny planet /
> to find her once again /
> on this cursed cradle, /
> on earth's desert?"
>
> Huseyin Yurttas
> (20th Century Laments)

"Pssst, if there's anyone in there who can hear me, reach for this rod! Psst! Anyone alive in there?"

When Duna heard the beckoning voice, he first thought it was an illusion.

"Pssst, psssst! Grab the end of this rod if you can hear me. Come on lads, come on fellas... go on, give it a try!"

Turning his head with difficulty in the direction of the voice, Duna saw a long iron rod being extended through a hole in the wall of the ramshackle hut. He tried to clarify the image by squinting but the pain he felt rendered him immobile. His hands and feet were bound, and he was slumped against a wall of the room. The place smelled even more intensely of rotten flesh than before. What made the stench worse than that of a rotten egg, old garbage, or cat urine was the consciousness that the object rotting into oblivion was a member of the same species. He was soiled from head to toe with blood, sweat, and urine. He overcame the frequent urge to vomit with a series of retches. Just as he was about to start feeling sorry for himself, he remembered that he must have passed out when they had killed Captain Birol. When they killed Captain Birol? Had they really killed Birol? Yes, in front of his very eyes. Yes, and what's more, in an ordinary, accustomed manner. Yes, with the ease of performing a daily, familiar chore. Like chewing gum, playing video games, or reading comic books... Like watching a Tarantino movie... They were cold blooded, professional killers, and what's worse (could it be worse?), it was obvious that they took pleasure from their job. What do you call people who find killing to be familiar and enjoyable? That was when he revived, immediately and completely. He suddenly realized that soon the terrorists would enter the room and kill him as well. All his pain and sense of despair disappeared and was replaced by a survival instinct that spread powerfully throughout his body. Even if this was a nightmare, he did not wish to die. A person must live, even in his dreams!

He lay down on the floor with an inhuman effort, and started crawling toward the hole from which the metal rod was extended. Although the battle he gave to cover that trivial distance seemed incredible, he did not have any other chance. He doubled up with pain at every move, but his survival instinct was much more powerful than he had imagined. When he reached the spot he was soaked with sweat and exhausted. He extended his bound hands with one final effort, caught the rod, and tugged on it.

"There you go, m'boy, just hang on to this pole, don't let go for a second, don't let yourself go!" whispered the voice outside.

Duna grasped the end of the metal pole tightly. This pole was the only link between himself and life.

As he held on firmly to the life he had caught in his hands, the whisper began to pull Duna outside, through a narrow hole in the slapdash fiberboard wall, which could barely accomodate a thin human body. This was a long, and arduous task for both of them. This struggle for survival, which for Duna seemed to last hours, started to bleed his wounds, re-bruise his already rotting flesh and reached an altogether unbearable pitch. Duna's face was covered in tears from pain, but neither one of them had any intention to quit. At long last, they managed to carry his wounded body outside.

Freedom was the color of twilight. First, Duna rejoiced with the clean air. Although his bruised cheek hurt when it grazed the ground, he felt glad to be touching the earth. Lifting his head with difficulty, he gazed at the sky, the stars had already begun to appear. He grew elated. What great hope it is to find the stars in their place!

"Is there anyone alive besides you inside?" whispered the savior.

"I doubt it," said Duna, but could not make a sound.

"Duna? That you my Kuzguncukite brother?"

"Sefer?"

"Those sons of bitches, look what've they done to my brother! May God damn them all, the vile bastards!"

"Sefer...is that really you?"

"Of course it's me, who else? Are you sure there isn't anyone else alive in there, Duna?"

"No, no one."

"Alright then, come on m'boy, let's get out of here. Here, let me untie you. Oh kiddo, what've they done to you, those cursed bastards!"

When, leaning on Sefer, he embarked on a long rescue trek that was a mixture of running and being dragged, Duna was mumbling:

"See, when I asked him 'Sefer, is that you?' he says 'of course it's me, who else?' Why does he say that? Very simple! My subconscious, which has written and directed this nightmare has already determined Sefer's role on this stage, that's why! And therefore... therefore what? What? That everything is fictitious, of course! So? So... none of this is real. None of it... If it were... If all the things I went through were real... I would have gone crazy! Yes, yes, I could not have stood this chaos and pain... This extreme familiarization of death would've driven me mad... Definitely..."

"Hold tight, m'boy, hold on, m'lad! Keep going, it'll all be over soon, by God! These dark days are going to end, we're going to show those traitor bitches, we're almost there m'boy, come on, you can do it brother!"

Stumbling, tripping, crawling, they fled and fled and fled for hours. They ran from death towards life. It was a difficult path. Whenever they stopped to rest, Sefer would feed Duna water from his tureen. Then Duna would open his eyes with an effort, look at his face with an empty stare, and glance at the stars lining the summer night with a crooked smile.

"Look, subconscious, whatever you do, you can't take away my stars and my sky from me! Just like, just like you can't take away Ada. Alright?"

"Sure, m'boy, sure kiddo, don't you worry. Here, have some more of this water."

"The skies will remain my own... Do you understand? The skies are everyone's country. The stars... they are the hope of us all... Don't you dare take them away from me, don't you dare!"

"That's right brother, that's true m'boy, come on now, hop to it, we're almost there, let me help you get up..."

"You're a bad, very bad subconscious! I've been feeding you like a snake for years in my head... Ada... No one could ever take Ada away from me! No one, not even Aras! Who the hell d'you think you are?"

"Sure Duna, sure, I understand. There you go, kiddo, try to walk now, lean on me, you got it buddy."

They arrived at the hill where the military unit was camped around midnight. After passing through several password and security circles they laid Duna down on a stretcher and transported him to the infirmary tent. Duna was in so much pain that he thought he no longer felt the aches of his broken fingers, cracked ribs, torn tissues, or his wounds, which were being dressed. He was perceiving the voices of the doctor and orderlies like mysterious signals coming from a distant planet. He passed out as the words painkiller shots, IV, and sanitation began to float through the air.

It was not dawn yet when he regained consciousness. Perhaps another day already elapsed. He was wearing a pair of shorts, an IV tube hung from his arm, and his entire body smarted violently. The sound of people moaning came from somewhere nearby, and he felt his heart sinking, ah he really felt his heart sinking!

"You sure had a close call, sir, you musta bin born lucky!"

Finally the sun had risen and the darkness had ended. The curtain door of the tent had been opened and sunlight had spilled inside.

"Thanks," said Duna absently, he could only think of the sunlight.

"You ain't payin' no heed, haven't you recognized me sir?"

"Hasan? It can't be you! What're you doing here?"

"Sir, whatever the reason you're here, it's the same as mine! National duty!"

"Well, what a believable coincidence it is that among all those orderlies, you should be the one to cross my path Hasan!"

"Yep, what're you gonna do sir, that's life. See, who'da known that you'd be the only one to make it out of that slaughter alive? They say great big soldiers are dead and gone, while you held out, though we thought you puny an' weak. You're finally a *ghazi*, good sir."

"A *ghazi*? Me?"

"'Sright, sir!"

"You mean I'm going to be crippled?"

"Nah nah, you gonna git better. That's what the doctor Major says."

"They kill men like flies Hasan! They slew Major Birol in front of my eyes. Right in front…Right in front of my very eyes, they…"

He was cut short by sudden tears gushing out of his eyes, and sobs bursting in his throat.

"You alright, sir? Now, now, don't you tire yerself out too much, if you please…"

"They're not human! They're not animals either! They're creatures, perhaps a kind we don't even know of… They're beings who kill in order to exist!"

"There's surely money behind it, sir. Money make a man do most everythin'… Well, we all been raised on raw milk anyhow!"

"What money are you talking about Hasan! These people're terrorists; they've been bathed in hate, malice, and humiliation! Neither their own, nor other people's lives carry any meaning for them anymore."

"You sure are naive, sir! There's money, tons of dirty money behind all these ter'rists and you still don't understand a single thing!"

"You're obsessed with money Hasan!" scolded Duna.

"Well, I dunno what that thing you say might be, but ever since this world been begun, money makes it go round, that's what I know, an' that's what I say!"

"Hasan! Where'd that sergeant go now? Stop yakking away and get over here!"

"Yessir, cap'n!"

"Now you just get well soon, sir, we'll see each other again nohow!"

Duna let out a deep sigh of relief, and relaxed. He looked out at the piece of sunny summer morning that could be glimpsed through the open curtain door. He loosened up. He smiled. His face hurt when he smiled, but he did not care one bit.

"Hey, there's my blue Kuzguncuk boy lookin' all better, smiles bloomin' on his cheeks!"

"Sefer! Sefer, I don't know how to thank…"

"Now, what're you talking about, what would the Kuzguncukite girls do if we hadn't saved you!"

"Thank you Sefer! Thank you!"

"Anyone would have done the same thing. If it were you, wouldn't you have saved me Duna? Come on, forget about that, but tell me, are you better?"

Sefer entered the tent with an amiable smile, and approached Duna.

"Sefer, I called you a spy and hit you, and you saved my life! Would it do any good if said 'forgive me'?"

"Forget it man… Long live the Motherland, Duna! These things happen between real men. You're a fine, patriotic kid. You've never been no atheist or communist. That's what's important to me, buddy. Things like this happen every once in a while. Love will get to even the best of men."

Duna kept silent.

"What was all that you were rambling about? Nightmares or something. You even made a Russian spy out of me, hah hah ha!"

"Not a Russian, a Nazi," said Duna.

"Don't you start with that again!"

"Alright alright, don't worry. I won't bother you on that subject anymore."

"There you go, m'boy!"

"What's going on, Sefer, what's our position, tell me."

"What else, buddy, soon, very soon we're going to break our silence and fall upon them when they least expect it. We're going to destroy all those vermins' nests in one night. Those sons of bitches are going to be sorry they were even born!"

"So, an eye for an eye."

"You got that right! Look, they've made you unrecognizable. How many other sons of this nation have they slaughtered mercilessly? Are we supposed to thank them for it?"

"Oh man, Sefer, violence always breeds violence, can't you see it still?"

"May god help you Duna, that's all I can say!"

Annoyed, Sefer shook his head.

"I've got to go. It's important that we go and finish this business! Well, give me your blessing, brother. Who knows, one can go down this road, but not return. Look, if I'm martyed, and can't make it back…"

He stopped. He was moved.

"If I don't return, tell my sons about me Duna. Say 'he was brave, he was fearless,' say 'he died for his country.' Let them go to school and complete their education. Let them love their country like their own lives! Let them be real men!"

"Don't you have anything to say to your daughter, Sefer?"

Sefer started, just as he was about to leave. He waited.

"Let my daughter be honorable and obedient."

"Shouldn't your daughter get her share of courage and intelligence?"

"Man Duna, why're you such a damn maniac?" grumbled Sefer as he came back.

He walked up to Duna and stood directly facing him. He looked into his friend's eyes defiantly. Then he bit his lips.

"Tell the girl the same things, she's one and the same in my heart, look, may God strike me dead if I'm lying. And quit that blubbering. Stop crying like a girl in front of me, will you? Ah my Kuzguncukite brother, you old disgrace to mankind!"

He touched Duna's unbandaged left shoulder, gave it a light squeeze, and left.

"You have my blessing Sefer," whispered Duna after him.

Despite the ebullient sunshine and birdsong that seemed to defy the late summer outside, he lay quietly crying on his gurney. His tears were marked more by the fresh, white narcissus scent of sorrow, than the heavy, rosewater smell of grief. As he attempted to take a deep breath of this gorgeous scent, he acutely felt all of his organs, starting with his head, ache terribly. Had he not noticed the pain before, or had it abruptly increased at that moment?

He tried hoping that someone would come by and give him some kind of painkiller, but no one was in sight. He shut his eyes, clenched his teeth, and searched for a few square centimeters of his body that did not ache, but there were none. He could not decide whether he should be glad for still hearing the birdcalls.

"Commander, is this soldier still unconscious?"

"No, he must be sleeping. Change his IV, give him a shot of painkiller, and then load him on to the ambulance with the other two without jolting him. Don't put these in the same ambulance as the critical cases."

"Yessir, commander."

"Place this soldier's folder on top of the others. His file should not be overlooked, he's a patient of the POWMITU."

"Is his condition critical commander?"

"He's going to recover physically, but his psychological condition is unstable."

"Poor fellow, he's such a young man!"

"He'll recover if he can find the strength to face reality. Such extreme reactions are common among impressionable and highly sensitive types like this one."

"They say he's also got a love story plaguing him. Doomed love or something, I heard."

"It's possible. But the realization of war is sometimes as powerful as the affect of war itself, major. Yes, carry the stretcher without jolting it, I'm going to visit the other patients."

"So it's real!" whispered Duna to himself.

"What reality? If this were all real, then why on earth would you come and have this conversation right next to me? If it were real, then why would Sefer, whom I tried to beat up for being a spy, end up saving me and not someone else? As if all that isn't enough, why is everyone dying but me?"

His pain had been allayed slightly.

"Because my brain doesn't want me to die. If I die this nightmare will end and I'll wake up. Ha, and I'm supposed to fall for all this, am I?"

"Commander, this patient's smiling!" yelled the major, as he carried Duna to the ambulance on a stretcher.

"Not yet," murmured Duna.

The ambulance started.

HELL IS PART OF HEAVEN

"Hostages to one arid climate, we have forgotten the rain, the earth within us has cracked, even the rocks have burned."

Huseyin Yurttas
(Dark History)

The first thing he saw was autumn peeking through the window.

"When did the leaves begin to turn yellow?" he asked.

No one replied.

He sat up slightly; everything around him was pure white.

That's when he recognized it:

"A hospital room again!" he groaned, and fell back on the bed.

He took a hesitant, sideways glance at his body. His arms and legs were in place. An intravenous tube hung from his arm. His toes, left hand, and right leg were in a cast.

The only thing he felt was weariness and intense exasperation. At this point, he found it difficult to believe that he had any chance left of being rescued from this nightmare. The state of dejection, despondency and resignation is a very exhausting one!

"Goood mornin' sir! You couldn't get enough o' them dreams, an' yet, lookee here, you finally all woken up."

"Hasan? Not you again!"

"Now don't you go makin' faces like that, sir! What I ever done t'you that you don't care fer me none? See, you're gettin' better, what else you want?"

"Are you kidding, Hasan? Everytime I meet you, I realize that I've fallen even further away from reality. As for recovery…"

"Right, right, sir, now you gonna start sayin' all your long, high-falutin' words again, but don't even bother."

Duna resembled a moviegoer who is annoyed at the director for stealing away valuable screentime from other actors to give an unnecessarily prominent role to an extra.

"You're around far too much Hasan."

"Whatcha gonna do, sir, that's our job!"

"Well, really, this is going too far!"

"Now then, sir, if you only knew what else there be, you'd count your blessings, upon my word!"

Hasan the orderly, who unsettled Duna with his wildly alert eyes and excessively curious stare, was a rather deft person. During this exchange he had already taken Duna's pulse and replaced his IV bottle.

"If you knew 'bout them others, your story would seem like a newborn babe next to theirs, sir! Ah, what troubles are on those other soldier's minds, ah me, ah my!"

"I don't have any troubles! The only thing I'm asking for is to get out of this goddamned nightmare and back into reality, do you understand? You don't! Because you all think I'm crazy! Because you only believe things that you're taught. None of you can dare to fashion your own truths yet!"

"Alright, sir, alright, don't go gettin' all crazy 'gain. See, your pulse an' everything is better now, so don't ruin your health. The doctors are gonna decide when it's right for you to go back home, not you sir."

"Could it be that there's a fate to dreams as well, Hasan?" Duna asked in a suddenly pacified voice.

"Well, I never go puttin' my nose in none o' that business. See, they even transferred you to POWMITU."

"What did they transfer me to?"

"You know, what they call the POWMITU unit!"

"Great, just what I needed! Ah my zealous brain, is that what you've come up with now?"

"What d'you mean 'come up with,' sir, it's all true!"

"Well, well, well, how's our second lieutenant doing today?"

"Doctor Kutlu! I am so glad to see you. I mean, what're you doing here?"

"Being here is my job, yet *inshallah* you will soon return to where you are meant to be," said Doctor

Kutlu in a cold voice.

"You mean I'm back in Istanbul?" asked Duna, brightening up.

"Yes, you were among the group that was brought back from the mobilization station last week. It turns out you have a strong constitution; we were able to save you."

"So there were those you were not able to save…"

"We are in war after all, second lieutenant. Life and death come this close only during a war."

They fell silent.

"It's autumn already," said Duna. "I'm very fond of the colors when late summer embraces winter. I have to get out of here as soon as possible and throw myself into the autumnal streets."

"All in good time. The behavior you have exhibited since the first day of your arrival is very hopeful."

Duna could not discern which first day it was that he meant. Neither could he gather up the courage to ask.

"What's this POWMITU business, doctor?" he asked, trying to quickly change the subject.

"The Post War Military Therapy Unit is a relatively new project for the Turkish army. It was actually conceived with specific units in mind, namely public order, internal security, and counter-terrorism, but we serve all the military divisions due to the current needs."

"Post-war military therapy unit, eh? Well, I'll be!" said Duna, revealing a mocking smile.

Pretending not to have heard him, Doctor Kutlu Chechen stood by the side of Duna's bed and went on, in his frigid voice:

"General difficulty in concentrating, fear of the dark, absolute intolerance to loud noises –such as car alarms, slammed doors, sudden laughter, children screams, or the sound of water pipes– and of course depression, fatigue attacks, and groundless fits of violent rage…"

"Fine, but doctor, after all these things you talk of, how can these people laugh, who can they trust, and… and how can they make love? I mean. who can claim the ability to treat fear, doubt, betrayal, and despair in a hospital?"

When he collided with Doctor Kutlu's surprised gaze, he collected his wits and remembered that he was not there for visiting purposes. They both remained awkwardly silent for a while, not knowing what to do. Doctor Kutlu was first to recover, and clearing his throat, he resumed speaking as if nothing had happened.

"It's difficult of course. Nobody wins in a war. All those who're left alive have in fact been defeated."

"I believe similar therapeutic studies were conducted on veterans of Vietnam and the Gulf War?"

"Indeed," said Doctor Kutlu, as he inspected the patient track record that was kept at the foot of Duna's bed.

"I'd read about them in magazines and newspapers," Duna mumbled absently. "It makes me very sad to remember that extremely young soldiers, who returned from a Vietnam they had not gone to willingly, could not adapt to social life and a state of peace. The remainder of those people's lives are now hell. The hell in heaven!"

"As a matter of fact, we received counsel from our American colleagues. Naturally, our own doctors comprise the core personnel."

"I'd found all this incredibly dramatic, and I'd been terribly moved."

"In all honesty, it is impossible not to agree with you, second lieutenant."

"Sure, sure," Duna started to scream with the fury of a wild beast which has suddenly become aware of the trap it has fallen into: "Sure, doctor, so you see nothing wrong in coming here and telling all these things in their minutest detail to a patient, do you? In fact, you even relate historical references, so nothing can be left lacking in my mind, isn't that so? Say something, doctor, why don't you? Of course, I'm such a raving lunatic that I fall for all this stuff! This is going too far, doctor! No, really, it's just too much!"

Doctor Kutlu, who was taken aback by Duna's sudden fit of rage, stood frozen, not knowing where to place the patient progress report in his hand.

"How well planned, how impeccably organized it all is, don't you think doctor? And you expect me to listen docilely to all these fairytales, am I mistaken Captain Doctor Kutlu Chechen, huh?"

"Look Mr.Duna, this sudden fit of rage, the cause of which remains vague, is an example of the behavioral complications we had indicated in our chat a minute ago. As for my being frank with you..."

He placed the patient progress report he was holding in the transparent plastic envelope at the foot of Duna's bed, and trying to appear calm, approached Duna.

"First of all, you are the POWMITU patient who has shown the most positive response to treatment, secondly, you are a highly aware and educated person. Therefore, I had no reservations about being frank with you. Thirdly,..."

"Humph! He had no 'reservations!' Don't make me laugh, hah hah ha!!!" said Duna, emitting a nervous laugh.

"See here doctor, why don't you just admit it, huh? You know just as well as I do that all this is in fact the designs and dreams of my own brain, these are my fears and nightmares. At least show some courage and call it a 'collective nightmare,' but for God's sake, don't just stand there lecturing me about reality!"

Doctor Kutlu heaved a regretful sigh. He hung his head and quietly reflected for a while. Then he spoke gently, in a sad voice:

"I think you're punishing yourself for a crime, the nature of which I cannot yet understand, but which I am convinced you did not commit, Mr. Duna."

Starting to wonder if the doctor was genuinely grieved, Duna calmed down.

"Your fears have formed a protective barrier which you employ to avoid confronting reality. Yet, as your fears grow more powerful they are reaching a pathological level. We have diagnosed you with traumatic war neurosis," said doctor Kutlu, sighing once again.

"This prototype is a psycho-neurosis based on excitation, and forms a psycho-physiological paroxysm model."

"Well, well, you don't say!" said Duna, beginning to laugh.

Doctor Kutlu, who did not seem very surprised that he had switched into such an involuntary peal of laughter following that sudden fit of rage, kept watching him patiently.

"Doctor, hah hah hah! Doctor, I swear, I can't believe this! Please excuse me... Hah ha ha, believe me, I'm laughing at this strange brain of mine. I mean, how could I have underestimated such genius as must have resided in it, hah hah ha! Just look at what grave and medical sentences it can devise when it fancies, and I was almost about to believe the reality of the situation!"

"Look, Mr.Duna," said doctor Kutlu, maintaining his level-headed and distant manner, "Naturally, we all have fears, and these reach back to our childhood years. However, in certain situations, the increase of terrorism, the complication of personal problems and the hopelessness that these will never be solved sweep us into states of panic and terror. Or as a result of artificial manipulation we reach a state which is termed hyperbolic."

"Well, I'll be!" interrupted Duna. "Upon my word, doctor, I'm bewildered at how well I must have processed the material I read on fear and psychology. In the past few years I've been very interested in the subject, and read plenty about it, but I thought that I had forgotten most of it. And yet, I realize now with surprise, that that was not the case. A person should not take his brain lightly!"

"How much longer do you think you'll be able to escape in this manner, Mr. Duna?"

He waited.

"You cannot get out of here in this way. Whenever you accept that this civil war, and your experiences are real, then you will able to regain your freedom!"

He stopped. The two young men looked at one another in silence. Their eyes remained interlocked, one of them half sitting up in bed, the other standing. They both knew that the most meaningful conversations are held in an exchange of silent glances.

"Then again, who can claim that what we are living through does not resemble a nightmare?" murmured Doctor Kutlu, concealing his eyes in the autumn that was visible through the window.

Duna smiled.

"I understand, doctor," he said.

Once again, silence came between them.

"Your glasses," said Doctor Kutlu, thrusting his hand into his pocket, "I remembered that you were three degrees short-sighted. I hope I'm not mistaken? I chose a frame like the one you had from the optician in the army bazaar, and had it fixed with the right lenses. If you would accept, the frame is my gift to you."

He produced a pair of thin, wire-framed glasses from an imitation leather case, and held it out for Duna.

"How kind of you, Doctor!" said Duna, joyfully grabbing the glasses.

"Thank you, I did not expect this at all."

He put on the glasses. The world around him had become clearer to a certain extent. When he tried to extend his hand to the doctor in gratitude he realized that he did not have the use of his left hand due to the cast, and his right hand because of the IV. Doctor Kutlu approached him with compassion and shook his right hand.

"You are a good person doctor. You are one of the positive characters in this dream, oh sorry, I mean war, of course. The type of person who knows his job well, who is principled and trustworthy."

"Thank you."

"The laid back male type who is sworn not to reveal himself, and who derives his strength from this silence…"

"Well, now," the doctor interrupted him, "At this rate, you'll soon be taking our job away from us, lieutenant."

He stopped.

"There is one point in which you're mistaken, Mr.Duna: I was once one who thought himself an ambling colt, who did not know what it was to walk, but galloped over hills and valleys like a Circassian foal."

"Sounds like *Engraved in the Mountains,*" smiled Duna.

"You've read that novel?" asked doctor Kutlu, animated.

Duna nodded.

" 'The mountains of Binboga were as the Turkoman bey, his face lathered and half shaved.Crocuses, and snowdrops bloomed on the first day of Spring. Sorrels, asphodels and purslane grew tall. And my nana would tell me 'sit back down, and stop whinnying inside the house.' "

They looked at each other, smiling. Sometimes even one second is too long to realize that camaraderie has fallen into one's soul.

"I will stop by again in the evening, Mr.Duna. I'll bring you books and magazines. Also, I shall try to find a walkman and some classical music tapes."

"Doctor Kutlu," Duna called out just as the other was about to leave, "I know that you know. That you know everything, starting from the fact that I'm not three but five degrees short-sighted, and that all this… and yet…"

He fell silent.

"And yet what?" paused doctor Kutlu.

"And yet, remember that boy who thought he was a Circassian colt? Well, he is the only thing that's real."

Doctor Kutlu turned around and walked up to the bed. "I'll miss you when you wake up from this dream, Mr. Duna," he said, and left.

HOMOSEXUAL, HETEROSEXUAL AND/OR BISEXUAL

"Traces of the opposite sex' sexual organs can be found in every man or woman."

Sigmund Freud
(Sexual Perversions)

"Honestly, a person should be ashamed of turning thirty!"

I looked at her, wondering if she was joking. No, she was dead serious. Turning thirty must have wounded her a great deal.

We were all gathered at the mansion, and none of us knew that this would be the final meal we were to have together at that house.

"Darling, you still have one year to go until you're thirty. You're finishing your twenty-ninth year today, what's the hurry Ada dear?"

It was the twelfth of March, and if Aras had lived the next day would have been the celebration of his birthday.

"Just an open rehearsal, queen mother! What does it matter if it's this year or the next? I have to get used to pronouncing this ugly and horrid number thirty. That's all!"

"If anyone were to hear you they'd think you were talking about age fifty. What're we to do then Ada, sweetie?"

"You're condemned to remaining forever young, queen mother!"

Although worn out both physically and emotionally by the health problems of Sureyya Mercan, who had been living with someone else's lung for the past three years, Pervin Gokay still managed to maintain the miracle of remaining trim, graceful, and considerate.

Instead of joining the legions who are afraid of aging, Ada thought she would ease the process by broaching the topic early on.

Yet the years had not changed her greatly. Though she had grown sadder she was still mischievous, and despite her endless flight from the past she was always the same Rain Girl!

"Hear ye hear ye, housefolk and friends from far away: this diminutive brunette dame standing before ye is now in her thirties! Hear ye hear ye!"

"Hooray for the old codger!"

"Long live Ada!"

"Happy birthday brunette Ada!" The mansion's living room rang with applause.

The short lived silence that ensued was broken by the poet Dogan Gokay's impressive, hopeful voice.

"How young you are, child!"

Since at this moment I think of how naive and young I was, three, only three years ago, when I was thirty. Uncle Poet was right once again.

"A toast to youth!"

Endeavoring to keep his frail body upright, Sureyya Mercan, who by then barely had the strength to even sit up, lifted the water filled glass in his hand with difficulty in honor of his daughter. His hand shook and he spilled the water over himself.

"Darling, you're always wasting our water, we're going to get a scolding from the mayor himself!" exclaimed Pervin Gokay as she ran to her husband's aid. She was grateful for every breath he took. Sometimes even we thought that her existence depended on the survival of her husband.

A few weeks after his daughter's thirtieth birthday Sureyya Mercan was once again hospitalized in critical condition, and died a short while later. Sureyya Mercan, who even on his deathbed dreamed of the movies he would make upon his release from the hospital, was given an official state burial. People from the remotest corners of Turkey flocked to Istanbul to attend the majestic funeral, at which the President himself was present. His name was given to the Kuzguncuk street which he would frequent to play backgammon. A film award was established in his name. TV channels and newspapers prepared documentaries about him, and his old movies were shown collectively. I suppose even he did not know how well-loved he was.

His death, which had been long expected, hit Pervin Gokay the hardest. When her tenderly beloved husband, with whom she had shared her life so closely for thirty-two years, passed away, she broke up with Kuzguncuk, and with a sudden decision, sold the mansion. She moved into an apartment in Valide Cheshme, which she had inherited from her father, so she could be close to Ada and to the poet Dogan Gokay. She then set to work investing the money she had in the Sureyya Mercan Foundation.

The new owners of the mansion tore it down, felled the trees, and hurriedly constructed two ugly and indistinct apartment buildings in its place. They raised the mansion's tomb directly before us.

"Since she's grown so old, what advice could Ada Mercan give us youngsters, I wonder?"

I knew that voice, I knew it all too well. I cast a searching glance over the group of eight or ten people who were present in the living room as Ada's friends, but could not recognize anyone. The voice was coming from behind me, and when I turned around, our eyes met. The first word that flashed in my mind was: "Impossible!"

How could I forget this predatory, aggressive voice, with the openly bleeding wounds?

"My advice, dear, is as follows," said Ada. "Live to the hilt. If you happen to be in love, eat your meal without letting it turn cold, sour or stale, youngsters! This is what your thirty-year old auntie deems good for you!"

We laughed.

It was Aliye. She had turned up years later to come and stand just a stone's throw away from me. People like myself think that when one bumps into his old lover, a slender thrill, a pale melancholy and a friendly warmth should spread across his heart. However, meeting Aliye had disturbed me as much as running into a vengeful old spouse who, after an extremely lengthy and troubled marriage, trembles with pleasure at revealing her entire private life in the courts and the media. Wherever she happened to be, Aliye could not rest unless she caused a scene and made a spectacle of herself for the sake of attention.

Merich leaned toward me and asked in my ear:

"Isn't this the woman who came and questioned me at the university years ago?"

Yes, it was her. A weary woman ravaged by alcohol had appeared in her prematurely aged face. There was still something sexy about her, but she was in her last act.

"Does Ada still see this woman?"

"I guess so," I answered Merich with a smile that tried to appear calm.

We had been married for four years, and resembled a pair of very close friends rather than newlyweds. I supposed that Merich was content. She was excited when making love to me, and smiled a gentle, quiet smile. That is how she has always been, gentle and quiet: she never opened up and talked about herself. It would have eased my mind to know that there was someone she confided in, but I was doubtful even of that. Perhaps what kept Merich alive was the constant battle to win my affections, I cannot say.

Merich had graduated from school a year after our marriage, and had initially insisted on remaining a practician. When I realized that the true reason for this was a self-sacrifice meant to preserve the male pride of her high-school teacher husband, I immediately objected. I was determined to support her to the highest and farthest heights she was capable of reaching.

"If a person is jealous of his wife's professional success then he's not a man, because he has not been able to become a human being yet!" I once declared.

She stared at me calmly, searched my face to see if I was joking, and asked: "Really?"

Was it true? I don't know! I suppose it was true, or at least it ought to have been true.

All I knew was that Merich was the only person I could please because of my unassertiveness. I happen to be one of those idiots with the underdeveloped egos who can find happiness in making someone else happy. (How many times have I told you this already?)

"You're so different!" cried Merich, throwing her arms around my neck. (Whatever that's supposed to accomplish!)

"Would it bother you if I wanted to choose psychiatry?"

"Oh for god's sake! Merich, dear, you're the one who's going to work on your specialization, how can I interfere with the field you choose?"

I do not know if there is a man who enjoys living with a woman who does not take a step without consulting her husband, but I admire women who make and execute their own decisions. Yet Merich even consults me on shopping!

"I don't know? Is there any man who would want to have a psychiatrist wife?"

"Merich, darling, what do we care what other men think? If you want to, you can be a psychiatrist, or I don't know, a pathologist, or anything. Who can interfere in your career choice except yourself?"

Since she perceived this attitude of mine as disinterest, it secretly hurt her. But I knew that however hard I tried, I would not be able to explain certain things to her. Merich was not dimwitted, insensitive, or lazy. No, she was extremely strong-willed, industrious, and intelligent. But Merich was nothing like Ada.

She went ahead and entered pathology. She told me that what led her to the choice was a lack of personnel. I never asked, but I have always been suspicious.

My mother moved downstairs as she had planned. We had a kitchen and a bathroom built there, and she moved into her new setting with such gladness that one would have thought it was a palace. Before long, she had turned the ground floor of our house, which I had always regarded to be an ordinary entrance, into a virtual heaven. Flowers started from the staircase and hallway, then overflowed into the windowsills and into the street. The return of the violets, which I had been accustomed to during my grandparents' lifetime, but which had disappeared noticeably after Aras' departure, made me feel surprisingly better. I suppose it will be difficult to explain this. To claim that flowers carefully tended inside and outside the home spread joy merely through their color and scent would in fact not amount to saying anything. For what makes such a home possible is constancy, a love of life, and hope for the future. These flowers symbolize a sense of being well enough to take on responsibility, they symbolize attention, saying "yes" to life, resilience and resistance. Dozens, scores of potted plants which demand individual care, require at least that one believe she can overcome her personal troubles enough to spare time for the problems of other creatures. To furnish one's home with flowers means that the person is tranquil, brave, and determined enough to settle down. Flowers are health! My mother and her numerous potted plants indicated better than all other signs that a new era was beginning in my life.

We had also succeeded, with what could be called wedding gifts from Merich's aunt, in renovating the small upstairs apartment into a more enjoyable setting. Taking a cue from my mother, I pampered the rather small balcony of what had become a modern and unassuming apartment (I should say our apartment) with an array of flowers.

"Ah, Duna Atacan! What a pleasure it is to see you!"

"Aliye, how are you?" I asked reluctantly.

"Never been better, how about yourself, Blue Danube?"

Her voice rang threateningly, dislodging poison arrocas in every direction. Her stare was pernicious. I did not want to have anything to do with her, but she had made up her mind a long time ago, and had perhaps come here for the sole purpose of being unavoidable.

"Aren't you going to introduce me to your wife, Duna?"

She was clad in black again. Wearing black combat boots, and a leather super miniskirt over sheer black hose, she fully exposed her still handsome legs. Her small breasts were bare under her flimsy black decolletage blouse, which defied the bitter chill of Istanbul in March.

"Of course, let me introduce you two," I said, patting Merich on the back, "This is Merich, and this is Aliye."

They shook hands. I grew worried that Aliye might have voluntarily hurt Merich while shaking her hand.

"I believe we've met before young lady!" said Aliye in a mocking tone.

"Yes, I remember. It was so kind of you to visit me!"

I glanced at Merich. She looked soft, gentle, and lovely as always. I had liked her reply. I caught myself thinking "Well, she does have Gokay blood in her after all."

"Do you always land on your feet, Duna Atacan?" Aliye asked me in an irritated voice.

So that silent, modest Merich had been able to stagger a professional fighter like Aliye in a single blow. Was it true that quiet horses have the more powerful kicks? However, I knew Aliye well, and she was not one to be knocked to the ground with such small slaps. It would only induce her to attack more angrily.

"So, what else are you two up to besides playing house? Anyways, can't you guys have kids or are there other plans in the making? You haven't been able to make an aunt of Ada for four years!"

It is not necessary to experience rudeness often to understand how cheap it is. As I tried to devise a level-headed answer, Merich spoke in a cool, collected voice (her usual, that is):

"Our honeymoon must have lasted noticeably long. I mean... Oh I'm sorry, did I misunderstand your question? Oh, if you're curious about the medical aspects of it, why don't you drop by the fertility clinic of my hospital sometime and I'll ask them to furnish you with better information."

I could not believe my ears! Merich, whom I had always known to be meek, quiet, accommodating, and gentle in every way, had a tongue sharp enough to make you cringe, and this was the first time I had noticed it. Well, I'll be damned!

It was not a question of doubting what I saw, for Merich was standing between myself and Aliye as simple and matter of fact as ever. Well then, if this curtness and snappishness of hers had not been a one time inspiration, why had she concealed this side of herself from me and from Ada's family for years? Perhaps this was part of a strategic tactic devised to attain whatever it was that she desired? Perhaps she had been hesitant to rival Ada, or had simply kept silent because of her affection. I could not tell. And even now I cannot say that I understand completely. Because Merich's tongue, which lashes out against others whenever appropriate, has remained decidedly silent against Ada and myself. If this was just a tactic, then Merich had an immense degree of control; enough to frighten me. I could not help but regard this as a threat.

Actually, I was the one who did not want to have a child. Not because I did not like kids, but... I think the idea of fatherhood scared me. A man fears becoming attached to certain women, and delights in the prospect of attachment to others!

Since Merich believed in smooth transitions, she did not pressure me in the least, and told the necessary people that we were delaying our plans for having children due to her specialization examinations. She was the one who had consoled me when a year earlier I had felt like a murderer after her abortion. I wonder if there is a secret allure to hurting those who love us?

"Hey, what's going on over there? Aliye, be nice to my kids!" said Ada, as she came towards us.

Dinner was over. Soon Ada would cut the birthday cake, and afterwards we young'ans would attend the opening of Ada's new photography exhibit, scheduled specially for that day. For the first time, Sureyya Mercan would not be able to take part in his daughter's gallery opening. Pervin Gokay would not leave her husband's side. Uncle Poet hated art openings. My mother who was not fond of crowds anyway was busy with my uncle Kemal's family, who had come to Istanbul to visit us at the time. I suppose Burkan was the only one who was going to join us.

When I noticed Aliye pursing her lips, I realized that she was about to launch a powerful new attack, and taking a deep breath, I prepared to weather the blow.

"So, have you told your kids that you happen to be my lover, Miss Brunette Ada?"

"What?" cried Merich.

No, the breath I took had not sufficiently prepared me for this blow. I fell to the floor of the ring, blood gushing out of my nose, knowing that I had been knocked out. Aliye was trembling with the joy of a great boxer who has saved the best punch for last.

My eyes met Ada's. We exchanged a brief, very brief glance. That was when, for some reason, I bit my tongue very hard. I reeled from the pain.

"Oh Ada, what for?" I asked. And she answered my glance with "But you too, with the same woman…"

Ada was the first one to recover. She spoke in a cheerful, blithe voice:

"You know what I suddenly thought of? That famous Bob Fosse movie that came out when we were kids."

It was Aliye's turn to be surprised. She stared at Ada, as if to say "So what?"

"Oh you remember *Cabaret!*"

"The one with Lisa Minelli and Michael York?" asked Merich, also attempting to gather herself.

"That's the one!" said Ada. "There is a fascist officer in that mo-
vie. He enters into sexual relationships with two very close friends, deceiving both of them in the meantime. I think the sense of humiliation that the woman and her gay friend feel upon discovering this charade tells us the true meaning of fascism."

I looked over. Ada had fully recovered.

"Because fascism begins in our own relationships, and consists of deriving pleasure from further hurting, wounding, embarrassing and humiliating others!"

Well, that was not so bad at all. Ada had been defeated but she was taking a stylish and noble leave of the ring.

"But they were both willing to sleep with that fascist! There's nothing that can't be bought!" yelled Aliye, as if spitting out the words.

Until that point we had looked like we were fervently discussing something in a corner, without attracting too much attention to ourselves, but when Aliye intentionally yelled out her last words, it caused everyone present to stare at us in surprise. (Oh how she loves that attention!)

"I want you to leave this place immediately, and forever!" whispered Ada in a sad but firm tone.

"You have never been able to take advantage of the chances given to you Aliye! A person has to deserve her friendships and loves. You don't deserve us!"

"I'll show Aliye out," I offered eagerly.

"So you're ending it, just like that?" said Aliye, making her final attack.

"It's long been over," said Ada, breaking my heart.

"You'll be sorry for this, you'll be very sorry Ada!" cried Aliye and stomped off, beating the floor with her combat boots.

There was a deep silence and curiosity present in the room, but no one had the courage to ask a question. It was unfortunate that an altercation should take place on such a day, but then again unpleasantness always flourishes on these days!

"Kids, come on, we still haven't cut the cake!"

Pervin Gokay called out to us in a voice that had not quite managed to hide its dismay. I went over to Pervin Gokay's side, taking care not to make eye contact with Ada.

"This midnight blue bolero jacket looks wonderful on you, ma'am. It reminds me that I have not designed any jackets for you lately," I said.

My tongue was throbbing painfully.

"Duna dear, teaching is such a holy profession in my eyes, that it prevents me from employing all the tricks I devised to steal you away into the world of design. But as you know yourself, should you work in fashion design, you could make a large fortune and acquire fame in no time at all."

"Merich, what kind of woman are you? Look, pay attention my dear girl, this auntie of yours is talking about stealing your husband away, right out in the open!"

Merich, who looked at her uncle with a crooked smile, must still have been thinking about Ada and Aliye's relationship. She looked bewildered.

Ada popped in a Nirvana tape. The music especially did her friends good, as they stopped paying attention to us family members and fell to having fun amongst themselves.

"Oh come now, Sureyya darling, stop teasing us. Don't you see, we are designers who realize what is on the page, but Duna comes from a true and expert tradition of tailoring. But as luck would have it, he insists on teaching. There is a lot we can learn from you."

"Not at all, ma'am. What can a princess learn from her subjects?" I replied, glad that the subject had suddenly been changed to fashion, but still awfully tense.

"There is a lot that can be learned from the people," said the poet Dogan Gokay as he stepped out into the garden, heedless of that cold March evening.

I got up and followed him. It was as if I was itching to get myself into trouble.

"You also knew, didn't you?" I asked, thrusting my hands in my pockets, and already beginning to feel cold.

"These things cannot be known, my boy, they can only be sensed!"

Hands in our pockets, we stood next to each other for a while, beneath the arbor which, despite its decrepit state, reminded us of past, cheerful days. I was so upset that I needed little pretext to find someone to pick on.

"For how long?" I asked furiously.

"I can't quite say," he replied in a preoccupied tone. "I do not think it lasted a long time. Ada is not a classic bisexual. If you ask me, Ada is still bent on punishing herself. And her relationship with this girl is the latest manifestation of her self-flaggelation."

"Still?" I moaned.

"She has to rid herself of the guilt which has plagued her for years. It is imperative that she finally liberate her spirit and find peace. If not, that child will not be able to live her own life!"

"It wasn't a murder! I was there, and I saw everything!" I cried.

"It is not as if your situation is any different, my boy. Both your spirits have been enslaved, you have buried freedom in Kuzguncuk together with a corpse. It is high time that you both liberated yourselves from this ghost!"

Suddenly I heard myself shouting:

"You won't be able to tear away the memory of Aras!"

Then, for the first time in my life I punched someone. Dear god, the person I punched was one of Turkey's greatest living poets, and he was thirty years my senior!

Just as I was throwing the punch, I saw Uncle Poet's estranged gaze upon me, as if I were from somewhere very distant, and knew that I would never forget that gaze as long as I lived.

The poet Dogan Gokay stumbled, and fell to the ground. He was not a frail, skinny person, but he did not possess a boxer's physique either. He was a perfect salon intellectual. He could have defended himself if he had wanted to, but I had attacked him unexpectedly. I perceived the force of the blow from the pain in my hand, and was petrified with shame.

Upon seeing the famous poet tumbled to the ground of the garden where we used to play as children; upon seeing this man searching for his glasses and attempting to pull himself together, my brain fried like an egg.

"My god, what have I done?" I said, and tried to help him to his feet.

He refused my outstretched hand, and got up slowly, on his

own. He was holding his chin with one hand and curiously inspecting his glasses with the other. At that point I saw the tiny rivulet of blood streaming from the corner of his mouth. Utterly ashamed, disgusted with myself, and at a loss for words, I was not even able to stand before him. The sight of blood makes me sick (as you know by now), and turning my head to one side, I began to swallow repeatedly.

Suddenly, Ada swept into the garden like a hurricane, and planted herself before me. She gave me a nasty glance. Did I say nasty? Wrong. Ada gave me a terrible, withering glance. That was it, it was all over for me!

"Uncle, what happened to you for god's sakes?"

The poet Dogan Gokay had recovered, and was wiping the corner of his mouth with a paper napkin he had produced from his pocket.

"This young man, offering me a compliment, attempted to tell me through unorthodox means that he thought I was rather young. However, as he himself has discovered, I am not quite so young anymore!" he answered in a sarcastic voice.

"You... did you actually hit him?" asked Ada, fixing her incredulous, bewildered brown eyes on my face.

"I was just being ridiculous..."

"I can't believe this! I really can't believe this." said Ada, after blowing a deep disappointment into my face.

"You were supposed to be the pride and joy of all men... But even you... even you like violence, and strike when you're in a fix, don't you? And whom? I don't even want to think of who it was that you..."

She ran crying back to the mansion, unable to finish her sentence. Never before had I hurt her to such an extent. In fact, I had never hurt her at all, not to any "extent."And what's more, on her birthday, as she was about to encounter the terrifying age of thirty, after Aliye's crudeness. And what's more I'm a damned idiot!!!

"Well, you and I can work this out, but what I cannot quite fathom is how you will be able to handle Ada," said the poet Dogan Gokay, now completely recovered.

"I don't know if my apologies would help anything, Uncle Poet?" I said shyly.

"How could they not, my boy!" he said, casting his mischievous, forever young and friendly gaze upon me once again.

"I apologize, I am so sorry. I will never forgive myself for this!" I said, extending my hand.

He took my hand and gave it a firm shake.

"One should first start by learning to forgive himself. These are trivial things, my boy."

We shook hands and took a short stroll around the mansion's garden, arm in arm.

"Even if Aras had lived, their marriage would not have lasted a long time," he said. "Ada is an independent, buoyant girl. Aras is an extremely handsome and old fashioned young man. In the beginning, these attributes fascinated them greatly, of course. But a consistent and stable relationship is a matter of discipline."

I was silent. Had I, like almost everyone else, believed all too often that if only Aras had lived, things would have turned out "happily ever after?" Or had I secretly anticipated a different ending? I cannot say. Even when I am most in earnest, I cannot fully face myself. Can anyone?

"However..." the poet Dogan Gokay continued animatedly, as if relating the plot of a novel, or movie.

"However, when Aras died prematurely, Ada remained fixated on his image. Instead of trying to become better acquainted with herself, and finding her own formula by reassessing the unsuccessful relationships she has had here and abroad, she... she lives miserably, with the sensitivity of a little girl who is still fixated on the notion of how perfect Aras was. Consequently, she repeats her mistakes and for a woman as intelligent as her that is very dangerous, my boy."

So, Ada had had boyfriends and lovers, however unsuccessful, domestically and abroad, and concealed it from me as if it was a crime.

"Ada's short lived experience does not mean that she is going to be a homosexual henceforth. A person is either born with homosexual tendencies, and in fact they are currently finding support for this theory through genetic studies, or he is not. Perhaps later on, one can consciously toy with sexual preferences. Such as the trend amongst feminists of the time to live together as lesbians, as a reaction to men. But that is all. Nature triumphs at the end, and everyone gravitates towards their natural sexual attractions."

It had grown dark and decidedly cooler. It was as if I were the one who had been punched, dozens, scores of times.

"I believe that Ada is a typical heterosexual. Believe me, if Ada had been a lesbian, she would never have concealed it."

I was heartened. While duelling with my rivals, however imaginary they may be, I prefer men. (I am such a hopeless case!)

"You're cold, my boy, perhaps we should go back inside?"

"How can I possibly apologize to you…"

"That matter is closed. But the true case that needs closure is Aras."

Grabbing hold of his chin, to see if he would suffer another punch, he threw me a mischievous glance.

"You two have to let go of Aras' memory, which you have almost made into something supernatural. It is imperative that you learn to be happy without Aras, my boy!"

"Uncle, Duna! What're you two doing out here in the cold? I swear, you're going to catch a chill!"

Just like always, Merich appeared on the scene at the end of the act, as the curtain was falling.

"Alright, Ms. doctor, alright, we're coming."

I looked up. The garden lights had been turned on. Merich had once again materialized on the mansion's steps with her clueless, innocent self. She was wearing what had turned into a symbol of unassertiveness: a ordinary pair of jeans and an ordinary sweater. She had tied her long blond hair in a ponytail.

"Now, of course, she's a whole other case…" whispered Uncle Poet.

Then he let out a crisp laugh.

"Didn't we all think someone was perfect in our youth, for god's sakes? Hah hah ha!"

The fresh wound at the corner of his mouth must have been stretched when he laughed, because he held his hand to his chin.

"You kids had better keep an eye out for that other girl, Aliye. That child is disturbed. She might be dangerous!"

"What're you two laughing at over there, uncle? Why don't you tell me? Oh dear! Your lip is bleeding. I'll treat it right away. Duna, really, uncle walks around with a bloody lip, and you don't even notice. Though the sight of blood makes Duna sick…"

"Don't be alarmed, my girl. It's just a minor scratch. And don't berate Duna in the least. In all honesty, he did his best. In fact, he did it so well that he made me feel like a young man again."

I hung my head in shame. We entered the mansion.

THE WITNESSES SPEAK

"The tree that is kept standing and prohibited from being cut down during a mass felling is called the witness tree."

Grand Larousse Dictionary

ADA MERCAN

Photographer. Single. Daughter of the famous Turkish screen couple Sureyya Mercan and Pervin Gokay. Niece of the poet Dogan Gokay.

I do not agree. Not at all!

I don't agree with the things that are said about me.

I tell you this plainly and simply.

Duna makes me out to be something greater than I am. He's not the only one. The majority of the people around me have been treating me in this manner ever since I was a child. Perhaps I'm the problem. Perhaps I'm guilty of exhibiting "a perfect image." People always find me to be extremely strong, intelligent, smart and successful. But of course they never stop to consider that by branding someone in this way, they are taking away her right to make mistakes or display any weaknesses. Even those I love most are taken aback when I make a mistake. They get harried and depressed when they encounter one of my weaknesses. There have only been two people, among everyone I know, who have been able to handle me.

I have always been told that I'm an attractive, striking girl. I have still not been able to figure out what part of me is attractive. I do not possess my mother's dizzying grace, or Merich's stencilled beauty, or Burkan's sexy femininity. I don't have any of these. The reason men find me attractive is a mystery to me. Now, if I came out and said that I was not pleased with my outward appearance, no one would believe me.

I don't say it.

The poet Dogan Gokay.

Extraordinariness! A miracle!

A model of wisdom and graciousness. My impossible, incestious love. My guru.

Duna, Mabel!

A daydreamer, my little one. The rebellious romantic!

The two of them... Only those two... Among everyone I know, only those two...

Then there was also Aras.

Aras, my lover. He was a phenomenon. A multi-talented beauty!

Aras and I resembled one another only in two respects: our excessive pride and our need to be applauded. While I enjoyed displaying these qualities openly, Aras stressed that they ought to be experienced in a deep, quiet manner. For example, Aras took great care to be a hero for his kid brother and his girlfriend, but when the fact was stated directly to his face he would become embarrassed, and even annoyed. Yet he would give his life to protect and maintain this image. And he did!

Now, at the age when I must become acquainted with the horrid number thirty, I realize that even I was unfair to Aras. While I can evaluate Aras with the help of all my accumulated experience, Aras has no such opportunity anymore! He is stuck being seventeen years old! But then again, who's being unfair to whom?

In the past few years I have been having a frequently recurring dream, and it almost perfectly summarizes my story. I usually have this dream toward morning time. When I awake, the morning prayer is called, and I cannot go back to sleep.

In my dream, I see Aras in a box made of glass. He is lying on his back, sleeping. He is so very handsome and young... Oh I cannot describe him. Only those who have known Aras, who have seen the defiant masculine fire of his beauty can understand this. The way my mother describes him as a dark James Dean is simply a cliché!

I start circling the glass box in which he is lying, taking care not to frighen him. I inspect his fine nose, his fleshy lips, his long legs and his hands with their slender fingers. I cannot see those sexy thighs of his, which I am so crazy about, but I know. I grow excited, thinking about how attractive he is. My excitement is tenfold that of a woman staggered by the incredible appeal of male beauty.

No, twenty, no, one hundredfold! Then I begin to desire what every woman caught in a man's field of magnetism does; for him to notice me. I want him to admire me and grow excited in turn. I wish this more than anything else. I feel as if he does not find me more attractive than any woman he has known, or will know in the future, then the world will grind to a halt, or all the volcanoes will erupt at the same time. I will either be incinerated or drowned in the ashes! I mean, if he does not like me I will die! I mean, if he is not smitten with me I will disappear! You know how women lose all their functions in this way when they fall in love… That is exactly what happens to me. Aras then wakes up, probably because of the vibrations I give off. He looks at me. Aras looks at me. In his eyes, the admiration that he can conceal from everyone but me! My god, Aras admires me, he still admires me!

Our eyes meet. He smiles at me. He smiles at me with his pearly teeth, his proud glance, and secret fragility. Just as I reach out to open the glass box in order to let him out, Aras' head begins to grow larger. Then his feet, and hands expand. As he is going through a horrible deformation, I scream and call to Duna for help:

"Duuuna, quick, for god's sake, come quick, something's happening to your brother, quick Duna, Mabel!"

But I cannot make a sound. I grab my throat in terror, and realize, panic-stricken, that I am out of breath. That is when I see that Aras does not fit in that glass box any longer, that he has started to become compressed and crushed. He is fighting for his life before my eyes, struggling to break the box, kicking, and emitting silent screams. I grow frightened of his deformity. I back away from the box. I feel precisely the grief and shame we experience when someone we have considered to be strong and resilient is rendered helpless in a situation. Our eyes meet. My god, our eyes meet. He gazes at me imploringly, saying "get me out of here Ada!" And from then on I can never forget that gaze!

"Set me free Ada! Please, release me." Release me!

I stand, frozen in place. Mad with grief, I watch him, my childhood sweetheart, whom I have imprisoned in a glass coffin at seventeen years of age. I wake up hundreds of times covered with sweat. The morning prayer is called, and I cry in bed: Oh Aras, where to?

I weep for the fact that, thirteen years after his departure, I have still not been able to set either of us free.

How realistic is it for a thirty year old woman to be in love with a boy of seventeen? What can a boy offer a young woman, and to what extent? It's a mistake. Weary of prolonging this mistake, I continue to have the same nightmare... Just before the call to morning prayer. And then I cannot go back to sleep.

I tell my uncle.

"Dreams do not bind anyone except those who sew them, my girl," he says, smiling. "Now, when the owners of dreams stop being tenants and pursue ownership, it is not at all a healthy sign. Do take my word, and move into other dreams, Rain Girl!"

And what about Duna? Me and Aras' cute little, emotional, floppy eared Blue boy. Little Duna. Mabel! Duna who makes me out to be much better than I really am, who idolizes me. Now he has two social labels: Duna the married man, and Duna the teacher. He is my infinite joy, my most important witness. My only consolation is that I believe I have set him free. Perhaps his marriage to Merich, and the life they are building together is the only precious thing that has been rescued from the ashes. Who knows?

Merich. Paleness. White waters!

The most beautiful, yet least prominent personality in every photograph. My cousin is expert in attracting shadows upon herself. To what extent does my mother's explanation cover Merich 's willful passivity? How different would Merich be, if she been raised with maternal love and paternal security? Fine, but isn't it the "passionate female" obstinacy that lies beneath her patient silence, which has, in the end, enabled her to attain everything she has desired since childhood? She always wanted Duna. She set her mind upon him from the very first day she saw him. And in the end, she got Duna. She wanted to become a doctor, and she did. She wished to live in Kuzguncuk, and she does. She was always jealous of Mrs. Zubeyde's admiration for me, and she even managed to take that away from me.

Only Merich, who seemed the frailest and most modest of us four, reached her goals one by one. While the three of us lay torn and bleeding, she walked on slowly, never taking off that costume of the wronged, well-behaved, innocent, and virtuous girl. She always advanced toward her goals by taking care to remain in the background. She sent her tears and sorrows masterfully to other adresses. She did not cry at Aras' death, but at the possibility that Duna would run to me as a result. I think I was in eighth or ninth grade when Uncle Mustafa, the veteran cafeteria attendant of Uskudar American College died of a heart attack caused by her and her friends' rowdiness. All the girls were crying. Only Merich was just standing there. Calm and quiet, as if nothing had happened! Supposedly some boys had hassled them, and they had gone and complained to Uncle Mustafa. And when poor old Uncle Mustafa tried to run after those little rascals... I know perfectly well that it was Merich who complained. She was definitely the one who went ahead and complained in her officious manner, wearing her beloved prim and proper girl costume. Everytime I asked her about it, she turned still as a stone and then calmly waved aside the subject, as if nothing had happened. That same year, as I cried for my classmate who had died from leukemia, she was stone cold again, gazing at me with a blank stare.

I presume that Merich regards my parents only as a source of financial support. She has always envied the special attention my uncle paid me. For I believe that Merich is driven by the desire to "possess" rather than "love." Therefore, I also do not believe that she loves Duna. Merich only wanted to possess Duna. Yet this is impossible! We know very well that no one, including Aras has been able to come between Brunette Ada and Blue Danube, and no such person as Merich will succeed in doing so in the future. We are attached to each other with a bond that they cannot comprehend. Ever since that first day he stepped into the garden of our mansion. Because... because in fact, Duna is one side of me, and I am one side of Duna!

Ah poor little pretty, sneaky cousin! Sweet, tranquil, still waters! Wandering upon surfaces always bears with it the heavy punishment of not ever being able to see the beauties of the deep!

I've never had a special affinity for Merich. Perhaps I pitied her during the first few years she moved into the mansion. I felt sorry that she could not fully experience the success that came through her beauty, her dilligence and her discipline. There were times that I genuinely tried for us to become closer, to become sisters. But she was like a brick wall. Nonetheless, I have to admit that I never hated her either. Merich did not even arouse hatred in me. She was not a fair match for me, she was too puny an opponent, and she always remained that way. Probably for this reason I can safely say that I was never jealous of Merich. The only woman who arouses my envy is Burkan.

I have never been independent of my uncle. Mine is a voluntary dependence. In order to quit smoking one has to first wish it. All addictions follow this rule. If it is against her will, one can only be freed forcefully from a serious addiction!

Every once in a while I sense that my uncle gets disappointed in me. The resulting pain is worse than having lost ten lovers, and makes me crawl in misery. I suppose there are very few things I would not do to keep my uncle's favorable opinion.

They say I resemble him. As a child, being likened to someone is pleasing, but if this delays the maturing process of an individual it loses all its charm. That is not what happened to me. I realized, growing up, that I already bore striking resemblances to my uncle. I think I have started to understand and judge him better through the years.

I believe that I'm not possessive in the generally accepted sense. I mean, I was never adamant that people I loved, people I was passionately attached to, should live near me, or that they should become something of mine. Perhaps, I should say, with the exception of Aras? Yes, I suppose it was that way... Aras was that way! However, after Aras, my loved ones do not have to be at my side. It may be that the desire to remain in someone's mind and soul is a more severely possessive urge. Therefore, I have always thought that my uncle belonged most of all to me. I was only scared once, when Burkan came on the scene. But Burkan became the queen of a domain which I could never have entered anyway. Actually, I might have wished to become my uncle's lover if I had not been his niece and if my age had been more appropriate... It staggers me to even imagine how difficult, painful, yet how fantastic and sweeping a love affair with him would be! It is as if the dream itself contains an incestuous mystery (is it?). Whenever I muse about my impossible love affair with my uncle, I become convinced that it would be the greatest classic of all time. This is the allure of the impossible. The incredible seduction of the unimaginable! No one knows this!

It is true that I was devastated when Aras left. However, some people's claims that I still have not been able to get my life back together seems ridiculous to me. Is there anyone who has been able to take complete control of her life? Is life something to be organized? For god's sake, what does it mean to organize your life in a time tunnel where anything is possible at any given moment, where no love, once possessed, can breathe freely, and where the thing called consistency is ripped to shreds? Who makes up these concepts and unleashes them upon society?

Aras' death left me absolutely shattered. I was very young, and I thought that those who left were only distant elderly people, and fictional characters. The first mistakes, the first betrayals, the first disappointments. But I did not die! Yet if my uncle or Duna were to leave, I would not be able to bear it. I feel as if I too would die and go with them... Those two are so important that... I mean... Anyhow, it pains me to even think about that subject. Extremely!

My mother and father have always been loving and supportive parents. Every once in a while I catch myself thinking that the only reason I have not gone insane or committed suicide has been due to my upbringing in a loving and stable mother-father relationship.

My father was a highly romantic child. He was wonderful as a father. My mother is a good friend. A superb confidante. In my eyes, she's a saint. I wish I could be as patient as her.

Aliye. Satan! Lucifer!

A demon who has ripped off every hand extended to her, who feeds on blood. All my life, I have never met a baddie whom I have provoked more than her! True, I have a stance, or an attitude that provokes people, even if I am not doing a single thing. Perhaps the reason some people dislike me before I even open my mouth is the same reason some men find me attractive, I cannot say. I'm not a psychologist.

When I discovered her in a photography gallery, she was an office-girl who longed to become manager of the place. She was talented and ambitious. Very ambitious! Initially, I took an interest in her simply to satisfy a charitable desire. Sponsoring a talented person in the same field as your own requires that you have a mature self-confidence, and a guarantee that the person will not become a rival at a later date. Whose guarantee? Of your own common sense of course! This is true of everyone, whether a person is aware of it or not. I do not believe anything to the contrary.

Her composition, focus, sense of lighting and ambition were ideal for becoming a photographer. She had no manners, education, or money.

I have never possessed a charitable spirit or a patient nature. I am not a ruthless, harsh person, but to tell you the truth, even as a girl, I cannot remember accompanying Merich, who derived pleasure out of weeping while reading Kemalettin Tugcu's tearjerkers.

Each time I returned to Istanbul for the summer, Aliye had made new progress. Obviously I was well aware of her temperemental and capricious nature, but I sensed that she could not rid herself from the trauma of the difficult childhood she sometimes told me about. Her past was filled with cold and merciless memories, or so she said. Perhaps even this attracted me. The worst childhood I knew of had been Merich's, and even that did not contain the beatings, torture, sexual abuse, hunger, and suicide attempts Aliye spoke of.

I was hoping that if her living standards improved, the hatred in her would decrease, or that she would channel it towards the art of photography, in which she was very gifted. Who knows, maybe it was my own arrogant desire to have a protege, to be able to say "I made her!"

She changed. She discarded her rural looks and her walk. The more she read the more occupied her blank stare became, and the more she thought the more her face gained meaning. She began to dress better. But her hatred and destructiveness increased. I was not surprised to learn that she started doing drugs. But nothing she tried had succeeded in purging her of her anger and violence.

It was as if Aliye derived a savage pleasure from going down faulty paths and getting wounded in order to deal with herself. The summer she adopted a noticeably sarcastic and defiant attitude toward me, she began to insert crude mentions of what seems to have been a considerably lengthy relationship with Duna into her sentences. She made rather dimwitted cracks and nonsensical remarks regarding Duna's body and sexual performance. I remember that she trembled with pleasure upon seeing the saddened expression on my face, when she was relating with hand gestures how Duna loved oral sex and how he was willing to be her slave for the sake of it. She must have been jubilant, thinking she had taken Duna away from me. And yet… Poor Aliye…

I heard that later on she got into the serial game of befriending happy couples and breaking them up. It must have been a triumph of destruction for her to cause several engaged and married couples to separate by taking advantage of men's sexual weaknesses.

I never asked Duna. He, in turn, never asked me about my experiences abroad. I never talked to him about my boyfriends, ranging from short and painful affairs to some who were worthy and nice enough to have been possibly lengthy relationships. I knew he would be hurt.

It was last summer. The start of the time when Aliye was ostracized from almost all social circles. One night, after seeing a movie with friends, I saw her walking all alone down Istiklal Avenue. She approached me and asked for a cigarette. She was a complete mess. Did I feel sorry for her? I don't know. Was it because I was a good person? Am I good person? I'm certainly not as good as Duna! No one can be as kind as Duna.

"Why don't you come over, we're all going to my place," I found myself saying.

She came. There was some eating and drinking. There was conversation. Old photographs were perused. Soon everyone left, but Aliye stayed. Between the pictures, liquor, and nighttime, all of a sudden I felt an incredible longing for the past… For the mansion, Kuzguncuk, my father, my uncle, my mother, Duna, Nanny Cihan, and Aras… Oh for Aras…

I was extremely drunk and nostalgic.

I remember that out of the blue I began to relate what it is like to miss a dead person. Did I cry out, sobbing, that I was actually the one who had killed him? I don't know, I might have. That is what I usually do when I reach that ultimate point. Suddenly Aliye began kissing me. She was very passionate, and was rapidly undressing me. I did not understand what was happening but I enjoyed that warmth, those passionate caresses. At the time, I badly needed to be touched and caressed. And I did not resist Aliye's lovemaking. The details are very vague. I had an awful headache and was swearing that I would never drink again. Upon seeing the next morning how Aliye had scratched and bled my body, I realized that I had certainly not been in my right mind the night before. No, I'm not saying this to make myself out to be innocent. In the beginning her kisses were pleasurable, and I'm not denying that I enjoyed them. Believe it or not, at that moment, I did not experience a pleasure different from that of being kissed and stroked by a man. However... however I was sober enough to notice that something very important to me was missing.

Just like a nature shot. In order to take a good nature picture light it crucial, and needs to be used well. That night I realized that for me, a good lovemaking had to be with a man. Because I was able to learn that without the meeting of a male body inside my own, sexuality seemed lacking and bland to me. It's a good thing that taste is the only inarguable subject!

When I woke up the next morning Aliye was gone. I only saw her half a year later. She showed up on my birthday. No, it was not I who invited her, as Duna thought. I had no idea that she was coming. Then, after wreaking havoc on everything, she left. I am positive that she made her way to the mansion in order to cause a scene.

Apparently rumors have sprung that I am a homosexual, a lesbian, similar to the ones which claim I was the one who pushed Aras into the sea on that night of terror. Well, let them! What am I supposed to do? People know me: if I were a lesbian I would not conceal it.

As for Aras... I did kill him, in a sense. This feeling is always on my view-finder. Once the feeling of guilt gets under your skin, it will dominate all the pictures you take from then on! Anyhow, aren't we all somewhat guilty for the deaths and miseries we were unable to prevent? Don't all of us have an element of the murderer, the thief, and the depraved when we are watching fires, breakdowns, poverty, war, and robberies? Come on now, don't be shy! That's how we all are!

Duna understands this best. Duna understands!

ZUBEYDE ATACAN

Housewife. Widowed. Mother of two male children. One of her sons is deceased. Exercised her right to remain silent.

MERICH ATACAN

Medical doctor. Pathologist. Married. Niece of the poet Dogan Gokay and the actress Pervin Gokay.

They are mistaken.

That is the only thing I can tell you.

They are mistaken about me. I mean, they look down on me.

Ada and Duna do this most, but that's just the way it is…

I mean, how should I say… none of them, not one of them ever really tried. All my life, no one really tried to get to know me. Maybe my Aunt Pervin and Uncle Dogan did, a little. But they too gave up quickly. One is an actress; thinks the scenes she plays in are reality, and her life a movie. The other's a poet; he lives in a world of images, and is in love with his own fantasies. Both are people with over-developed egos, and therefore have little time to spare for others. They were impatient toward me. I mean, umm, that's what happened.

Of course, things were different for Ada. Her case is invariably special. Everyone always has time for her. As for me, I mean, even my own mother was impatient toward her child, and had no time for me. In short, none of my relatives, friends, and even my husband, have accepted me into their hearts, or their real worlds. I mean… I have always been a guest, a background image in all these stops. If life really were a play, as Uncle Dogan says, then I would be a pathetic actress who sneaks into the theater unnoticed after all the strong characters have long taken the stage, and all the large parts have been distributed, and agrees to take the last walk-on part that no one wants. I don't know how to say it, but they, the ones I shared the same stage with, were such powerful personalities that, you know, I had lost my chance from the very beginning.

I think, I mean, in my opinion, the personalities of the witnesses are important. Criminal clues can be deduced from the genetic make-up of people, behavioral analyses can be made from their endocrinological inheritances. Mine is very typical and simple. Merih, the very young, pretty, but weak-willed flight attendant marries Demir Gokay, the wealthy, handsome, middle-aged womanizer. Naturally, they immediately have a kid and the man goes off to further conquests without wasting a precious moment. I mean, what do they call it, you know, a perfect cliché!

Here's the truth: I think both my mother and father are people who were defeated in life. A man who is constantly and selfishly running around after younger women's bodies must be wretched enough to realize that he does not deserve his own self-respect. In my opinion, that's the kind of person my father is.

Somewhere, I have two or three step-brothers, and an uncertain number of step-mothers, cursing after my father who cannot accomplish anything besides deserting people. And now I have a step-father.

That is the reason I commend Uncle Dogan for never wanting to have children. How should I say, he found this responsibility to be excessive and made his decision from the start. Unfortunately, for the same reason, I despise my father. The most distinct feeling I have toward my mother is pity, I suppose.

I mean, there is a serious reason why I cart around the childhood hell I had to live through, to all my new addresses in the form of nightmares. When I was a tiny little girl, my mother would lock herself in the bathroom and refuse to come out for hours. On the weekends, I would wait at home, alone and hungry, and I would be terribly scared. I mean, I would really be terrified. The house was dead silent. My father would never come by. I would see the neighborhood kids out walking with their parents, or going on picnics, and I would ache with envy. I would wait all by myself in that huge living room, filled, like a museum, with expensive furniture, and wait for someone to come and rescue me. I thought that maybe my mother would come out of the bathroom, my father would return home, or... I don't know, umm... you know, I thought there would be someone who thought about me... But when the phone rang the person calling would always be my Aunt Pervin.

"Merich, dear, it's me, Aunt Pervin. Is your mommy home, sweetie?"

"No mommy. Mommy went to the bathroom. She didn't come. Mommy locked the door. She never came."

"You aren't all by yourself again are you, my little one?"

"But I have my dolls. I brushed their hair. No mommy. She's go-one. Mommy went to the bathroom!"

"Did you eat, Merich, dear, are you hungry, sweetheart?"

"No food. Mommy go-one. Daddy didn't come. The babies are very hungry."

"Oh dear god!.. Well, now..."

"You come here, auntie, why don't you come here auntie dear! It's very black here."

"Look Merich, now you just turn on the lights, and the music, and tell your mommy 'Aunt Pervin says please can you come to the phone,' alright, will you do that?"

My mother would not come out. She would moan, whine like a puppy, and lapse into an infinite silence. I mean, that's what I thought.

"Mommy's dead, auntie dear. She won't come out at all. Mommy's go-one, gone to heav-een."

"Now, now, stop crying. You be a good girl, sit down and wait for me. I'll be there right away. Don't let anyone in except me, alright Merich, darling?"

After what seemed like hours a taxi would pull over in front of our building, and my Aunt Pervin, always stylish and graceful like a princess, would come running in. I mean, how do I say it, I found her very beautiful... I would open the door for her, she would give me a loving hug, and cry indiscreetly. I mean, how should I say, my aunt felt sorry for me. Everyone felt sorry for me. They still do!

Then Aunt Pervin would wash my face in the kitchen. I think... then she would open our completely empty refrigerator and inspect it sadly. She would ask me to get dressed. After that, I mean while I got dressed, she would start pleading with my mother, and minutes later, succeed in getting her to come out of the bathroom, semi-conscious, half-naked, and looking like a ghost. Anyway, then she would get her dressed, while talking to her as if she were a baby. She would put us in a taxi, drop off my mother at her sister's, and take me to her own house. I really liked their house. It was cheerful and safe there. There, everyone would act nice to me. I mean, even Ada would be nice.

And Ada... Unarguably the only center of attention, the irresistable queen, the vain goddess!

Yes, I suppose... I mean, I suppose no one, not even a sibling, a cousin or anyone else could have spoiled Ada's reign. She was so self-assured, so self-satisfied that everyone who approached her would sense the flames of the self-love that emanated from her, and would have to understand that they would not be able to get any closer. She even loved her mistakes. She was a year older than me, but in my view Ada was a big girl who was very smart, confident, and who knew everything. Maybe that's why there was not a rivalry in the generally accepted sense, I mean a classic and visible rivalry, between us. She was already the winner of every race I might have entered, I mean, I guess...

After they moved to the mansion in Kuzguncuk, I liked visiting them even more. How can I tell you, the mansion seemed like a palace, and it's garden like heaven to me. I did not feel unwanted there. But I did not belong there either... I mean, all the real roles had been distributed before my arrival, and once again, I was too late. Around that time, my mother was hospitalized for alcohol, and my father got re-married. They told me that they had gone on a long journey, but I think I'd understood.

I would want to believe that the disasters befalling me were a bad dream. Before going to sleep I would pray to God and ask Him to protect me if He loved me. When I woke up my mother and father would be in the same house again, and we would live together without ever fighting. And then I would become the Ada of our house. The more my prayers failed to come true, the more I would pray, and cry. I guess those fantasies I made up while praying would give me happiness, I mean, that's what I suppose...

It was during my weekend stays at the mansion that I met him. The first day I met him, it was like my life changed. You know, I don't mean to exaggerate, but, really, it's true... The first time I saw him, it was as if I felt that someday he would be mine. He would be mine, only mine. I guess he, he wouldn't, he wouldn't even remember this, I mean that first day. He was there in the sandbox, making sand castles. He did not wear glasses yet. He was wearing short red overalls and was practically panting for Ada's favor. (That's what everyone does!) His curly black hair was long, and I had not yet seen his baby blue eyes. I stared at him, spellbound. His big old ears were very cute. I went up to him. I mean, umm… How do I say it? I stood around next to him to make myself noticed, but it didn't work. I tried helping, but it didn't work. So I placed a small white oval stone that was on the ground on top of his sandcastle. That was when he noticed me. But I guess he was angry…

"Don't ever touch that stone!" he said, snatching it away from me, and put it in his pocket.

Ada came up to me and scolded me. Ada scolded me for the first time. Her subsequent admonishments always came when I approached Duna. I suppose, maybe that boy was important to Ada. But Ada already had everything. Everyone was her friend. Ada has always gotten what she wanted. As for me, I only wanted him.

His name was Duna!

Actually, I know that Ada calls Duna "Mabel." As if I haven't figured out that that word means "Ma bella," i.e., "My Lovely!" They must have adopted it from a song they knew. I mean, it must be the song's name or something… I've known this code between them for a long time. I guess they don't know that I know. It doesn't matter at all. Anyhow, I had learned to mask my fears and loneliness with my silence (or should I call it taciturnity?), when I was just a little girl. They're clueless about some of the other things I also know. For example, I'm aware that Duna had a serious relationship with Aliye. Because I… how to say this, it might seem odd, but I would follow Duna… I mean, especially when I left Kuzguncuk to live in the dormitory, and never got to see him. I would miss him an awful lot, but I knew that he did not miss me very much. Sometimes I would go and secretly watch him in the school cafeteria. I also went to that tea garden in Sultanahmet a couple of times, where he liked to drink tea and study. I would love Duna from afar, as he sat, usually alone, poetry books in hand, and sometimes with his friends. I always loved him from afar… Actually, even now... how do you say it, I guess I'm not very close to my husband... And he's not to me... I mean, I think I still love Duna from afar. However, this does not make me very discontent. What's important to me, I mean, the real issue, is that Duna is together with me. Moreover, that he's mine!

Then, seeing Aliye and Duna together in that tea garden... I recognized her. She's very eye-catching. I mean, she's extremely sexy. Utterly sexy... When I saw her there, being intimate with Duna... I mean, she was bending over to kiss Duna's ear... something shattered inside me. I mean... I mean, after I'd even managed to keep Ada from getting Duna, to lose him to someone like that... Then I began to follow Aliye. It was easier than I had thought. She was in a miserable state. The people she met and talked to would shove her around. It was not difficult to figure out that she did drugs. When I realized that she was sleeping with Duna, I mean, of course, one uses her instincts a little... I began sending anonymous letters to Aliye in the beginning of the summer. Somewhat harsh letters, warning her that she would get in trouble for her drug abuse... I suppose she began to get suspicious around that time. She had come to my school to interrogate me, but had left thinking that I was too innocent to ever do anybody harm. Too clean, innocent, too quiet and naive to the point of stupidity!.. That's what everyone thinks about me! You know how some people think they have a monopoly on intelligence, and that everyone else was born yesterday? Well, Aliye is a prime example! Ada is not like that. Ada could not care less. Ada does not even pay attention to those who she does not consider worthy.

I suppose that the letters might have affected their break-up in the following manner: You know... Aliye might have become more angry and aggressive, and Duna might not have been able to stand it, or something like that... I don't know. In my opinion, Duna would not have been able to establish a long-term relationship with her in any case, but perhaps Aliye might have hatched a plan and married him or something... I mean, I was really afraid of that... But it did not happen. I managed to win Duna over once more. Duna was fated for me, and I knew it.

I was terrified once, only once, when Aras died. Every single person mistook the deep sorrow I felt at the time to be for Aras. Yet

I was going insane, thinking that now Ada would steal Duna away from me. I mean... all my dreams would be shattered due to a completely unexpected death. Ada did not suspect anything. Because she was hospitalized for two weeks. She did not talk to anyone, and did not want to live. If she had been around, and seen that Aras' death grieved me more than anyone else, she would have caught on. Ada would have understood right away. Duna did not even get it.

I had no particular affinity for Aras, but to me he was a guarantee! I don't think he ever took me seriously. I mean, umm, in my opinion, Aras was very arrogant, and his passion for Ada had to do with capturing the daughter of the neighborhood's most wealthy and important family. All the girls were after him, and naturally, Aras was well aware of this, but... Ada's different. I mean, I believe that Aras did not really love Ada. Duna, on the other hand... He was always crazy about Ada. He still is. I play a game, where I regard Ada as my sister-in-law. You know, to me, Duna is a husband who is madly under the influence of his dominant older sister.

I have always been told that I was beautiful. I suppose it's true that I'm pretty, though not as much as my mother... but I think the woman who is pleased with herself when she looks in the mirror is the truly beautiful one. I mean, I think that's why Ada is prettier than me. Because, I think Ada must tremble with pleasure when she looks in the mirror.

All my life, I mean, ever since my most formative memories, the only person I have really felt safe next to has been Duna. Ever since the first time I saw him, his presence gave me comfort and solace. I would do anything not to lose him. Since he thinks of me as innocent and guileless, I will not spoil his image. I would do anything to keep him belonging to me. Soon, I will also have his baby. I will have a child, and experience everything I wanted to as a child, with her. Everything.

Duna is soft hearted. Once we have a child, he can never leave me, I know... But there's no hurry. Quietly, without frightening him... I never saw any harm in advancing slowly, but stealthily.

Finally, I would like to say that I silently laugh at those people who make fun of the triumphs I won through the power of silence. I believe that people who underestimate or deny the power of silence are unaware of an important weapon. Silence spreads slowly, and turns into a great contolling power over your opponent. I mean, silence, coupled with patience and consistency, becomes the most important force in the world... And that's why I became Merich Atacan, whereas she is still Ada Mercan! I think, I mean, I guess she'll always remain that way... My aim was never to steal her life. Why would I want to cause her any harm? I just, you know, I just wanted to be Ada, that's all.

ARAS ATACAN

High School Student. Deceased.

DOGAN GOKAY

Poet, writer, journalist. Married.

The kids exaggerate a little.

Then again, is not youth the lingering of dreams upon their pupils, like so many daytime ornaments?

Indeed, it is true that I do not relate my personal affairs to them. Their tendency to regard me as a fictionalized hero might be partially rooted in this fact. The way one always does in youth... In all honesty, I myself used to idolize Nazim and Marx a little, when I was young. In those first hours of youth... In any case, after one chooses to follow the path of socio-realism, the childish notion of edifying any one person becomes out of the question.

"Liberty is the perception of necessities," says Marx. My own comprehension of my responsibilities coincides with my sixteenth or seventeenth year. Since then, I have expanded my personal freedom by consciously keeping the responsibilities of my private life to a minimum. First and foremost, I have erased the concept of "ownership" from my life. Now, nearing the close of my fiftieth year, I neither have any taxable property, nor any stocks. I still rent my lodgings, and I own neither a house nor car. I merely save a sum of money in the bank for an emergency medical siuation, that is all. It has been a matter of choice for me that my wife is a working, independent woman. She has a domestic automobile of her own, and money in the bank. I neither know the amount, nor inquire about it. Burkan is a girl who would appreciate this.

All too often, women shortchange their intellectual capabilities because of an infatuation with their own femininity. And upon meeting a man who is aware of this fact, they assume that they are being complimented. Actually, girls today have realized that they possess both qualities, but it has taken a long time. If you ask me, the vitality and mental capacity of the female human being, whom we call woman, is one of nature's greatest miracles. Therefore, the essence of that tale called life consists of wandering about the lilac colored maps of women. Some men experience this with pleasure, others with rage and violence. Yet women were born well aware of everything, and whatever fits men might want to throw, it is only women who hold the map of life. After making this discovery, you have no choice but to love them dearly.

The rent and household expenses have always been my responsibility. I have always made my living through writing. Occasionally, the income that falls to my share, from the property my late mother held in Alanya, is sent to my bank account, after being divided between Pervin, Demir, and myself. I do not understand anything about money matters, that is Burkan's area of expertise.

If I had so desired, I could have accepted the frequent offers of a political life that are posed to me, and become a man of a wholly other, ostentatious lifestyle. Those who know me well are aware that. I have refused these offers without so much as a second thought. I am not a member of any party or group. If I were, I would lose my chance to criticize, I would be bound and gagged. We see the charlatans around us.

It is true that they are intimidated by me as a result. Never in my life have I taken or given bribes, in any sense of the word. I neither submitted to anyone, nor did I ever force submission. Now, I have had many opponents whom I have intellectually defeated, but that is a whole other matter! Hah hah ha! I have not taken pity on anyone on that subject. Basically, I do not owe any debts or favors to anyone, and this is a great liberty as well as a great loneliness!

They have tried to wear me down by labeling me as a homosexual, an Ottoman elitist, and a liberal socialist. However, they have never been able to cast a shadow on my literary course, my political opinions, or my private life. As for sexuality, nowadays they call it things like "action," or "intercourse," but the appropriate word is sexuality, and it is most certainly a matter of private taste. Sexuality renders anyone except the participants unnecessary. No one should have to answer to anyone else! Burkan knows everything, absolutely everything that they are curious about.

My professional side is as clear as daylight. My books go into numerous reprints, and I have a good connection with young people. My relationship with the public is very broadly based. Devout people, atheists, socialists, nationalists, lesbians, homosexuals, women, and men, they all come and find me. Because I have always maintained my line. I have respect for myself and most important of all, I am an occasional partner-in-crime to youth. Hah hah ha! This is a very simple and vital issue. Accompanying youth in a small act of insurgence opens an air hole for them, as they are smothered with sins and prohibitions, and it allows them to breathe. That is all! The kids know that I am sincere and consistent.

To fall behind his times during his own lifetime is one of the greatest misfortunes that can happen to a writer. Ever since the *Tanzimat* period most of our intellectuals have been conformists, hedonists, and opportunists. They have never succeeded in leaving their social ambitions behind those of their intellectual ambitions. They continue to repeat the mistake of being severed from both the public and their era. They do not read much, and believe that they can manage to maintain their occupation by depending on their talent alone, with misinformed, one-sided partialities for the rest of their lives. And, naturally, they are mistaken! The Turkish intellectual does not regard himself as a Turkish intellectual, but rather as say, a French, Soviet (back in the day), or currently, American intellectual. Well, is that any way to go about things? You laze about, derogate your own culture, as well as anything that is different from you, and then you dream of being a widely loved writer! Well, that simply will not fly! And it does not. That is why writing books which no one except one's own friends and yes-men read is considered "a sad fate."

A writer must be as concerned with remaining up-to-date and in touch with the people as with his talent. It is important to be reinvigorated. Young people know this. Youth is the only true age when one knows. When one grows older, he only remembers. Old age is the realization of one's own ignorance and misperceptions. That is why I like young people: they know. Also for the same reason, youth can immediately discern empty, hollow, pretentious, and pushy old people from a mile away. And young people are merciless!

I can safely say that those four spent their formative and adolescent years under my guidance. Thus, even though they have reached their mid-thirties they are still, in a sense, children to me. If their lives, that of Ada, Merich, Aras and Duna, were to be written down, it would make a highly interesting novel. They have gone through intense and complicated paths. And they are still in the process? Who can know what life will bring?

I liken Ada to myself, somewhat. However I am noticing that the older she gets, the more like her father she becomes. Sureyya was the son of a poor family with many children, and was extremely emotional. He lived according to whimsy, and died in the same manner. I was never able to comprehend the love my sister bore for her husband, how she put up with his irresponsible drinking, ridiculous womanizing, capriciousness, and childish changes of temperament. I have considered Pervin's steadfast devotion and faithfulness to be a type of love in which addiction manifests itself as passion. Naturally, there are thousands of different kinds of love, and love hurts. And Ada is the fruit of of a love that has been thus pruned. She was not like any of the other children I knew. She was a sensitive, excessively proud, intelligent, and strong child. She was at peace with herself from a very early age. Unfortunately life, just like nature, is meaningless and unegalitarian. We humans have been the only ones who have endeavored to attribute meaning to this.

Ada's misfortune was having made long-term plans inordinately early on in life. In this mistake lay the clues to her unwillingness to grow up, which has surfaced noticeably at present, and the extreme emotionality she inherited from her father. These two matters still cause me slight apprehension, but in the end I believe that she is smart enough to take care of herself.

I cannot say the same for Merich. I suspect that, despite all the calm, proper, consistent, and successful aspects of her life, that child is in terrible private fear and unrest. She, of course, has been the victim of an egotistical father and a wretched mother. Even as a boy, my older brother Demir was extremely irresponsible and spoilt. And because I adopted his responsibilities, everyone thought that I was the older one. However, what strikes me as even more grave than Demir's thoughtlessness is the mothering desire of that poor stewardess Merih. I have always pitied women who believed they could keep a man by having his baby. Because I liken them to soldiers who do not recognize their power, and who fight with the wrong weapons. I do hope Merich does not take after her mother.

The only thing Merih counted on was her beauty and her youth. She really was very beautiful. She was one of the loveliest stewardesses at Turkish Airlines. And like most girls in this situation, her fear of losing the treasure she held was debilitating the working energy of her other talents. If she had not given birth, Merih might have gotten away from that marriage with less damage and refashioned her life. She ruined both herself, and that child. Although her parents were alive, Merich was a foundling and an orphan. Thankfully, Pervin and Sureyya turned out to be merciful, and raised the girl themselves. I could not have done it. No, I could not have. Due to a decision I had made in my early youth, I had crystallized the notion that I could only advance toward my goals by keeping my personal responsibilities limited. Therefore, I was not going to have any children. Children are binding, coercive, and pushy creatures for their mothers and fathers. They take no pity on their parents, they are always right and always demanding. If you had infinite time they would take it all up and ask for more. I could not have flung myself into a life which was out of my control. This is one of my most crucial reasons for marrying Burkan. She has accepted this desire of mine from the very beginning, and has not requested anything to the contrary, so far. Burkan's most important quality is that she knows what she wants. I do not know whether she has her moments of wanting to be a mother, but if that is the case we both know that this marriage cannot be forced to continue. Her age is still suitable for motherhood, if she so desires. But frankly, her leaving me for this reason is the last thing I could wish for.

Now, about Duna. Regardless of how this boy seems to have been left in the shadow of Aras, in my opinion, he was the healthier and livelier of the two until they reached puberty. His sole misfortune was falling in love with the same girl as his brother, and as always happens in love triangles, this created a tragic situation for all three of them.

Aras was an extremely introverted and irritable boy. He was too ambitious to stand failure or being second place. He was ill-tempered when he lost, passionate when he acquired, and dogmatic when he made up his mind.

He was gifted and intelligent, but above all Aras was a very hand-some and masculine youth. You know, one of those rogues born with a certain *je ne sais quoi*. He was a combination of slightly dangerous looks, vain indifference, and somewhat excessive self-confidence, packaged in a handsome physique. There are not many women who can resist that! If he had lived, women would never have left him alone, and since Ada is not by nature one to pursue a man, they would have separated. However, prior to that, much different reasons for their break-up would have occurred, and the relationship would have ended before they reached the episodes of jealousy. Because it was evident that Ada would become a colorful, lively, avant-garde woman. Aras, on the other hand, was going to turn out a measured, straight-laced, monotonous, and traditional man, and together, these two dispositions would have suffocated one another. Had Aras lived, their relationship would have ended naturally, and Ada, lacking any guilt, would have discovered the man with whom she could have found true happiness: Duna. Yet it was not to be!

Duna is not mysterious. Regarded from the outside, he does not promise any adventurous back streets with which to sweep girls off their feet. Yet he has subtleties, and a very deep inner world. He is shy, and has been badly crushed under his older brother's dominant character. But life does not resemble a novel in the least, and even if some of us can sense very early on what is to come, we cannot change the course of history. We can only accomplish this feat in novels and movies, and that is why we so adore cinema and literature.

Ada is passionate, like her father. Aras was a passion of hers. After losing him, she made an unnecessary effort to stay away from Duna. Yet it was those two who were genuinely meant for each other.

Someday, women and men will acquire equal rights, but it will never be possible for them to comprehend one another. This is always the case since the masochistic pleasures nature endows to women, due to the physical structure of sexuality, develops in the direction of sadism in men. I know women well. I have known the dark, the white, the black, and also the yellow skinned of the East. What women have I encountered... What is universal is that no matter what their race or class, women are ready and willing to forfeit their righteous competition with men in bed. Aras, who was Ada's sexual preference, would have been unable to provide for her emotional needs, as is often the case with the misguided relationships educated girls fall into, but Aras died, somewhat unfairly, before she had a chance to make this realization.

Aras did not like me in the least because he sensed my reservations. Even if he could not label it at that age, he perceived my suspicions that he would not suffice for Ada. It is a pity! It is honestly a pity for all three of them.

Merich is the most fortunate one among them. It can be said that Merich finally found her own harbor, and established a home where she is safe. However, I doubt that this harbor is constructed in an appropriate location. I do not think that Merich will be enough to soothe the raging storms of the sailor's heart, who is in her harbor. Therefore, I am glad that they do not have children.

Merich can save herself. She has a profession. She is resilient. So is Ada. What really worries me is Duna's state. I do not like how he has been behaving lately. He has become alarmingly introverted. If human life were a novel, I would have written Duna as the only son of that family, and would have saved him from many a misfortune. Nowadays, the blue gleam has disappeared from his eyes, and he resembles fictional characters who cannot find the time to live from reading too many books. I am extremely worried that that child might fall ill. Perhaps he should travel to a distant country with a third and new woman... I feel as if soon a deadly civil war will erupt inside him. Dangerous, and grave! He needs to stay alive. If anything happens to that young man, four women, including my sister, my two nieces, and his own mother, will be irreperably devastated. Someone has to help this boy, but who? We writers and poets cannot heal people. We warn and shake up people, and this can sometimes create a worsening effect. Those who are sturdy and strong then go on to write their own books. Those who are frail go to psychologists. Perhaps Duna will be saved by writing his own book. Who knows? In the end, which one of us has not been the victim of some war during his lifetime?

ALIYE YILDIZ

Secretary. Single. Has criminal record.

They're all liars!

These maniacs're all cowards and liars. I don't agree with anything that's said about me. Anyway, when I'm the subject, people always lie. They always think they can destroy me, wipe me off the face of history. But no way! No one's been able to destroy me so far, and no one can! There's only one person who can annihilate me, and that's me! Yeah, so I have a record. So what? Who doesn't? Now, don't anybody go giving me the old good, clean cut kid bullshit! Everybody knows their own criminal records. Like hell they do!

Those two bourgeois bastards kicked me out of their house. They kicked me out in front of everybody! They just dumped me out of their house, their lives, and their futures. Just like that, BAM! See, that's how easy everything is for them. These people, whose every need has been readily provided for, are dandies who know nothing about what it feels like to struggle for one cup of tea, one single cigarette, for a tiny bit of love and acceptance! It's easy for them to kick people out. They kicked me out. No one can stand me anyway, I get booted out of everywhere in the end. Only he, he seemed to have some balls… It was like he was brave, like he loved, would love forever. Duna! Yes, Duna. I thought he'd be able to stand me. Hah! Stupid of me, of course. He got spooked too, and ran away. He kicked me out as he was fleeing. But I make those who get rid of me regret it. In the end, I make 'em sorry they were even born. They know it!

And those who don't will soon learn!

Lots of people piss me off. In fact, I might get pissed at anyone. I fuckin' hate bourgeois ethics, "good little girl" acts and "I'm not like other guys" speeches. I think everyone's the same, and fronting like you're any different really makes me mad. All girls and guys look for an opportunity to screw, and pounce on it when they find one. You can't tell me anything different! But no, they all wear some sort of label now. Love, or passion, or art, or religion, then manners, or society, or this or that or the other!

Oh yeah? Man, are you all blind or something, the only legitimate shit in this world is the law of the jungle, then why're you still acting like you don't know? Everything's based on power, are you dumb or something? Whoever's strong wins, the rest bite the dust. Sex and money are the only rulers of this world, man. Nothing else! So everybody stop the bullshit!

I swear, no one's ever pissed me off as much as those two: Ada and Duna! I didn't hate that perverted dad of mine, or my maniac mom as much as I hated them! Alright, so my dad was a scumbag. He didn't love us one bit cause even his seventh kid was a girl. I mean, he didn't love us like his daughters, but he sure knew how to love us as something else. He would corner us here and there, he'd fondle and kiss every part of us, and steal our childhoods away. But what happened? He supposedly got shot "by mistake, while out hunting in the woods." Don't make me laugh! Then why'd he get shot right between his legs? Why didn't he mistakenly get shot in the heart? Cause he didn't even have a heart, the bastard! Well, then, who shot him? Why didn't the village residents pursue it, instead of burying him quickly and getting rid of that scum? Could it be, eh? Hah hah ha! I know who finished him off. I know real well.

My maniac of a mother, knowing my dad abused us in every possible way, knowing full well that the miscarriage my sister Meryem had was my dad's seed, would still lie down below that bastard and try to make a boy. Shameless hussy! But what happened? Turns out the last one she was trying to pop out was a boy too... she died bellowing like a cow at forty. Supposedly from "bleeding!" Don't make me laugh! What possibly could have caused the bleeding? I wonder, could there have been a certain situation somewhere, somehow, that caused the bleeding?

All brats who've had a comfortable, happy childhood are the same! That's what those two proved to me. I despise both myself, and them for thinking that they were different! That's why I hate them so damn much. I hate myself for having loved them!

Anyway, loving is not for me!

And of course, I'm beginning to understand way too late that Ada and Duna are taking their inability to screw each other out on me, then kicking me out of their lives. When Duna thought that Ada, who could never sleep with him, was my lover, he went nuts. Man, what kind of love is it that the guy feels for that frigid bitch who walks around with the blue little girl picture on her face! What fuckin' luck for that narcissistic creature called Ada! Yeah, Duna went crazy with jealousy, he really went crazy. Or he simply revived. Maybe he went into electroshock. I know all about electroshocks. They put a little rubber pillow between your jaws so you don't bite your tongue. Duna really bit down hard that day, 'cause he didn't know this! I know from the way he lolled his tongue around in his mouth, and from the face he made. They give us barbiturates before electroshocks, but poor little Blue Danube didn't even have that. I don't know if after I left he took his anger out on his serpent of a wife, who plays the innocent little girl. Merich isn't like them, I know those types. Ada and Duna are naive enough to think that they are smart, but Merich's a good actress. Looks like she started out with a small, trivial role, but she's now snapped up the lead part. The vestal virgin plays a hell of a part.

She was drunk. Ada was really drunk that night. When she was picking up the photographs after everyone left, out slipped a picture of that famous dead hero, Aras. Seeing him, she suddenly began to cry. She was crying like crazy. She was retelling that flashy childhood of hers, that childhood filled with nannies and cooks, with a disgusting modesty, as if it were oh so ordinary. She even missed her dog Sivri. Oh such noble yearnings, such sickening nostalgias!

Even though I'd never met him, I was hearing for the thousandth time what a superior, what a so and so creature that Aras was. That was when I realized that it wasn't Merich, but Ada who took Duna away from me. And I saw very clearly that all my life I'd actually wanted to be in Ada's position. Who wouldn't want to be in her place? A small, tiny little thirst for revenge spread across me. I love it when that shiny proud snake slithers its way inside me. It extends its head in such an attractive, seductive manner. I'll never believe there ever was a person who could resist it! Revenge is a glistening, coy snake that does not come when it's invited, but only starts moving after it has really, really been wished for, and even sex pales in comparison to the ecstasy it gives me when it arrives. It fills my lungs like oskigen.

That night the serpent came, and flickering out its gorgeous tongue, allowed me a kiss. There and then I decided to take my revenge on Ada. I stripped and made love to the talented, successful, famous, smart, and attractive Ada Mercan, who was practically drowning in a pool of love and trust I had never tasted. She was in no state to object, but I understood that she also liked it. I possessed her body, tearing and hurting every inch of it! The whole time she was crying, moaning, and murmuring "Aras." When she finally curled up like a cat, I heard her say "I killed him."

"Who'd you kill?"

"I killed Aras. I was the one who caused his death!" she groaned, and then passed out.

Alcohol, sex, and remorse. No form of torture can make a person talk as much as these three. Duna's eternal love had spilled the beans. So, I threw a few pictures I found lying about into my bag. These were mostly group shots of Ada and Duna, taken at restaurants and gallery openings. I knew they would come in handy some day. I knew it well!

They kicked me out. They not only kicked me out of their house, but also from their lives and futures. I'll make them sorry. I'll take such revenge on them that from now on, they'll never be able to stand on their feet again! I'm going to hit them in their weakest spot. And with a single blow.

"The murder committed by photographer Ada Mercan, darling of our famous movie stars and poet, and our great source of international pride…"

Hah hah ha! They'll be done for. I'll even go tell the district attorney. Well, is it a lie? Didn't she admit the murder to me, and in our lovebed? Damn, this's going to be a first class, top of the line scandal, I swear. Will I or won't I plant myself in the forefront of newspapers, in the most serious news programs, at the micro-phones of the most intellectual, pseudo-leftist announcers?

Come on then, let them see who's kicking who out of where, and good luck! This's going to be a lesson to everyone who has ever screwed me over, left me out, pushed me around, or witheld the smallest crumbs of love! Of course, I also know that by punishing those two pigs, I'm doing a service to humanity. Crime should not go unpunished! Like my mom's and dad's crimes... Now it's Brun-ette Ada and Blue Danube's turn.

Good. Very good. Perhaps this'll be the best thing I have ever done in my life!

PERVIN GOKAY

Movie actress. Entrepreneur. Married. Has one daughter. Wife of the late actor Sureyya Mercan, sister of the poet Dogan Gokay.

The assumptions are false.

First of all, I would like you to know that they are mistaken. They think that I do not see, know, or hear.

I always sensed Sureyya's escapades. Later, I also began to know of them.

Once you become a public figure, you are forevermore a public character. From that moment forward, your private life is constantly observed. You have no more privacy. In fact, people appear around you who are actually paid to follow you and create scandals by wearing down your private life, believe me.

And god forbid, if you have dreamt of establishing a stable, lasting family life as I did, this is brought before you as a greater issue, than female artists who frequently change lovers, or get divorced. The magazines continue to hound you, and sometimes even friends you truly believe in do not conceal their discomfort from you. Perhaps they are afraid that you might set an example?

"The marriage of two artists never lasts long, so what's your formula for happiness?" they ask disconcertingly. No, really, and I'm someone who believes in things like the evil eye. I swear, I panic everytime this question is asked. What if it jinxes us? Besides, how can there be a recipe for contentment? Come on! There is a price for every love affair. In long term relationships, sacrifice is always required of one of the parties. In a sense, there is an oppressor and an oppressed in all romances. Sureyya and I had an incredible love affair, and naturally, its costs were high.

Perhaps, an ideal method of paying this price would be for the oppressed party, or to put it more lightly, the one who makes the sacrifice, to switch sides for certain periods of time, although of course, this cannot be simply done with work distribution. Sometimes events can take place so unexpectedly, at such extreme hours that the person in control makes a great mistake, and a change of guard becomes likely. Then he or she assumes the sacrifices. That has been the case with us.

Therefore, I get annoyed at people who sigh: "Oh, Pervin Gokay is so lucky! She's beautiful and famous, and has a handsome, ideal husband, and family!" For one thing, I'm terribly afraid they might put a curse on us. Oh dear me, god forbid, sometimes one even jinxes herself!

Such talk also makes me laugh secretly. Pervin Gokay has worked very hard to become chic and famous, and to remain that way. They do not know that her husband, whom everyone swoons over as a dashing gentleman, is in fact an unstable, infantile man with a roving eye, nor are they aware of all the things that "the lucky" Pervin Gokay has quietly put up with to save this family. The grass is always greener on the other side, of course!

How many of you know the feeling of living under "probation," in addition to the extraordinary difficulties of maintaining a lengthy relationship? A part has been set for you, and you are left captive to it; a victim of your image! Mine was the role of a noble, chic, graceful, young woman, and from then on I was expected to not only play that part in my movies, but also in my private life. Especially in our youth, in those heydays of Turkish Cinema when there was no TV, only one radio station, and a small number of newspapers, we, a handful of movie actors, were constantly under surveillance.

Afterwards, young people appear on the scene waiting to snap up your place, and defending your status becomes as exhausting as the effort it took to attain it. Soon you notice that your thirties are looming ahead of you, and that everybody favors younger and younger women as if they themselves were not growing old.

My greatest fortune has been my elder brother, Dogan. I always, gratefully repeat that he has been the one who educated and guided me. Culture renders one more resistant to both the monotony and the sorrows of life. His contributions, coupled with my enjoyment of reading and learning, which are treasures we inherited from my dear, late father, have led me to act calmly and intelligently at many forks in the road. My father was a highly enlightened educator, an admirer of Ataturk, and he gave all three of us an equal education. Unfortunately, my brother Demir, choosing to live only by his instincts, ruined both his own life and the lives of those around him. My mother used to say "that Demir has been jinxed by the evil eye," god bless her soul. Maybe there is a bad seed in every family, who knows?

In my day, it was not at all accepted for "proper family girls" to choose such professions as acting or singing. Had my father been alive at the time, he would never have given me his permission, despite his open-mindedness. The freedom his generation granted their women and daughters contained a concept called "honor," the limits of which were indefinite, yet the meaning of which was greater than that of freedom. Such was the case.

My father had passed away around the time I registered for the Academy of Fine Arts. My brother Dogan had just returned from abroad, and he would take me out to wine and dine with his friends. And that was when his moviemaker friends grew determined to include me in their films. It's a long story. Finally, Mr. Sherif won me over. Even in his youth, Mr. Sherif was the huge, bulky, endearing fellow that he is today, and he was also very strict and authoritative. Yet it turns out that he was only eight years older than me at the time.

"This girl has a European manner. Our cinema is in dire need of such elegant and educated girls! Poet, do what you can, convince your sister, make her come to the movie set tomorrow!"

Since Mr. Sherif is always self-assured, neither my mother's weeping, nor my bashfulness could deter him, and I began my acting career with the movie "Mournful Roads." I thank god a thousand times that before passing away, my darling mother was able to see how honorable, dignified, and successful women actresses can exist in a Moslem country, and that she felt proud of me. Girls nowadays don't know this.

I was awfully stilted and unsuccessful in my first movie. I was embarrassed of the people on the set. It was during my second movie that things fell into place, and the course of my life was altered. In fact, "The Last Train" is still among the important works of Turkish Cinema. I met Sureyya during the shooting of that movie. He was a young actor who had long achieved fame and a place in the hearts of women. A dark Mediterrenean beau, with dangerous looks, a very charming man. Dogan used to say "that rascal's born with a certain *je nais sais quois!*" Believe me, I get excited talking about it even now. Look, I'm getting goosebumps, I swear. God bless his soul, maybe my positive energy is soothing his soul right now, who knows! Oh dear, see, I've started crying again. To think that I used to berate him for being such a sop, now I've gone and become the same way. As my mother used to say: "Those who age on the same pillow always exchange their habits in the end!" If you'll excuse me, I'll go find a handkerchief…

That famous parting scene in "The Last Train", which was filmed in the Sirkeci train station, is in fact the live footage of the moment we fell in love, and it was shot with great difficulty. But it is so genuine that I can safely say it has become the "Casablanca "of our cinema. I remember even the laborers on the movie set were crying.

"Pretend that we are madly in love, Ms. Pervin. Pretend that I adore you so much, I cannot spend a second in your absence. The wondrous visage upon your graceful neck is the sunshine of my life and the sorrow in your languid eyes, my destiny!"

Embarrassed, I had hung my head. Everyone was grumpy and tired because of a parting scene I had not been able to pull off for hours. It was a chilly winter morning, we were freezing from being on our feet, and I worried that I had certainly caught cystitis. Just as I started to panic, thinking that they would give up on me, he cupped my chin in his hand, gently lifted my head, and looked all the way into my heart with those lovely hazel eyes of his.

"And once more, pretend that you are crazy about me. You melt in my arms with a single touch, enough to imagine that you would prefer death instead of a life without me." His voice was soft, but full of secrets that peaked one's curiosity.

"They're separating us. This is our last meeting, due to gang law, and the social differences between us. We will never, ever be able to see one another again! Farewell forever!" he whispered, stroking my hair.

He had made such an impression on me that my lips had begun to tremble, and I felt wrecked with sorrow. I was suffering unbearably at the thought of losing a man who, until a week ago, I had only known from his movies. I could not comprehend it the least bit, but I suddenly threw my arms around Sureyya's neck and started to weep.

"Action!" yelled Mr. Sherif.

"Quick, quick! It's going to happen this time, finally the girl got it! Very good! Excellent, kids! Embrace tighter, this's your last contact!"

Oh, what an embrace that was! What a clutch, dear god! And what a kiss! We were all stunned.

Hours later, when we were sitting alone, and holding hands without saying a single word, I was still sniffling, while he was busy drying my eyes, and hushing me. Really, if someone were to tell me the same story I would tease them, but when it happens to you... I think I had been overly affected, and was subsequently unable to discern reality from illusion. Sureyya, who until that point had been watching me with slight perplexity, finally burst forth in excitement:

"All right girl, then we'll never part again!"

And we never did!

I received great support and assistance from him in my later films. Sureyya was a born actor. He was natural, he was casual. He would act in real life as well; he got a great kick out of testing himself.

It is not true that Sureyya compared me to either Ingrid Bergman or Grace Kelly. He always thought I resembled Audrey Hepburn in "Breakfast at Tiffany's."

When we decided to get married, Sureyya began studying like crazy to earn his high-school diploma from equivalency examinations. He hired a tutor, attended classes, and I helped him, taking care not to hurt his pride. As you know, men are terribly depressed when learning something from a woman. By the time Ada was born, Sureyya had earned his high school diploma, and cheerfully adopted the role of an in-law trying to be worthy of what he called "an educated class" family. He would be particularly influenced by my brother Dogan, tracking down and reading every book that Dogan mentioned. Nevertheless, in some ways Sureyya always remained the neighborhood hoodlum, which I think was an unusual and attractive draw for me.

This roguish aspect was fun the first few years, but later it also brought home a drinking, noisy, rambling, and messy man. Such was the family in which he had been raised, and such had been his experience. But I loved him. I always loved him, and was aware of being loved in return. There was something in him which most men lack, and which attracted me for years. Sureyya was compassionate and sincere. I believed that he was earnest even when he was lying, and that he did this in order to spare me any grief.

If it had been another woman, she would have left Sureyya many times. He was like a baby, now growing animated, then sinking into despair, and never knowing himself how he would act at any given time or place. But worst of all were his numerous infidelities!

The first time, when I learned that he had had an affair with a dreadfully base woman, Ada was still a baby and I was disgusted with him. At that point I was determined to leave him. He did not deserve to live with us!

"This is the last time!" he had said.

"It won't happen again, Pervin! Don't take my family, my daughter, my friends, and yourself away from me! I worked really hard to attain these. Give me one more chance, angel!"

The years passed with minor escapades, and plenty of gossip, but the matter was never even mentioned between us until that disaster. In other words, he led a loving and attentive life toward myself and our daughter, without making a fool of himself. However… however, while I was staying in North America, where I had taken Ada after the accident which befell that strapping young fellow, that darling Aras (and that boy was definitely jinxed!), he apparently had an affair with a famous lady pianist. I would rather not disclose the lady's name. By the time I learned of it, Sureyya had fallen ill, and that lady had married an extremely wealthy businessman. I never told Sureyya that I knew of this relationship. Yet it's odd, perhaps some sort of confessional yearning takes over people before they die:

"Pervin, darling princess, your mournful eyes really did turn out to be my destiny, you see girl? I tried very hard to be worthy of you... but, you know, there've been many times I caused you grief. I've never asked you, and I wouldn't, I mean, it wouldn't even cross my mind, but I, I screwed up when you two were abroad..."

We had cried, hand in hand, in the hospital room. Just like the parting scene in "The Last Train." With one difference, this time we knew that we were really parting, and there were no spotlights or cameras around us. Of course, I never told him about Mr. Sherif. Even my brother Dogan doesn't know.

Moving into Kuzguncuk was also Sureyya's wish. Kuzguncuk reminded him of the neighborhood he grew up in. I took a shine to both the mansion and Kuzguncuk. We have had some very good times there. My brother Dogan, Burkan, and Merich were always there to share that Bosphorus village with us... And then the Atacans. Oh that family! What unfortunate, ill-fated folks they were. We were, all of us, jinxed, I know it! In fact, my darling Aras and my little Blue Danube were also our children, in a sense. If it hadn't been for that dreadful accident, Aras would have become my son in law.

I mean, one loses her mind just thinking about it... That superbly intelligent, accomplished, handsome, brilliant youth goes and dives into the sea in the dark, and never comes out. Oh, we were so overcome with grief, so heart-broken. I know that I was genuinely worried something might happen to Ada. My lark of a daughter simply froze up. She did not eat, drink, or speak for days. I was faint with worry. She loved Aras very much, she was absolutely crazy about him. And what about that poor Mrs. Zubeyde? How much has that self-educated, reserved woman suffered? First she lost her son, and then her husband. May god never give such pain to anyone, not even my enemies. After that event, the Atacans and ourselves almost became one family. Our fates were thrown into the same track. Our children grew up so close together that they were almost like brothers and sisters, and we only realized it during that cursed accident!

Ada is a lot like my brother Dogan. She is confident, just, and has a generous heart. Neither of them pay any attention to trifles, if their noses fell off they would not bend down to pick it up. Perhaps it is for this reason that after Aras, she simply could not return to Duna, who I believe was the one she really loved all along. She turned it into a matter of honor. Duna, poor dear, who is sensitive, romantic, and mad about my daughter, has withered and wilted, my good boy.

I have tried to talk to Ada many times. Although my daughter and I are friends on every subject, she even treats me like a younger sister at times, when the topic comes around to Duna she becomes silent as a rock, and refuses to speak to me.

"It's true that Duna and I care deeply for each other, mom, but I love him too much to want to marry him."

My brother Dogan had also caused my mother grief with similar words for years. My dear mother passed away before she could see Burkan. Same expression, same pride. What truly worries me is the possibility that Ada might see herself as unlucky, and think that, after Aras, she might also cause Duna harm. My poor dear, she even regarded her left-handedness as a sign of misfortune for years. And yet my late father was also left handed, and he was a lucky person.

When one becomes a mother, staying alive ceases to be her primary instinct, and it is replaced by the desire to keep one's child alive, to protect her. Undoubtedly, my primary wish is in regards to Ada's life and happiness, but I love Duna as if he were my own son. Of course, I was glad to witness his matrimony to Merich, yet I would be blind to not notice him wasting away and going to pieces before my eyes. I am not at all happy with the state Duna is in. Lately he has become very introverted, he has turned into a preoccupied, brooding man. He used to drop by the studio and draw up tasteful designs, he would bring us a youthful touch. Now he has stopped doing even that. I am afraid that he might fall ill. If something happens to him as well, neither his mother, nor Ada can bear the burden. If anything wrong should befall Duna it will be the end of both families! I've had many a prayer conducted on his behalf, and yet…

Merich is level-headed. The poor dear has had a dismal childhood. She's a good girl. She is a year older than Duna, but I have always thought that she has loved him like a father. Duna has a compassionate heart far beyond his years. I think it's unfortunate what's happening to that boy. Really, I do not think anything good will come out of this silence of his. He needs help, maybe professional help! What should we do, I don't know? My brother Dogan says "he will pull through!"

How the departure of an actor from life's stage can damage the work. The poet who said "every death is too soon," was right.

BURKAN GOKAY

Businesswoman. Wife of poet and writer Dogan Gokay.

Every human relationship contains its king, queen, and slave(s). A union with Dogan meant blessing his sovereignty. It still is. He is firm. Obstinate. Temperamental. He does not want children, and he is always right. I mean, he really does end up being right in the end. He is elegant. Well-dressed. He knows everything. He is incredibly talented, particularly on the subject of how to treat a woman. He is polite and mature. He never confronts a person. Dogan is a man of great subtleties. I mean... we all have our weaknesses. I don't know. Dogan is difficult. How much longer can I remain his voluntary slave? I don't know that either.

I'm not sorry. I have had a very colorful life with him, one that was enriched with incredible experiences, one that is hard to imagine. And I have nothing more to say!

SUREYYA MERCAN

Famous actor of Turkish Cinema. Married. Father of an only daughter. Real name: Abidin Olcer. Deceased.

CIHAN UMAR

Caretaker. Nanny. Retired. Single.

They have always been very kind to me. I mean, why should I lie to you now? Both the lady and the gentleman are very good people. God bless them. God rest the gentleman's soul. There never was a day of ill-will or double-dealing in their house.

I was young when they took me in, not even twenty yet. Ada, my cherub, my doe eyed girl, was only a month old. Oh what a lovely baby she was, how plump and cute, my God!

Turns out my little one had a mean destiny. She never could recover after what happened to Aras. Now, may god forgive me for this, but I had never been able to like that Aras. He would always sneak in over the garden wall and scare the daylights out of me. He would never speak to us. He wasn't spoilt, but arrogant maybe... Yes, he sure was good looking. Well, so what, after all he's just the son of a Bulgarian immigrant tailor. My father used to be a saddler, but it seems he died before I was able to see him, so me and my mother came to Istanbul and started working at strangers' houses. No, I don't look down on people's occupations, but. that Aras... god forgive me. But then, you see, that blue-eyed brother of his, Duna, is something else entirely. Everyone loves him. Oh, what an unfortunate boy he is. Duna was a sweetheart, even as a kid. He's talkative, kind. If I have an armful of packages he can't help but run to my aid. Ever since he was five, he's been this way. He would never leave the side of my little princess, grew up mad in love with her, that boy did.

There's fate for you! In the end, that Aras-like Merich caught

Duna, strung him up, and placed him right in the palm of her hand. I swear, my heart aches for both my mournful princess, and for my blue boy. Just like that saying, the good always lose.

I live in my lady's house at Valide Cheshme as a caretaker. Cooking, housekeeping and that sort of thing. Mostly we keep one another company. Bless her, she's even got me insurance. I get both social security and monthly wages. May god bless them! If I could just see the happiness of my luckless girl with worldly eyes, I would be content. *Inshallah,* she will make a home with a decent, honest fellow. After all, I raised her, I'm practically half her mother.

What can I say, may God grant us peace. May this be our worst day to come. I've got nothing more to say.

THE ME IN THE MIRROR

"When we begin to dream within our dreams, the hour of
waking is near."

Friedrich Leopold
(NOVALIS)

It was nighttime when I awoke.

*At first, I saw a bare mirror. Rectangular, and unframed. It
hung by a crude nail, on a naked wall. It was crooked, and
coarse. Must have been twelve by twenty inches. The edges of
the mirror were jagged, chipped away. It looked extremely dangerous; sharp enough to slice off one's finger entirely, if touched
by accident.*

*I was standing in front of the mirror, putting on shaving
cream. But the cream stuck to my face like glue, impossible to
spread. I tried several times, but the more I did, the more a
white mask formed on my face. White, cold, and hard.*

*That was when he appeared. Right then. He is a head taller
than me. He was standing right behind me. I could not see his
body, the only thing visible in the mirror was his head. A head
with short, brown, wavy hair. A small, shapely nose, olive skin.
It looked like an Apollo head. Yes, yes, just like one. But still,
neither man nor woman. I mean, a man at first glance, but his
beautiful face contains both masculine and feminine features.*

*He is standing behind me, and staring straight at me in the
mirror. His gaze is not hostile. Ponderous, maybe. Not frightening, in fact, one could even speak of a very faint smile.*

*These are not what startle me. It's his sudden appearance in
the mirror, behind me. I neither feel nor hear him arrive. He
disappears when I turn around to look. When I turn back*

around and try to put on that terrible shaving cream, he reappears in the mirror. Gone when I turn around, but there in the mirror!

After repeating this game a few times, I grow irritated. I mean, what's going on? I decide that I'll foil the game of this uninvited guest, it's getting tiresome!

When our eyes meet again in the mirror, I slowly lift my hand, taking care not to scare him away, and extend it backwards. He does not back away from the hand I am holding out, as I stand still and watch in the mirror. I reach out as patiently and gradually as if we were in a non-gravitational field. My heart begins to beat faster, and an abrupt heat spreads throughout my body.

Suddenly, I'm afraid. I shudder, thinking of the moment of contact between my hand and the face. I sense the fear of falling into a deep vacuum. My heart skips a beat. But I am also aware that I cannot turn back. And my hand touches the face of that curious stranger who appeared behind me.

At first my fingers touch warm skin, then I freeze with the terror of what I am feeling. The shaving cream drops out of my other hand, my blood runs cold, and my heart turns into a hysterical time-bomb. I cannot move a muscle. My legs must be paralyzed. My body has revolted against me, and is asininely watching the distress signals sent by my brain. I feel close to suffocation. "I'm done for!" I say.

At the same moment, the Apollo head in the mirror smiles. A cool smile. I become even more anxious. My god… because, because… because that strange face I am touching is in fact my own!

The stranger I see in the mirror is actually "me"!

"I" am actually in that head, but I do not know it. "I" am that stranger!

"I" am he. He is "I."

Then, who's this other person I have been mistaking as "myself" in the mirror for years? Which one am I?

Did "I" ever exist?

No! I do exist! I always did exist! I will exist!

I wake up screaming. I am covered with perspiration. Instead of rejoicing that it was all a nightmare, I still see, terrified, the "me" in

the mirror. That head is always before me eyes, whether they are closed or not.

Someone is watching me! Upon turning to my left, I come face to face with Merich, who is lying down. I turn on the bedside lamp.

"Are you alright?" she asks anxiously.

"Of course I'm alright," I say, feeling bad.

Merich studies my face. Which "me" does Merich see when she looks at me?

"Go on, go back to sleep. Tomorrow's Tuesday, your lucky day," she says, as if it were any help at all.

I try to cheer myself up by thinking: "Tomorrow's Tuesday. I can prepare a nice breakfast on the balcony." But it does not work. The terror I felt at the moment I touched that strange head and myself simultaneously, has burrowed inside me, and refuses to leave.

"I'll go wash my face," I say. I am afraid of meeting the "me" in the mirror. As I get up and head toward the bathroom to overcome this fear, Merich is already fast asleep.

WE HEARD THE SOUND OF PAIN

"The mass annihilation of Jews at Auschwitz has unequivocally proven the failure of culture."

Theodor W. Adorno
(Negative Dialectic)

"It's winter!" exclaimed Duna in amazement.

"Now then, are you still starin' out that there window, sir? Lie down, rest a wee bit, come on, good sir!"

"How quickly did all this happen? When did the trees undress, when did the sky turn unfriendly, why was autumn in such a hurry to leave this year, Hasan?"

"Well, every little thing has its own, proper time, sir. This way's better than if it were to be untimely."

"It's winter, and I'm still here. What sort of nightmare is this that I still cannot wake up, huh? You must know, Hasan. You're the most realistic character in this nightmare, what with your common sense, your pragmatism, and your faith. Come on, tell me."

"Oh dearie me, you gettin' all wistful again, sir. But that's winter for you, what're you gonna do, there's a spring at the end of every winter. The wonder of it all is makin' it through the winter, sir. Y'understand, don't you?"

"How could I not, Hasan. Is there anyone around me who speaks more clearly or correctly?"

"Now, now, that's not true, sir. You're an educated, learned man, far be it from me to advise you… I'm just talking, 'cause I like you, that's all."

"To make it through the winter in order to reach the spring!" sighed Duna. "Isn't that the hardest thing after all."

"Lookee here, good sir. You're just never grateful for what you got! That's your real trouble! If you only knew what types are in this POWMITU service, you'd take a look at yourself and start dancin' a jig from joy, but... what you gonna do, mankind's already suckled raw milk. See, there's a new patient, I mean a reserve officer, they brought him in two weeks ago. Now, that fellow's in a sure pitiful state. He was a lawyer, poor man, he's all skin 'n' bones, a dark, shrivelled thing. He jest talks to hisself day in, day out. He don't eat or drink or nothin'... He never looks at us, or recognize us, or anything. Poor dear didn't have no fate like his name. His mamma called him Mutlu, and yet..."

"A lawyer called Mutlu? What, is Mutlu the lawyer here?" asked Duna, surprised.

"That's what they call him, but the poor wretch's just miserable. An' those damned terrorists sliced off one of his ears."

"I wonder if it is him? Hasan, why don't you take me to him, maybe it's the Mutlu I know."

"Well, I can't say what Mutlu it is, sir. But, I mean, I can't take you."

"Come on Hasan, just do me this favor. If it's the person I think, it'd make me very happy to see him again."

"But then my doctor commander will see, and he won't let me get away with it none."

"No, no, he won't find out. Besides, if it's not the Mutlu I know, I won't even talk to him. Well, why're you looking at me that way? Look, I promise!"

Upon entering the room at the end of the hallway, they saw a thin, dark young man in army-green sweatpants. He was leaning his back against the wall, and carefully inspecting his hands.

"There, that's the man I'm talkin' about, sir."

Duna peered carefully. He squinted from behind his weak glasses, trying to clarify the image.

"Mutlu? Mutlu, is it you?" he asked hesitantly, as he slowly went up to the man.

The man did not pay him any attention. It was as if he were absorbed in the most crucial part of a deep personal showdown, and he had closed all his gates to the outside world.

"You are him! You're the poetry-loving lawyer Mutlu! The

Mutlu whom nobody likes because he's a Kurdish intellectual!" cried Duna delightedly.

"Hush, don't go gettin' all crazy, sir, for God's sake! They'll hear, and you'll cause me trouble, I swear."

"Well, so be it Hasan. If that is the way this man defines himself, what else can anyone do about it now?"

"See here, you promised, don't forget!"

"Alright, alright Hasan!"

Mutlu raised his head and looked indifferently at Duna. All the lights in his eyes had been extinguished.

"It's me! Remember, that summer night we recited poetry, and talked of love? I'm the teacher, Duna Atacan."

"My hands have aged," said Mutlu, holding out his hands.

Duna looked down at the small, dark pair of hands held out to him. They were trembling.

"You got a cigarette?"

"No, I don't smoke. But maybe Hasan can get you one, what do you say, Hasan?"

"No sir, I can't get no cigarette," said Hasan tersely, and then whispered to Duna;

"Well now, you got him talkin'!"

"Come on, go find a cigarette Hasan, look he's a terrible addict, maybe you'll be doing him good. Eh?"

"Ah, my innocent sir, how can a cigarette be a favor? But, let me go and see. You did get this poor soul talkin'… Only, 'til I get back, neither you nor this nicotine-freak lawyer's gonna do nothin' crazy, alright?"

"Okay, okay, you're the best, Hasan!"

"It was long. So long," whispered Mutlu, continuing to inspect his hands with great care.

"It was a long civil war. We had many deaths on all sides, all with extremely good reasons to fight. They're all our dead, we are every one of the dead! We saw blood, we smelled rotting flesh, we heard the sound of pain. It was the deepest of civil wars, the most layered, the most painfully close to home… and it lasted so long, so very long."

"Mutlu, I don't think you recognized me. Remember how that night, you'd read some Onat Kutlar poems, and I had read Dogan Gokay."

"There were those who rejoiced, of course. Arms dealers, drug smugglers, and merchants of faith and nations. Do you know that some of them can be called businessmen, and even businesswomen, and others can be called politicians? Ironic, isn't it?" He shook his head, staring down at his hands.

"There were also those patriots whose hearts swelled at the diminishing population problem, and the disappearance of unemployment. But the strange part was that we were always dying!"

"Mutlu, Mutlu, look at me! I too know that what we've lived through is inhuman. And I swear, I understand how depressed you are. Maybe that's why, yes that's the reason you and I are thrown together in this same hallway, exactly at this point of the nightmare. Do you understand?"

This time Mutlu looked at Duna's face with a concerted effort, and studied it suspiciously. His attempt at recognition had given Duna hope.

"Mutlu, look, this is all a nightmare. Everything will be better when I, or perhaps you, wake up. Believe me, do so that you can read poetry once again. Just think about it, do you suppose this senseless slaughter could be real? Huh? See, you're silent, it can't be true, can it? Hadn't we learned a lesson from the Nazi terror? Hadn't we become civilized, even walked on the moon, and proudly entered the age of the most advanced technology and communication in human history? Huh? There's something amiss here, isn't there? Of course there is."

Mutlu, who was biting his lips and watching him, suddenly made a face as if he had a toothache, and grasped his cheek.

"You might find it difficult to believe, but I did not kill anyone," he said, moaning.

"I was sent into exile for refusing to bear arms. I was under probation. Four separate cases filed against me are still continuing. Attempted non-murder, spreading peace propaganda, weaning soldiers away from guns, and reading Finnish, Spanish, and Turkish anti-war poets."

Duna sank down at the edge of his bed with a sigh.

"Then the others kidnapped me. They actually put on a circus called a public trial. They called me a sell-out. They declared that they would slash anyone who dared deny the truth, and see, they cut off my ear."

When Mutlu turned his head sideways, the gruesome sight he revealed forced Duna to shut his eyes. He felt queasy.

"I roamed the mountains for months. I had plenty of time to think, and to go insane. I was so hopeless that my only wish was for death itself. Death was under every rock, at the end of every other step. But the death that brushed by everyone around me would simply not pay me a visit. Let me tell you, there is nothing, absolutely nothing worse in this world than a young, healthy person regarding death as salvation. Never, ever forget this! Alright?"

"Alright Mutlu, I won't forget," replied Duna, with a sigh.

"Because there cannot be a more cruel or awful system than the one in which conditions make death look like a way out!"

"See, I'm even smuggling cigarettes for your sake, sir. Here it is, it's American too, besides!" said Hasan the orderly as he entered the room.

When he saw the cigarette a faint light appeared in Mutlu's face. He immediately reached over and took it. After lighting Mutlu's cigarette with a match produced from his pocket, Hasan went over to stand guard at the door. He kept an attentive ear on the conversation between the two men.

"I saw hell. I saw hell with my own eyes," said Mutlu, as he lustfully smoked his cigarette.

"Do you know, they broke me like a twig? From now on, however I might turn out, I will never again be the same old 'me.' My eyes cannot gaze the same way after having seen all that evil. The texture of my skin has changed. And strangest of all, my hands have aged, see!"

Placing the cigarette between his lips, he held out his hands once again. Whatever it was that he saw in his hands must have disturbed him greatly.

"Those who have personally witnessed the fact that man is the cruellest and most vengeful creature on earth, are doomed to be alone forever, my friend. They will not ever want to be relatives, friends, or even acquaintances with any man or womankind again. And that's the reason I am orphaned! Now I am utterly alone!"

"Mutlu… They really have devastated you. But I swear, you are not alone!" said Duna, having difficulty holding back the tears welling in his eyes.

"While boasting that I had not allowed myself to be used by them, I realized that they had already used me as a witness. But it was too late," murmured Mutlu.

"This 'ere lawyer ain't recognized you at all, sir. He's talkin', but see, he's just talkin' to plain air!"

"Odd, isn't it, I used to think that emotions were made out of cartilage. But it was my bones they broke!" said Mutlu, staring at Duna.

"It's almost gettin' around five, we'd best be goin' sir. My commandor doctor might show up any moment. C'mon!"

Duna got up reluctantly.

"Farewell Mutlu. Now I want to wake up, not just for my own sake, but yours as well. I really want to wake up from this nightmare!"

"We all died, so very much," said Mutlu, staring at the floor.

"You're right Mutlu. You're right."

Just as they were about to step out into the corridor, Duna halted, and spoke numbly, with the puzzled expression of having suddenly remembered something for the first time in centuries.

"Mutlu, I could have killed those maniacs who, in front of my eyes, scourged the bound and helpless Captain Birol for minutes upon end with their machine guns," he said.

"If I had a gun, I, who try to walk without stepping on ants, would have killed all those murderers without batting an eye, and would have never regretted it!" he said.

There was a surprised tone in his voice. He sighed, after hearing and comprehending what he had just uttered.

"So, that's that Mutlu. You take care."

Then he began to drag his feet back to his own room. That was when Mutlu's deep voice echoed through the hallway:

"Haven't you still found that girl, 'Brunette Ada?' "

INTERSECTION

"Perceptions can reverse suddenly, much like an optical illusion."

Hans Magnus Enzensberger

"Surprise, surpriiise! I got good news for you, sir!"

Entering Duna's room with envelopes in hand, Hasan the orderly was yelling at the top of his lungs and sporting a grin that exposed his rotten teeth in their entirety.

"Well, I'll say, it seems like you're gonna like me after these here news I bring."

Duna, who was stretched out reading on his bed, paid no attention. The book in his hand was Thomas Hobbes' *Leviathan,* and he had been told that it had been sent to his name a week prior. The envelope had born neither the name nor the address of the sender. The stamp had been torn. The book was published by Penguin.

"There's letters for you, my good sir. Four of them, no less, and three of them being from women!"

"Letters?" asked Duna, astonished.

"For me?"

"Yes, but I ain't standin' for no plain thanks this time, sir, I mean, it's time you did us a favor back."

"There're letters for me!" repeated Duna.

"Bah! You ain't gonna listen to me no more, are you."

Duna looked in bewilderment at the envelopes given to him.

It was as if he had never seen a letter before in his whole life, and had given up hopes of ever laying eyes on one. From the outside, he gave the impression of one examining UFOs. After handling the envelopes for a long while and fully immersing his skin in the texture of the paper, he began to grow animated. His heart became a wild bird, longing to break through his ribcage and fly away.

"Well, you sure are somethin' else, sir, really. Why don't you jest open 'em and start reading, instead of daydreaming like that."

Two of the envelopes were long and slim; the other two were smaller. One was blue, one yellow, another was white, and the last a pale recycled brown. The name Duna Atacan was inscribed on all of them in various handwritings, but the addresses had been scrawled over with black pen.

"Why, all these envelopes have already been opened! What the hell is that supposed to mean?" cried Duna suddenly.

"For your own good, sir. 'Cause you're a little... I mean, sensitive and all... So if there were anything to upset you... you know..."

"They're checking! They're even going through my private mail, they're keeping me here by force! God damn it, I just want to wake up!"

"Hold up, hold up, now, there you go gettin' all crazy again, instead of rejoicing! Why don't you jest open these 'ere letters, then... See what them women been writin' you, then!"

His voice contained the saccharine tinge of a grown-up awkwardly trying to calm down a troubled, naughty child. Duna wiped his hands, as if they had become covered in slime.

"Leave me alone, Hasan!" he scolded. "Surely you must have read every single line in these!"

Hasan skulked off without a word. Upon exiting, he closed the door halfway.

Now that he ws alone, Duna surveyed the envelopes in his hand once again, and a smile first appeared on his face. These were letters, they were written documents, definitive proof. Therefore? Could it be? And if...

He laid out the four letters side by side. He stroked them, and first picked up the brown envelope, without any hesitation.

• • •

Wednesday, February 7th. Istanbul.

Dear Mabel,

I've missed you terribly.

I really wish I could see you.

It turns out that being left without you is much different than wondering what it would be like to be left without you. I found this out, Mabel. It's unbearable. If I didn't know you were alive, I probably would have gone insane.

Ever since that horrible Tuesday morning, my god, how long it has been... Ever since that Tuesday, everything has been spoiled! You left, I left. We left, Mabel!

And the way the newspapers attacked me like that! Without inquiry or investigation. It's awful, Duna, really awful when it happens to you. Neither the memory of Aras, nor his family, nor I... No one gave a damn about any of us! One realizes the value of genuine love at those hours and geographies where no one cares about anyone else. Though belated, one understands. I understood Duna.

I collapsed, as if I had been delivered a powerful punch on the nose. My initial reaction was to escape. Far, very far away. Somewhere nobody could find me. I fled and fled and fled. I traveled far and wide, and when I turned around to look, what do you think I saw? I had taken refuge in Kuzguncuk.

I rented a house there. I stayed in Kuzguncuk a long time. I tracked the footprints of our childhood. This did me good. Because it seems that the present can't fit into yesterday's shoes. They're far too small, Mabel!

Aliye. Poor little scorpion! It turns out that she's the traitor in this story.

Apparently she not only went to the newspapers, but also to the attorney general's office and made a public accusation. An investigation was started about me. You would've been overwrought to see my trips to the courthouse, dear Mabel. The exaggerated attention paid by certain newspapers and TV stations to this subject was beyond belief. As if we were not the ones living through a civil war, as if we were in any state to heed sensationalism. All the living witnesses of our childhood went before the judge and testified, one by one. I think it grieved us all to relive that event. Your mother in particular. So basically, my sweet, total fame has been bestowed on all our kith and kin! We are all celebrities now!

The final day of the trial was a very important one for me. I understood, with terrible tardiness, that Aras was dead, and that I was still alive. And yet, what a long time it takes to sincerely grasp such a simple truth! Furthermore, whatever my crime might have been, I had done my penance. Quite possibly I had been freed from my past.

Do you know what I did yesterday? Remember that pair of "converse" sneakers Aras tied together and slung over my shoulder before he left? Well, I finally took them out of the closet and gave them away to the doorman. The doorman took one look at them and said, "Ma'am, these're a size 13, ain't nobody got such giant feet!" So I threw the giant shoes in the trash. Duna, I managed to do it!

Oh Blue Danube, light of my life, my child, my brother, my Mabel, my one and only, my beloved, dearest to my heart, how much I've missed you, how very much!

Many have been the times I've set out to visit you. But they simply will not let me inside. Well, fine. They can't keep us apart, rebellious romantic!

I know that you will soon be receiving news from home, so I'm not going to tell you any. Someone will take care of this anyway. I want to tell you something else. Listen carefully, my emotional boy:

Never, ever let yourself go, Duna. It doesn't matter in the least what they tell you, what they say to you. Wherever you believe you are, and whatever you think you are doing, then that's the truth of it! I believe you, even if no one else does, and I will always vouch for you Mabel! Never give up, little sweetheart. What really matters is that you return here in one piece, the rest, what is said and what remains to be said is just words! Never start doubting yourself. Whatever that place looks like, then that's what it is, and in my opinion, you're surely right Blue Mabel.

With you, and always with love,

ADA.

P.S. You remember Musa the grocer, don't you? Your grade school friend, you know, the Musa who turned religious, stopped greeting us, and regarded us as enemies? He lost his entire family in a terrible car crash. One of his legs have been amputated, and he's crippled. But he married an Alevi nurse whom he met during the operation, and ended up going to Sivas as a groom. Can you believe it Duna? Perhaps life's appeal is nestled in this mystery? What do you say?

That was the end of the letter. Duna stroked the handwriting on the paper. He gazed at the envelope, face aglow with a brilliant smile. The beloved who is far away smells of a mossy sea. Her color is turqoise. Duna took long, deep breaths. He went over, took out the white pebble he hid in the drawer, and caressed it for a while.

Then he picked up the yellow envelope. He fell to reading that letter which his mother had inscribed with the docile, round handwriting of her generation.

Saturday, January 27th, Kuzguncuk

Dearest Son, My Only Child, Duna,

Thanks be to God, we receive news of your health, and pray for your speedy return home. My sole wish in life is for your health and happiness, son. Of course, I also pray, by the grace of God, for peace in our country and in the world, and for the preservation of all people from the pain of child-loss, no matter what their religion. You keep yourself healthy, and the rest will sort itself out, son. Don't you worry your sweet soul. Be strong, do not lose your faith.

Merich and I are doing well, thanks be. Merich has a heart of gold, the darling, and she is like a true daughter to me, may God bless both you and her... Mrs. Pervin comes to visit us regularly once a week, together with Nanny Cihan, such a fine lady she is. Even your "Brunette Ada" has started dropping in on us. She's not so cold and vain as before. As a mother, I have now decided that she truly loves you. May God forgive me for thinking badly of her once. *Inshallah,* she too will find an honest, decent young man for herself, and be content, what else can I say in this situation, son?

Merich has some joyful tidings, but I will leave that for her to tell you, it's a husband and wife matter. Your cat, Brunette is fine, don't worry. The little fiend missed you quite a bit in the beginning, she even lost her appetite, but she's fine now. Well, as you know, cats are devoted not to their masters, but to their homes! She even goes out romancing at night. Naturally, since it's nearing March.

I just wish I could see your baby blue eyes, son. I've missed your infant smell, my boy. *Inshallah* we will be reunited soon, and this longing will come to an end. I await you with fortitude, my Duna. I've prepared that Grandma Murshide coffee you love so well, and I'm waiting.

Your loving mother,
Zubeyde Atacan.

Note: Son, I don't know if it matters, but I thought I should tell you. The other night your boyhood friend Sefer the baker stopped by, kissed my hand, inquired after you, asked when you'd be released, I mean… discharged.

You might not remember, he has one daughter and two sons. His daughter, may God keep us all, developed a tumor in her brain and died before you knew it, the poor thing. She was barely ten years old, the girl. Sefer grasped my hands and cried, saying "Auntie dear, I used to treat my daughter different from my sons. I used to love my sons better, now God has given me what I deserve!" He broke my heart.

I knew him to be a rather gruff and mean sort. They used to say he was somewhat merciless. In his youth, he used to pester our neighbors whose roots were not Turkish. But, may God never teach any of his subjects through death, he has changed immensely. The boy has become repentant. He wept, "Mama, tell Duna there'll be no more gender discrimination, tell him Sefer is repentant!"

I could not understand why he told me to tell you this, but I'm writing it in case you have any insights.

Peace be with you, son."

Duna sniffed the letter in his hand, exclaiming "Oh mommy!" Then he leaned his head against the letter and stroked his hair with it. On his face was the natal gaze and naked smile which, at any age, only appears in the presence of one's mother. "Maternal longing" smells of freshly baked, homemade cookies. Its color is green. Duna deeply inhaled the scent of maternal longing.

"Now we're definitely going to make that trip to Igdir, Mrs. Zubeyde!" he whispered in the letter's ear.

He picked up the blue envelope third. And he spoke to envelope:

"Cats are devoted to their homes!"

The script on the envelope had the ciphered, barely legible quality of a doctor's prescription.

Monday, February, 12th

Dear Duna,

I'm no good at writing letters, as you know. But I need to write now, I mean due to the conditions we're in.

But I don't quite know what to write. When a person's husband is a literature teacher, well, it just gets you all nervous... You'll just have to excuse me...

I'm well. Your mother is well. The cat's also well. Aunt Pervin, and Uncle Dogan are well also. Ada stops by often. I think she's doing better than everyone. I wonder, is she in love? Because she's grown very pretty. I mean, it seems to me as if Ada has recovered. Don't ask me for whom, I don't know.

She is exhibiting two photography shows called "Civil War Landscapes." Both of them gained very favorable reviews. Foreign news services purchased her pictures. I think interest in her pictures increased because her name was all over the press due to those absurd trials. Given how people love that sort of thing, you know... Anyway, she probably writes to you, doesn't she?

We're still working a double shift at the hospital. The number of dead and wounded has really gone up because of obvious reasons. Apparently a new head doctor is going to be assigned to our hospital. I can't quite remember his name, but it might be Dr. Kutlu. They said "your husband knows him well," but as far as I'm aware, you don't know all that many doctors. Anyway, maybe they're getting you mixed up with someone else. Right now, I'm on leave for a special reason.

Duna, I don't know how to tell you this, but I'm pregnant. That is, you're going to become a father. The ultrasound revealed that we're going to have a little girl. Of course that's not a hundred percent certain, but it'll most likely be a girl. Ada suggested the name "Irmak" for our daughter. "You two are both rivers, so your child should be a 'stream.' And her middle name Gokay," she said.

Irmak Gokay Atacan.

What do you think?

Don't be surprised to find Irmak on my lap when you return; I'm due in two months.

So, there you have it. I wish you good luck.

Love.

Your wife: Dr. Merich Atacan.

Note: Your friend who's a professor of philosophy at Bosphorus University, you know, the one who's related to Grandpa Muharrem's first wife, what was his name, Besim or Nesim or something... do you remember? Well, he dropped by Kuzguncuk last month. He said he was going on a long journey. He had come to wish you goodbye. He looked very subdued and tired. He asked me to relate to you the following, word for word:

"On every long journey we undertake to find 'the other me' the same head resting on the same body travels with us."

There's a philosopher for you! Just like something Uncle Dogan would say. Oh, and he said he'd send the book he promised you, whatever that is.

That's all.

M. A."

"So I'm going to be father?" said Duna, stunned.

It was not clear whether he was thrilled or unsettled. There are times when anxiety and jubilation play tag with one another.

This was the time. Finally, he smiled.

"A little lady, eh?"

He was obviously having difficulty imagining it. A person is still young when it comes to areas beyond his expertise!

"Hasan, did you hear that, I'm going to have a daughter!" he cried ebulliently.

"A new life, a new person… Dear god, what a miracle!

For a while, he fell to blissful musing. Then he frowned:

"Why am I calling to Hasan anyway? If this is a civil war, he must be savvy to the news, since he reads all my private mail. And if this is just a nightmare, then there is no way I will be a father!"

Then he realized in terror:

"So it's been seven months."

He got mad and harshly tore open the last white envelope he was holding. This one was inscribed with a masculine handwriting, and came from the poet Dogan Gokay.

"My dear boy,

I have received news of your well being, and harbor no doubts as to your recovery. Things are the same with me. I write, not stopping to consider who might hear poems or read novels in these dark, turbulent days. Writing is an act, and a political one! As you know, I have not been working much on prose in the last few years, but after your departure I sat down and started a novel. I had told you that I initially work with the characters while writing a novel. Once the characters of a novel have been fleshed out, putting the thatchings on the roof is mere child's play.

This time around, my characters were awfully animated from the start. Brace yourself, for I am in the process of penning the story of you kids, and the story of the nation and the world as it relates to your personal dramas and pursuits of happiness, starting with your childhood in Kuzguncuk. It is evident that the lot of you; Aras, Merich, Ada and yourself, have extremely suitable character parameters for the socio-realist viewpoint. Your tendencies, your occupations, and your lives is a fine portrait of the Eastern Mediterranaean in the 1990's. For those who know to look.

The novel is almost done, and I am considering naming it Mediterrenean Waltz. I am telling you first because I thought you might like it. Even Burkan does not yet know about it. However, you will find out the ending when you return, as I have not written it yet.

Son, I can imagine what you are going through over there. I withstood an arduous military service, and was forced to undergo a period of psychotherapy due to the crimes against humanity committed towards me on account of my intellectual dissidency. As for nightmares, there never was a lack of them. Therefore, son, I am fairly familiar with whatever they call your plight, and/or whichever one you believe you are experiencing. It is difficult, but you will withstand it. You will not give way. And when you return, you will stand firm on your feet and raise youth who do and will take pleasure out of life, despite all the executioners, fanatics, and dictators who oppose life itself. You will, at least, pave the way for these youths. I believe that you are strong and equipped enough to do this, son. Ignoramuses are often cowardly. We will struggle, even if there is only a handful of us left to establish a more civilized and humane world on the road that passes through light and education. We have no other choice!

I miss you and await you, rebellious romantic!

Take care, son.

Your Uncle Poet.

Sunday, February 18th. Validecesme, Istanbul.

N.B: Last week, upon a friend's request, I attended a book signing at the new Leviathan bookstore in Kadikoy. (These people don't even know that Leviathan stands for bureucratic dictatorship, I think they take it to mean the sea-monster in the Torah.) A young girl, graceful as a drop of rain, sought me out. Like a pale, wounded bird. Her name was Neshe. The fiancée of the martyred Captain Birol. She said she had come to pick up a book of poems in my possession, which I had autographed for her. If you touched her she would shatter like glass, her hands like autumnal leaves… I was not aware of any such book, but wouldn't you know it, the moment I looked at the kid I realized I had been waiting for her a long time.

"I had been awaiting you for a while, and I had guessed correctly the color of your hair," I said. A wistful 'joy' like the meaning of her name, fell on her cheeks from her red locks. I went to the restroom of the bookstore, on the pretext of picking up the volume her fiancée had left for her, and there autographed the new edition of "Brunette Ada", which I kept in my pocket.

She caressed the book gladly. It seemed to me that she was in fact touching her dead fiancée. I cursed once again all the causes that played executioner to dead youths!

Just as she was leaving, she shook my hand and said "Please give my regards to Mr. Duna." Now, what on earth? I could not make head or tail of this, but I have related it to you in case you might have an idea.

Once again, I send you my love, son."

After reading the last letter Duna sighed, and fell deep into reflection. "Paternal longing" smells of tobacco. This longing is the color of camel hair. Duna inhaled the tobacco smell longingly. Odd… Neither he nor Uncle Poet used tobacco. His father, Naim the tailor? All of a sudden, he could not remember. It was as if his father had chosen to always remain in the background, as a distant memory. Now, even his habits had been erased from Duna's memory. He did not recollect himself, or his brother, ever being coddled in a father's lap. On the other hand, how lovingly Sureyya Mercan used to spoil his little girl…

When Duna came back, after a considerable time, he had on a serious and determined expression. He got out of bed, went over to the door and called out in a very firm voice:

"Hasan! Hasan, take me to the head doctor. I need to have a word with him!"

THE BLUE DANUBE WALTZ

> *"Only someone who has escaped a death sentence can regard time as a gift."*
>
> John Berger

"I'm getting excited, I'm really getting excited for the first time in a long while," said Duna, smiling.

"I sense something is going to happen. A man can only get this feeling when he's ready. I think I'm… I'm finally ready."

"You'd do better getting up and getting dressed, instead of jest sittin' there like that, all grinning and whispering to yerself, sir. Don't suppose you'll be goin' over to the brigadier's house with them sweatpants on. See, your uniform waits in the closet, ironed and clean as a whistle. Now, jest you get up, get yourself a sharp shave, an' let's see your face a little. Honest, that beard don't look too good on you."

Duna quickly jumped out of bed. After many days he had given up hope on Hasan, who had not taken his request to see the head doctor seriously, and he had finally made his case to Major Dr. Kutlu Chechen. Shortly afterwards, he received an invitation from Brigadier General Turhan Ozsoy, instead of the head doctor.

"Well, well, my fine sir, so you knew the Brigadier General and everythin', and we didn't have no idea of it. Well I'll be…. Turns out you ain't so shy as you look. I mean, if we'd known, we'd have acted accordingly… I mean, naturally… you know, mayhap we might have a business that needs to be taken care of…."

Putting on his glasses, Duna took a long good look at Hasan through the faulty lenses. For the first time, he saw the good and the bad in his plump, round face without getting angry. He smiled.

"Wait jest a minute, something's happened to you sir. Did you get charmed or something? All that grumpiness of yours has melted away, thank goodness!"

Although he needed to go down to the barbershop, this time the barber himself came over to his room and gave him both a haircut and a shave.

"Well, from now on you got some pull, sir. Ah, my, if only we'd known from the beginning, d'you think it woulda turned out this way?"

After donning his uniform, Duna inspected himself in the mirror above the sink. There were no bruises or bumps in the face he saw now. Except for the stitches above his right eyebrow, his face finally resembled himself. He was pale, and had lost a considerable amount of weight, but apart from these things there was something else, a tiny but more noticeable change had taken place in his face. His gaze had grown deeper. It was as if the blueness of his eyes had intensified.

When evening came, a jeep was waiting for him in front of the hospital. The chaffeur of the jeep, a private, ran up to his side, gave a salute, and opening the door, stood to attention as Duna got in. This private bore a strong resemblance to the general's service private. But there was no trace of previous recognition on his face. There was no trace of unrecognition either. In fact, the chaffeur's face remained expressionless.

Brigadier General Turhan Ozsoy's house was a two story villa located at the end of the officer's lodgings and nestled in a garden of flowers even in the middle of winter. The entrance to the garden had been converted into a parking lot, and had already begun teeming with cars, some of which bore diplomatic license plates. Duna noticed a profusion of security measures and soldiers touring the grounds.

The door to the general's lodging had been illuminated with colorful lanterns, and decorated with small Turkish flags and red and white balloons. A cloth banner caught the eye, bearing the words "Peace at home, Peace on Earth," together with its English translation.

"Peace and the army" smiled Duna as he alighted from the jeep. Night had fully descended. The stars had already popped up in the sky. The air was cold and crisp. Duna inhaled the clean air exuberantly.

As he entered, another private checked Duna's name off the guest list. Inside, it was more crowded than he had expected; well dressed women, glasses in hand, were chatting and laughing with high level officers, some in tuxedos, but most in uniforms. Foreign words drifted from conversations, and the scent of perfume imparted a female hue to the atmosphere.

All the doors to the salon had been flung open, and a vast, rich buffet had been set up in one corner. The gossamer strains of a waltz could be heard around the room.

"This must be more of a celebration than a dinner party," thought Duna.

"Something is being celebrated here tonight!"

After having experienced a long, very long period of silence and lack of civillian life, Duna was suddenly overwhelmed by the voices of people, the smell of alcohol and food mingling with perfume, and the sound of music weaving through it all. His vision dimmed, and he grew dizzy. He leaned against the wall to steady himself, and waited for this brief faintness to pass. Yes, these existed. Music, good food, women, men, having fun, conversing, loving… These still existed and life went on.

How difficult it is to take that first step back into life, after having been excluded from it for such a long time!

"Could it be that this nightmare is drawing to a close?"

"Second Lieutenant Duna Atacan, welcome!"

Turning around, he came face to face with the confident, paternal, and imposing general Turhan Ozsoy.

Eyes glittering brilliantly, he had thrown open his arms wide, as if he wished to give Duna a hug. Or perhaps Duna wished it was so.

"General!" said Duna, jumping to attention with a sharp salute. Yet what he really wanted to do was run over and embrace the other, or grasp his plump, large hand and give it a shake.

"Ah, forget the formalities. Welcome professor, you look very well," said the genral, as he threw an arm over Duna's shoulder and gave him a friendly pat.

That was when he missed the whole lot of them. His grandfather, his father, Aras, Sureyya Mercan, Nesim, Birol, Sefer, Tarkan, and even Musa, but most of all the poet Dogan Gokay. That fleeting contact, and the general's warm attention made him miss all the men who had been his friends. His nose tingled with sorrow. He was hesitant to openly display his longing. "Yet how easily women manage to do that," he thought enviously.

"See, here we are at the end, son!" said the general, "It was tough, but we succeeded. I had told you so!"

"Is the war ending?" asked Duna jubilantly.

"Any day now, teach!" said the general, pulling him by the arm.

"The nightmare is ending!" Duna translated.

"What was that, teach, I couldn't hear you? Here, come on, I would like to introduce you to a friend of mine."

That was when he saw the four musicians: an accordionist, a violinist, a bassist, and a drummer.

"The music's live!" he rejoiced.

"Over here professor, allow me to introduce you."

"That's the Blue Danube Waltz!" whispered Duna, thinking he was talking to Ada.

"Muzaffer, dear boy, here's the young teacher I have been telling you about: Duna Atacan. See Duna, take a good look at this man, he's one of the few names in the world on the subject of future science. Mr. Muzaffer's mind, having long settled the present, is now concerned with futuristic projects. Our pride and joy!"

"Oh come now, dear Turan, you're embarrassing me in front of the young man. Hello Mr. Atacan, Turan has talked a great deal about you."

Mr. Muzaffer was incredibly thin and tall. He must have been six foot three, and was slim enough to be called skinny. With his bald head and long nose he looked like an affable kingfisher. His tiny green eyes glowed with a surprising intensity amidst his unusual dimensions, as if they were scanning his surroundings. His lips, which circled his huge mouth like a slender thread were stuck in a mischievous, mocking smile. He must have been in his late fifties or early sixties like the general. It was apparent even from the way he extended his hand to Duna that he was an energetic person.

"Glad to have you with us!"

"Thank you," Duna had to reply, acknowledging their acceptance.

"And here is our genetic engineer Feza!" said Brigadier General Turhan Ozsoy.

Feza was a dimpled, curvy woman in her thirties who wore a stylish green dress-suit, and who bore an uncanny resemblance to Turhan Ozsoy.

"This girl is an agent of the science that will turn the world and the future on its head. She rejuvenates us with her modern knowledge, better watch out for her, teach!"

"Oh daddy, you still introduce me to your friends the way you did when I was a little girl. Honestly, it's embarrassing! Don't mind him, ours is a typical father-daughter love! How do you do, Mr. Duna?"

The dimples crowning Feza the genetic engineer's gorgeous smile cheered up Duna.

"Actually, it's hard not to envy you," he heard himself say, as he shook Feza's hand.

"He also loves you like a son, you must have noticed long ago!" whispered Feza, with a wink.

"This boy must be hungry, he should eat something, and we'll talk later," said Brigadier General Turhan Ozsoy, goading Duna toward the open buffet.

"Once you're full, come up to my study on the second floor. The password is *cybernetics*, don't forget Second Lieutenant!"

Duna smiled.

"Is that clear, officer?" asked the general sharply.

Duna faltered, confused as to whether this was facetious or not, just the way he doubted nightmare and reality.

"Yessir, commander!" he said, and gave a salute.

Since he had done this rather loudly, a brief silence ensued in the salon, and everyone turned to look at him.

The Brigadier General received the salute as if nothing had happened, and disappeared after replying "At ease, Lieutenant!"

The Blue Danube Waltz had ended, and Master Dede's "Gulnihal" waltz had been struck up.

"We are still alive, and we definitely must have this waltz Ada!" he whispered, smiling.

Then, for a while Duna remained motionless before the white porcelain plates, raki glasses, and crystal goblets. Even the sight of real plates and glasses excited him now.

"These are signs!" he whispered, with the thrill of being able to get excited once more.

He picked up a plate and began a lustful trip around the table. What he first saw were the things he had missed most. Stuffed dolmas made with olive oil were lined up side by side, gleaming like they had been varnished. Lemons that were carved in the shape of roses had been placed among the grape leaf and bell pepper dolmas. Then he blissfully observed the garlic yogurt dip, the eggplant salad in tomato sauce, the zucchini patties, the Ladies' Delight meatballs, the Circassian chicken, the raw koftas, the canellini bean salad, the fried crepes, the thin beans, the delicate, multi-layered borek pastries, the mushroom pilaf, the "Imam's favorite" stuffed eggplants, the artichokes in olive oil, the Albanian style liver, the lentil balls, the hummus, the almond tartar dip, the Russian salad, and the hot sauce salad, which all beckoned with seductive appeal.

On a large wooden platter decorated with tomatoes and parsley, slabs of feta, aged sheep cheese, goatskin cheese, smoked mozzarella, walnut Kars cheese, and dilled Erzincan cheese waited side by side, making his mouth water. Right in the middle of the cheeses, he spotted black Gemlik olives, and their green counterparts stuffed with red pimientoes, lounging around leisurely in a dressing of oregano and olive oil. Immediately next to him were salted, dried mackerels, which were presented in a lemon dill sauce, placed on lemon peels that resembled sailboats about to take off. The stack of small Turkish pizzas and Black Sea flatbreads which was frequently replenished piping hot, was being consumed rapidly.

However, what really blew him away were the pickles. The various kinds of pickles, ranging from cornichon, to cabbage, hot peppers, wild cucumbers, carrots, melons, eggplants, zucchini, red bell peppers, and watermelons were painted like a still life on dimunitive serving plates. As for the cornucopia of salads, they had truly gotten out of hand, and were presented in a manner so appetizing as to tempt the most hardheaded carnivores.

The varieties of breads and flatbreads were confidently couched at the head of the table, emitting a bountiful scent.

When he arrived at the head of the handsome cauldrons which contained the hot entrées, there were a few dolmas, sone walnut Kars cheese, salad, pickled cabbage and garlic yogurt dip on his plate. A waiter had also handed him a goblet of musket wine made of central Anatolian grapes.

"We have spiced pastrami bean stew, Sultan's Favorite, lemon sauce kofta, meat filled chard, Turkish ravioli, anchovy pilaf, and doner kabab, sir," said a cheerful young cook, in a starched white outfit.

"Amazing, incredible!" said Duna, beaming.

"Thank you. Because of limitations of space, we did not at all go into kabab and fish varieties, sir."

"This culinary diversity reminds me of the wealth of characters in Karagoz and Hacivat shadow plays."

"Excuse me?" asked the cook, surprised.

"Nevermind. I will be back in a short while."

The table displaying desserts was smaller, and was situated at the other end of the salon. Duna first noticed the various kinds of baklava. The walnut and pistachio filled baklavas were simply crying out in invitation.

Delicate pastries and cakes of all kinds, including nightingale's nest, lady's navel, vizier's finger, semolina sponge cake, crumb cake with cream, and crumpets in syrup were waiting with a maddening appeal. The vast sampling of puddings were grouped together, some baked with rice, others made with almonds, chicken breast, grain and beans, or rose-water. Desserts of dried apricot and quince with cream, zucchini, walnut and fig tarts, cheesecakes, and sour cherry bread, were arranged in the lovely blushing hues of autumn, and awaited enticingly. Then there were the fruit platters...

Duna did not know what to eat. A few dolmas and a piece of cheese had already made him full. In fact, it was his visual hunger that had been satisfied, for he had lost his appetite in all the excitement.

"Really, sir, how can you walk around with an empty plate like that tonight?"

"I just feel full all of a sudden," replied Duna, but as soon as the words were out of his mouth, he swerved around in the direction of the voice.

It came from an extremely young waiter serving drinks. One of his eyes was covered with a black leather pirate patch.

"That old eye of mine's gone the way of the dogs, sir! Oh well, god save the rest, don't you think?" said the youth with a dark smile.

"Tarkan?"

"That's correct sir, you get an A plus!

Duna closed his eyes and tried to overcome the blow he had just been delivered.

"Aw, sir, it really isn't all that terrible. See, you too have aged, and you've lost a lot of weight. Naturally, peace will have its price, isn't that what you taught us? 'We're growing enlightened kids,' and all that sort of thing."

Duna stared at Tarkan, clenching his teeth.

"Come on now, sir… It'll all come to pass. At least they didn't lock me up in that place called POWMITU. Apparently only those who've gone nuts are taken there. At least I haven't lost it yet. Besides, this eyepatch just might drive the girls wild!" he grinned. His voice betrayed a bitter yellow frustration, which he tried to hide with childish pride.

"Is the war over, Tarkan?"

"You're even testing me here, aren't you? I think it's over. That is, the violent part is over. From here starts the war of the civillians, sir! So I'll see you in school."

"Second Lieutenant?"

A private saluted Duna and stood to attention.

"The Brigadier General is expecting you in his study, Second Lieutenant!"

When he turned around to say goodbye to Tarkan, the latter had long vanished.

After following the private up to the second floor study, Duna knocked before he entered. He heard the general's deep voice from inside.

"Password?"

"What?" asked Duna, startled

"This must be a joke," he thought, but this time the general's voice asked even more sternly from the inside:

"Password?"

"Cybernetics," said Duna.

THE FUTURE OF THE FUTURE AND
CYBERNETIC WARFARE

"Those who are expert in combat do not fly into a rage, and those who are expert in winning do not grow afraid. As a result, intelligent people win before they fight, and ignorant ones fight in order to win."

Zhuge Liang
(The Art of War)

The general's study was a spacious setting, its walls covered entirely with books except for a window which caught the eye with its vertically striped yellow and turqoise drapes. The room was extremely tasteful, modern, and sparse. The floors had wall to wall grey carpeting. The wide desk was made of a single piece of glass, and stood on two Z shaped legs fashioned out of black metal. On the left stood an Art Deco divan of bright turqoise color. The tassled yellow cylindrical cushions, placed on either cheek of the divan were as attractive and whimsical as candy wrappers. The nearby coffeetable could be deemed a spitting image of the desk. The blue and yellow striped-armchair, which looked comfortable with its accompanying ottoman foot-rest, looked exactly like the one Dogan Gokay favored at the mansion. A huge, illuminated globe was set on the desk, and certain cities upon it had been marked with crosses.

"Could a general possibly have such modern taste?" wondered Duna.

General Turhan Ozsoy and Mr. Muzaffer the futurologist were huddled over the desk, carefully studying a map. After standing in place for a while, he felt the need to remind them of his presence, and gave a cough.

"Ah Duna, here, come have a look at this!" said the general without lifting his head.

On the table was a galactic map, drawn on jet black paper. The planets of the solar system, the stars and constellations were spread out before them as an extraordinarily appealing geometrical work of art. At the same time, the map was frightening in the way it beckoned toward a mysterious journey, replete with long, cool, and dangerous surprises. Gazing at it, one felt the vertiginous depths of the concept of infinity threatening loss and disorientation.

"A three dimensional, unlimited vacuum in which exist only objects and events that possess a relative direction and position to one another!" said Mr. Muzaffer, pointing to the map.

"Well?" asked the general, with the air of someone taking pride in his own work.

Duna, who had been enchanted by the geometrical aestheticism of the map, peered at the Earth, which was barely visible in space, and sighed disconsolately.

"Oh, I hope my subconscious doesn't go getting involved in star wars, amidst the whole civil war scenario!" he thought quickly.

"Now, let's not get the young man too excited yet, Turan. These maps look extremely complicated at first glance."

"Let him just take a peek at Feza's genetic maps, then he'll really understand about complexities, hah hah ha!"

"Daddy, you just have to tease me don't you!"

That was when Duna noticed Feza the genetic engineer leaning against one of the bookshelves by the entrance of the study, cognac glass in hand. Obviously unfettered by her plumpness, the young woman was once again bejewelling her confident smile with her dimples.

"Ah, I should have some right to brag about my daughter, shouldn't I?"

"After the Chinese invented the magnetic compass, explorers were rescued from remaining blind under foreign constellations. Consequently, the fate of explorers and humanity was altered."

"And a good thing too! In the seven hundred years since Marco

Polo, we're almost done with the solar system, my dear fellow! That is unarguably an achievement of mankind."

"Actually, we're only at the very begging, Turan, old boy! Here, let me put it this way, if we were to squeeze the entire history of the universe into a year's worth of time, we would end up with roughly the following calendar: Now, let January, the first month, be the beginning of the cosmos. So, we'll say the Big Bang happened in January, alright?"

"Alright, alright, then what?" nodded the general enthusiastically.

"If the first stars, galaxies, and nebulae formed in February, only by September would the sun begin to shine, and the meteors start to shower down on what would be considered our infant Earth and its Moon. Let's see now, if we assume the first atmosphere and algae began forming in October, the Moon would pull away from the Earth in November, and only by December…"

"What about December?"

"Only by December would early mammals begin to appear!"

"Well, I'll be! But what an awful calendar that is, Muzaffer, dear. I mean, our planet is already a mere speck in space. And you're telling us that even our appearance on that planet is a one in twelve in the notion of time. Just as I was beginning to brag about how we discovered so and so, and invented such and such…"

"What's more," laughed Mr. Muzaffer the futurologist, "What's more, within the history of the universe, which we have condensed into a one year time period, the history of civilization, from the earliest recorded caveman to the present, would take up just forty seconds on December the 31st!"

"What? Oh no, that's going too far!" exclaimed the upset general.

"On the other hand, man is the only creature that has brought meaning into time and life!" Duna interrupted against his will.

"True! Although we are at the very beginning of our evolution, consciousness differentiates and rescues us from all the other beings we know of so far," said Feza the geneticist.

"Well, it's a little unclear whether it rescues or ruins us!" sighed Duna.

"In the future, biotechnology will succeed in accomplishing what biology could not accomplish alone. It will increase the capacity of the human brain."

As she said this, Feza's voice was calm, and her face clear.

Duna suddenly had the idea that she was not a passionate person.

"Tell me, how familiar are you with the subject of nano-machines, Duna?"

"Nano-machines?"

"Yes, nano-machines assist us greatly in foreseeing the future of the future. Thanks to them, we can devise scenarios reaching the year 2100," said Mr. Muzaffer.

"I don't know anything other than that a nanometer is a billionth of a meter," interjected Duna, in curiosity.

"Nano-machines, which are the size of large atoms, are like micro-robots and will be playing serious roles in many vital functions, starting with the reparation of living creatures in the very near future," said Feza the geneticist, smiling her dimpled smile.

"So are you telling me that these little robots will be inserted into human bodies in order to repair the diseased areas?

"Yes, but this is not as mechanical a procedure as you fear. These molecular robots will repair the human body by exactly replicating human cells. As a result, life expectancy in the future will be much, much longer than the ones dreamed of today."

"While we can't even properly furnish and live our lives in this short state..." grumbled Duna.

"Besides, isn't all this what my students call techno-utopia?" he then added.

"Not quite," smiled Feza, displaying her dimples in all their nudity.

"It cannot be called a utopia anymore. Genetic engineers have already succeeded in programming bacteria DNA with nano-machines in order to create insulin."

"Meanwhile," Mr. Muzaffer joined in, "The day is close when human learning capacity will be increased beyond imagination through the insertion of a pea-sized nano-machine into the cranium."

"Naturally, I don't even want to think about the kinds of social and ethical problems all these will present for us, hah hah hah!" chuckled the general.

"So are you saying that in the future we will hand over the world to robots?" asked Duna, annoyed.

"In a way, yes," replied Feza.

"But don't you forget, Duna, that those robots will still be the offspring of our intellect."

"Repulsive and confusing!" sighed a dejected Duna.

"Nothing is as confusing as it seems, but what I really want to know is how Turan will simplify those military maps of his in the future."

"What? Now you're trying to tell me that military service will continue in the future?" cried Duna in amazement.

The other three glanced at each other and kept a brief silence.

"We're not completely in agreement on that matter, professor!" said the general in his most authoritative voice.

"It is not exactly prophetic to say that the wars of the future will employ computers instead of guns, and logic bombs in the place of nuclear bombs…"

Once again they were silent.

"In Europe there is the ongoing project of downsizing troops and making the switch to professional militarism by the year 2000. And then there's the instance of Bill Clinton, who is personally against military service and who has had the courage to defend the rights of homosexuals in the army, being elected to the presidency of the United States. It is not a coincidence that these two events have happened to fall toward the end of the twentieth century," added general Turhan Ozsoy.

"But in fact, you all agree that there will be military service in the future!" protested Duna.

"Not as we know it! Mass killings and civillian bombardments will cease. Technology and production wars will be settled at desktops, like computer games. Of course, one does not need to be a futurologist to predict that the first quarter of the next century will be a period of terrorism!"

"Feza, why don't you get us some cognac as well? And some coffee on the side wouldn't be bad either."

As a waiter was summoned for the coffee, the sound of voices and music seeped in through the opened door. The little orchestra was now playing an Azerbaijani waltz.

"We're not alone!" thought Duna.

The topics which they were discussing had abstracted him so

much from the present and the world at large that it made him rejoice:

"There're people outside!"

"The present time, and the world at large? So am I finally feeling these... for real?" His head spun with gladness. He discreetly leaned against the wall.

"In countries that use advanced technology," the general picked up from where he had left off, "a control mechanism similar to those in planes has already begun being employed in the military as 'the smart helmet.' The smart helmet, which is manufactured bulletproof out of lightweight plastic, determines the effects of nerve gas and biological warfare through its bioelectric sensors, and provides nightvision through its infrared glasses. In addition, it projects tactical information according to the soldier's line of sight by means of a plastic holographic projector. The radio connector included in the smart helmet constantly informs the soldier of his location, and relays tactical orders from the commander. The helmet also contains a camera, a microphone, earphones, a visual system and a wrist terminal."

"You hadn't told me about this wrist terminal before, Turan, my dear fellow!" said Mr. Muzaffer as he sipped his cognac.

"It's simply a terminal attached to a wristwatch for purposes of translating the information from the helmet computer into script and graphics," answered the general, shaking his head from side to side in awe. "Advanced technology is an incredible thing, my boy!" he exclaimed.

Duna assumed that the intense pain he felt in his abdomen was due to having drank cognac on an empty stomach.

Just then, a waiter brought in the tantalizingly scented coffees.

"What is this logic bomb you speak of, general?" inquired Duna, clutching his stomach with one hand.

"There, you see, the thing that peaked his interested happened to be the most crucial weapon! Didn't I tell you he was an extremely smart young man?" smiled the general.

"The logic bomb could be termed a type of computer virus. For instance, it's the story of a virus that can cripple the communication and transportation networks of a country in order to topple a dictatorial regime with a four or five level operation, but a single blow. Certainly, the country in question must be entirely governed through computers, and that is not in the very distant future."

"Computer viruses and logic bombs will also be made use of on the subjects of counter-propaganda and psychological demoralization, of course," added the general smugly.

"In other words, winning the war before engaging in it!"

That was when Duna realized that the true cause of his stomach pain was disillusionment. He quietly rose to his feet, and began speaking, this time without at all getting angry or raising his voice.

"To tell you the truth, all three of you have disappointed me to-night, and now my stomach is aching from distress. Even though all of you possess admirable reserves of strength and enlightenment to devise dreams or scenarios pertaining to the future, the things you speak of, and the plots you have produced, while technologically impressive, have one grave deficiency. You are overlooking such an important factor that my stomach has started aching from desperation."

"Well, will you listen to this young man! And what might that be?" asked the general.

Inwardly, Duna was glad to observe that he could object without flying into fits of rage, and speak without being afraid.

"What is it you think we are overlooking, Mr. Duna?" asked Mr. Muzaffer the future scientist, his interest aroused.

"Emotional perception, what else?" said Duna.

He had neither started yelling, nor had he worked himself into a frenzy, but nevertheless he could be effective. Yes, he could be! Just like Aras, like Ada, and like Dogan Gokay. He was not superbly handsome or talented, or incredibly special, or even a great poet, but he could finally "be!"

"Tonight, we are repeating the mistake that we have been making for centuries. You are discussing the future and the wars of the future as if our emotions and our thoughts were separate from one another."

As always happens when thoughts related indirectly to a subject are initially introduced, the words first froze like ice in the air, then clattered to the floor. But this time around, Duna did not cringe or squirm. He smiled. When he smiled, the other three fell to thinking that they may have been the ones who had failed to make the connection.

"While for centuries we regarded thought as the crowning glory and deemed it fit on the heads of men, we dismissed emotion, which secretly burned within us, and which we had buried behind our sexual identities as belonging to women, and often as a symbol of weakness. Yet toward the end of this century, people, among them male scientists, stepped forward who understood and confessed that all our perceptions were primarily emotional. Most important of all, they emancipated us men a tiny bit by conceding that what lay at the heart of it all was 'emotional intelligence.'"

"Emotional imprinting is very fascinating to geneticists," remarked Feza, as she listened attentively to Duna.

"So, young man, you're saying that all logical deductions, all intellectual conclusions are first perceived emotionally and later transferred to other areas. I too read a few articles on the subject of this emotional intelligence, but to tell you the truth, I did not take them very seriously."

"Mathematics, physics and even cybernetics are the same way. Because logic is initially perceiving everything emotionally, and not denying it! Every type of intellectual activity is necessarily processed through an emotional understanding, and this is not anything to be ashamed of."

He felt the pain in his stomach diminish. Or he thought it did.

"The point we have reached by trying to deprive a person of his or her emotional perception has not made him or her happy. Come, let us not do this in the upcoming centuries. Let us not enter genetical engineering or future science by stripping a person of his or her nervous system."

He sat down on the Art Deco divan, and took a sip of his coffee. He felt good.

"And therefore, no offense anyone, but the fancy scenarios you write on the future's combat uniform will only serve to make the future more ostentatious, and not, in my opinion, any better!"

"This kid's an idealist!" said general Turhan Ozsoy in a fatherly voice.

"A romantic!" said Feza the genetic engineer.

"And a rebel!" added Mr. Muzaffer the futurologist.

Duna pushed back the glasses that slipped down his nose.

His stomach did not ache anymore.

He smiled, thinking that had Ada been here, she would have exclaimed: "Good for you, Mabel!"

"I've always wanted to be a medical doctor," sighed the general suddenly.

"You never told me that, daddy!" said Feza, staring in surprise.

"And I'd wanted to be a professional scuba diver when I was young, hah hah ha!!"

"You did, Muzaffer? Hah, hah, ha… honest? Hah ha!"

"I swear it's true… hah hah hah!"

"What about you Feza?"

"I'm content with my lot, but…"

"But what?"

"But frankly, I would badly dream of becoming a singer when I was a girl. Just imagine me in a nice black lace dress, singing by the piano, daddy."

"I had no idea!" said her startled father.

"And yet, it's true, you have a lovely voice. You drove all the neighbors crazy when you were a kid… Why of course…"

A silence spread over the room. Everyone had embarked on a journey into their dreams when Duna spoke up:

"What I want most of all is to wake up, I mean, to go back home," he said.

"Huh? Oh, of course!" sighed the general.

"Oh dear! I had invited you here tonight to congratulate you on your return home tomorrow, but you see, I forgot to tell you!"

"Oh daddy, really! You mean he didn't know?"

"I wanted to be the first to tell him, you know, he was entrusted to me by Birol."

"What, I'm going home tomorrow?" cried Duna, almost swallowing his tongue, "I'm going home tomorrow. The nightmare is ending!"

First, his heart began to bounce. Then it went out of hand and began to beat his body and cut off his respiration. His eyes grew dark. But this time, he did not faint. He did not want to miss his awakening. He closed his eyes, threw his head back, and smiled infinitely.

TUESDAY MORNING ONCE AGAIN

"If thou were not here… If I did not behold thou for one instant
Dost thou know what would happen?
If thou were not here… If finding you were a vain dream
Dost thou think I could live?"

Tevfik Fikret

I awoke that morning.

It was a Tuesday.

That Tuesday morning I finally awoke.

The nightmare had ended. I was free to go home.

I had left home on a military truck. Now I was returning home in Brigadier General Turhan Ozsoy's official automobile. I had on the same light blue t-shirt and blue jeans I wore when I left home. Also the burgundy coat belonging to the general's eldest son who had died in the war. My hand was in the coat's pocket. In that hand there was a small, white, oval stone. I was clutching the stone tightly.

It was late winter, the weather was forbiddingly cold, but the sky was a clear blue, and soon it would be springtime.

The Brigadier General's chauffeur knew the way to my house, and was recounting how Turhan Ozsoy had paid two previous visits there. My mother believed that I was taken away from home in an ambulance. And perhaps she would tell me that the general was in fact the head doctor. Perhaps Mr. Muzaffer the future scientist was, in reality, a world-renowned underwater researcher, and Feza the genetic engineer was a well-known jazz singer.

Perhaps Merich's sole interest had become our daughter Irmak, and her greatest desire had always been to relive her lost childhood with Irmak, who knows?

Perhaps the poet Dogan Gokay had at last managed to complete the conclusion of his novel *Mediterranean Waltz*, which had been giving him such difficulty.

And as for Ada… She finally knew that she loved me!

I watched with a smile the pictures of Istanbul streaming by the window of the official automobile.

It is Tuesday.

I am thirty-four years old.

I am a bespectacled, clean-shaven man of medium height, with curly black hair.

I am a teacher.

I am an ordinary person, and of course, like all ordinary people, I am unusual.

I do not smoke, but I do like to drink every so often.

My father was a tailor, and my mother a housewife. My brother was a student.

I am returning from a civil war.

I am awaking from a long and very trying nightmare.

I have learned the meaning of Leviathan.

I am tired. I am very tired, but I am, nevertheless, able to feel well. At this point, I am ready to be well. Now, I deserve it.

Soon I will be back in my neighborhood, in the streets where I played, laughed, and made merry, where I tasted love, disillusion, pain, and loneliness.

When I look out from inside the car, my old footsteps will seem foreign to me. But in a few minutes the car will come to a stop, and I will move to the other side of the window. The soil is ready, and I am ready to form new and real footprints.

I am returning.

Home.

To myself.

I smile, thinking it is lovely to awake.

No matter what the situation might be, it is lovely to awake!

My countenance on the window smiles back at me.

What's more, blood does not make me queasy anymore.